DRIFTER™

vol.4

REMAINS

DRIFTER created by Ivan Brandon and Nic Klein
AN OFFSET COMICS PRODUCTION

Drifter Volume 04
Originally published as DRIFTER #15–19

Story: Ivan Brandon & Nic Klein
Script: Ivan Brandon
Full color art: Nic Klein
Lettering: Aditya Bidikar
Logo and design: Tom Muller
Original Cover artists: Nic Klein, David Rubin, Mike Hawthorne,
                 Thomas von Kummant, Ben Caldwell.
Editor: Sebastian Girner

Special thanks to Holley McKend

IMAGE COMICS, INC: Robert Kirkman—Chief Operating Officer / Erik Larsen—Chief Financial Officer / Todd McFarlane—President / Marc Silvestri—Chief Executive Officer / Jim Valentino—Vice-President / Eric Stephenson—Publisher / Corey Murphy—Director of Sales / Jeff Boison—Director of Publishing Planning & Book Trade Sales / Chris Ross—Director of Digital Sales / Jeff Stang—Director of Specialty Sales / Kat Salazar—Director of PR & Marketing / Branwyn Bigglestone—Controller / Sue Korpela—Accounts Manager / Drew Gill—Art Director / Brett Warnock—Production Manager / Leigh Thomas—Print Manager / Tricia Ramos—Traffic Manager / Briah Skelly—Publicist / Aly Hoffman—Events & Conventions Coordinator / Sasha Head—Sales & Marketing Production Designer / David Brothers—Branding Manager / Melissa Gifford—Content Manager / Drew Fitzgerald—Publicity Assistant / Vincent Kukua—Production Artist / Erika Schnatz—Production Artist / Ryan Brewer—Production Artist / Shanna Matuszak—Production Artist / Carey Hall—Production Artist / Esther Kim—Direct Market Sales Representative / Emilio Bautista—Digital Sales Representative / Leanna Caunter—Accounting Assistant / Chloe Ramos-Peterson—Library Market Sales Representative / Marla Eizik—Administrative Assistant / **IMAGECOMICS.COM**

CHAPTER 15
BROTHERS

CAN'T HEAR A THING.

I WANT MY BONES TO SHAKE, THE WHOLE WORLD SCREAMING UNDERNEATH.

BURY US UNDER ALL WE WROUGHT.

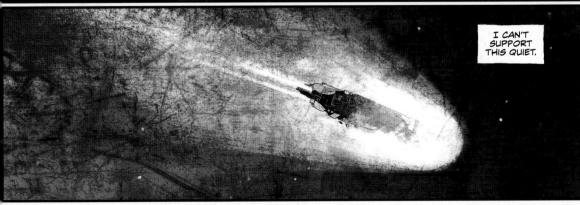

I CAN'T SUPPORT THIS QUIET.

SHORT OF ALL THAT I'M STUCK WITH ME.

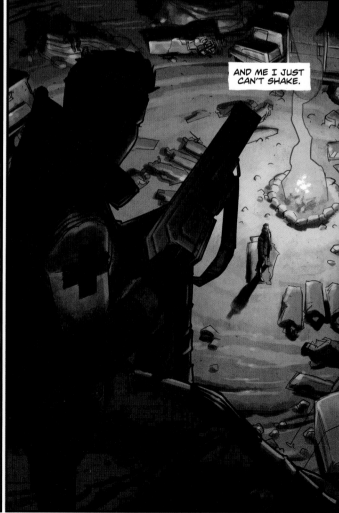

AND ME I JUST CAN'T SHAKE.

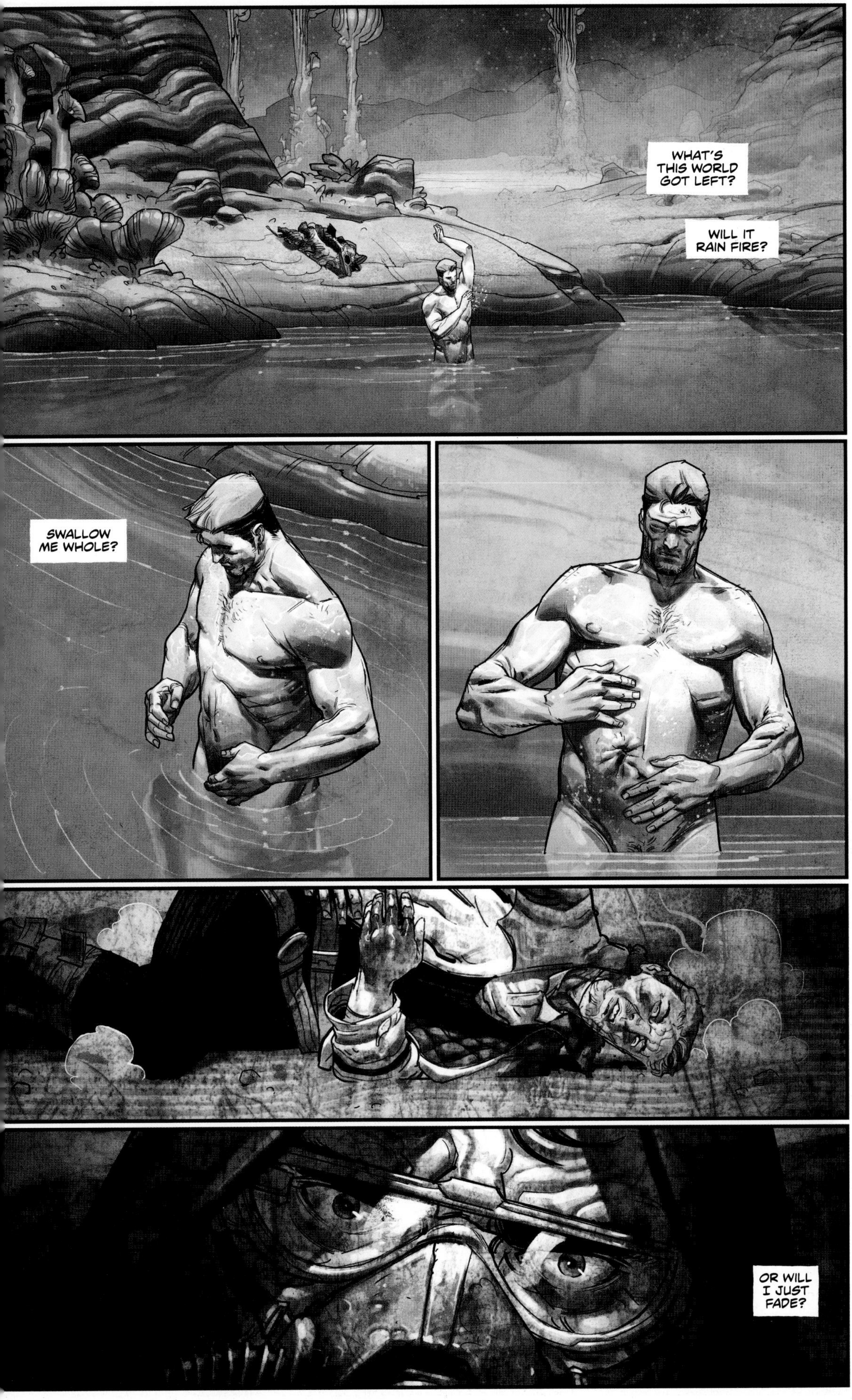
WHAT'S THIS WORLD GOT LEFT?
WILL IT RAIN FIRE?
SWALLOW ME WHOLE?
OR WILL I JUST FADE?

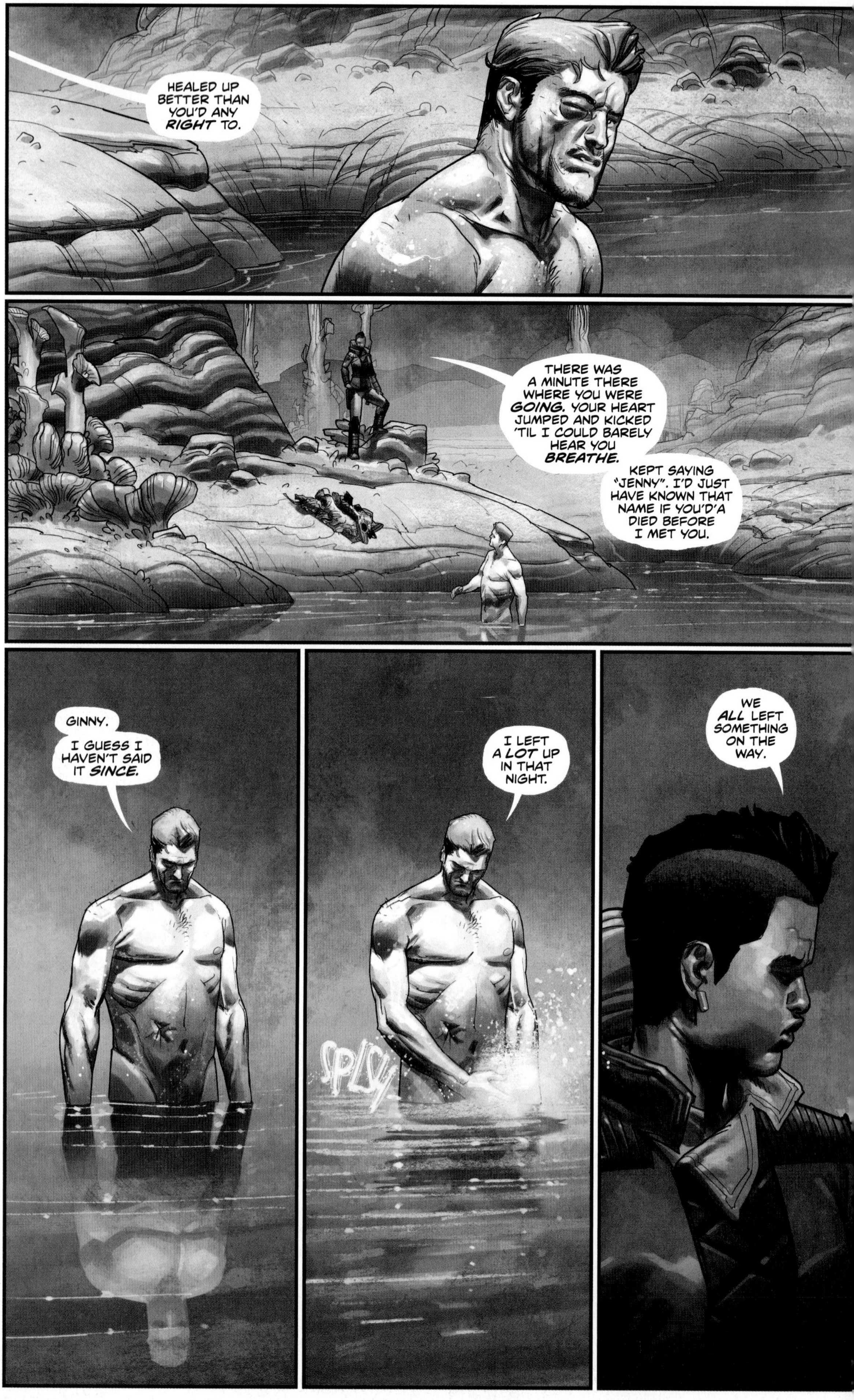
HEALED UP BETTER THAN YOU'D ANY RIGHT TO.
THERE WAS A MINUTE THERE WHERE YOU WERE GOING. YOUR HEART JUMPED AND KICKED 'TIL I COULD BARELY HEAR YOU BREATHE.
KEPT SAYING "JENNY". I'D JUST HAVE KNOWN THAT NAME IF YOU'D'A DIED BEFORE I MET YOU.
GINNY.
I GUESS I HAVEN'T SAID IT SINCE.
I LEFT A LOT UP IN THAT NIGHT.
SPLSH
WE ALL LEFT SOMETHING ON THE WAY.

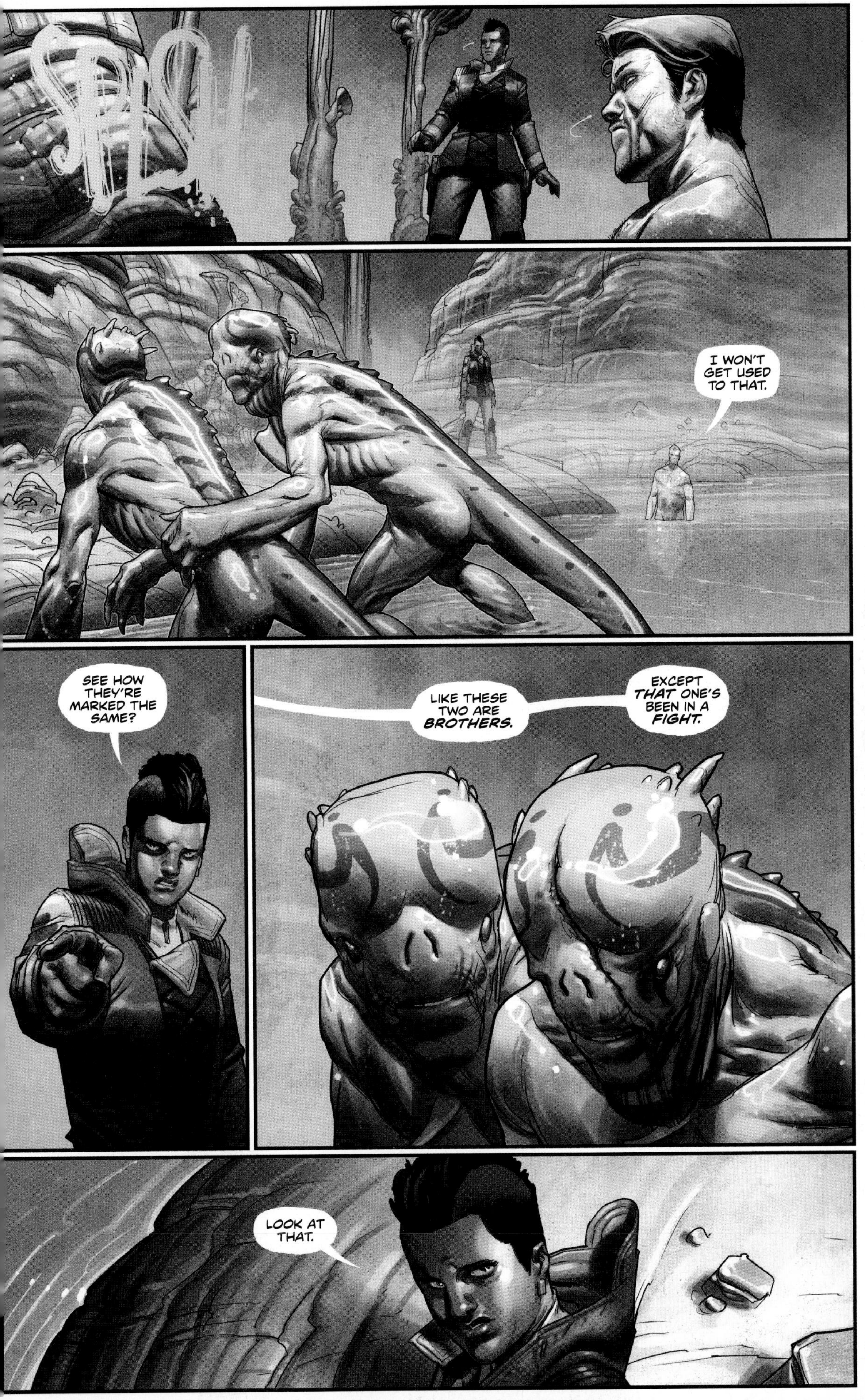
SPLSH
I WON'T GET USED TO THAT.
SEE HOW THEY'RE MARKED THE SAME?
LIKE THESE TWO ARE *BROTHERS.*
EXCEPT *THAT* ONE'S BEEN IN A *FIGHT.*
LOOK AT THAT.

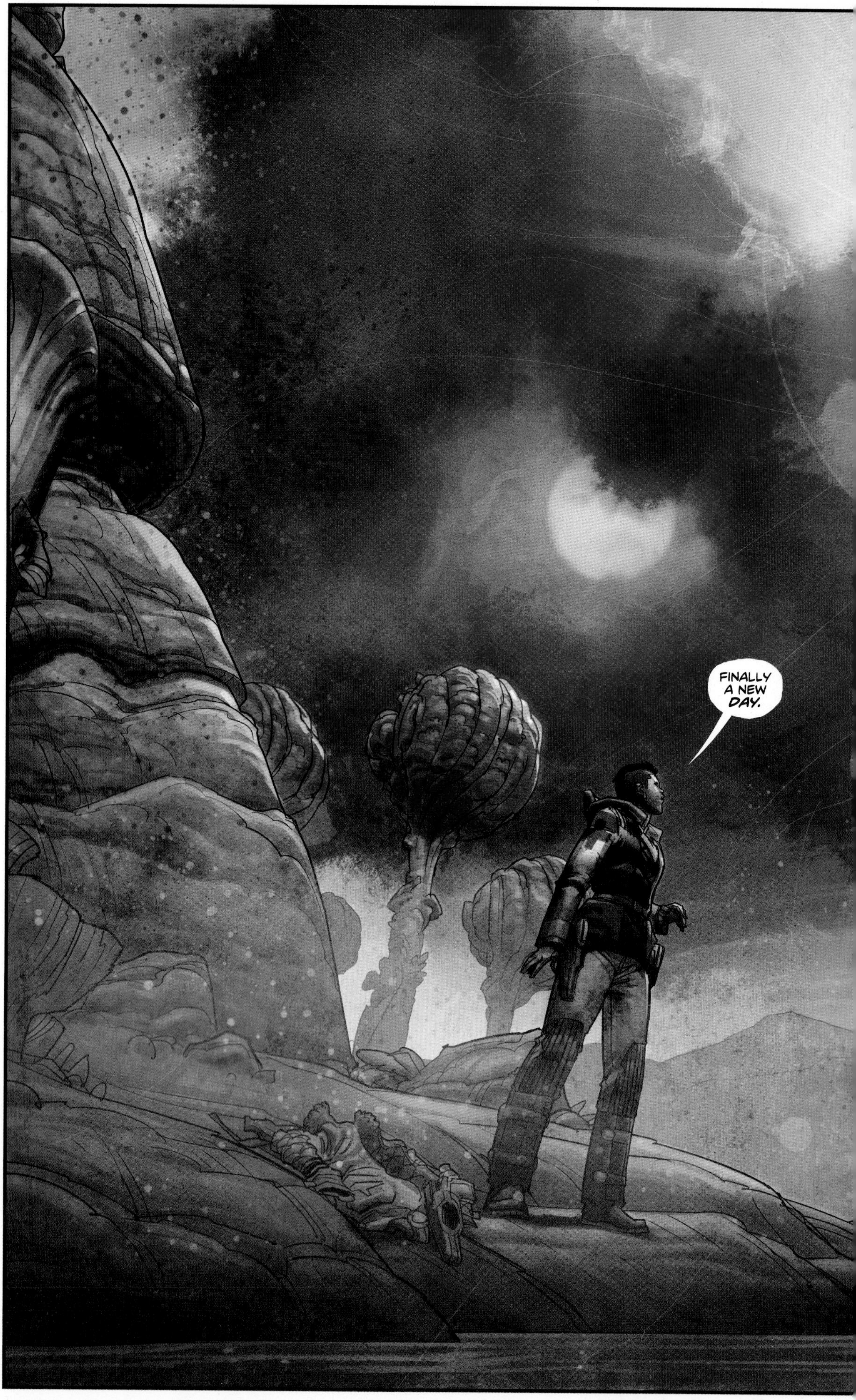
FINALLY A NEW DAY.

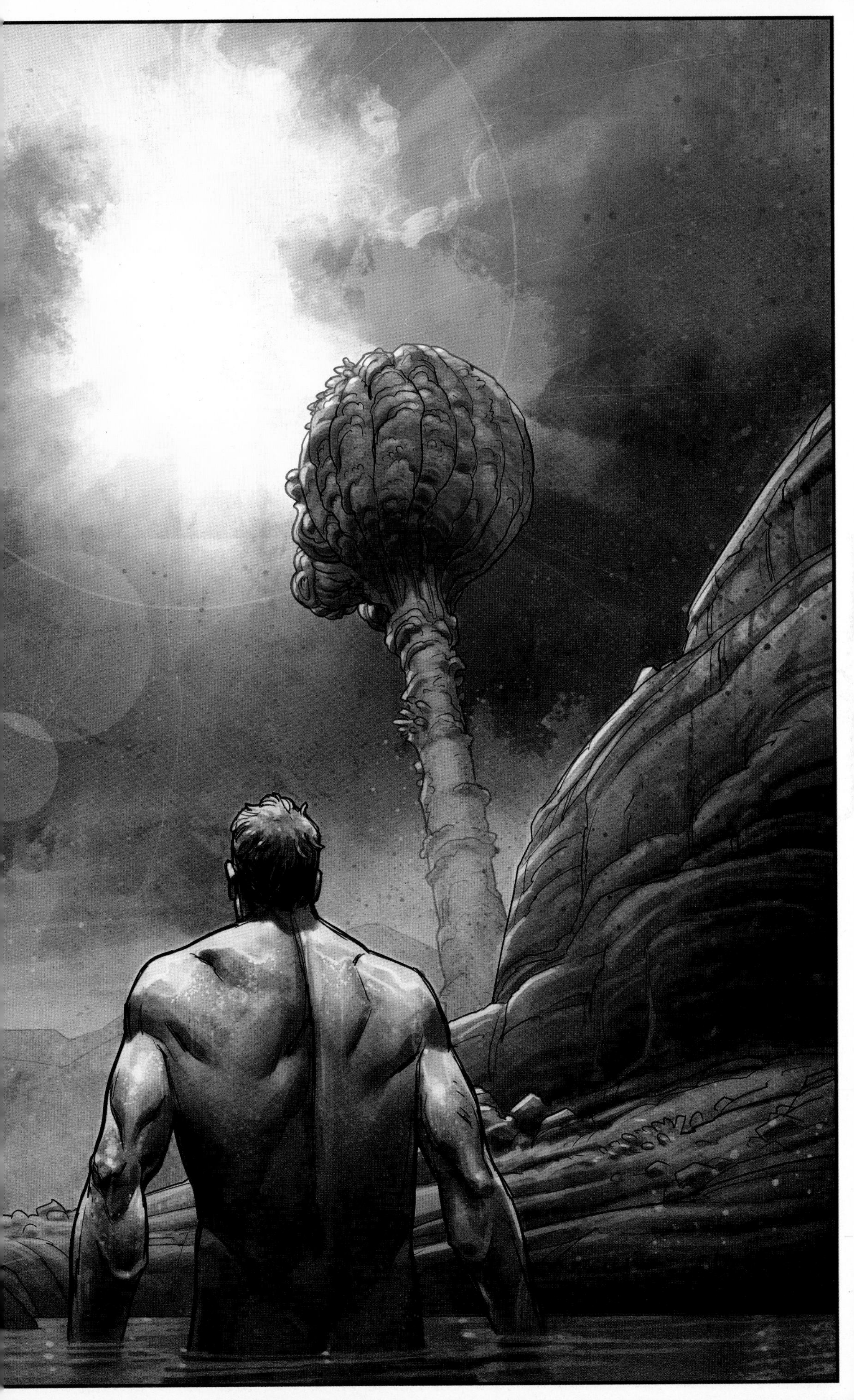

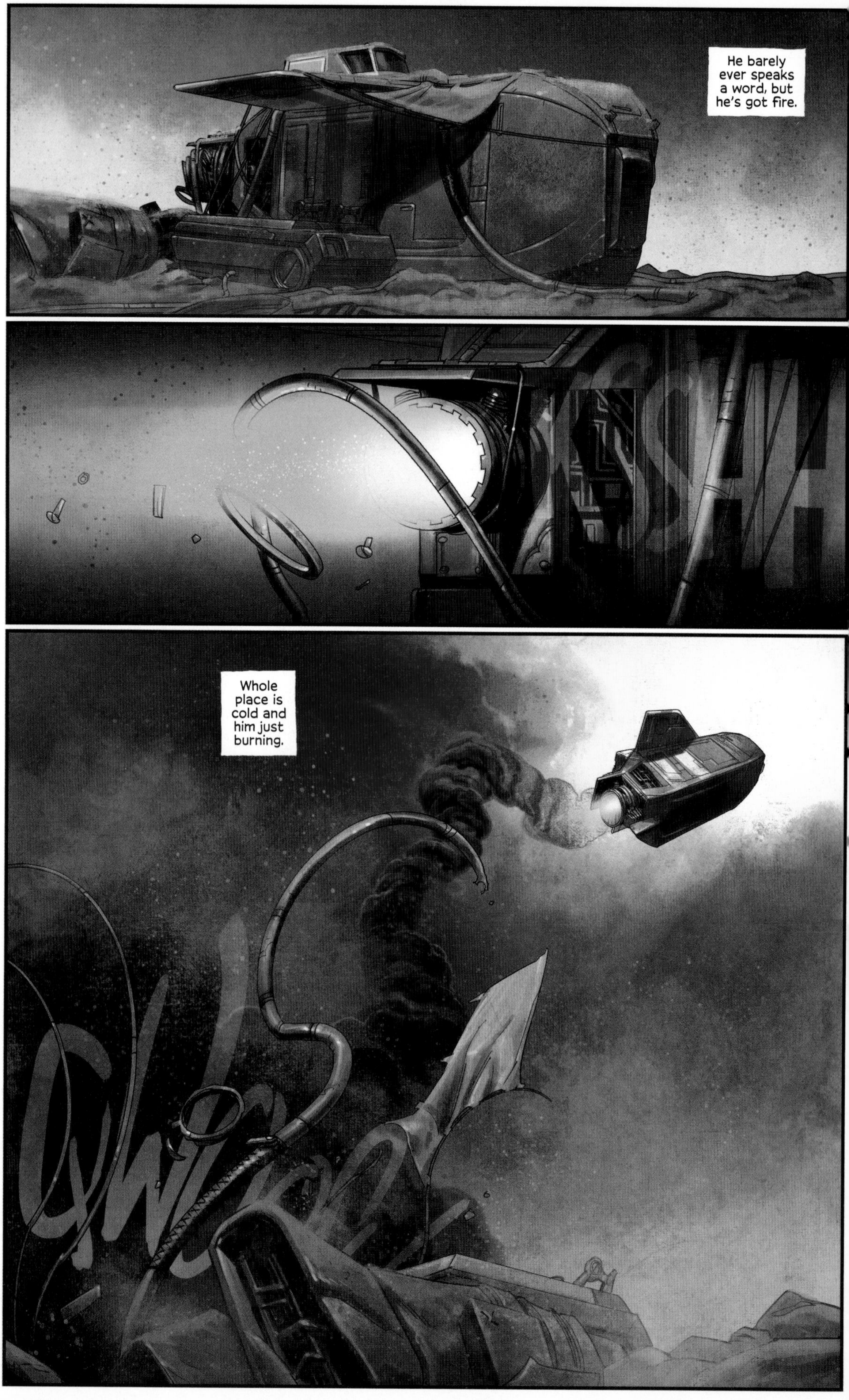
He barely ever speaks a word, but he's got fire.
Whole place is cold and him just burning.

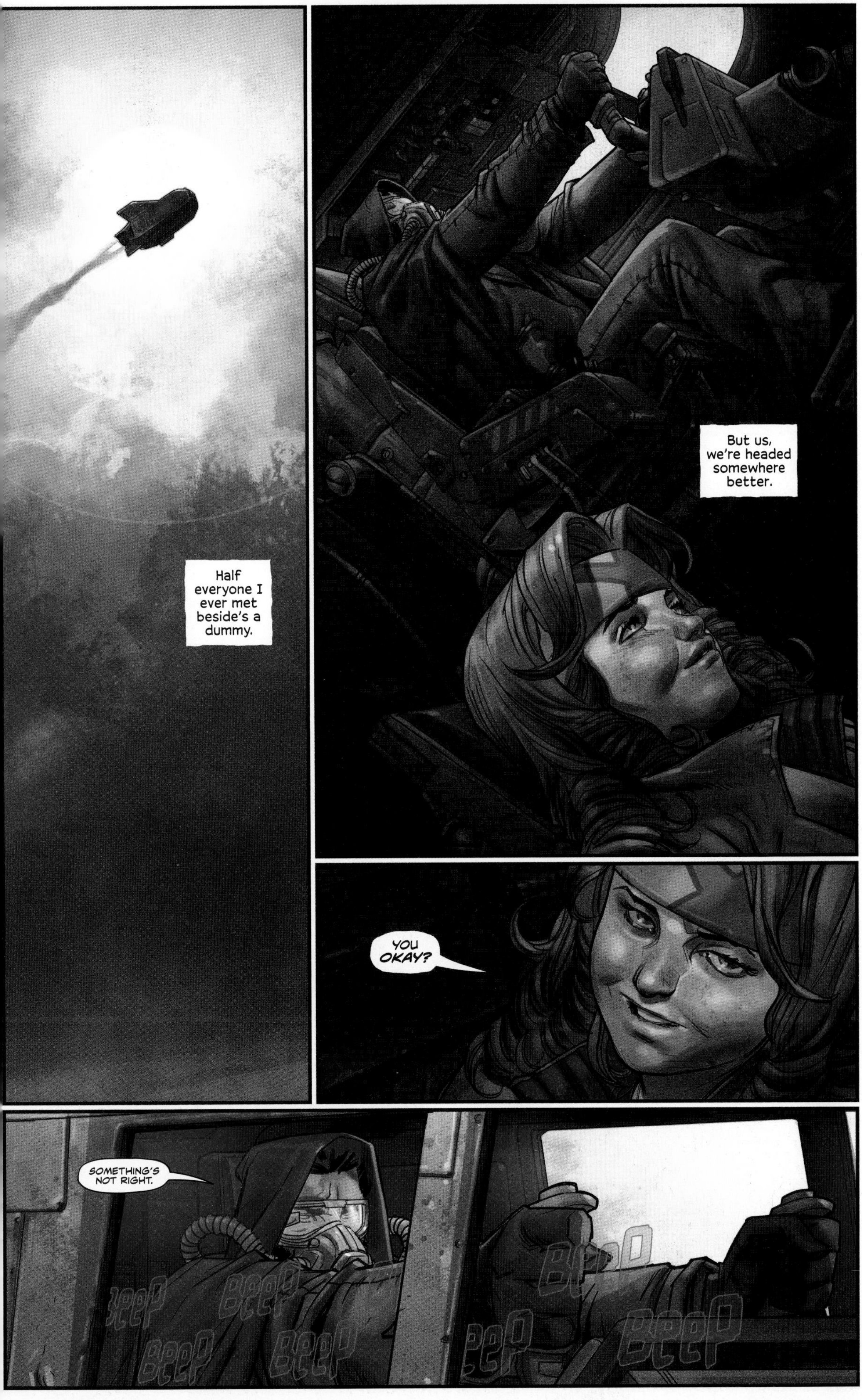
Half everyone I ever met beside's a dummy.
But us, we're headed somewhere better.
YOU OKAY?
SOMETHING'S NOT RIGHT.
BEEP
BEEP
BEEP
BEEP
BEEP
BEEP
BEEP

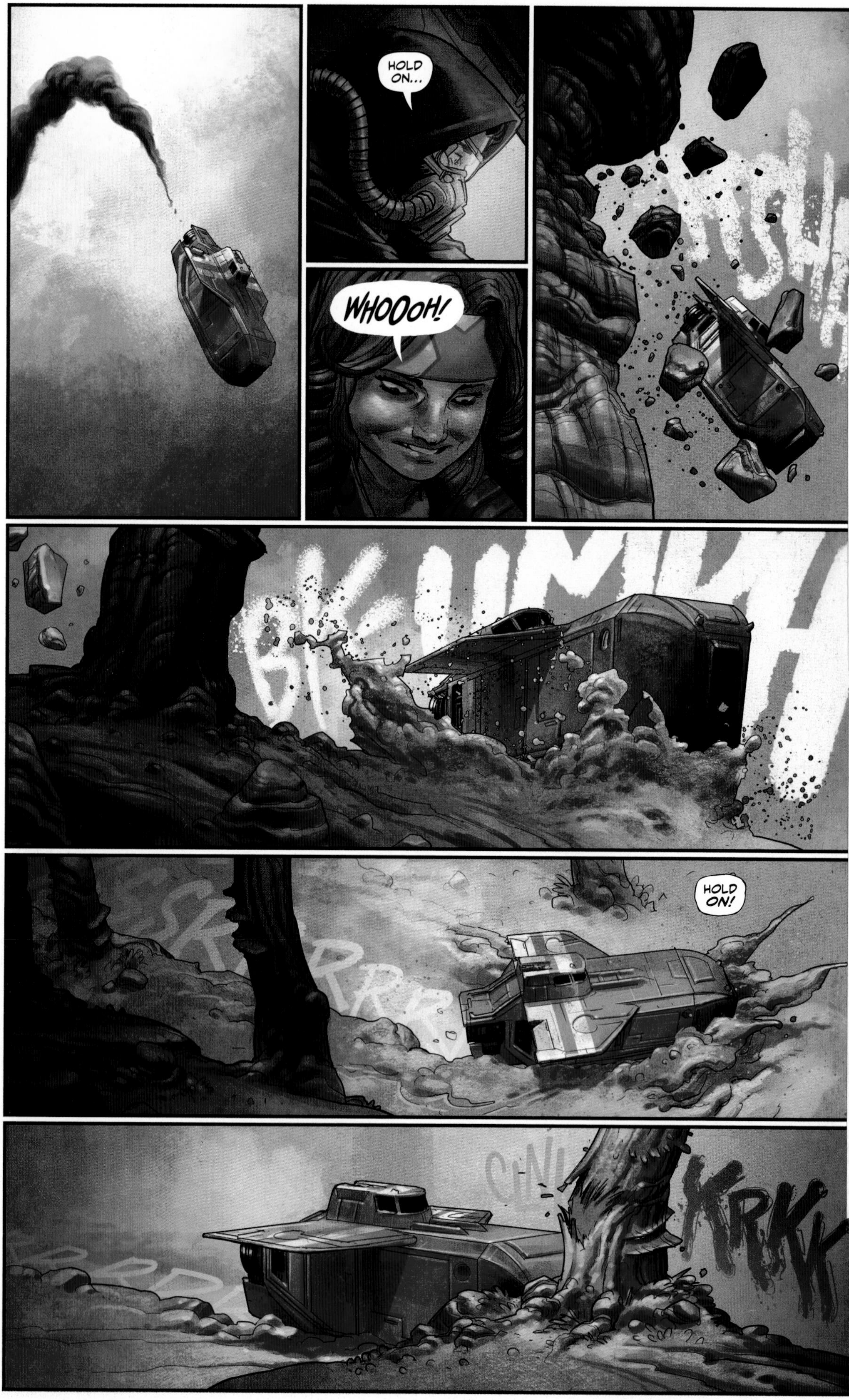
HOLD ON...
WHOOOH!
HOLD ON!
KRKK

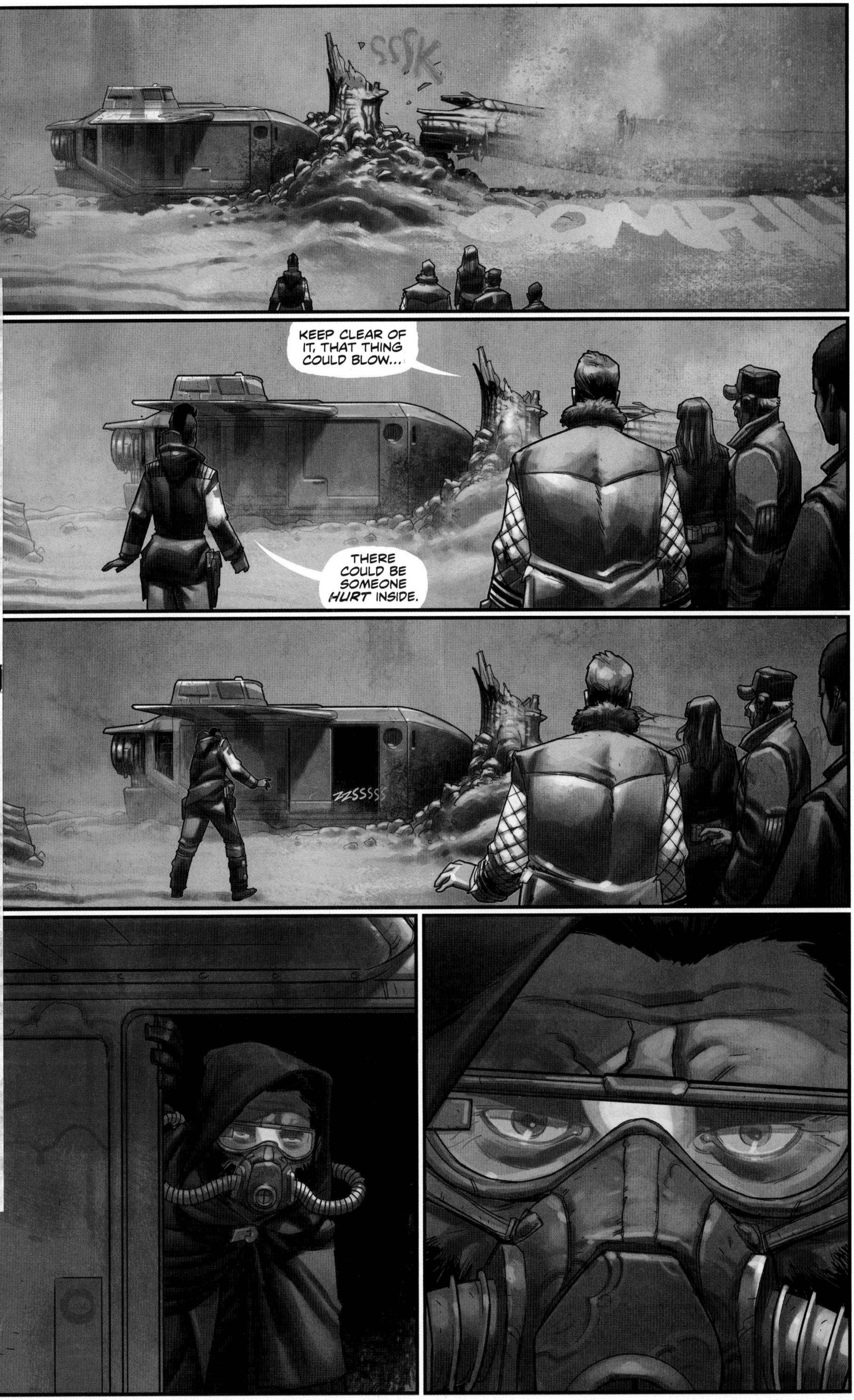
SSSK
KEEP CLEAR OF IT, THAT THING COULD BLOW...
THERE COULD BE SOMEONE *HURT* INSIDE.
ZZSSSSS

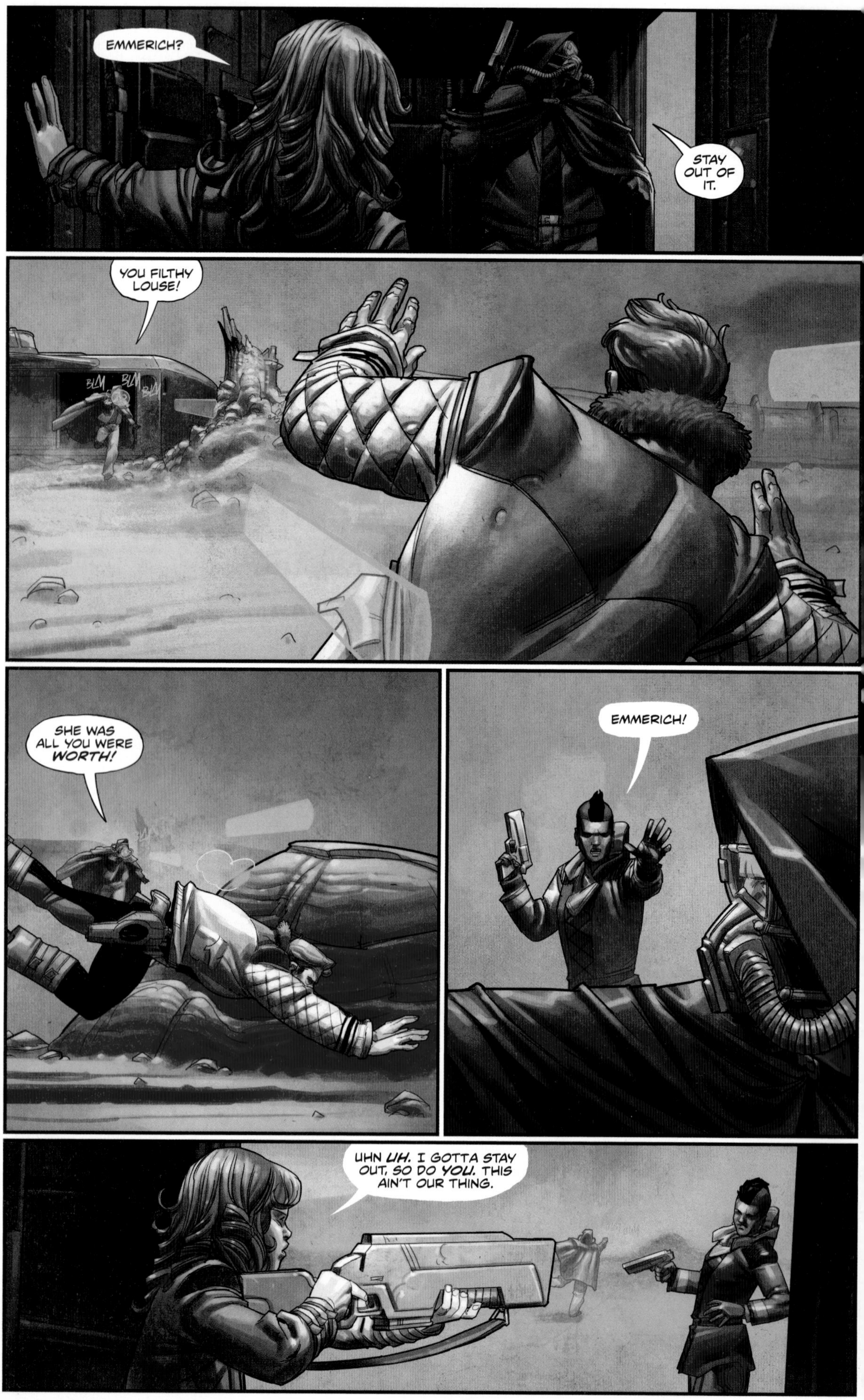
EMMERICH?
STAY OUT OF IT.
YOU FILTHY LOUSE!
BLM
BLM
BLM
SHE WAS ALL YOU WERE *WORTH!*
EMMERICH!
UHN *UH*. I GOTTA STAY OUT, SO DO *YOU*. THIS AIN'T OUR THING.

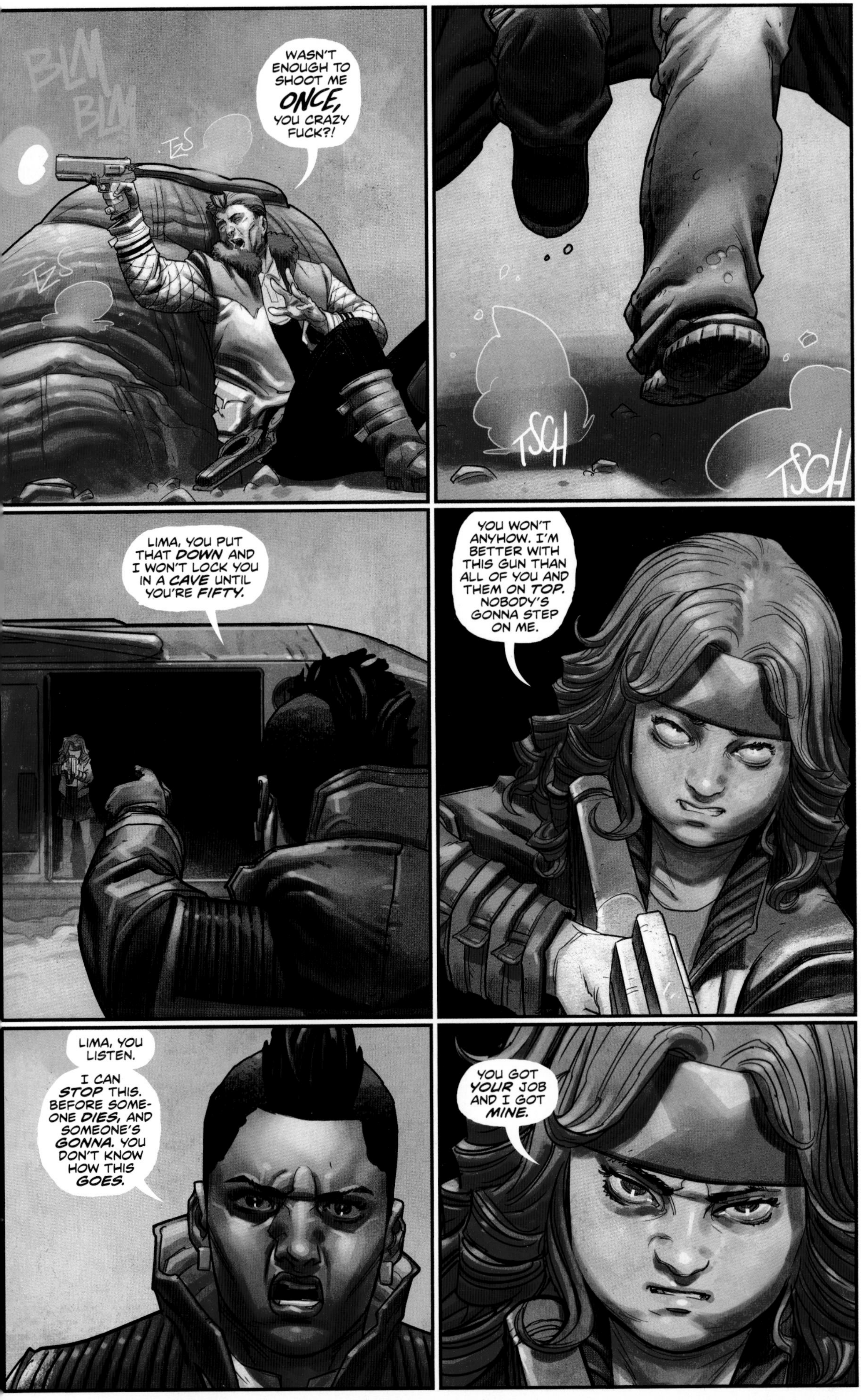
BLAM BLAM
WASN'T ENOUGH TO SHOOT ME ONCE, YOU CRAZY FUCK?!
TZS
TZS
TSCH
TSCH
LIMA, YOU PUT THAT DOWN AND I WON'T LOCK YOU IN A CAVE UNTIL YOU'RE FIFTY.
YOU WON'T ANYHOW. I'M BETTER WITH THIS GUN THAN ALL OF YOU AND THEM ON TOP. NOBODY'S GONNA STEP ON ME.
LIMA, YOU LISTEN.
I CAN STOP THIS. BEFORE SOME-ONE DIES, AND SOMEONE'S GONNA. YOU DON'T KNOW HOW THIS GOES.
YOU GOT YOUR JOB AND I GOT MINE.

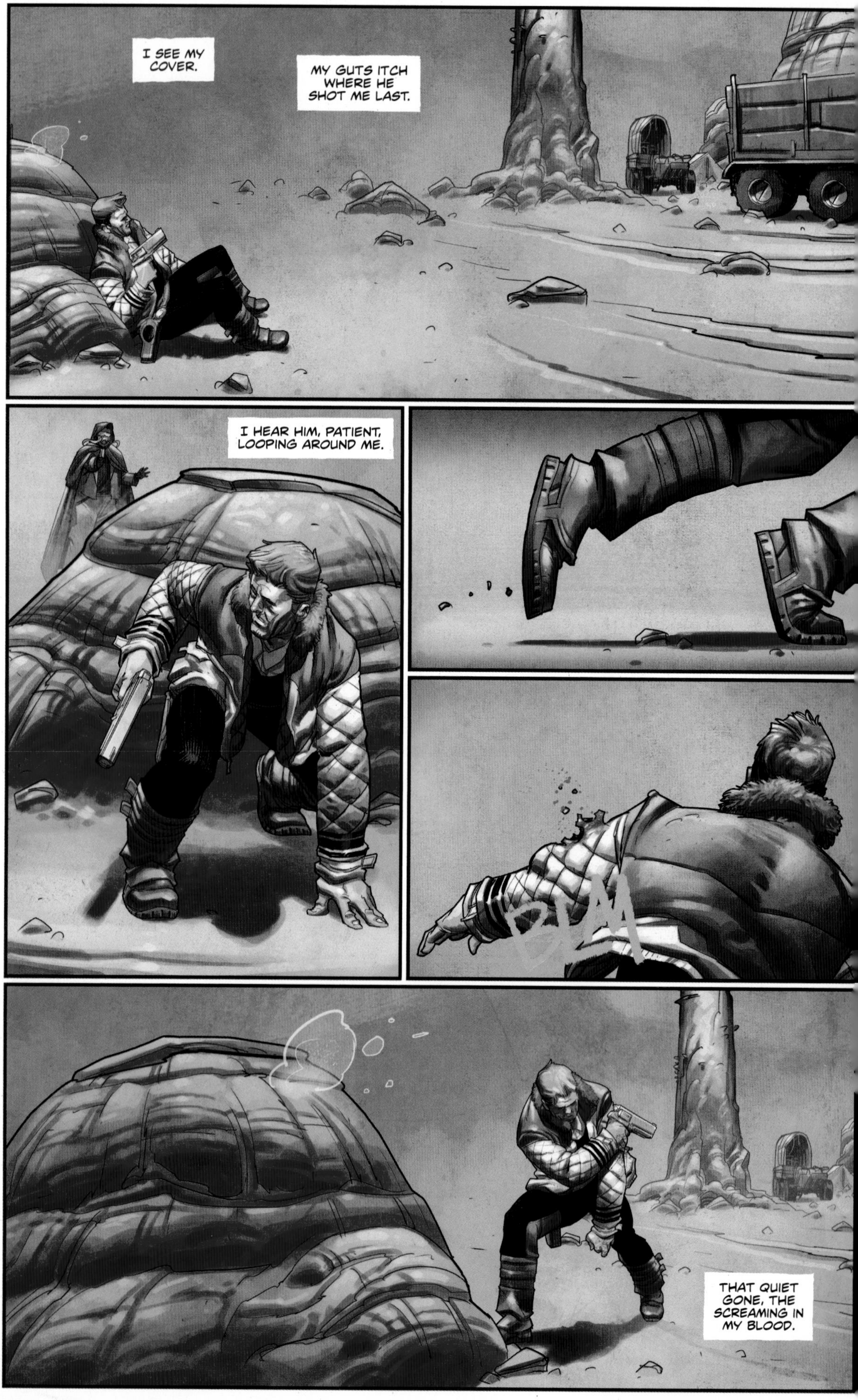
I SEE MY COVER.
MY GUTS ITCH WHERE HE SHOT ME LAST.
I HEAR HIM, PATIENT, LOOPING AROUND ME.
THAT QUIET GONE, THE SCREAMING IN MY BLOOD.

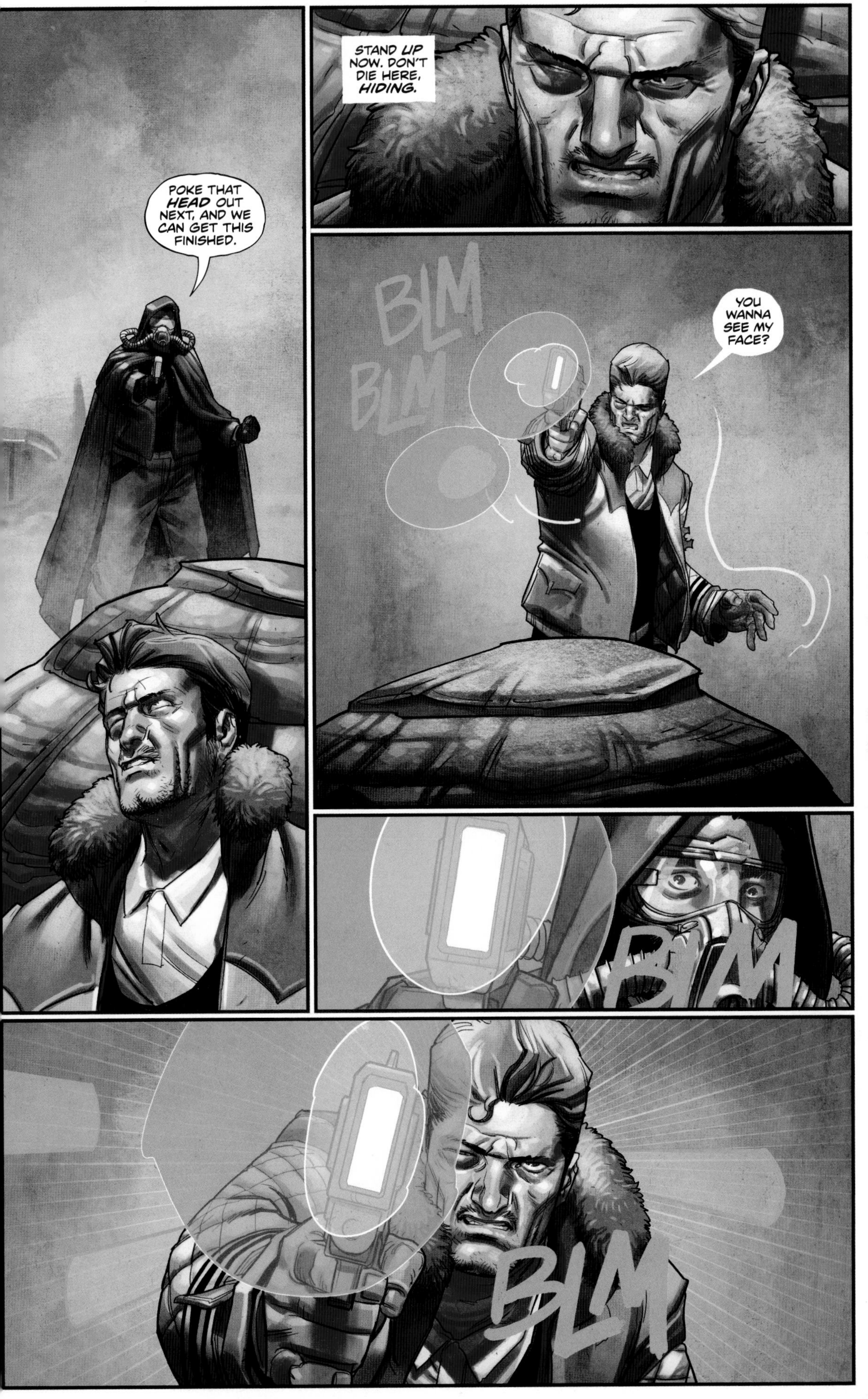
POKE THAT HEAD OUT NEXT, AND WE CAN GET THIS FINISHED.
STAND UP NOW. DON'T DIE HERE, HIDING.
BLM
BLM
YOU WANNA SEE MY FACE?
BLM
BLM

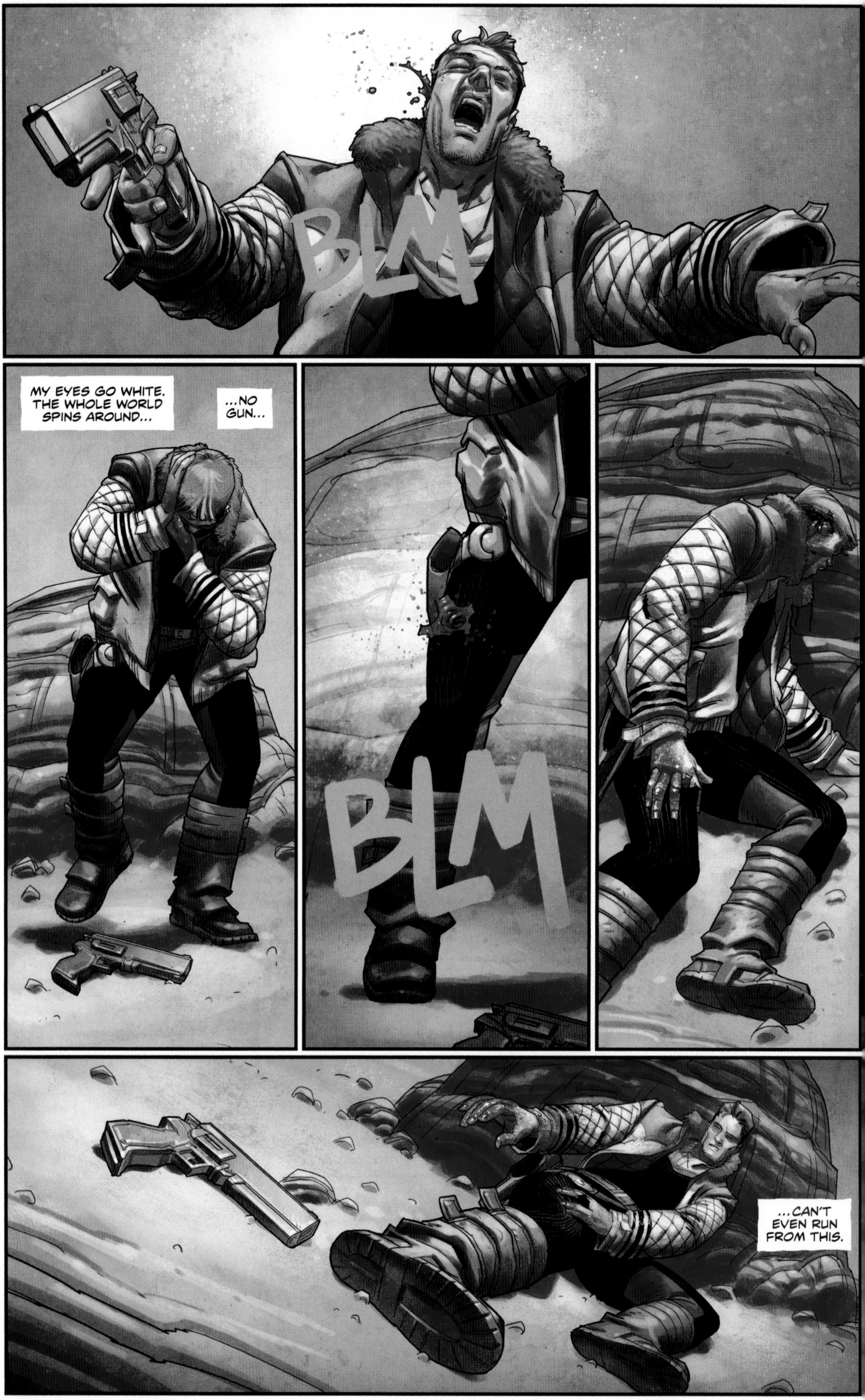
BLM
MY EYES GO WHITE. THE WHOLE WORLD SPINS AROUND...
...NO GUN...
BLM
...CAN'T EVEN RUN FROM THIS.

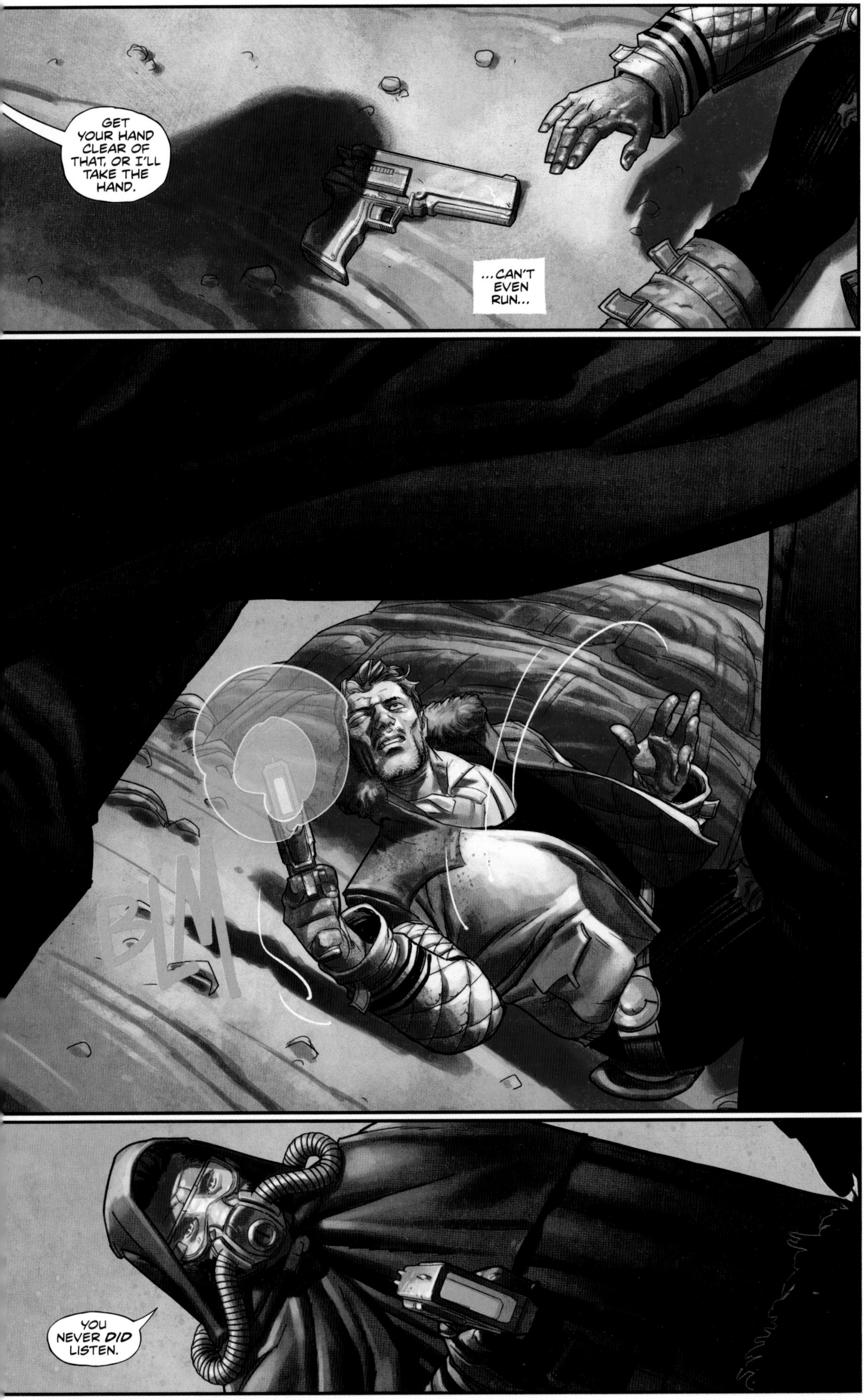
GET YOUR HAND CLEAR OF THAT, OR I'LL TAKE THE HAND.
...CAN'T EVEN RUN...
BLM
YOU NEVER *DID* LISTEN.

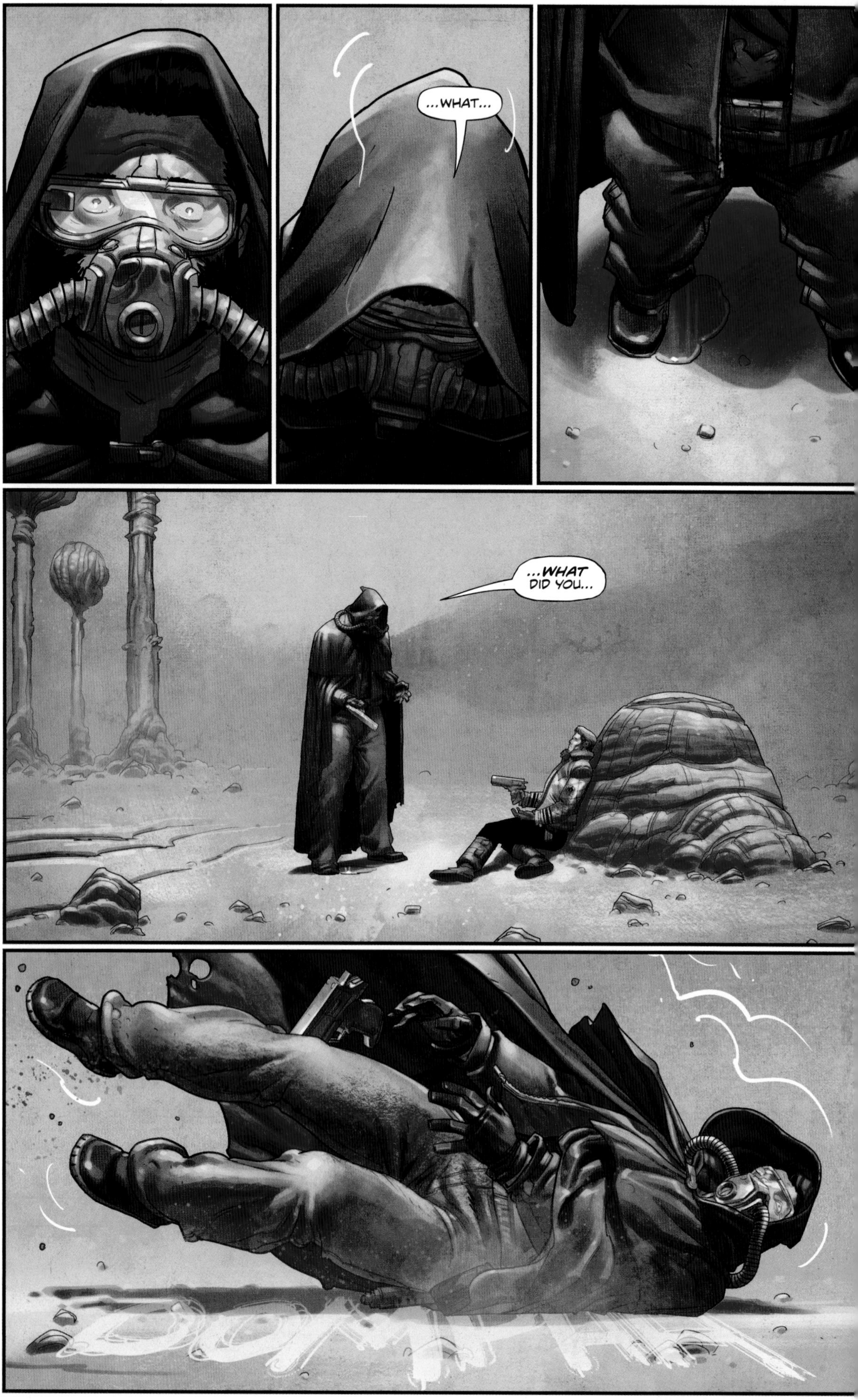
...WHAT...
...WHAT DID YOU...

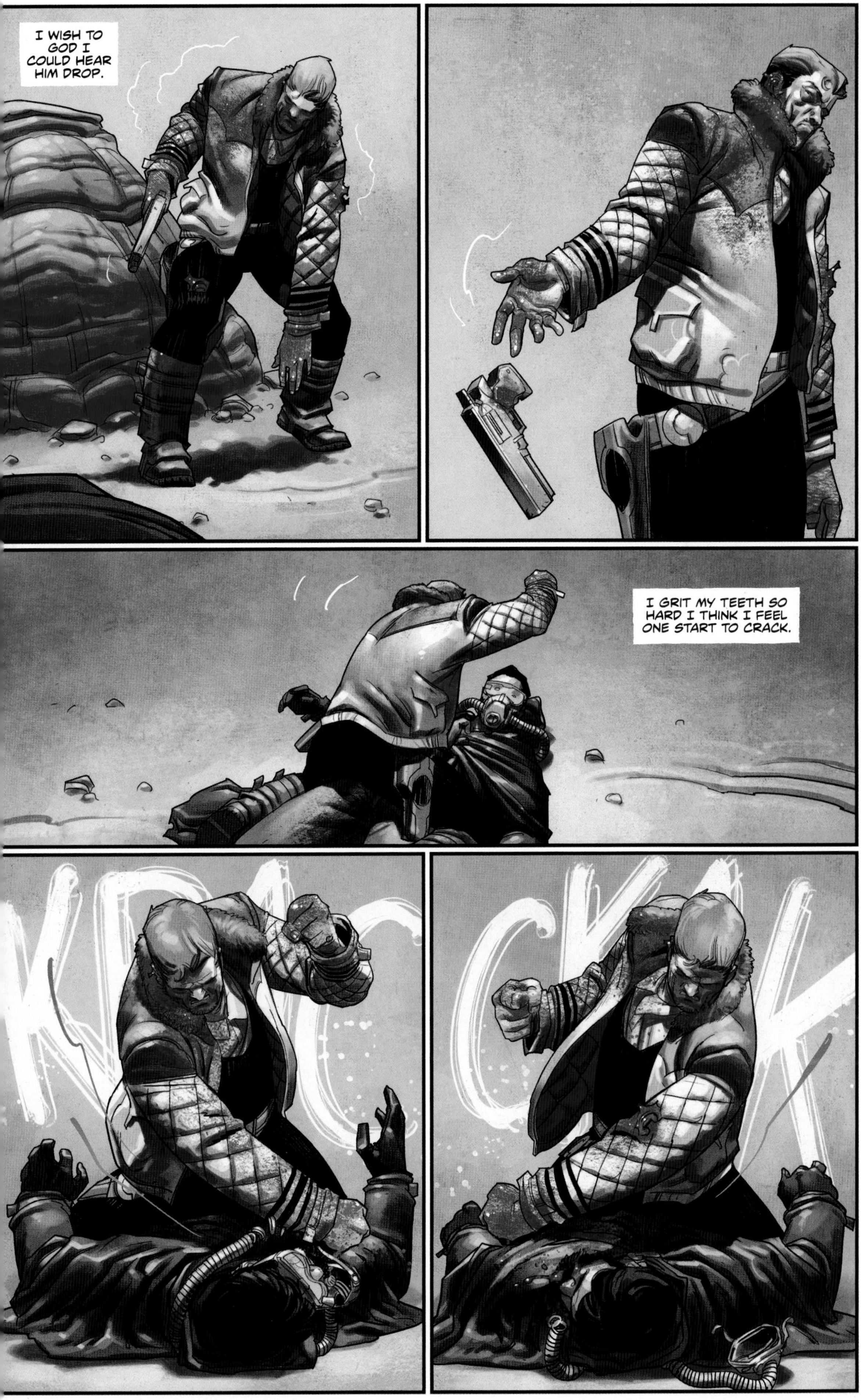

I WISH TO GOD I COULD HEAR HIM DROP.
I GRIT MY TEETH SO HARD I THINK I FEEL ONE START TO CRACK.

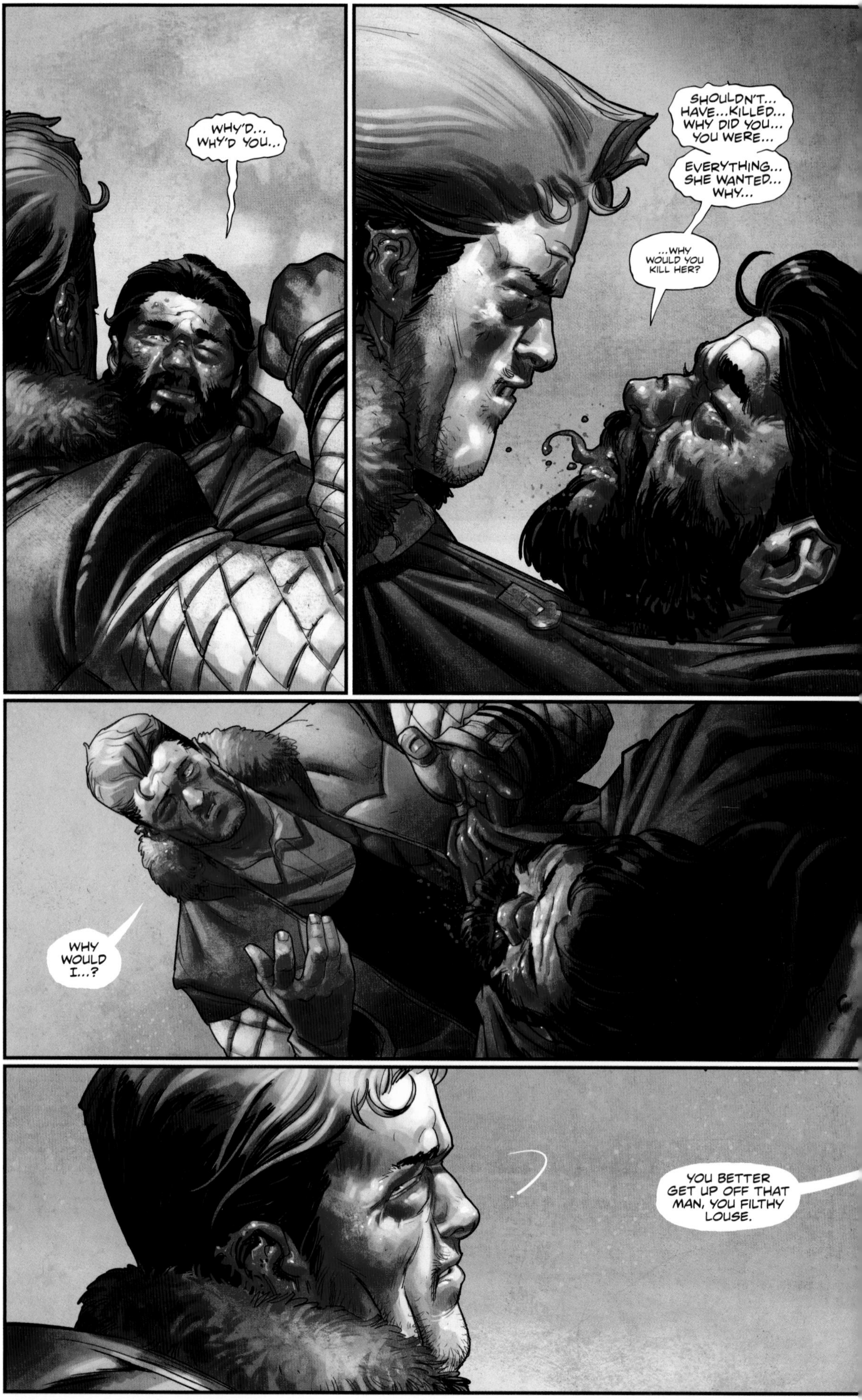
WHY'D... WHY'D YOU...
SHOULDN'T... HAVE...KILLED... WHY DID YOU... YOU WERE...
EVERYTHING... SHE WANTED... WHY...
...WHY WOULD YOU KILL HER?
WHY WOULD I...?
YOU BETTER GET UP OFF THAT MAN, YOU FILTHY LOUSE.

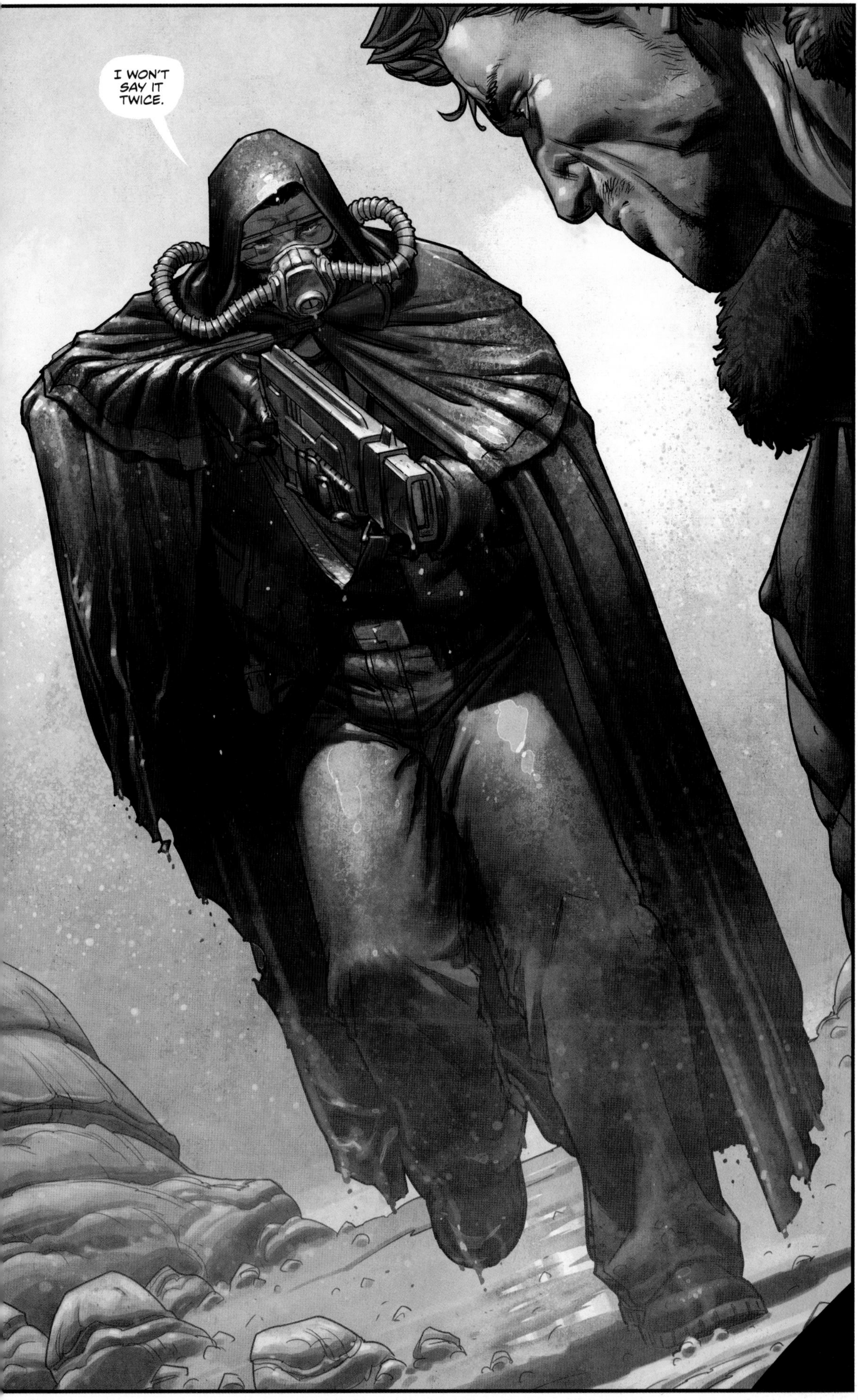
I WON'T SAY IT TWICE.

CHAPTER 16
TILL DEATH US PART

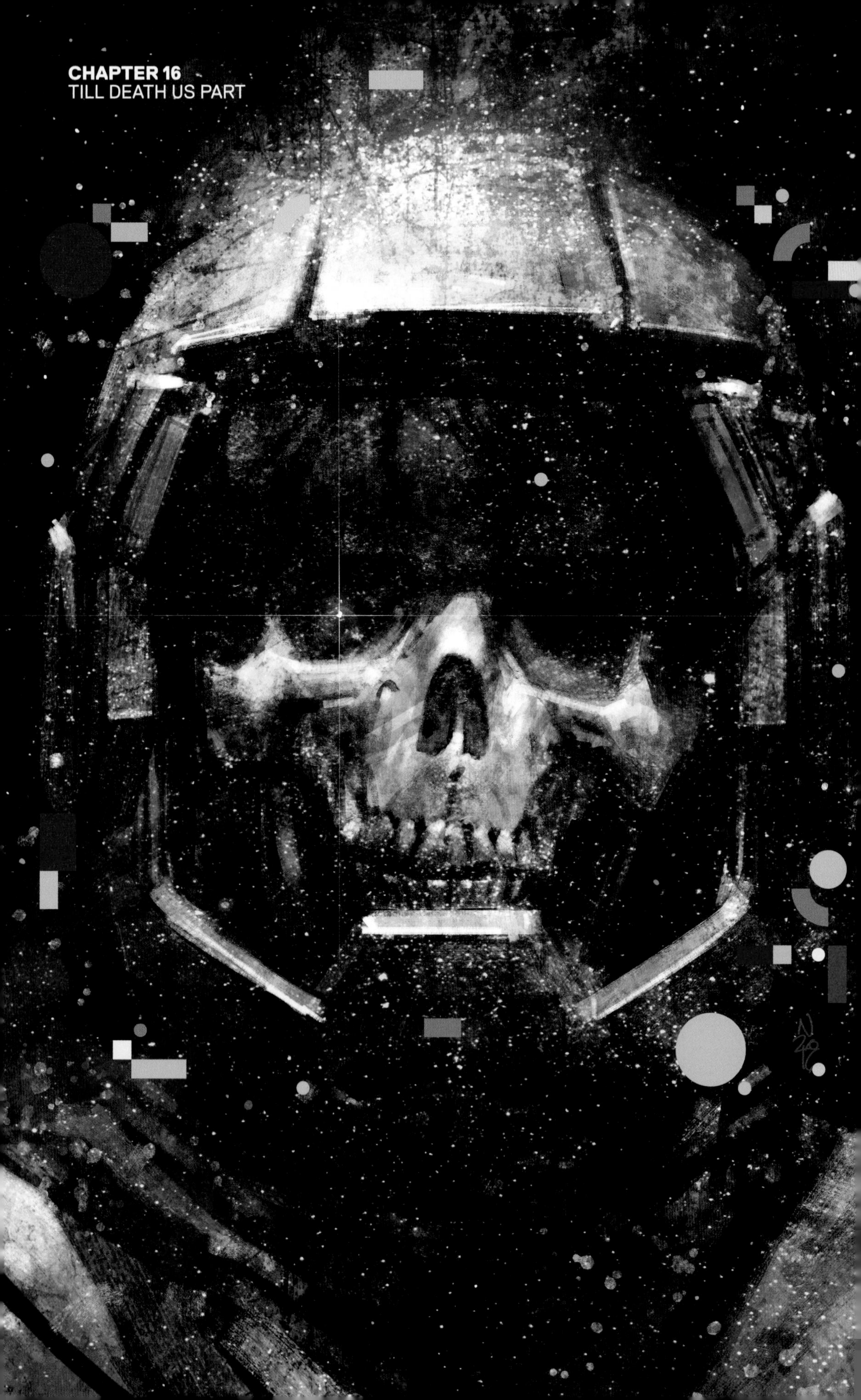

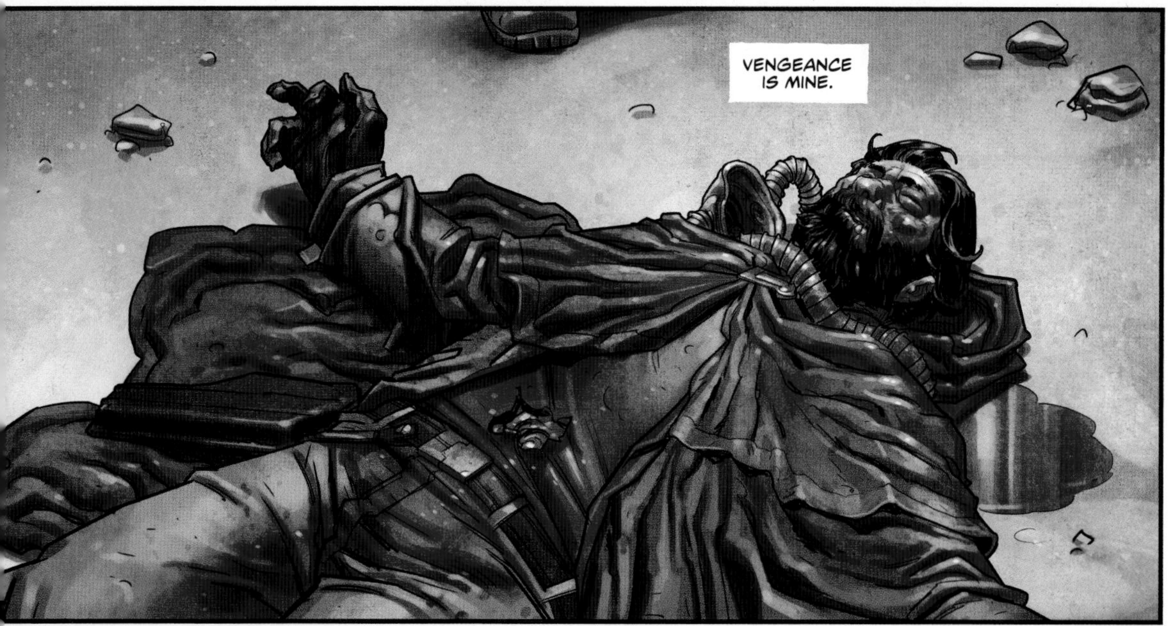
VENGEANCE IS MINE.

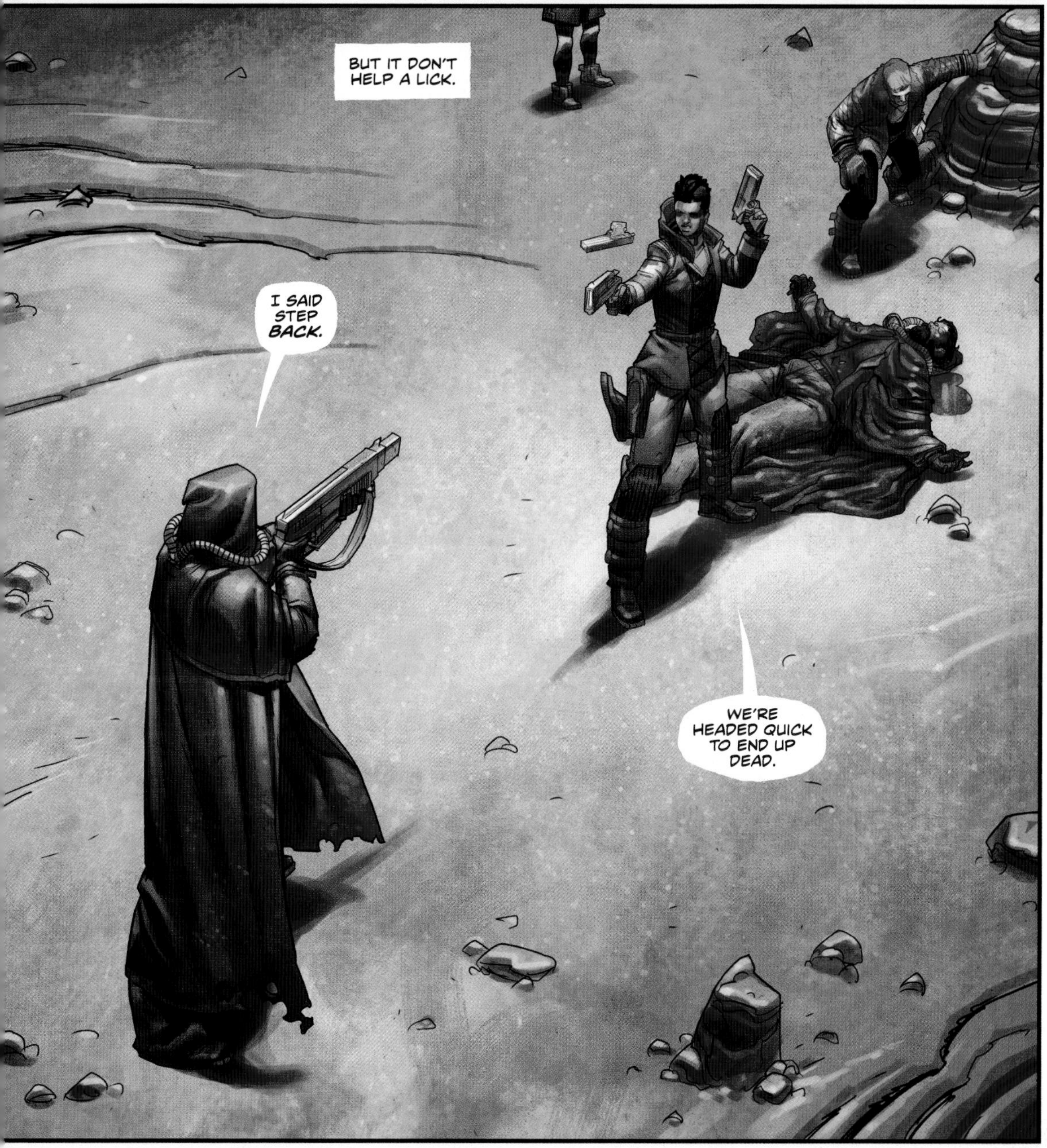
BUT IT DON'T HELP A LICK.
I SAID STEP BACK.
WE'RE HEADED QUICK TO END UP DEAD.

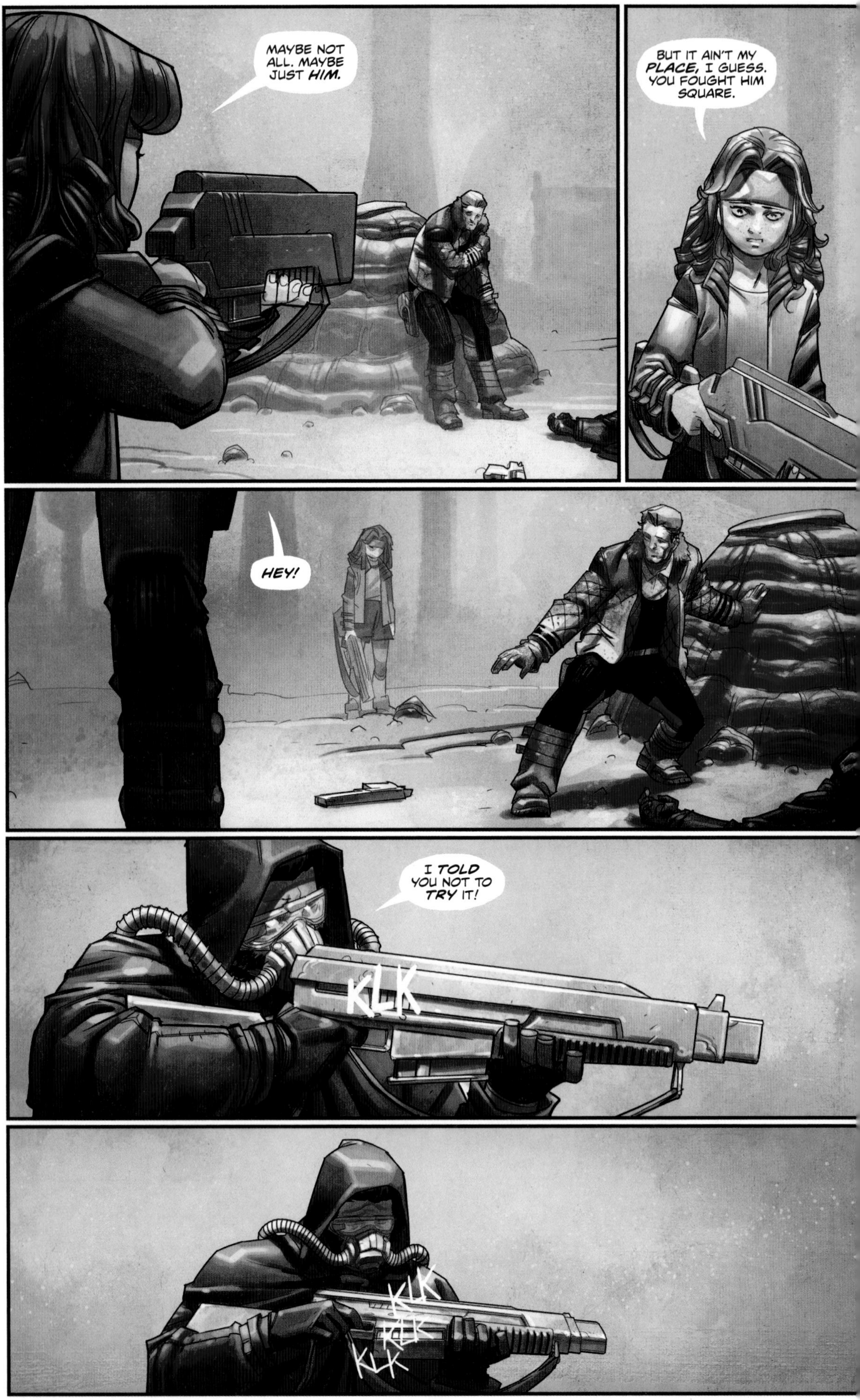
MAYBE NOT ALL. MAYBE JUST *HIM*.
BUT IT AIN'T MY *PLACE*, I GUESS. YOU FOUGHT HIM SQUARE.
HEY!
I *TOLD* YOU NOT TO *TRY* IT!
KLK
KLK
KLK
KLK

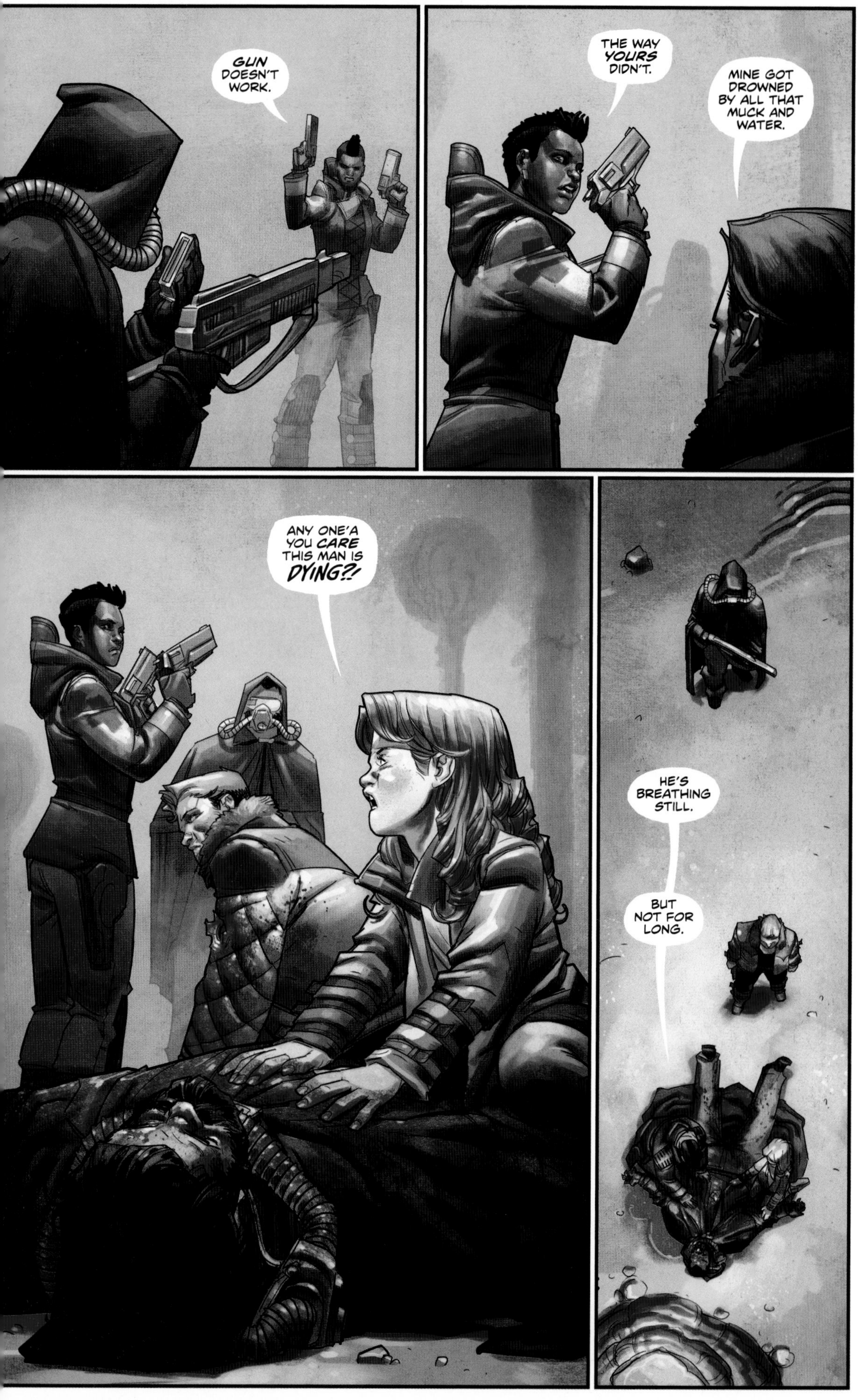
GUN DOESN'T WORK.
THE WAY YOURS DIDN'T.
MINE GOT DROWNED BY ALL THAT MUCK AND WATER.
ANY ONE'A YOU CARE THIS MAN IS DYING?!
HE'S BREATHING STILL.
BUT NOT FOR LONG.

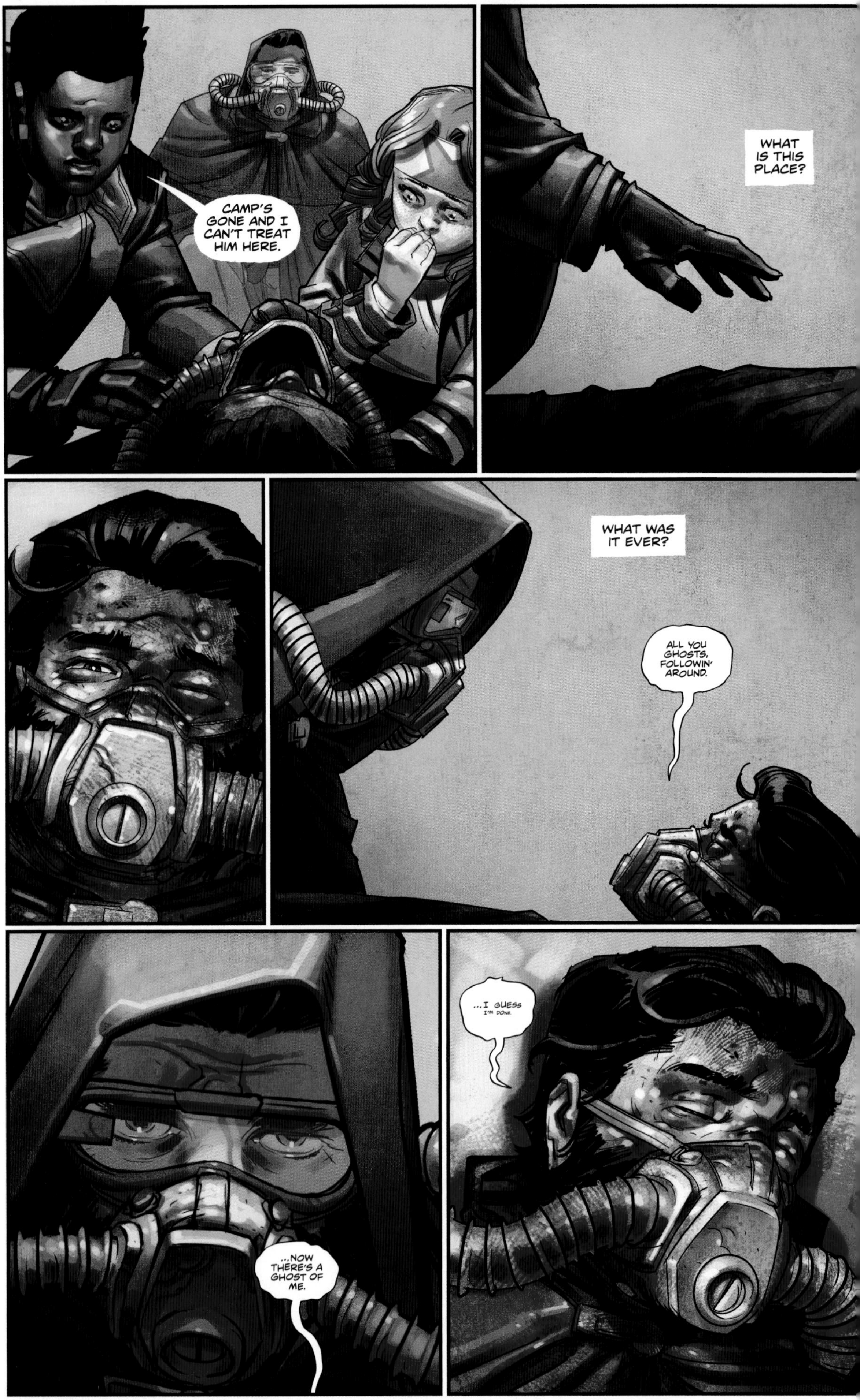
CAMP'S GONE AND I CAN'T TREAT HIM HERE.
WHAT IS THIS PLACE?
WHAT WAS IT EVER?
ALL YOU GHOSTS, FOLLOWIN' AROUND.
...NOW THERE'S A GHOST OF ME.
...I GUESS I'M DONE.

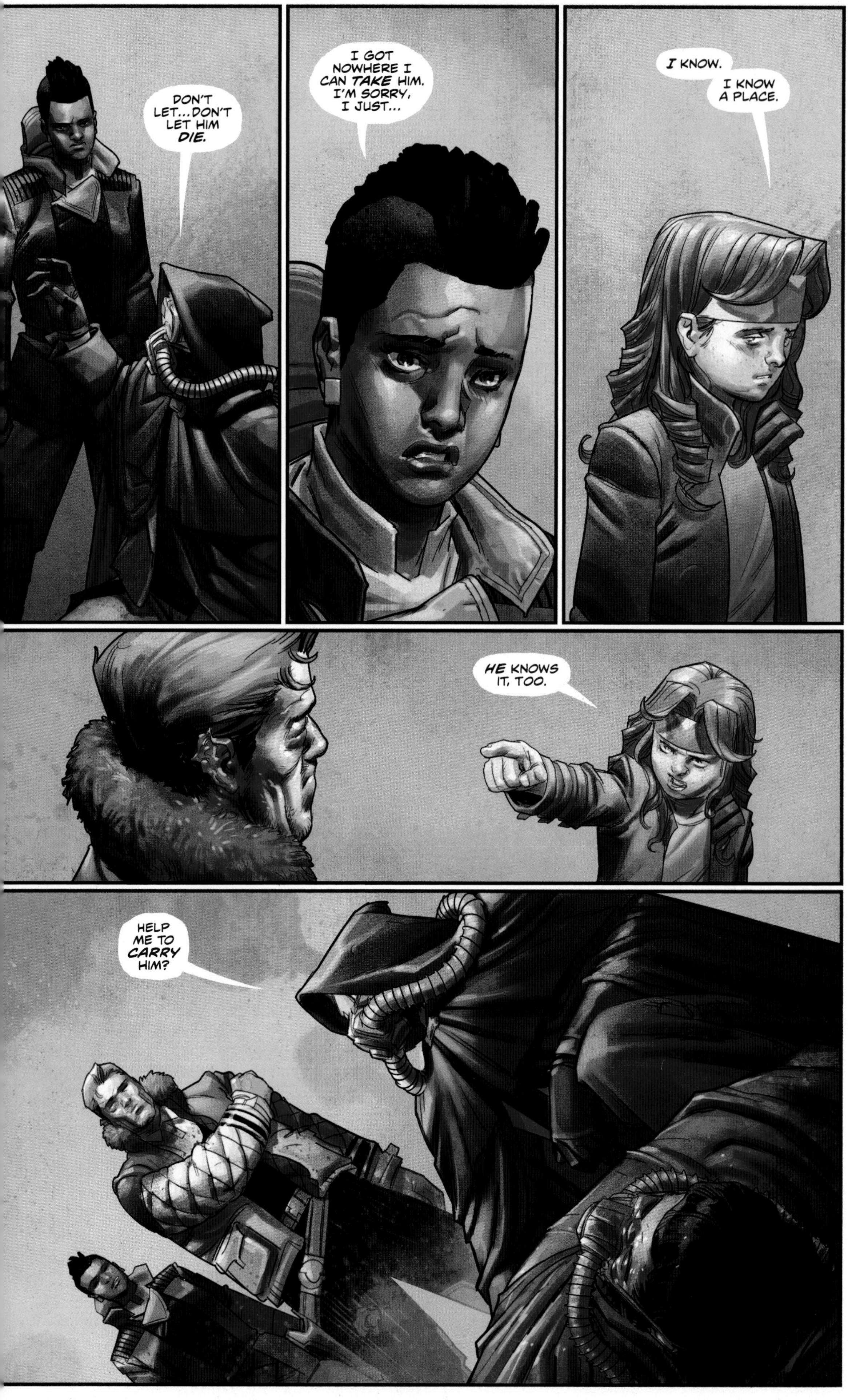
DON'T LET...DON'T LET HIM DIE.
I GOT NOWHERE I CAN TAKE HIM. I'M SORRY, I JUST...
I KNOW.
I KNOW A PLACE.
HE KNOWS IT, TOO.
HELP ME TO CARRY HIM?

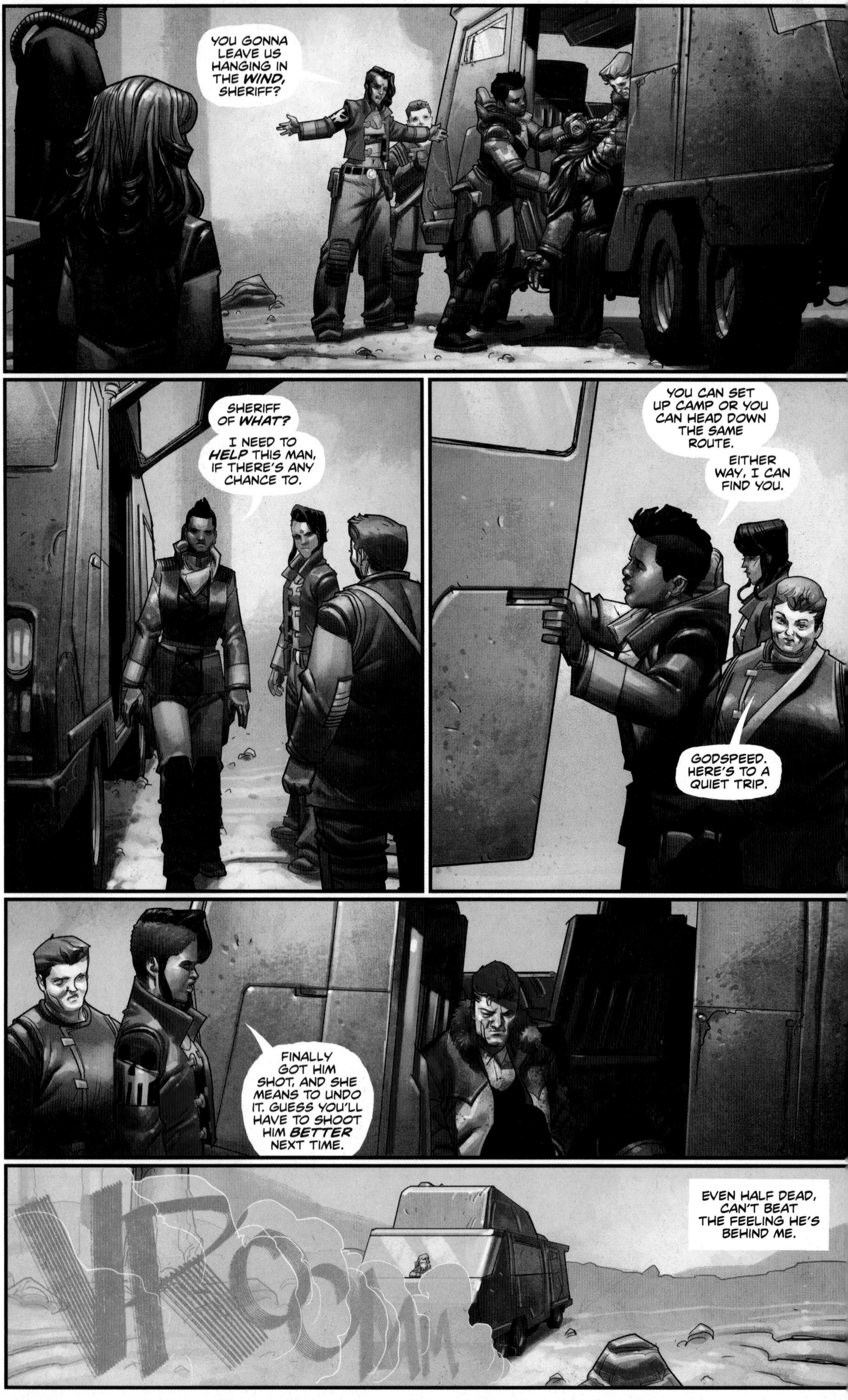
YOU GONNA LEAVE US HANGING IN THE *WIND,* SHERIFF?
SHERIFF OF *WHAT?*
I NEED TO *HELP* THIS MAN, IF THERE'S ANY CHANCE TO.
YOU CAN SET UP CAMP OR YOU CAN HEAD DOWN THE SAME ROUTE.
EITHER WAY, I CAN FIND YOU.
GODSPEED. HERE'S TO A QUIET TRIP.
FINALLY GOT HIM SHOT, AND SHE MEANS TO UNDO IT. GUESS YOU'LL HAVE TO SHOOT HIM *BETTER* NEXT TIME.
VROOMM
EVEN HALF DEAD, CAN'T BEAT THE FEELING HE'S BEHIND ME.

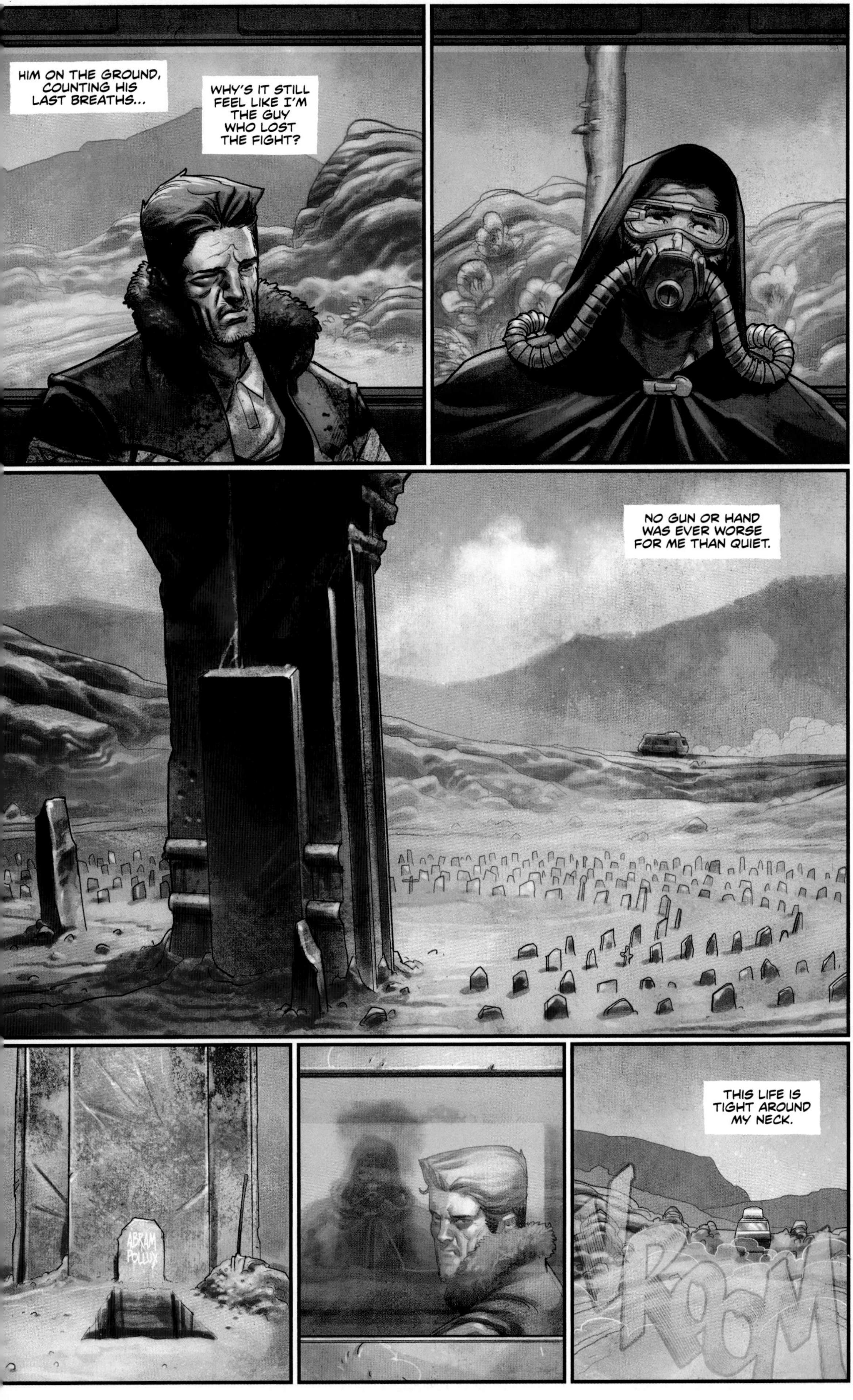
HIM ON THE GROUND, COUNTING HIS LAST BREATHS...
WHY'S IT STILL FEEL LIKE I'M THE GUY WHO LOST THE FIGHT?
NO GUN OR HAND WAS EVER WORSE FOR ME THAN QUIET.
ABRAM POLLUX
THIS LIFE IS TIGHT AROUND MY NECK.
VROOM

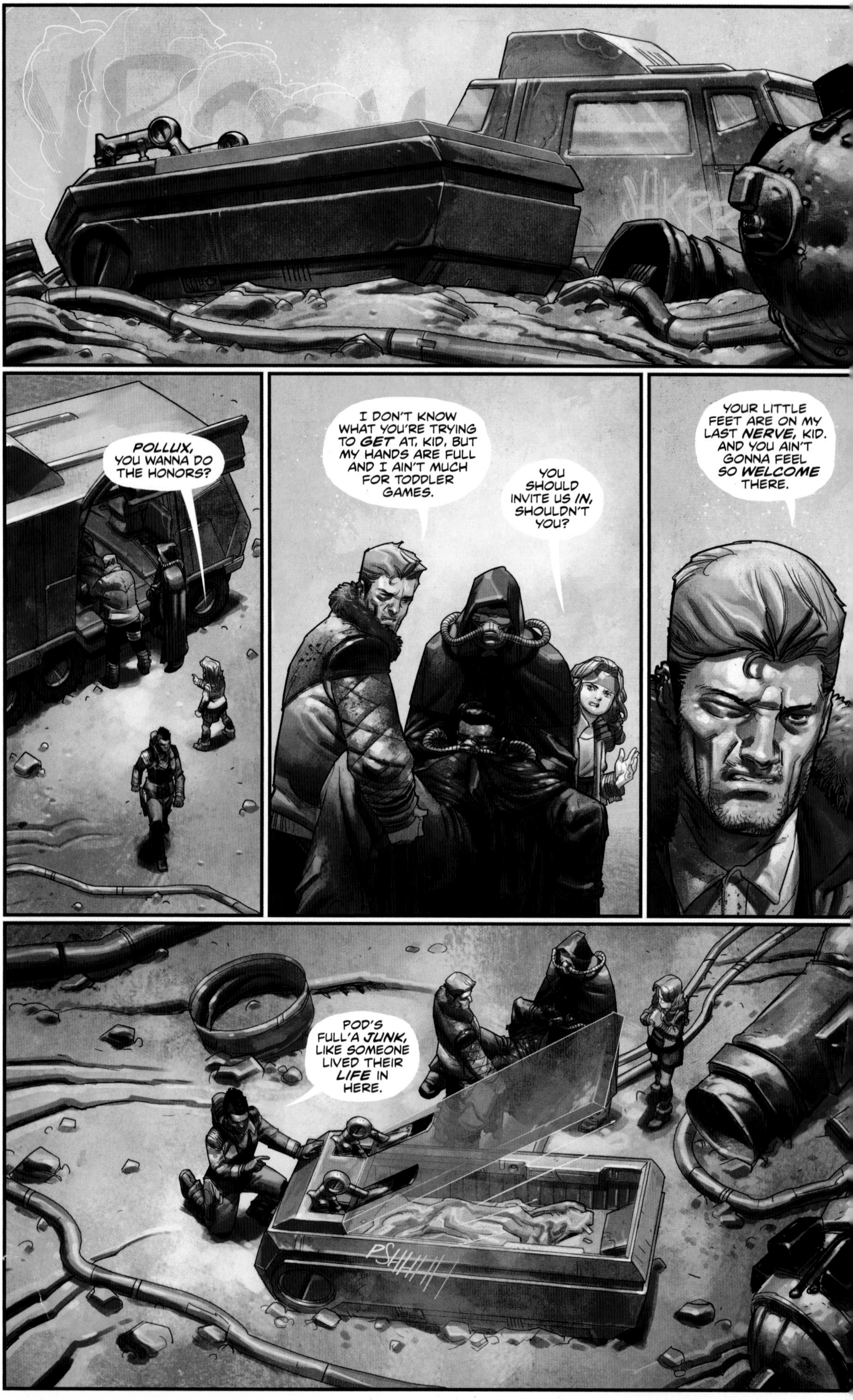
SHKRR
POLLUX, YOU WANNA DO THE HONORS?
I DON'T KNOW WHAT YOU'RE TRYING TO GET AT, KID, BUT MY HANDS ARE FULL AND I AIN'T MUCH FOR TODDLER GAMES.
YOU SHOULD INVITE US IN, SHOULDN'T YOU?
YOUR LITTLE FEET ARE ON MY LAST NERVE, KID. AND YOU AIN'T GONNA FEEL SO WELCOME THERE.
POD'S FULL'A JUNK, LIKE SOMEONE LIVED THEIR LIFE IN HERE.
PSHHHH

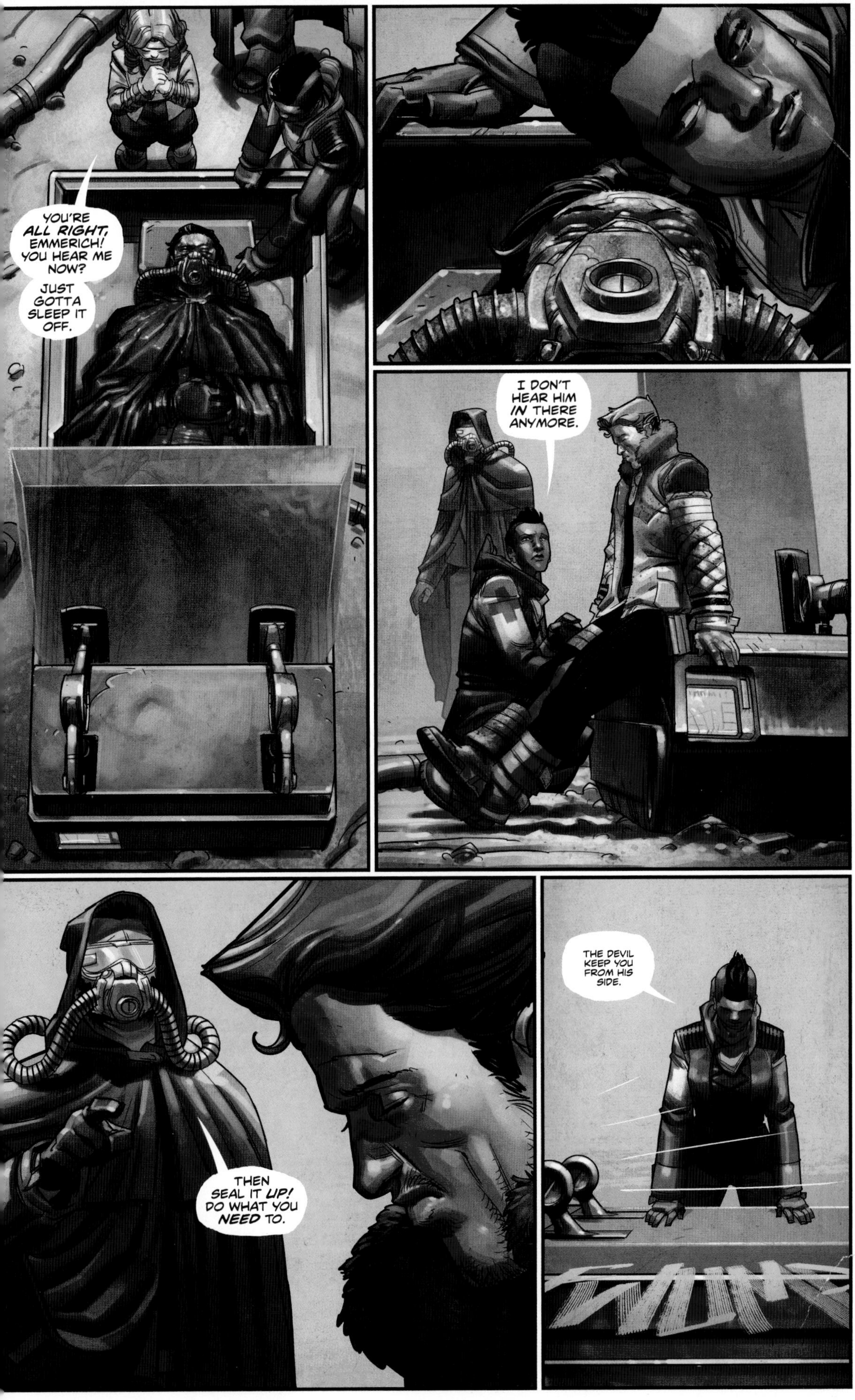
YOU'RE ALL RIGHT, EMMERICH! YOU HEAR ME NOW?
JUST GOTTA SLEEP IT OFF.
I DON'T HEAR HIM IN THERE ANYMORE.
THEN SEAL IT UP! DO WHAT YOU NEED TO.
THE DEVIL KEEP YOU FROM HIS SIDE.

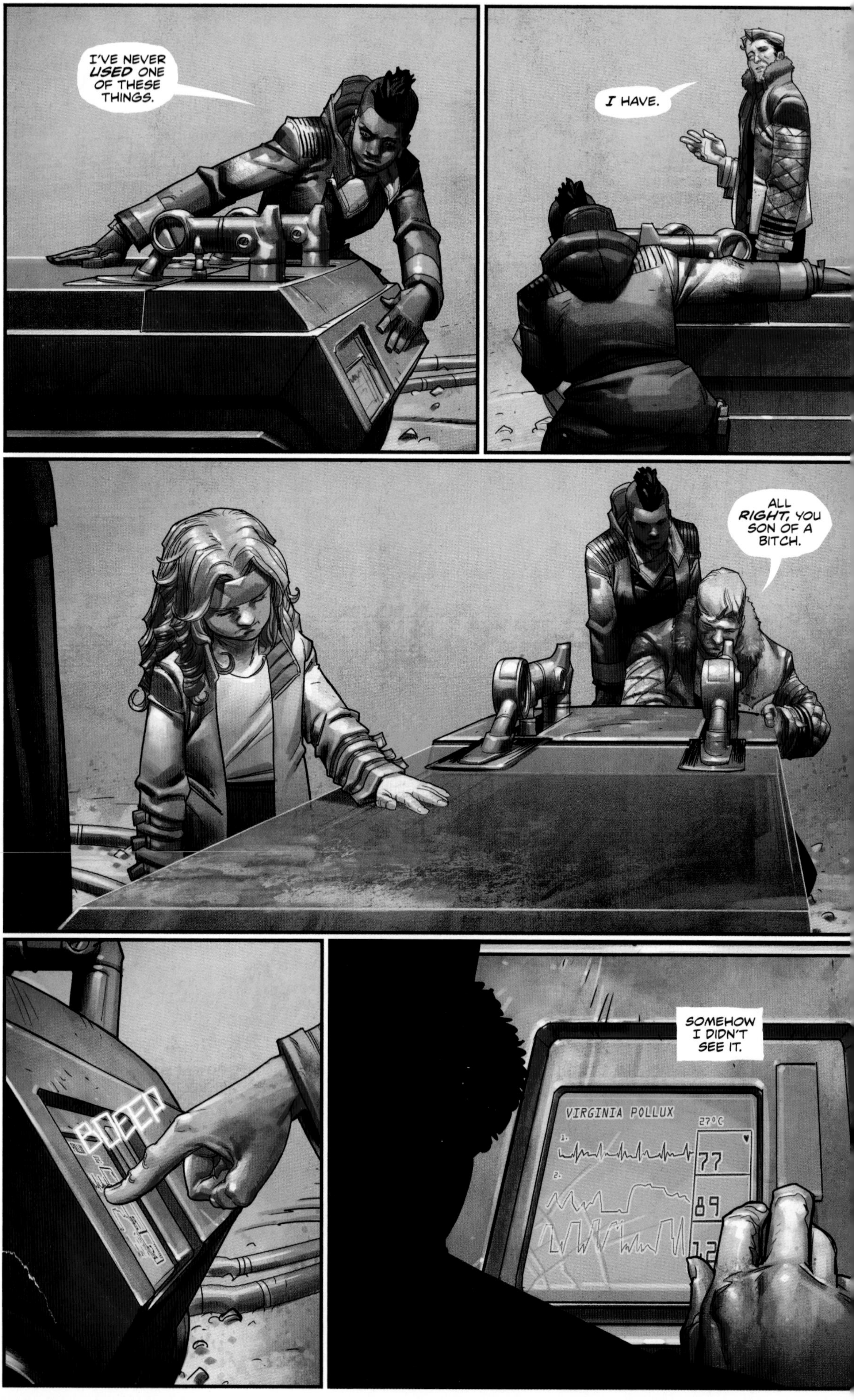
I'VE NEVER USED ONE OF THESE THINGS.
I HAVE.
ALL RIGHT, YOU SON OF A BITCH.
BEEEP
SOMEHOW I DIDN'T SEE IT.
VIRGINIA POLLUX
27°C
77
89

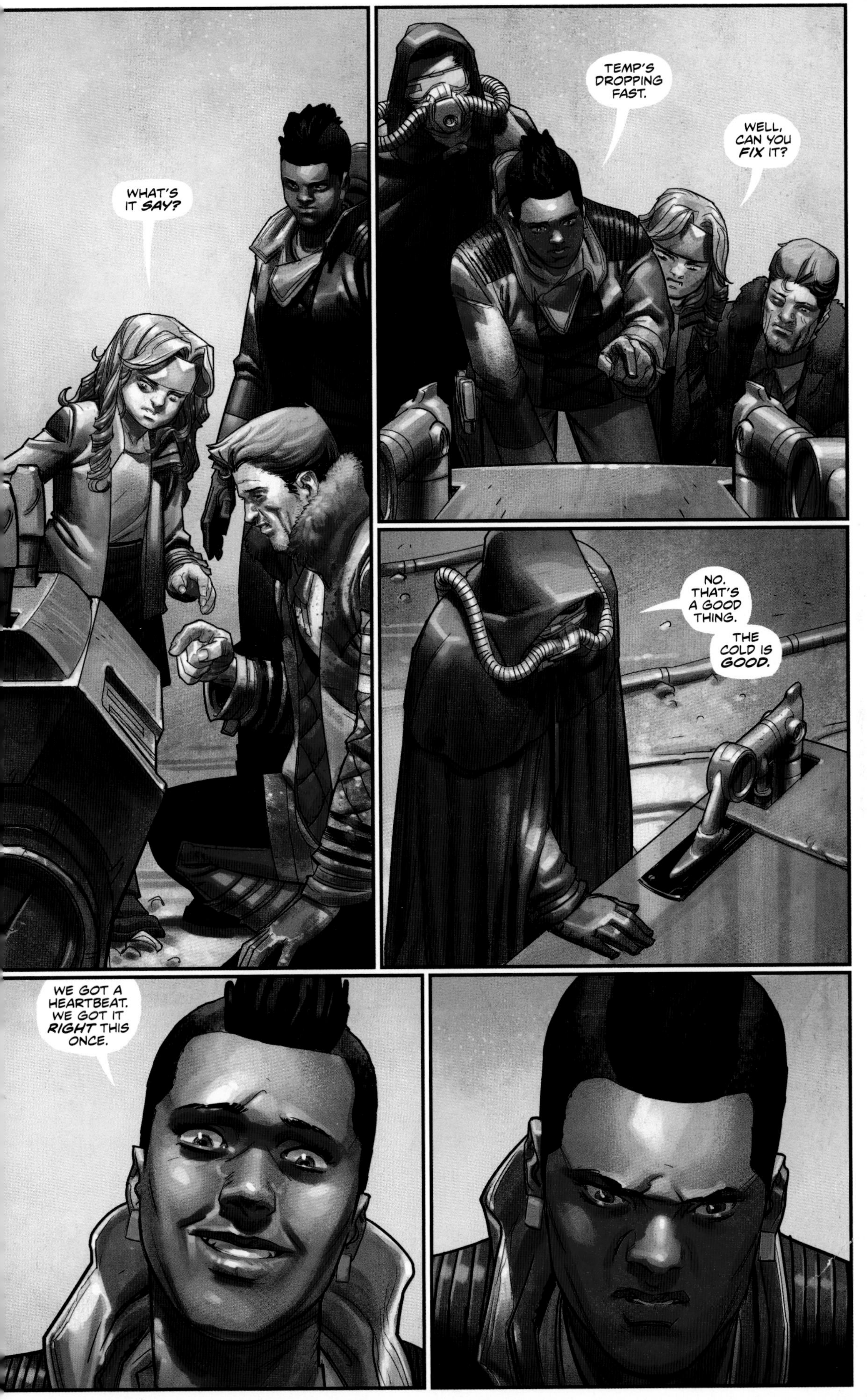
WHAT'S IT SAY?
TEMP'S DROPPING FAST.
WELL, CAN YOU FIX IT?
NO. THAT'S A GOOD THING.
THE COLD IS GOOD.
WE GOT A HEARTBEAT. WE GOT IT RIGHT THIS ONCE.

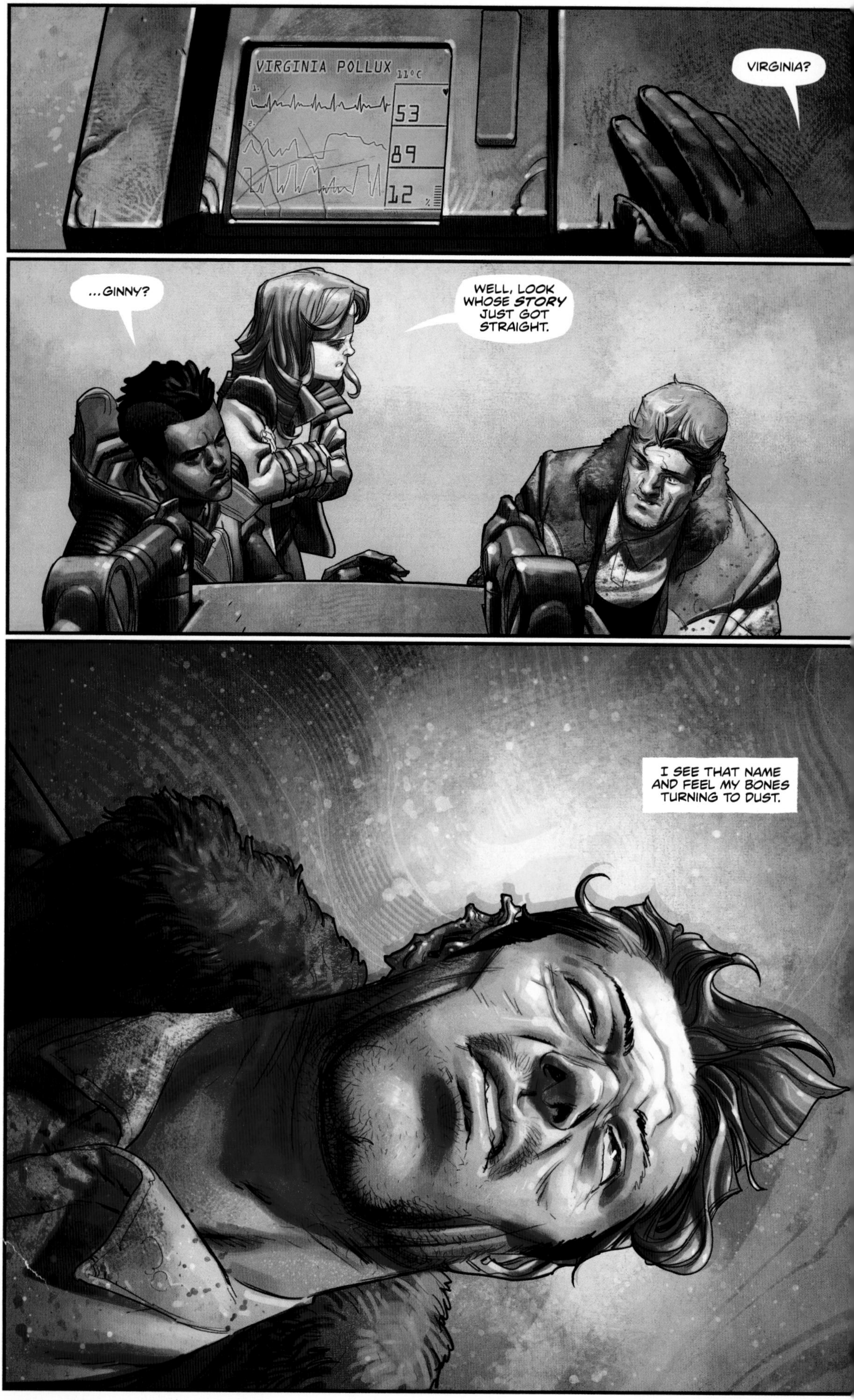
VIRGINIA POLLUX
11°C
53
89
12 %
VIRGINIA?
...GINNY?
WELL, LOOK WHOSE STORY JUST GOT STRAIGHT.
I SEE THAT NAME AND FEEL MY BONES TURNING TO DUST.

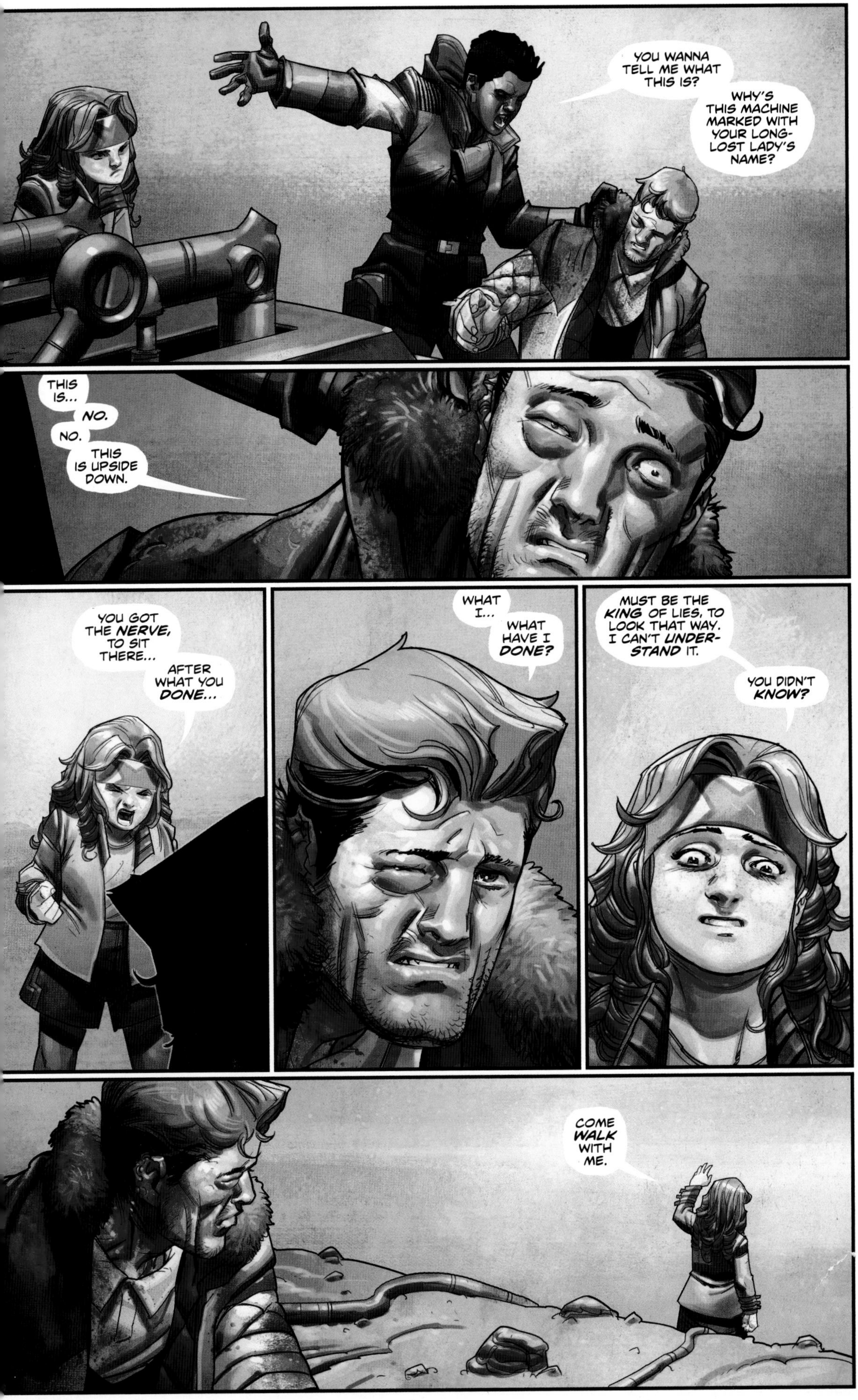
YOU WANNA TELL ME WHAT THIS IS?
WHY'S THIS MACHINE MARKED WITH YOUR LONG-LOST LADY'S NAME?
THIS IS...
NO.
NO.
THIS IS UPSIDE DOWN.
YOU GOT THE NERVE, TO SIT THERE...
AFTER WHAT YOU DONE...
WHAT I...
WHAT HAVE I DONE?
MUST BE THE KING OF LIES, TO LOOK THAT WAY. I CAN'T UNDER-STAND IT.
YOU DIDN'T KNOW?
COME WALK WITH ME.

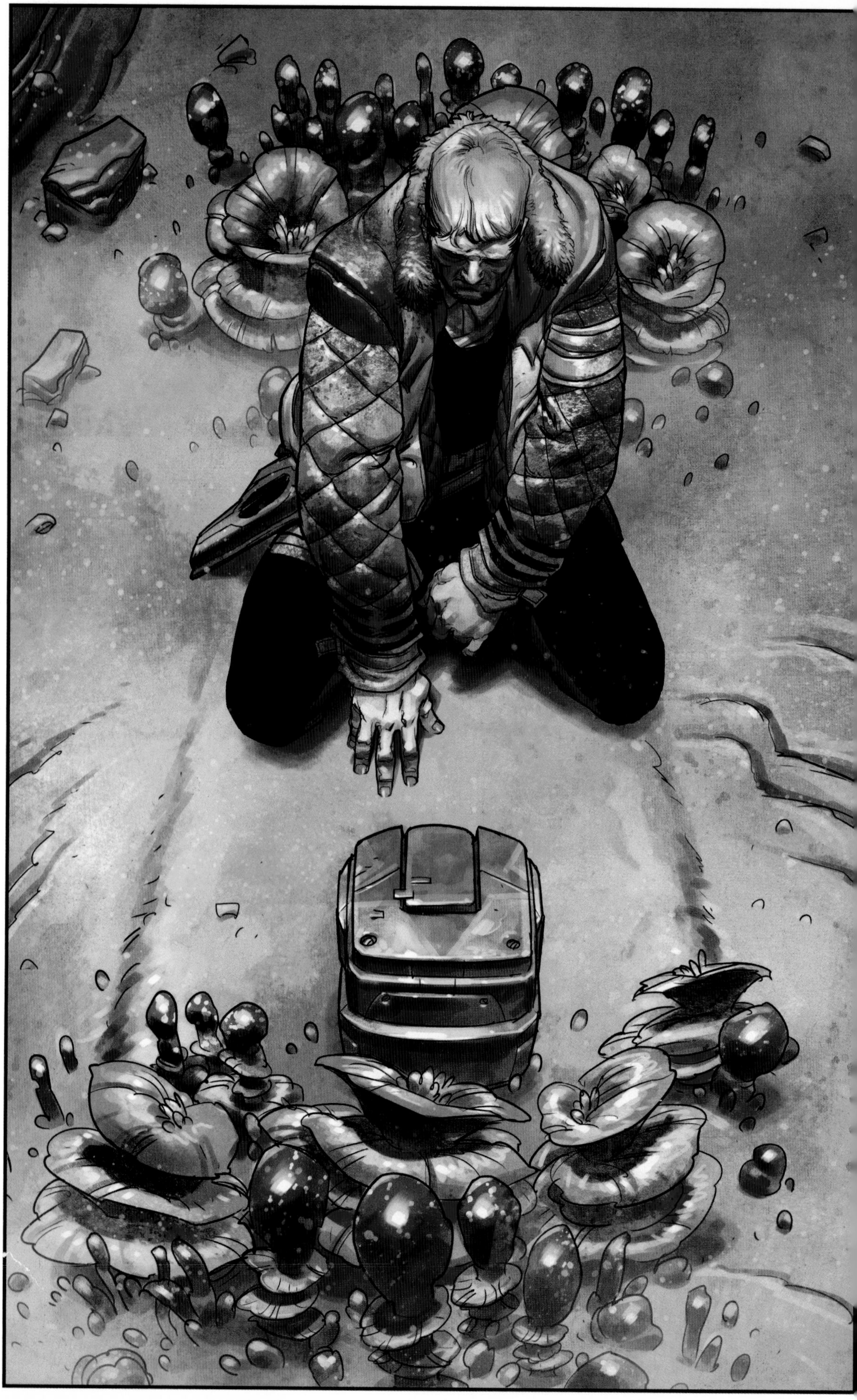

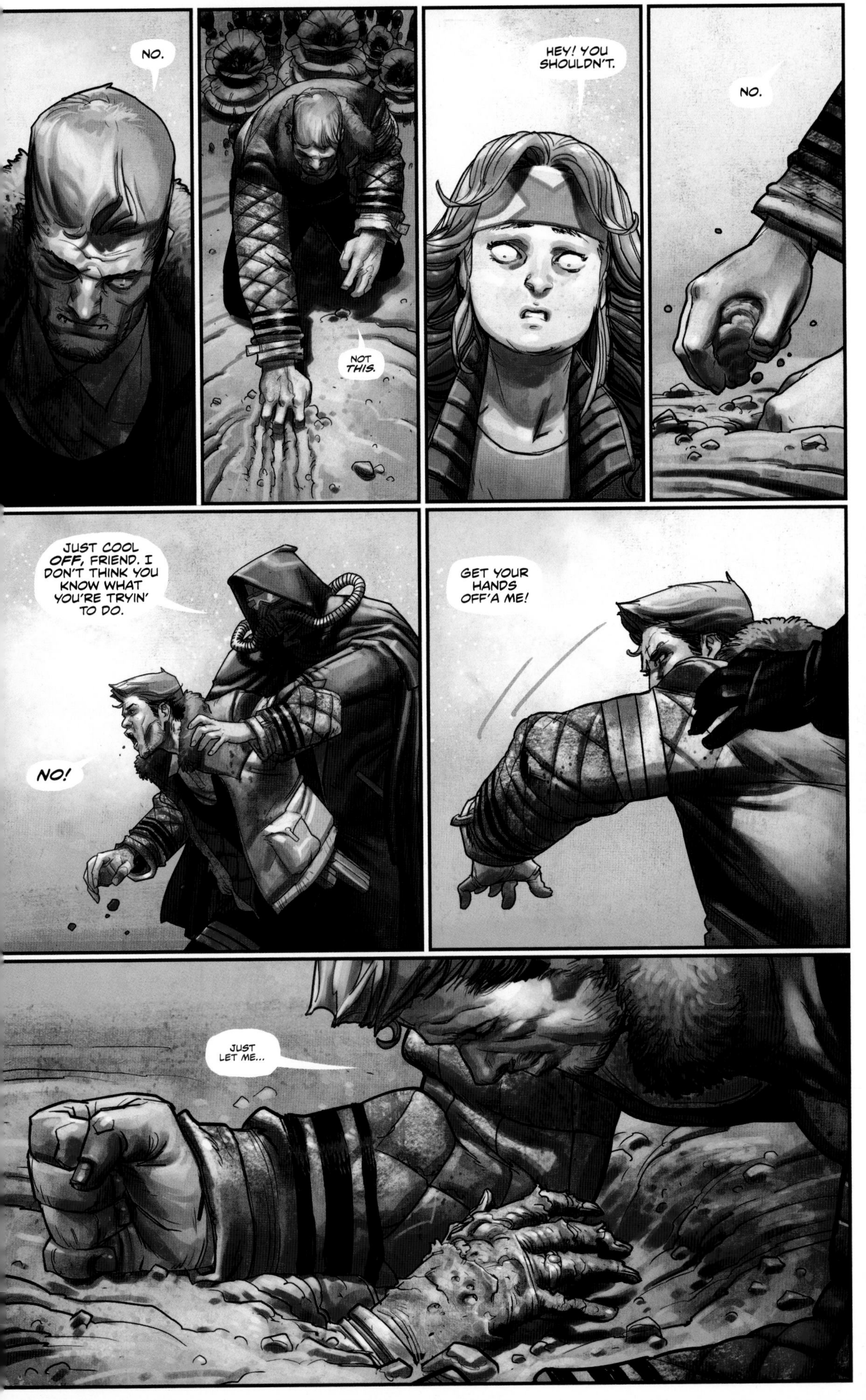
NO.
NOT THIS.
HEY! YOU SHOULDN'T.
NO.
JUST COOL OFF, FRIEND. I DON'T THINK YOU KNOW WHAT YOU'RE TRYIN' TO DO.
NO!
GET YOUR HANDS OFF'A ME!
JUST LET ME...

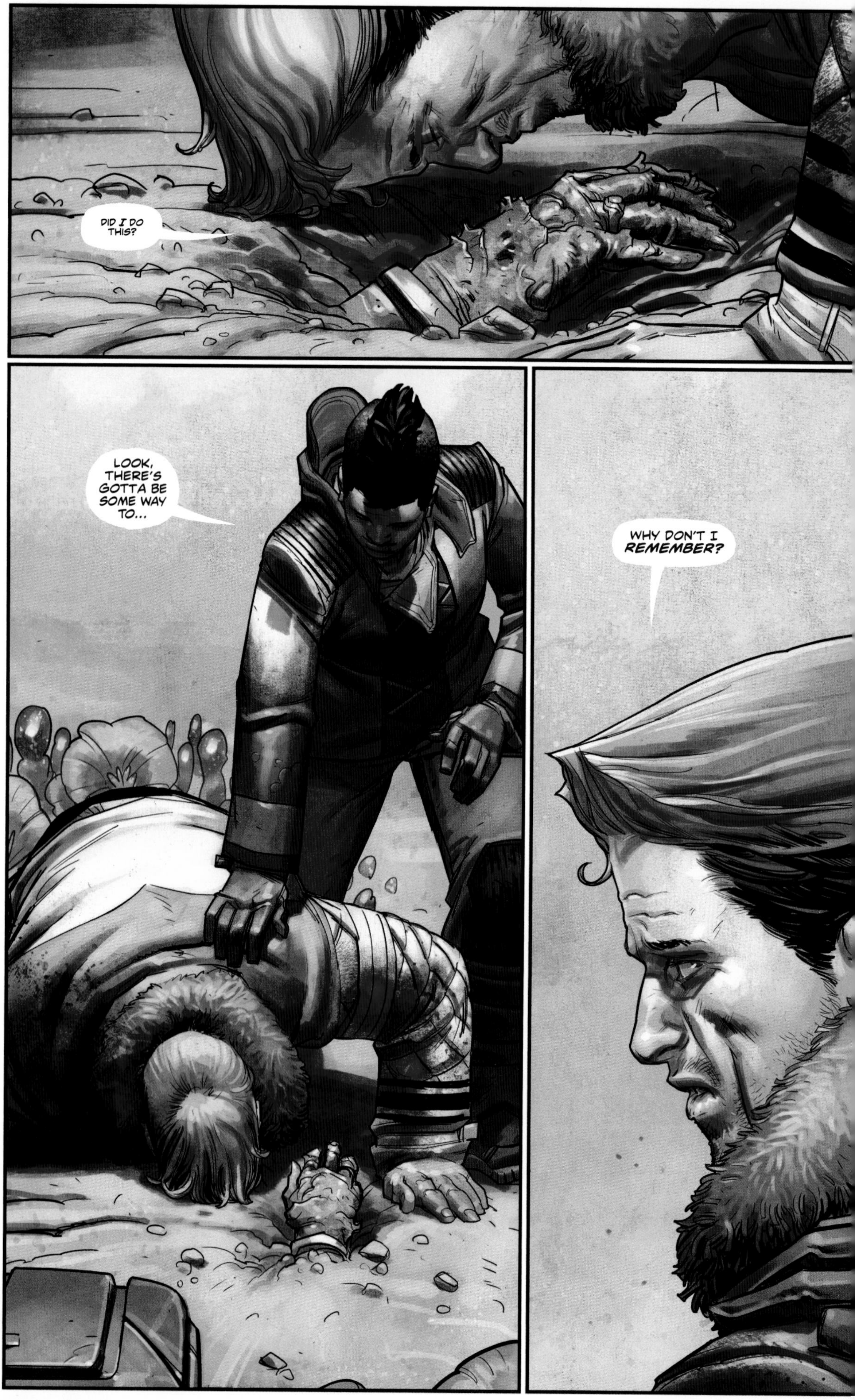
DID I DO THIS?
LOOK, THERE'S GOTTA BE SOME WAY TO...
WHY DON'T I *REMEMBER?*

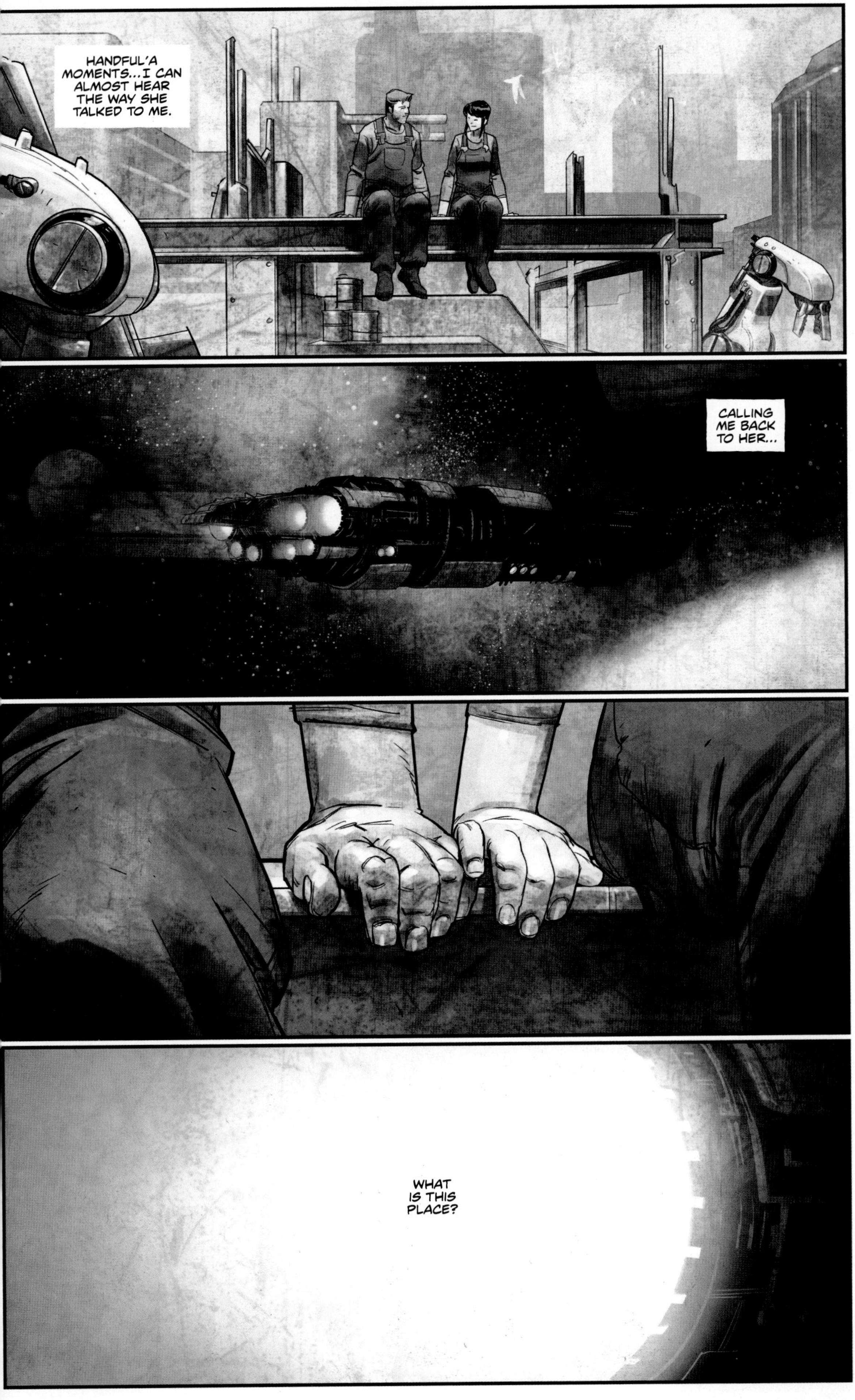
HANDFUL'A MOMENTS...I CAN ALMOST HEAR THE WAY SHE TALKED TO ME.
CALLING ME BACK TO HER...
WHAT IS THIS PLACE?

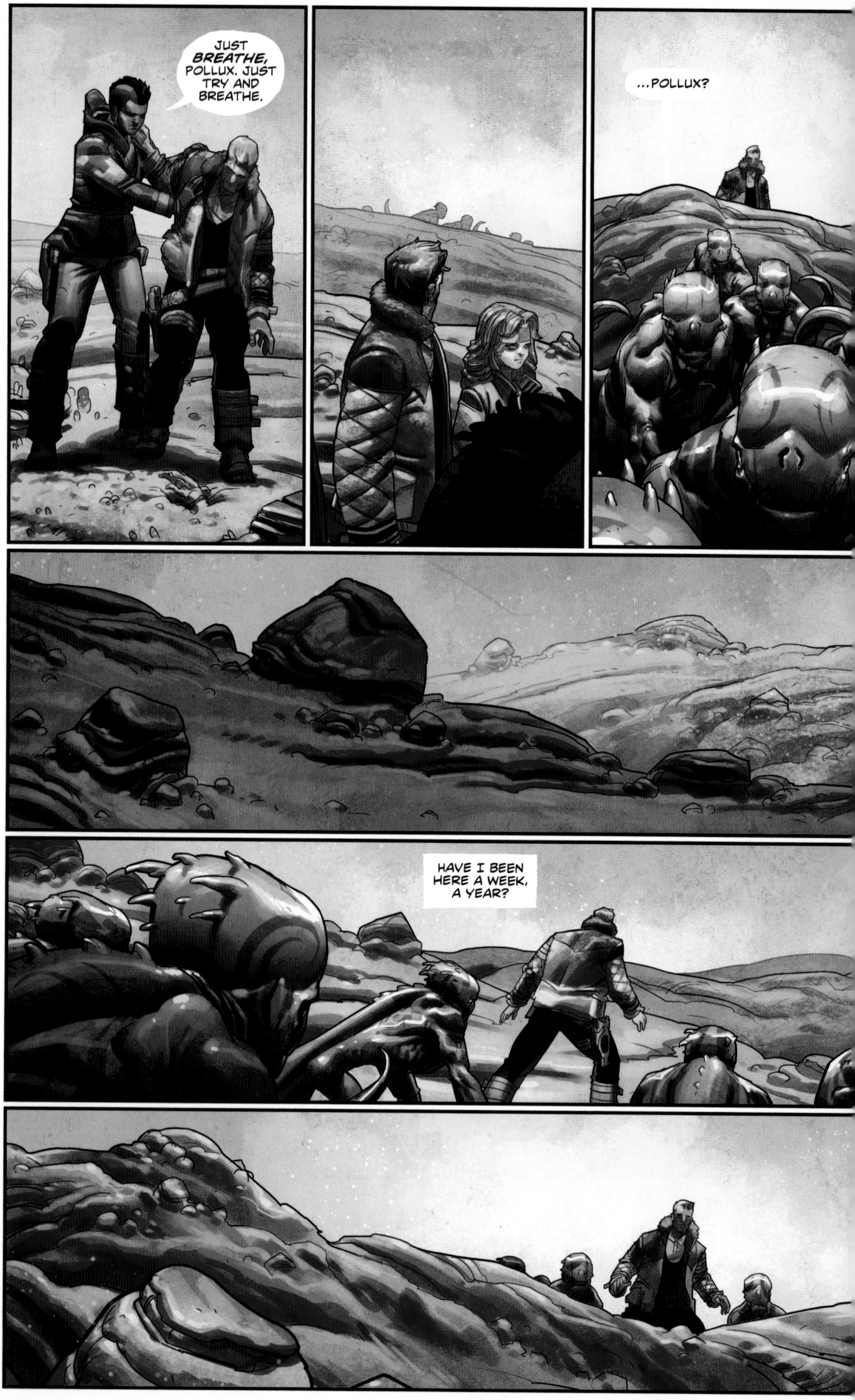
JUST BREATHE, POLLUX. JUST TRY AND BREATHE.
...POLLUX?
HAVE I BEEN HERE A WEEK, A YEAR?

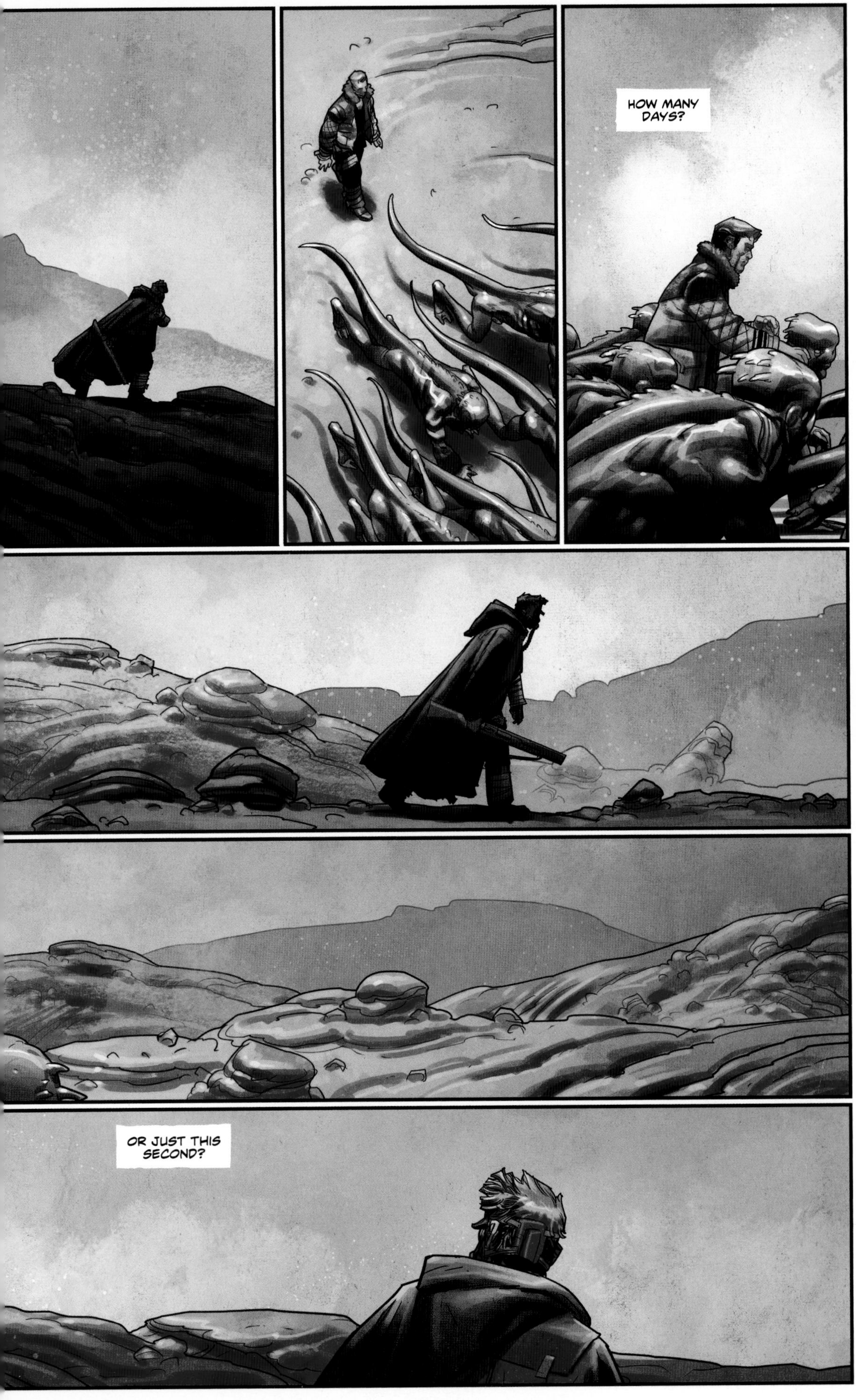
HOW MANY DAYS?
OR JUST THIS SECOND?

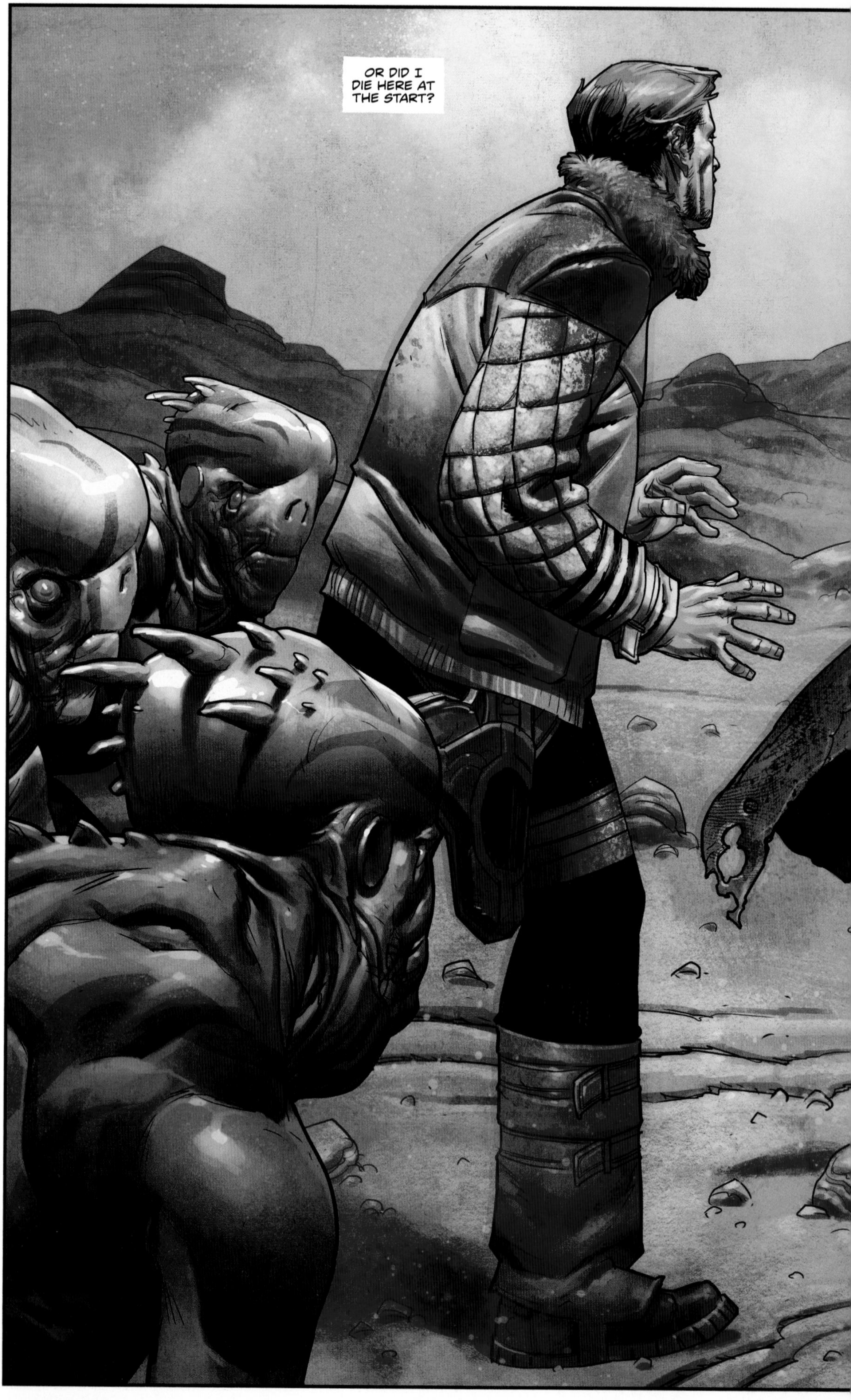
OR DID I DIE HERE AT THE START?

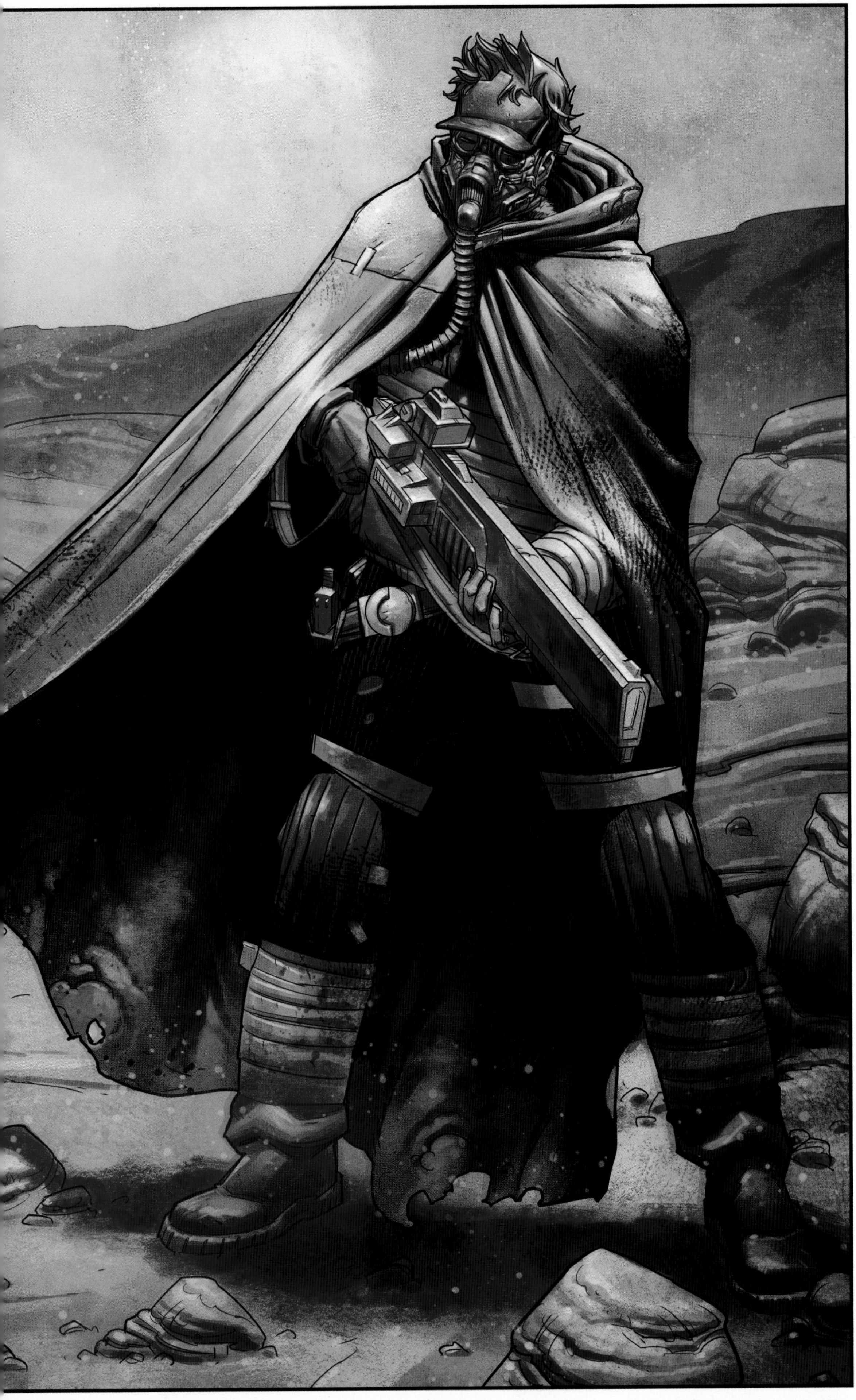

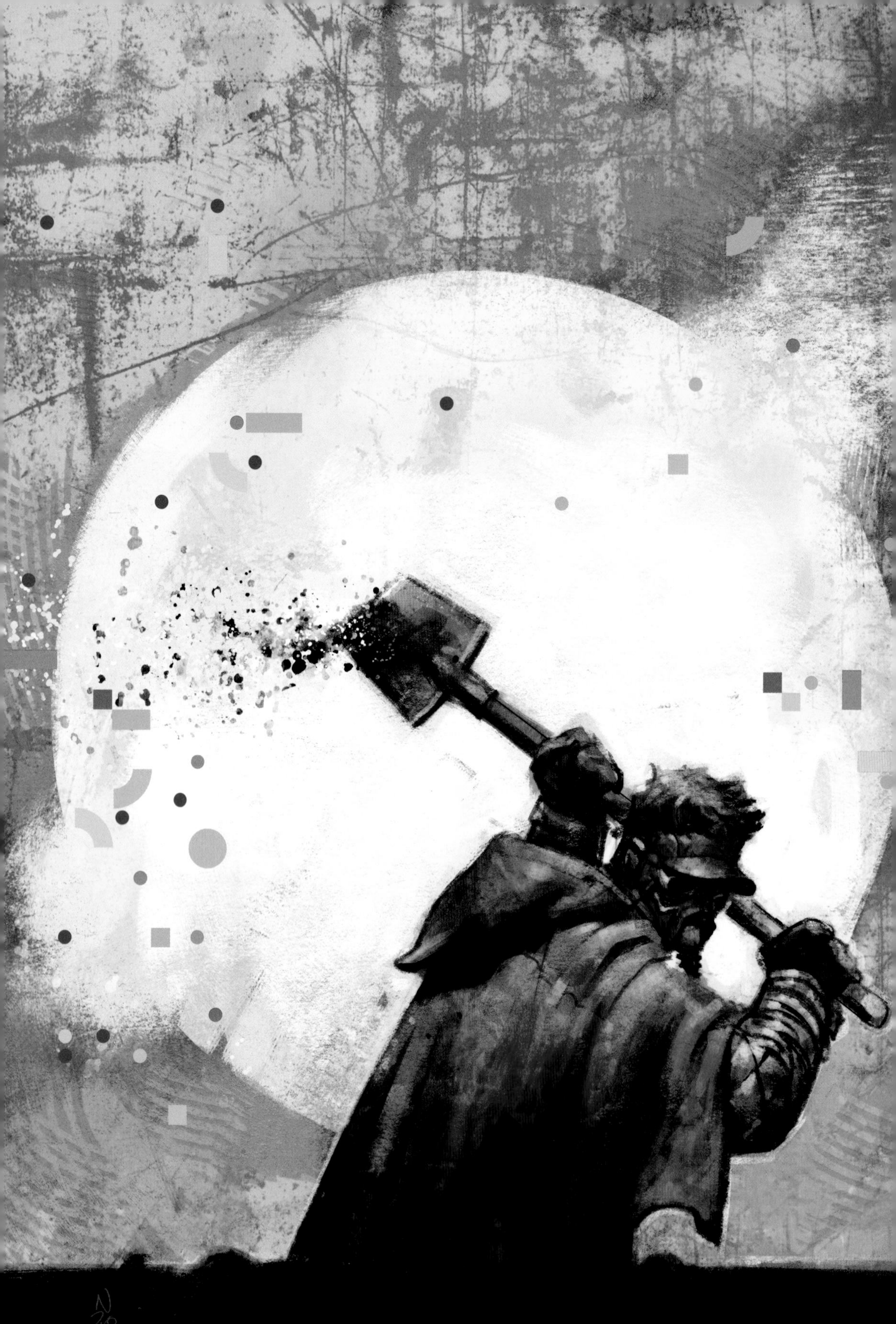

CHAPTER 17
EVERYTHING FOR YOU

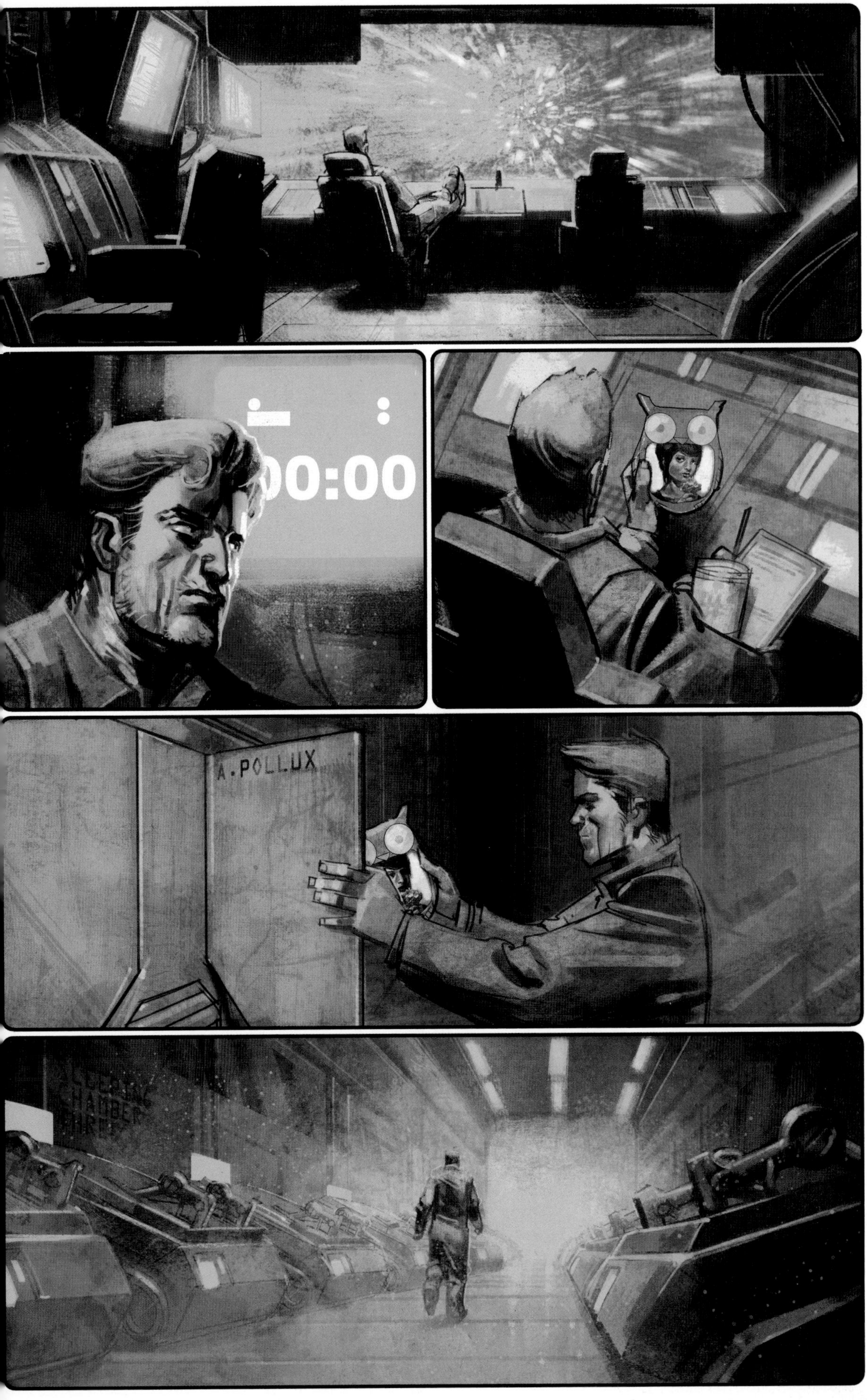
00:00
A.POLLUX

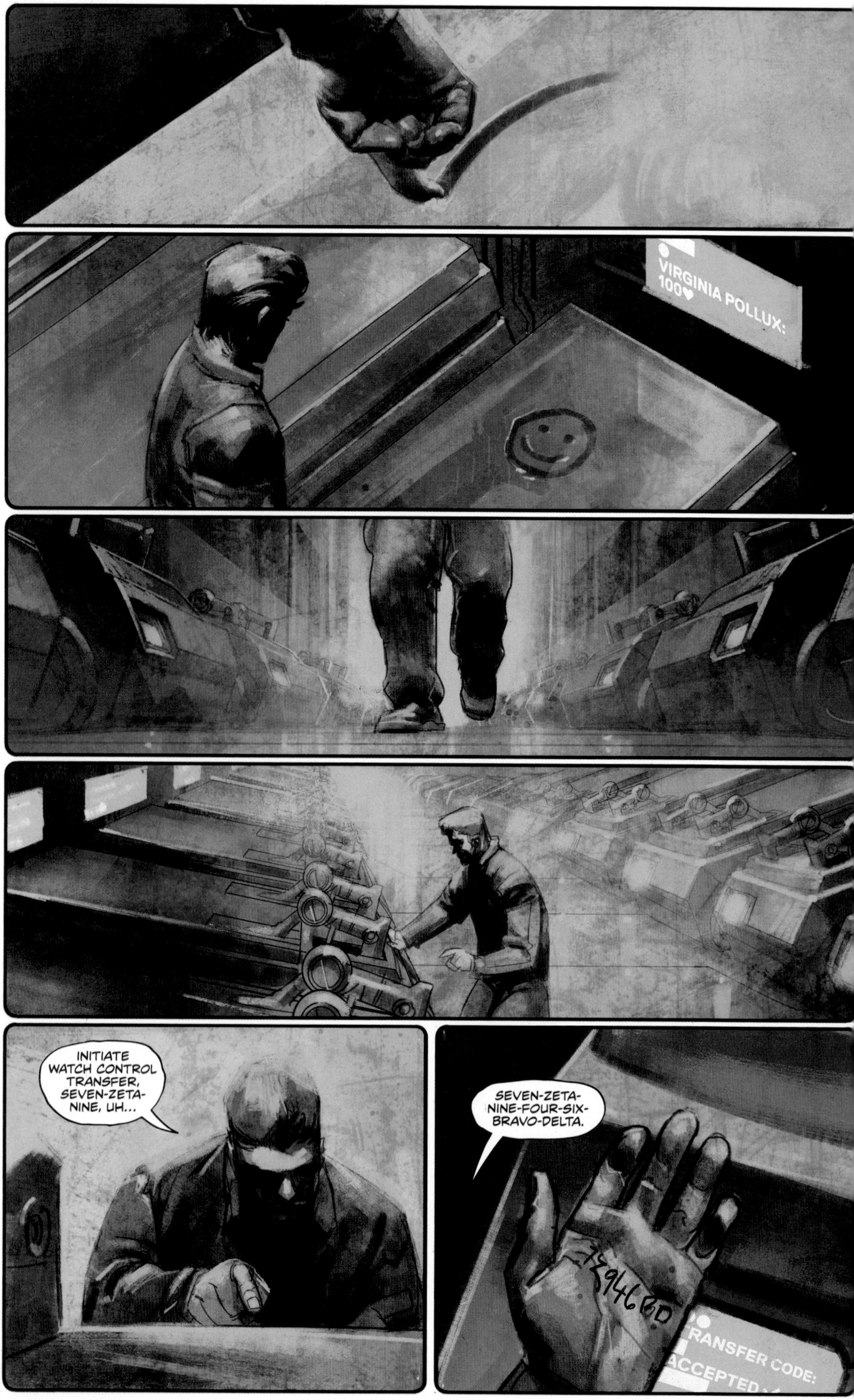
VIRGINIA POLLUX:
100♥
INITIATE WATCH CONTROL TRANSFER, SEVEN-ZETA-NINE, UH...
SEVEN-ZETA-NINE-FOUR-SIX-BRAVO-DELTA.
7Z946BD
RANSFER CODE:
ACCEPTED

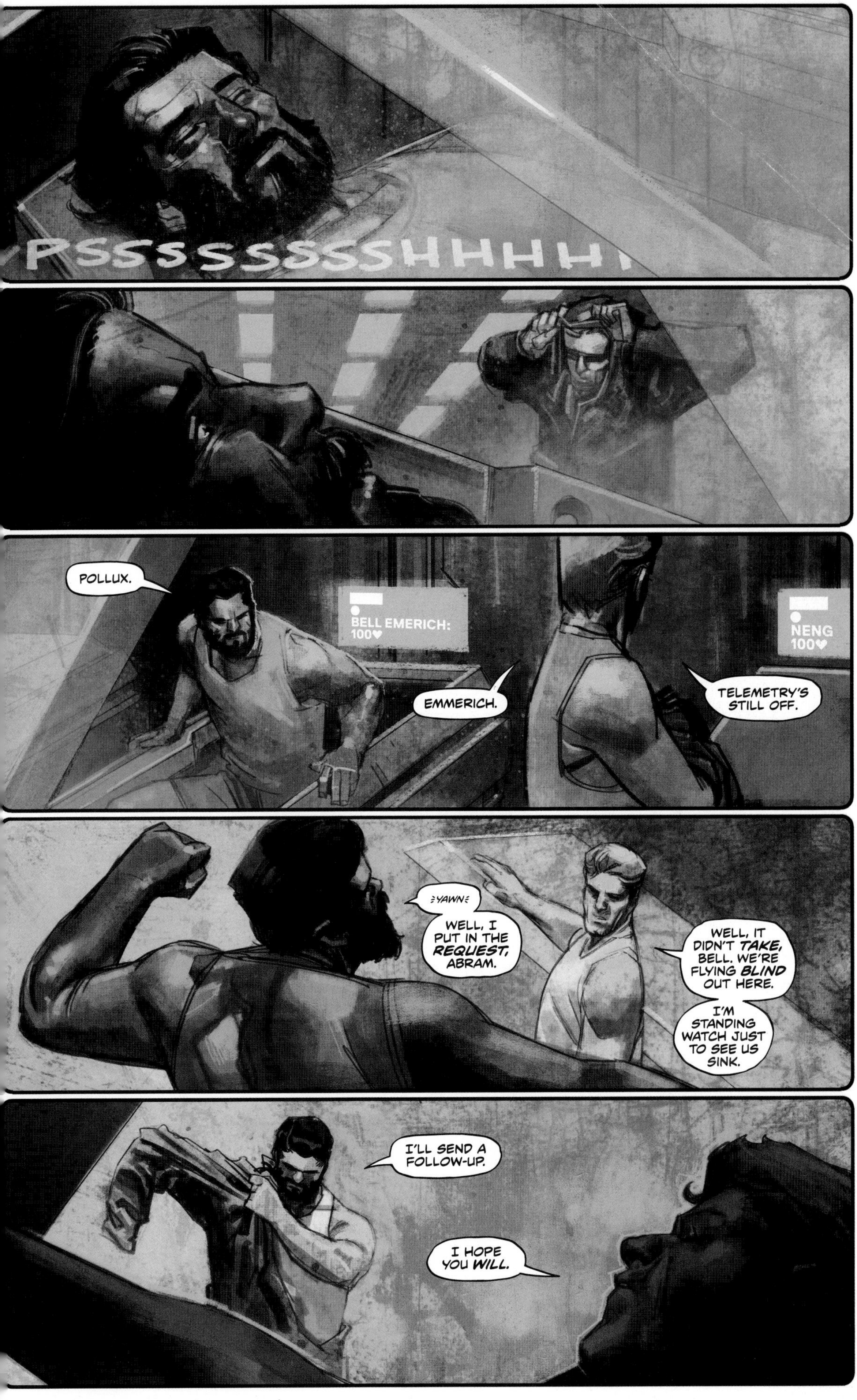
PSSSSSSSSHHH
POLLUX.
BELL EMERICH: 100♥
EMMERICH.
NENG 100♥
TELEMETRY'S STILL OFF.
YAWN
WELL, I PUT IN THE REQUEST, ABRAM.
WELL, IT DIDN'T TAKE, BELL. WE'RE FLYING BLIND OUT HERE.
I'M STANDING WATCH JUST TO SEE US SINK.
I'LL SEND A FOLLOW-UP.
I HOPE YOU WILL.

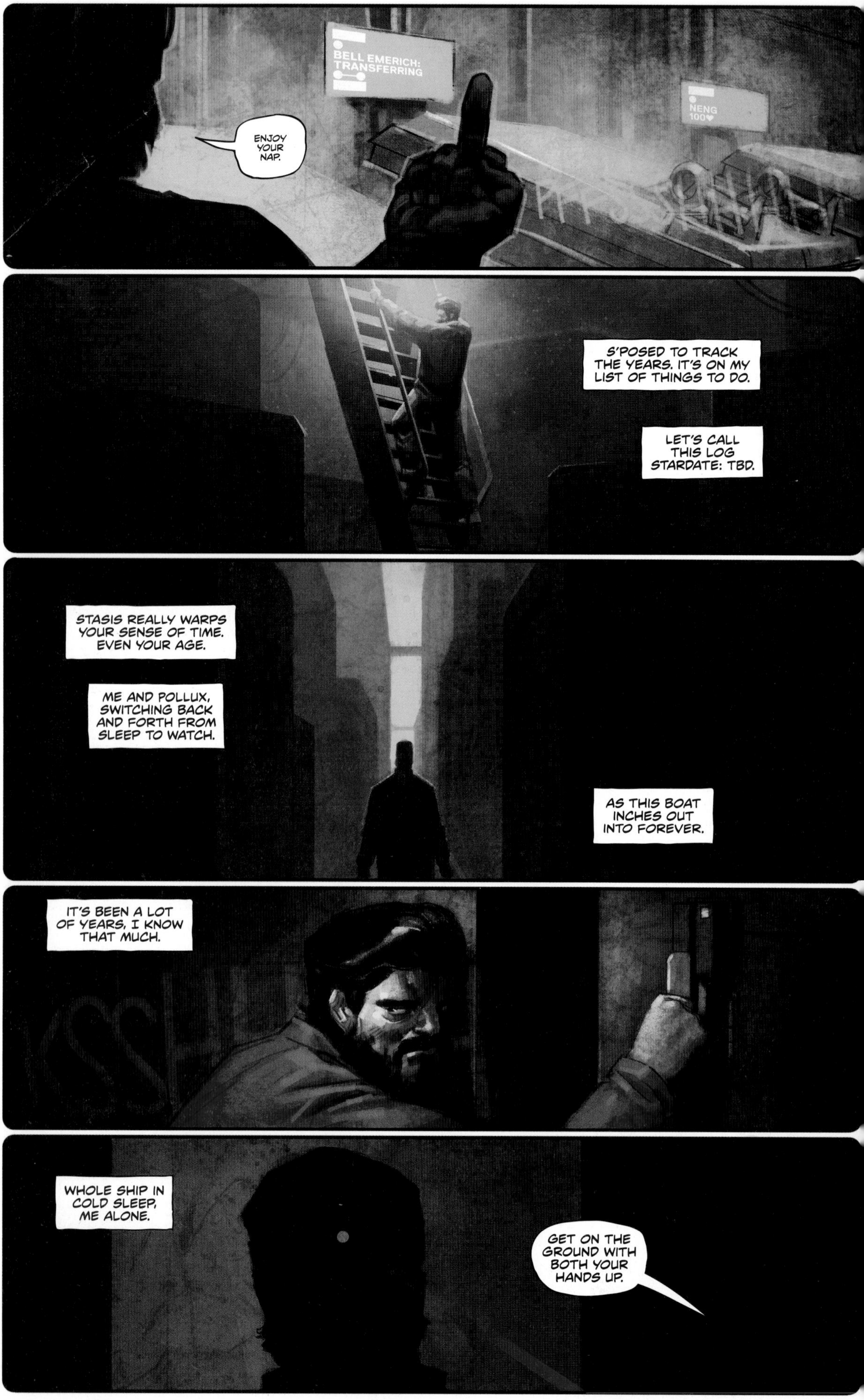

BELL EMERICH: TRANSFERRING
NENG 100
ENJOY YOUR NAP.
S'POSED TO TRACK THE YEARS. IT'S ON MY LIST OF THINGS TO DO.
LET'S CALL THIS LOG STARDATE: TBD.
STASIS REALLY WARPS YOUR SENSE OF TIME. EVEN YOUR AGE.
ME AND POLLUX, SWITCHING BACK AND FORTH FROM SLEEP TO WATCH.
AS THIS BOAT INCHES OUT INTO FOREVER.
IT'S BEEN A LOT OF YEARS, I KNOW THAT MUCH.
WHOLE SHIP IN COLD SLEEP, ME ALONE.
GET ON THE GROUND WITH BOTH YOUR HANDS UP.

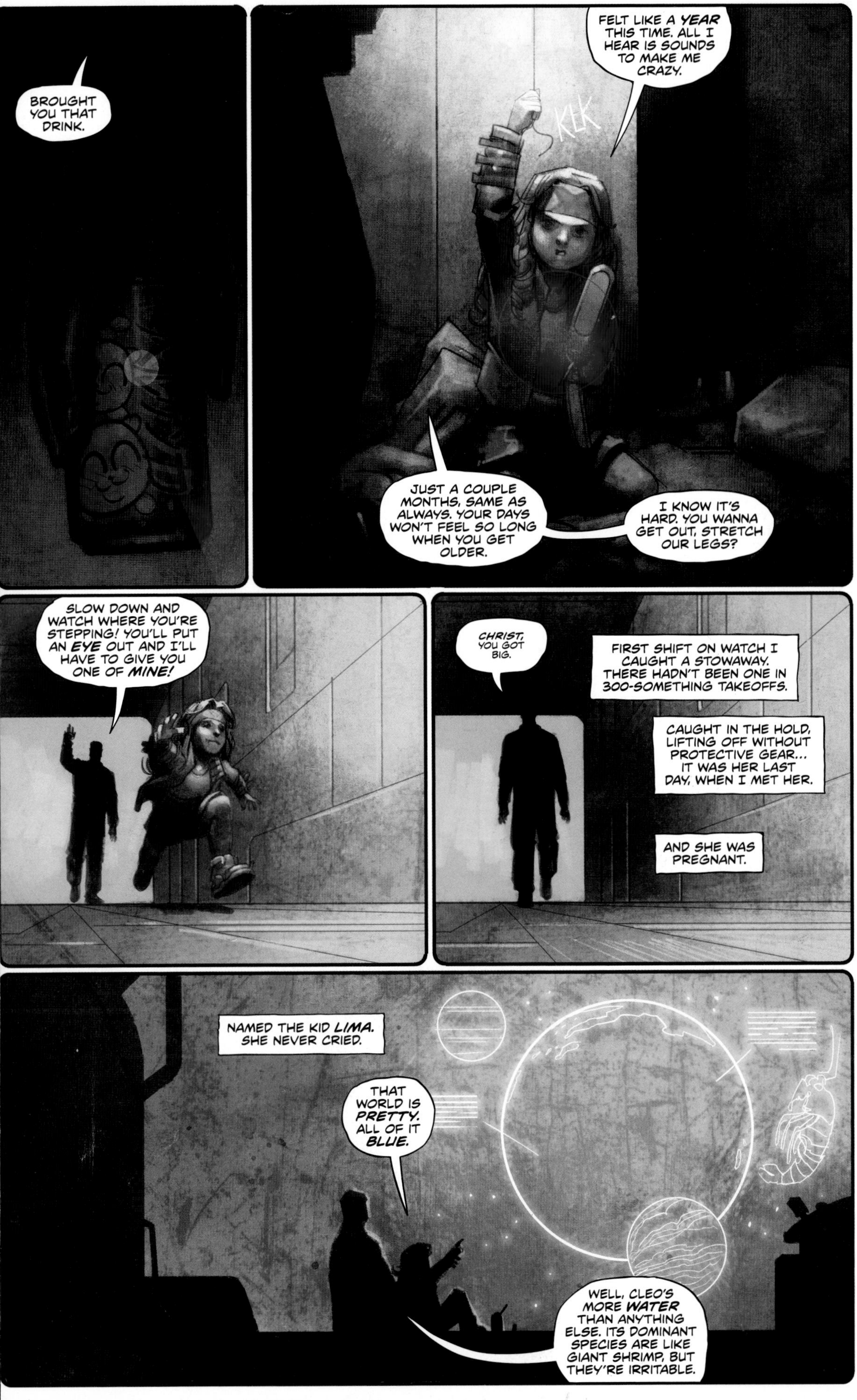
BROUGHT YOU THAT DRINK.
FELT LIKE A *YEAR* THIS TIME. ALL I HEAR IS SOUNDS TO MAKE ME CRAZY.
KLIK
JUST A COUPLE MONTHS, SAME AS ALWAYS. YOUR DAYS WON'T FEEL SO LONG WHEN YOU GET OLDER.
I KNOW IT'S HARD. YOU WANNA GET OUT, STRETCH OUR LEGS?
SLOW DOWN AND WATCH WHERE YOU'RE STEPPING! YOU'LL PUT AN *EYE* OUT AND I'LL HAVE TO GIVE YOU ONE OF *MINE!*
CHRIST, YOU GOT BIG.
FIRST SHIFT ON WATCH I CAUGHT A STOWAWAY. THERE HADN'T BEEN ONE IN 300-SOMETHING TAKEOFFS.
CAUGHT IN THE HOLD, LIFTING OFF WITHOUT PROTECTIVE GEAR... IT WAS HER LAST DAY, WHEN I MET HER.
AND SHE WAS PREGNANT.
NAMED THE KID *LIMA.* SHE NEVER CRIED.
THAT WORLD IS *PRETTY.* ALL OF IT *BLUE.*
WELL, CLEO'S MORE *WATER* THAN ANYTHING ELSE. ITS DOMINANT SPECIES ARE LIKE GIANT SHRIMP, BUT THEY'RE IRRITABLE.

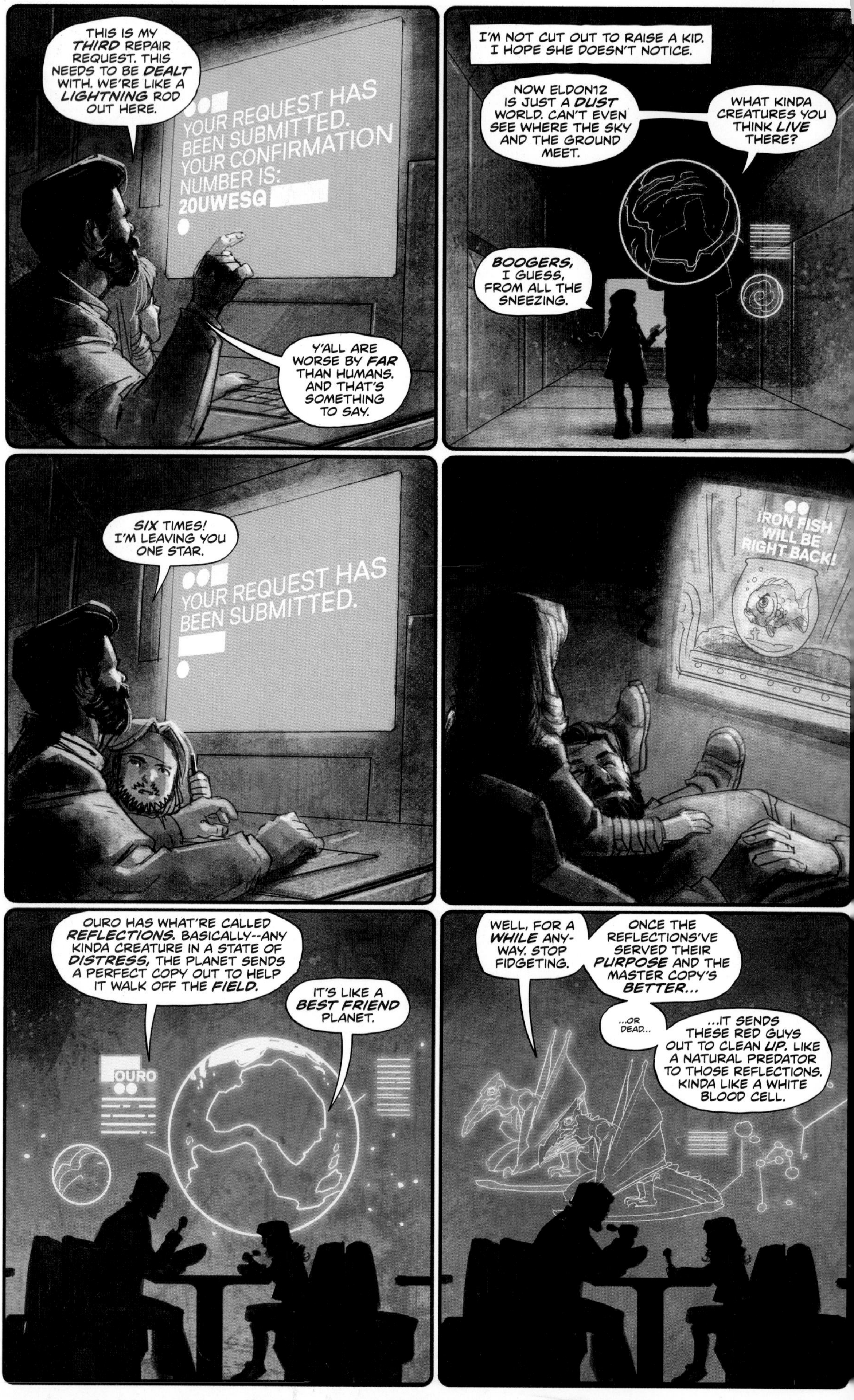
THIS IS MY THIRD REPAIR REQUEST. THIS NEEDS TO BE DEALT WITH. WE'RE LIKE A LIGHTNING ROD OUT HERE.
YOUR REQUEST HAS BEEN SUBMITTED. YOUR CONFIRMATION NUMBER IS:
20UWESQ
Y'ALL ARE WORSE BY FAR THAN HUMANS. AND THAT'S SOMETHING TO SAY.
I'M NOT CUT OUT TO RAISE A KID. I HOPE SHE DOESN'T NOTICE.
NOW ELDON12 IS JUST A DUST WORLD. CAN'T EVEN SEE WHERE THE SKY AND THE GROUND MEET.
WHAT KINDA CREATURES YOU THINK LIVE THERE?
BOOGERS, I GUESS, FROM ALL THE SNEEZING.
SIX TIMES! I'M LEAVING YOU ONE STAR.
YOUR REQUEST HAS BEEN SUBMITTED.
IRON FISH WILL BE RIGHT BACK!
OURO HAS WHAT'RE CALLED REFLECTIONS. BASICALLY--ANY KINDA CREATURE IN A STATE OF DISTRESS, THE PLANET SENDS A PERFECT COPY OUT TO HELP IT WALK OFF THE FIELD.
IT'S LIKE A BEST FRIEND PLANET.
OURO
WELL, FOR A WHILE ANY-WAY. STOP FIDGETING.
ONCE THE REFLECTIONS'VE SERVED THEIR PURPOSE AND THE MASTER COPY'S BETTER...
...OR DEAD...
...IT SENDS THESE RED GUYS OUT TO CLEAN UP. LIKE A NATURAL PREDATOR TO THOSE REFLECTIONS. KINDA LIKE A WHITE BLOOD CELL.

PIOTR GALKOVICH: 100♥

ABRAM P TRANSFER

I PUT IN FIFTEEN REQUESTS.

YOU WANT THE CONFIRMATION NUMBER?

SO MANY YEARS OUT IN THE NIGHT I CAN'T REMEMBER HOW IT FEELS TO SEE A SUN.

EVEN IN STASIS, IT'S ALL I EVER THINK ABOUT.

PSSHHHHH

EMERGENCY SETTINGS

POLLUX?

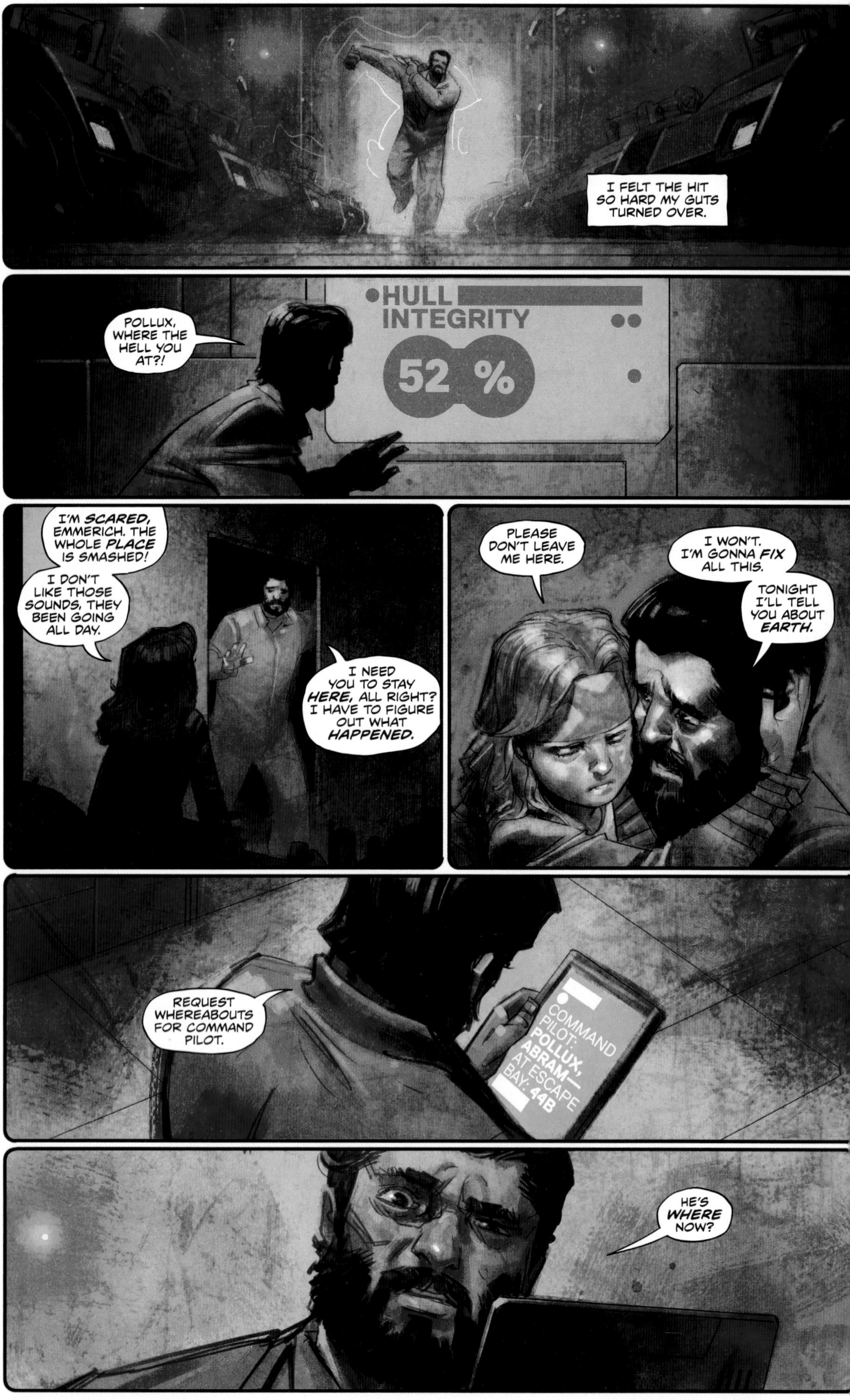

I FELT THE HIT SO HARD MY GUTS TURNED OVER.
HULL INTEGRITY
52 %
POLLUX, WHERE THE HELL YOU AT?!
I'M *SCARED*, EMMERICH. THE WHOLE *PLACE* IS SMASHED!
I DON'T LIKE THOSE SOUNDS, THEY BEEN GOING ALL DAY.
I NEED YOU TO STAY *HERE*, ALL RIGHT? I HAVE TO FIGURE OUT WHAT *HAPPENED*.
PLEASE DON'T LEAVE ME HERE.
I WON'T. I'M GONNA *FIX* ALL THIS.
TONIGHT I'LL TELL YOU ABOUT *EARTH*.
REQUEST WHEREABOUTS FOR COMMAND PILOT.
COMMAND PILOT: POLLUX, ABRAM— AT ESCAPE BAY: 44B
HE'S *WHERE* NOW?

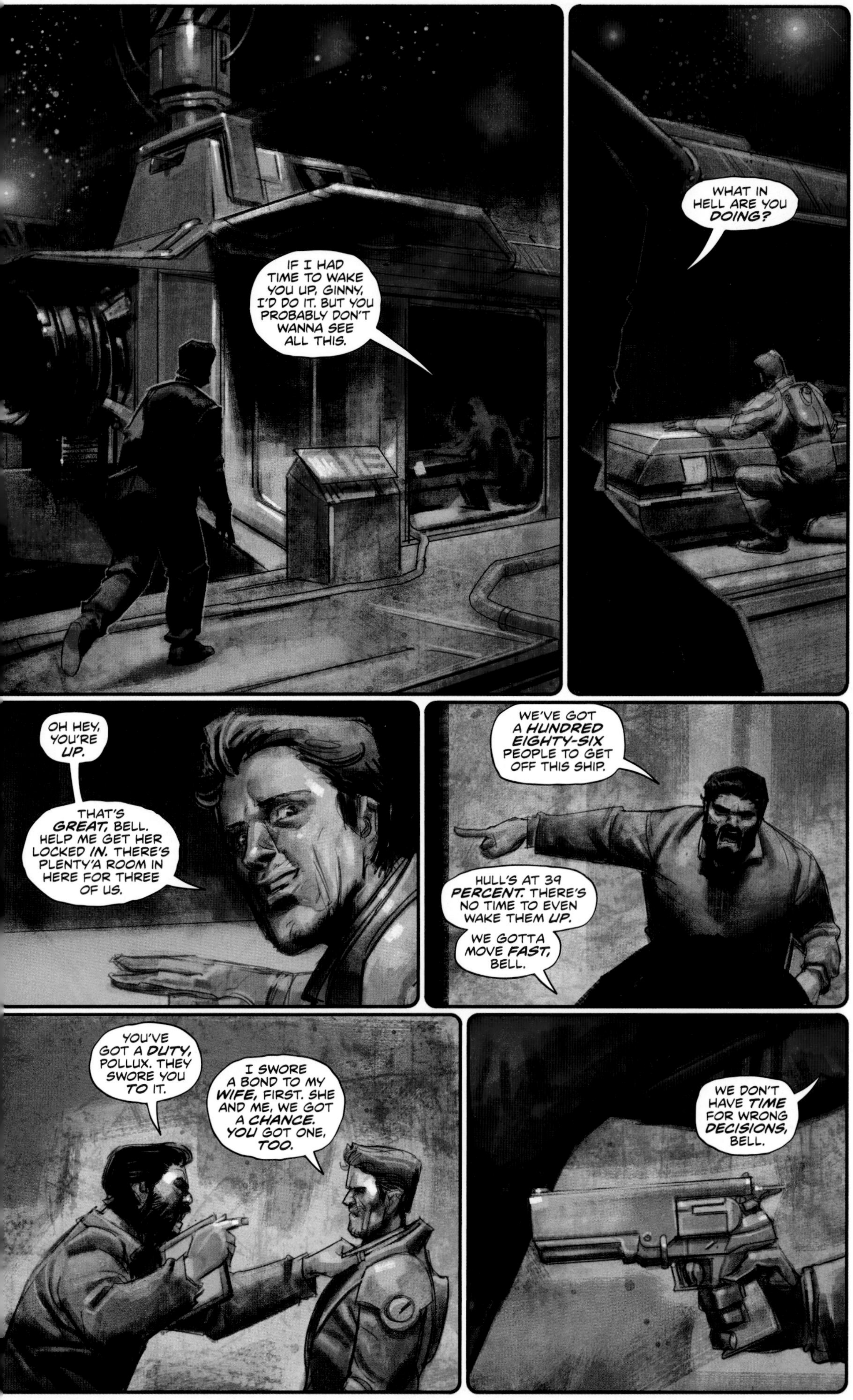
IF I HAD TIME TO WAKE YOU UP, GINNY, I'D DO IT. BUT YOU PROBABLY DON'T WANNA SEE ALL THIS.
WHAT IN HELL ARE YOU *DOING?*
OH HEY, YOU'RE *UP.*
THAT'S *GREAT,* BELL. HELP ME GET HER LOCKED *IN.* THERE'S PLENTY'A ROOM IN HERE FOR THREE OF US.
WE'VE GOT A *HUNDRED EIGHTY-SIX* PEOPLE TO GET OFF THIS SHIP.
HULL'S AT 39 *PERCENT.* THERE'S NO TIME TO EVEN WAKE THEM *UP.*
WE GOTTA MOVE *FAST,* BELL.
YOU'VE GOT A *DUTY,* POLLUX. THEY SWORE YOU *TO* IT.
I SWORE A BOND TO MY *WIFE,* FIRST. SHE AND ME, WE GOT A *CHANCE. YOU* GOT ONE, *TOO.*
WE DON'T HAVE *TIME* FOR WRONG *DECISIONS,* BELL.

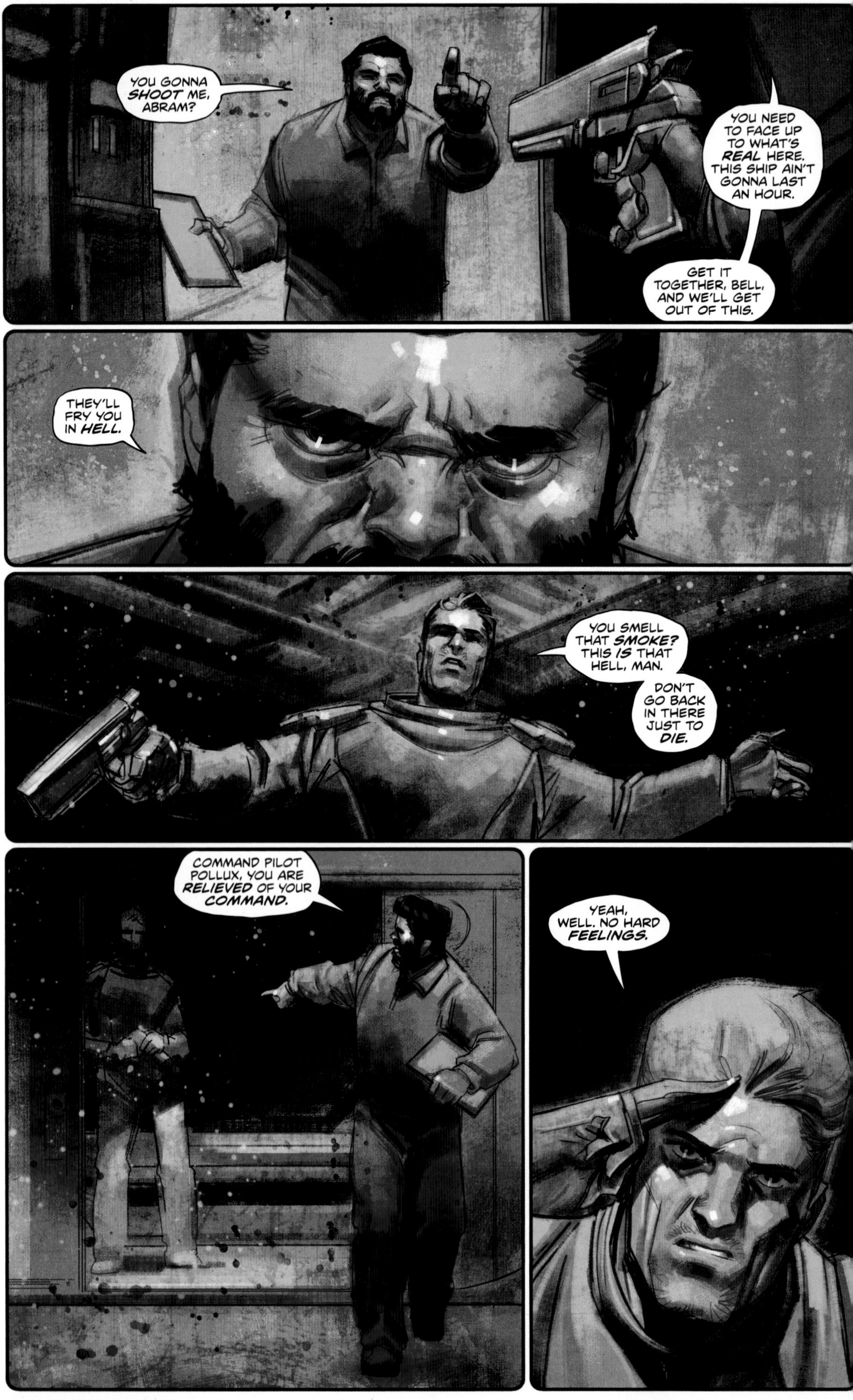
YOU GONNA SHOOT ME, ABRAM?
YOU NEED TO FACE UP TO WHAT'S REAL HERE. THIS SHIP AIN'T GONNA LAST AN HOUR.
GET IT TOGETHER, BELL, AND WE'LL GET OUT OF THIS.
THEY'LL FRY YOU IN HELL.
YOU SMELL THAT SMOKE? THIS IS THAT HELL, MAN.
DON'T GO BACK IN THERE JUST TO DIE.
COMMAND PILOT POLLUX, YOU ARE RELIEVED OF YOUR COMMAND.
YEAH, WELL. NO HARD FEELINGS.

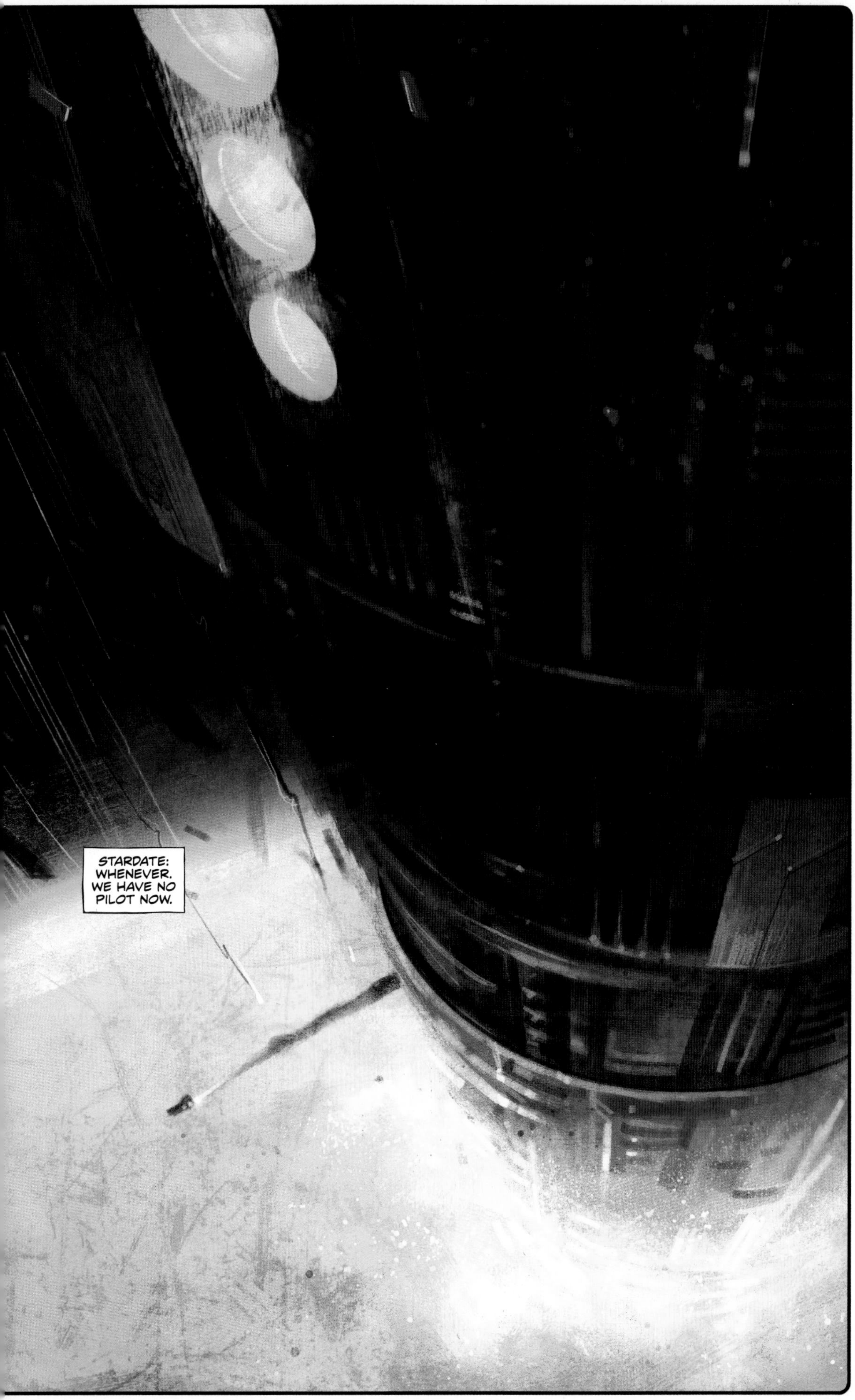
STARDATE: WHENEVER. WE HAVE NO PILOT NOW.

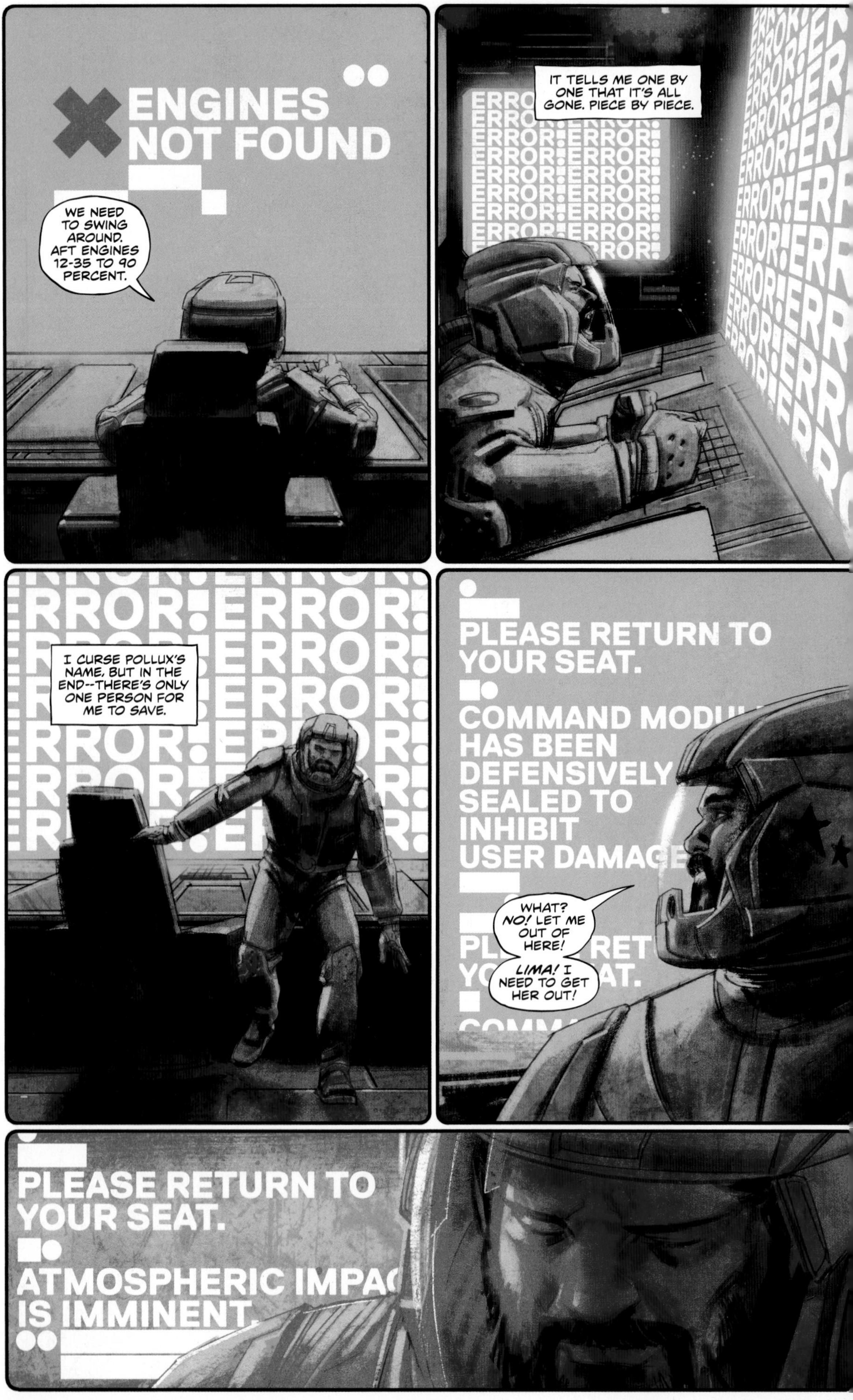
ENGINES NOT FOUND
WE NEED TO SWING AROUND. AFT ENGINES 12-35 TO 90 PERCENT.
IT TELLS ME ONE BY ONE THAT IT'S ALL GONE. PIECE BY PIECE.
ERROR!ERROR!
I CURSE POLLUX'S NAME, BUT IN THE END--THERE'S ONLY ONE PERSON FOR ME TO SAVE.
PLEASE RETURN TO YOUR SEAT.
HAS BEEN DEFENSIVELY SEALED TO INHIBIT
WHAT? NO! LET ME OUT OF HERE!
LIMA! I NEED TO GET HER OUT!
PLEASE RETURN TO YOUR SEAT.
IS IMMINENT.

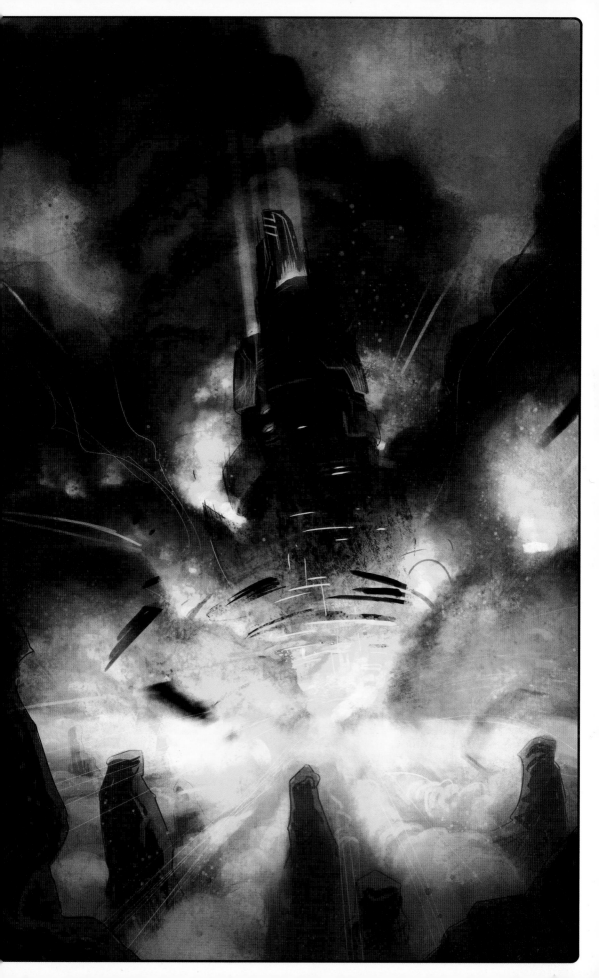

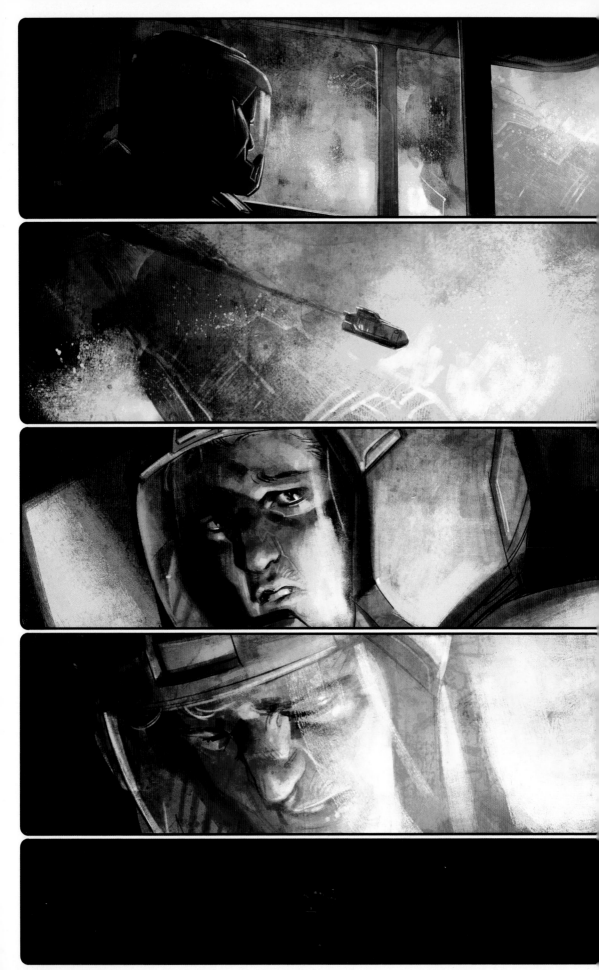

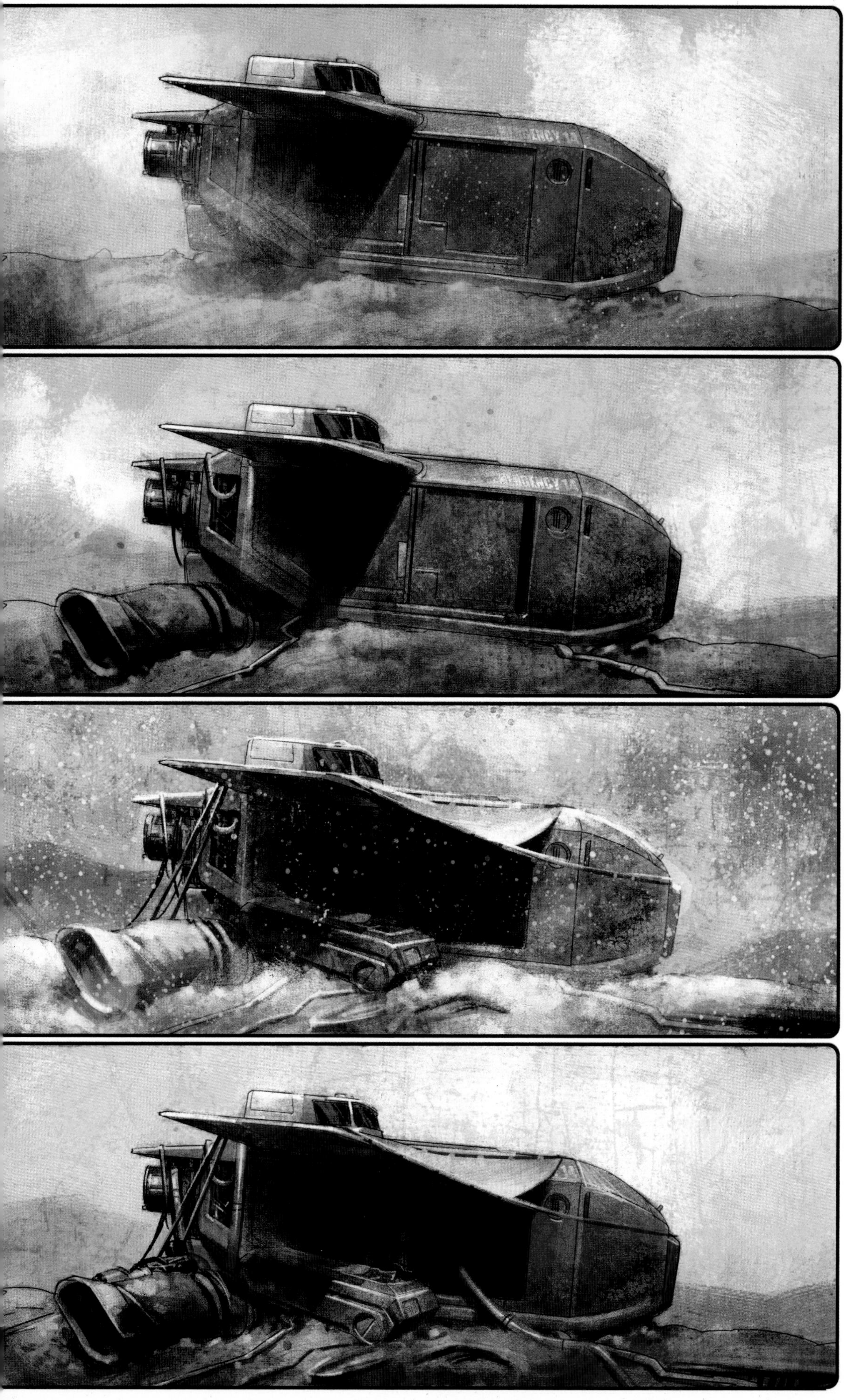

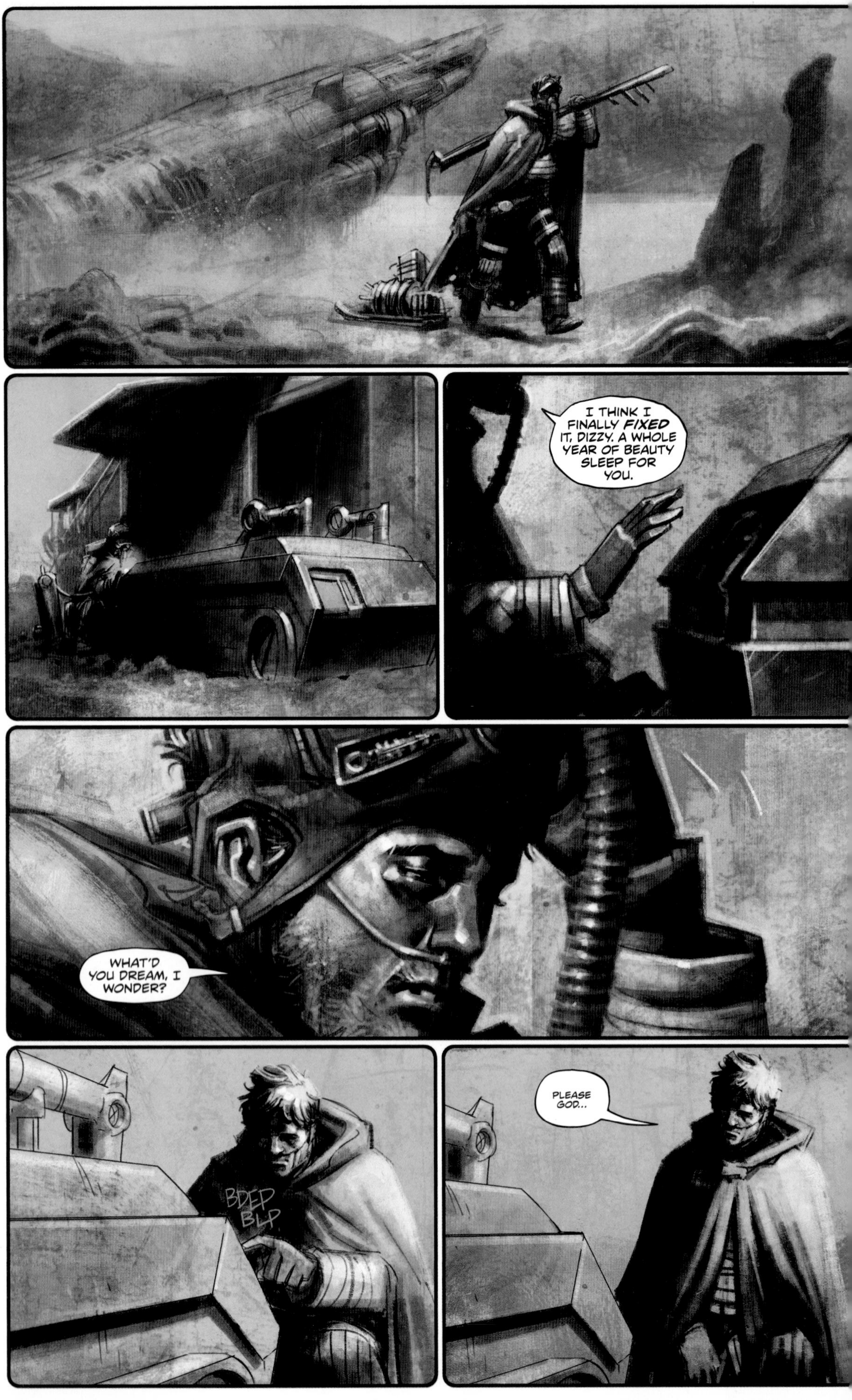
I THINK I FINALLY FIXED IT, DIZZY. A WHOLE YEAR OF BEAUTY SLEEP FOR YOU.
WHAT'D YOU DREAM, I WONDER?
BDEP BLP
PLEASE GOD...

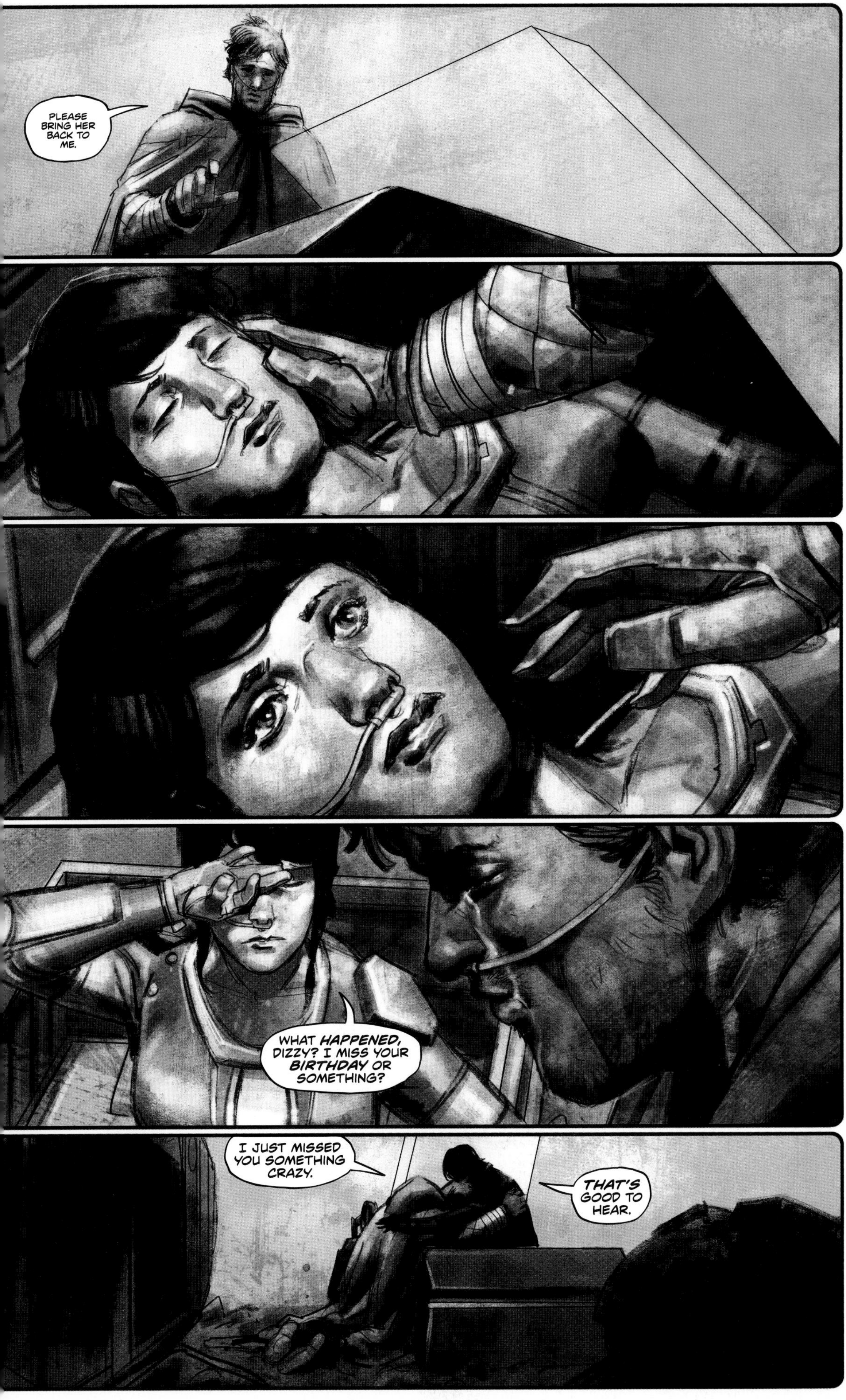
PLEASE BRING HER BACK TO ME.
WHAT HAPPENED, DIZZY? I MISS YOUR BIRTHDAY OR SOMETHING?
I JUST MISSED YOU SOMETHING CRAZY.
THAT'S GOOD TO HEAR.

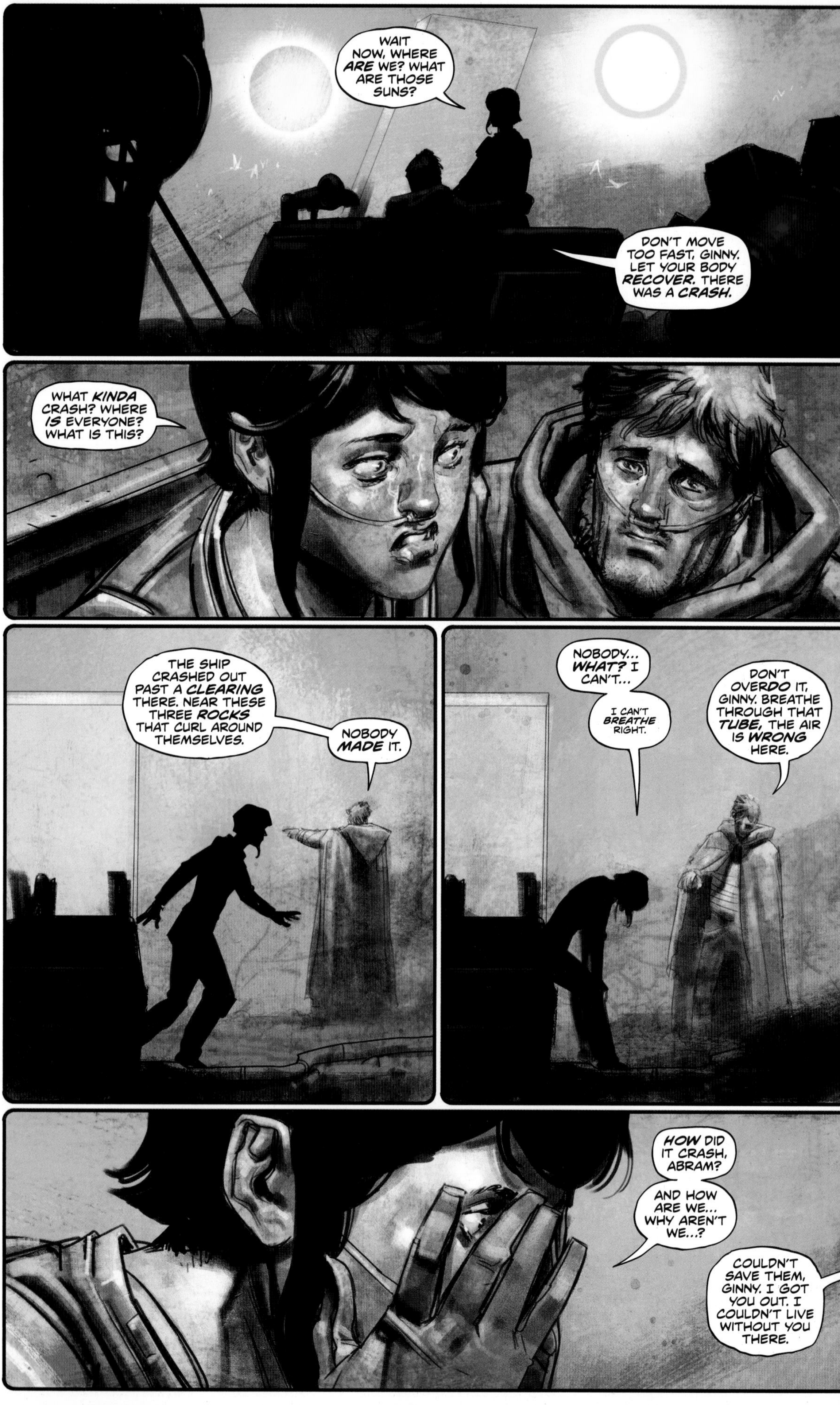

WAIT NOW, WHERE ARE WE? WHAT ARE THOSE SUNS?
DON'T MOVE TOO FAST, GINNY. LET YOUR BODY RECOVER. THERE WAS A CRASH.
WHAT KINDA CRASH? WHERE IS EVERYONE? WHAT IS THIS?
THE SHIP CRASHED OUT PAST A CLEARING THERE. NEAR THESE THREE ROCKS THAT CURL AROUND THEMSELVES.
NOBODY MADE IT.
NOBODY... WHAT? I CAN'T...
I CAN'T BREATHE RIGHT.
DON'T OVERDO IT, GINNY. BREATHE THROUGH THAT TUBE, THE AIR IS WRONG HERE.
HOW DID IT CRASH, ABRAM?
AND HOW ARE WE... WHY AREN'T WE...?
COULDN'T SAVE THEM, GINNY. I GOT YOU OUT. I COULDN'T LIVE WITHOUT YOU THERE.

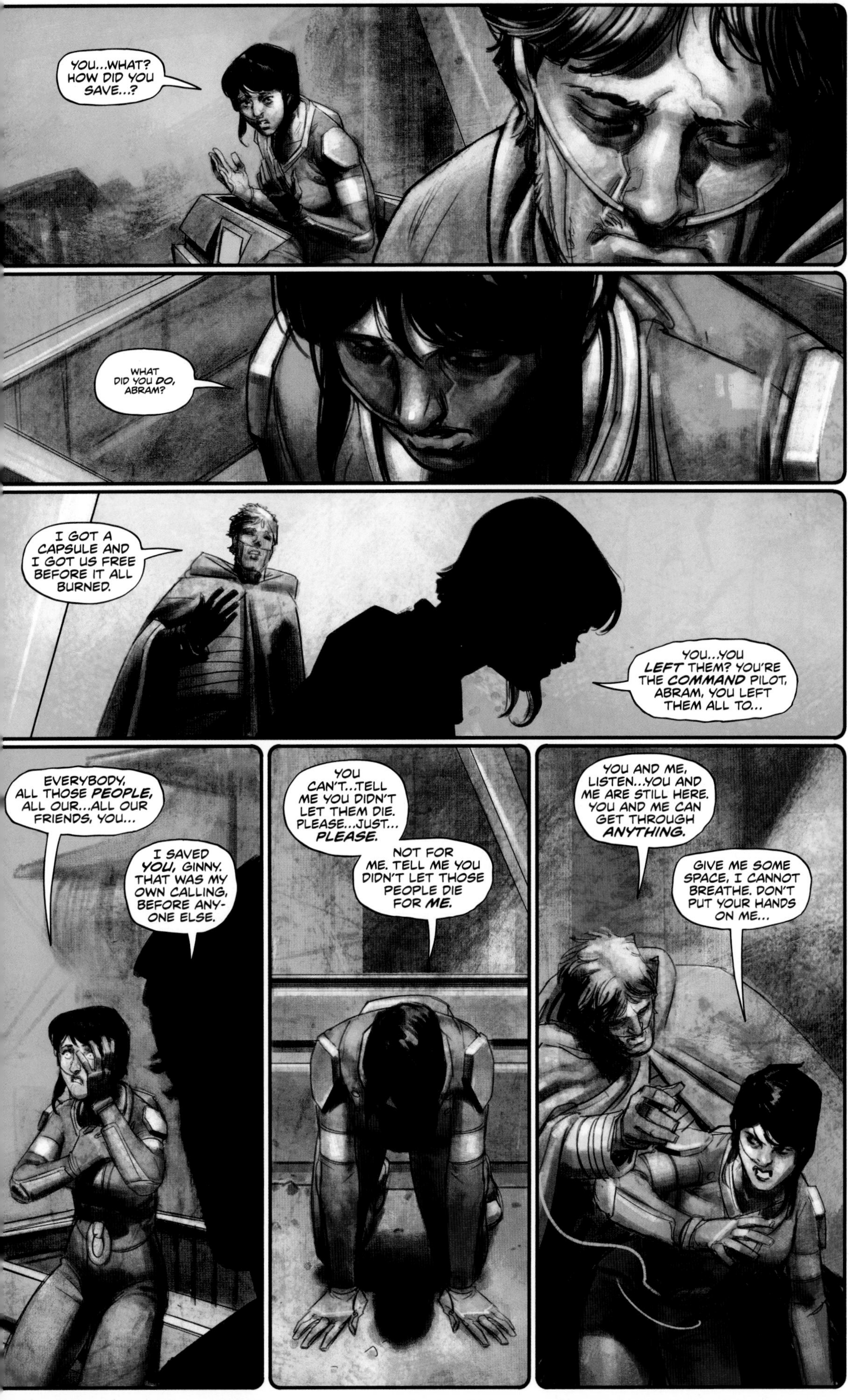
YOU...WHAT? HOW DID YOU SAVE...?
WHAT DID YOU *DO*, ABRAM?
I GOT A CAPSULE AND I GOT US FREE BEFORE IT ALL BURNED.
YOU...YOU *LEFT* THEM? YOU'RE THE *COMMAND* PILOT, ABRAM, YOU LEFT THEM ALL TO...
EVERYBODY, ALL THOSE *PEOPLE*, ALL OUR...ALL OUR FRIENDS, YOU...
I SAVED *YOU*, GINNY. THAT WAS MY OWN CALLING, BEFORE ANY-ONE ELSE.
YOU CAN'T...TELL ME YOU DIDN'T LET THEM DIE. PLEASE...JUST... *PLEASE.*
NOT FOR ME. TELL ME YOU DIDN'T LET THOSE PEOPLE DIE FOR *ME*.
YOU AND ME, LISTEN...YOU AND ME ARE STILL HERE. YOU AND ME CAN GET THROUGH *ANYTHING.*
GIVE ME SOME SPACE, I CANNOT BREATHE. DON'T PUT YOUR HANDS ON ME...

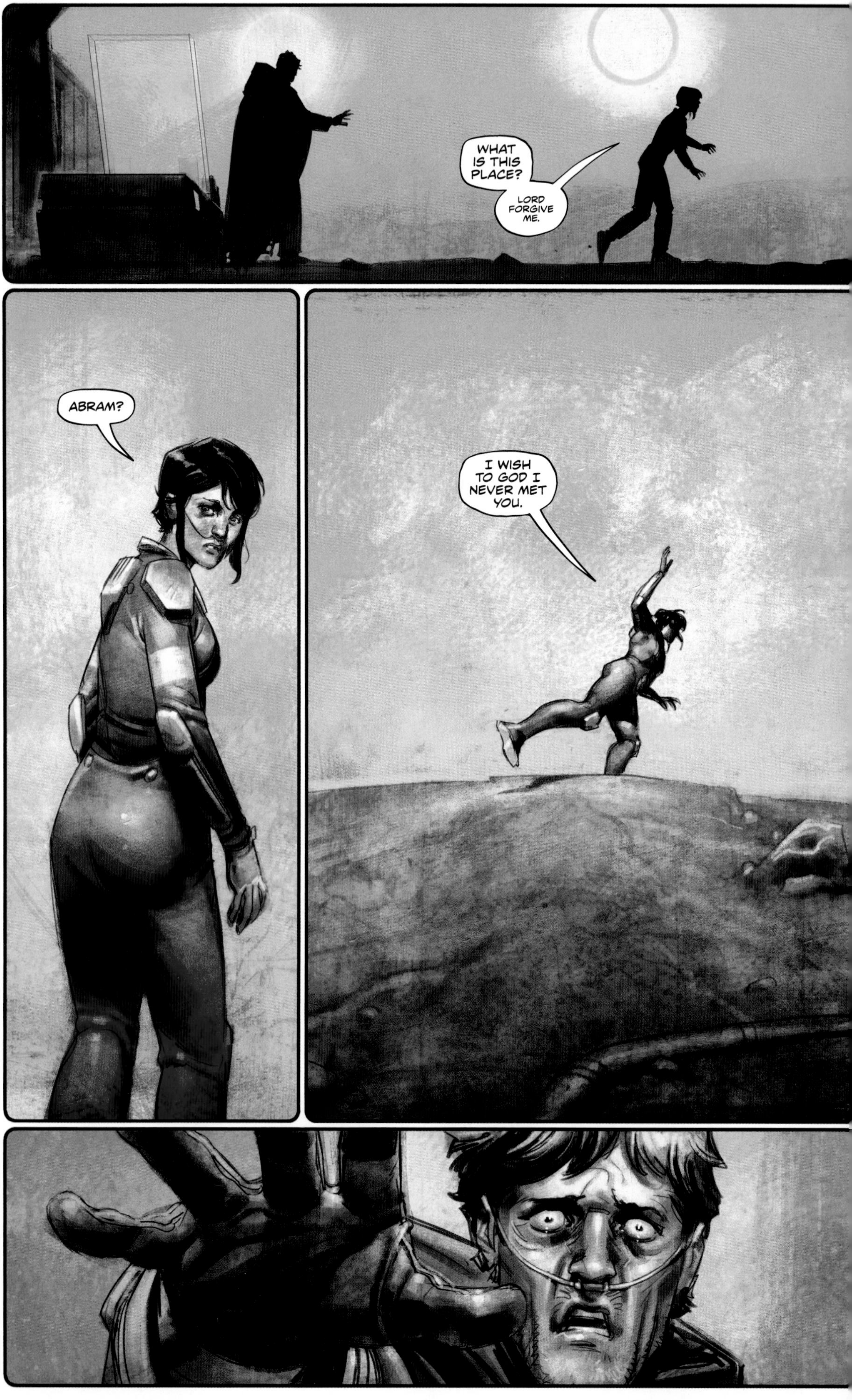
WHAT IS THIS PLACE?
LORD FORGIVE ME.
ABRAM?
I WISH TO GOD I NEVER MET YOU.

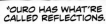

"OURO HAS WHAT'RE CALLED REFLECTIONS.

"BASICALLY--ANY KINDA CREATURE IN A STATE OF DISTRESS..."

CHAPTER 18
SOME KINDA RECKONING

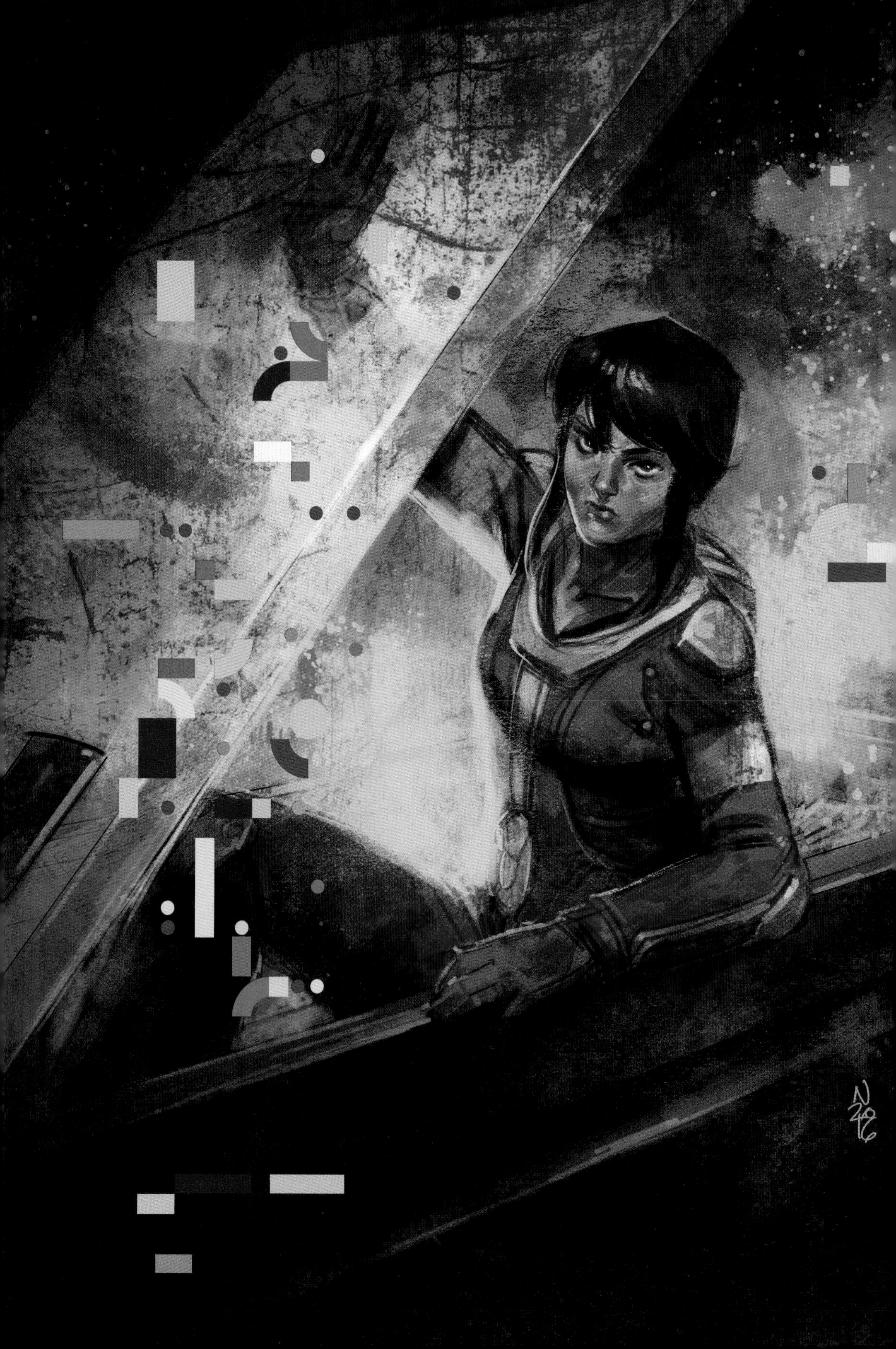

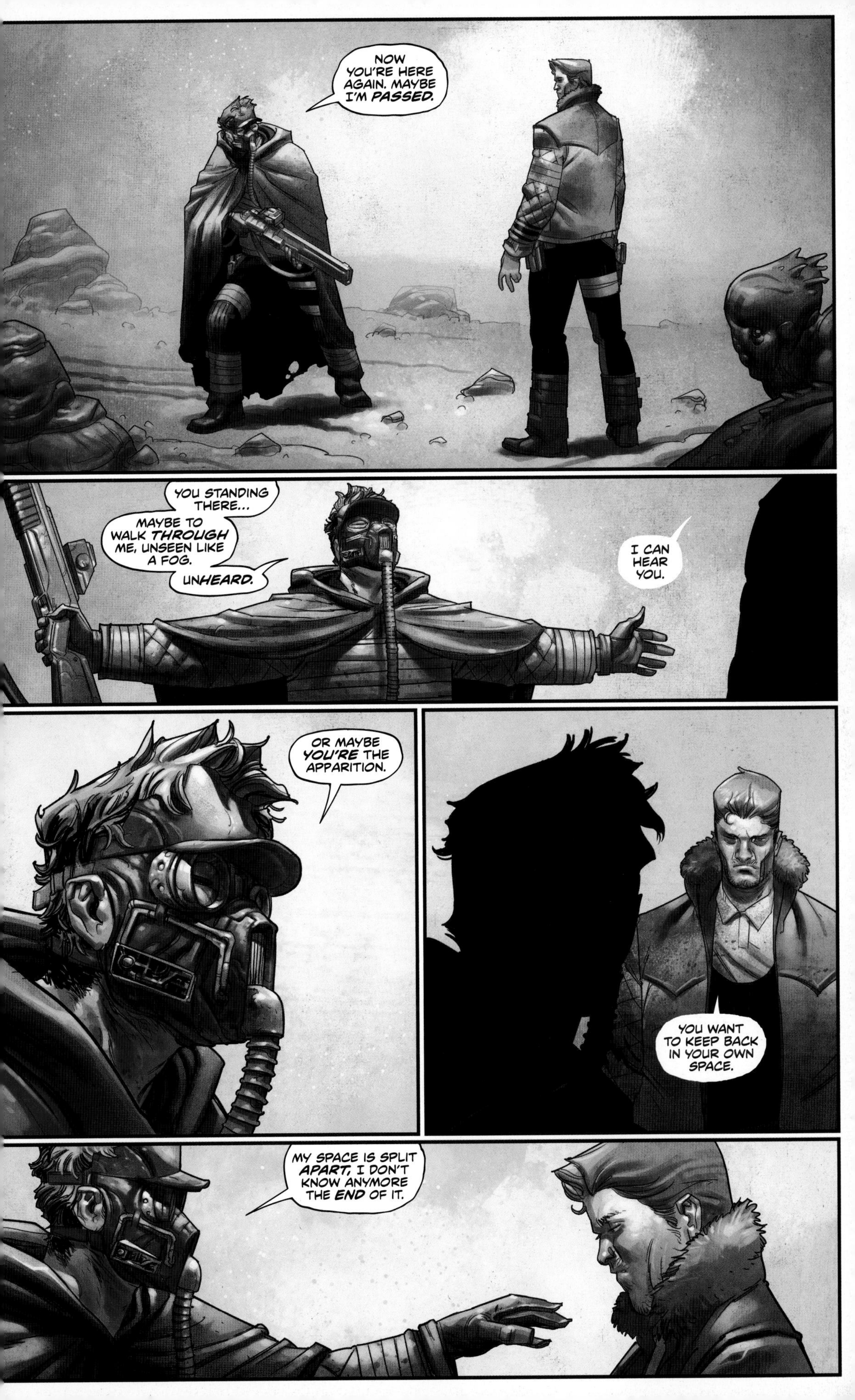
NOW YOU'RE HERE AGAIN. MAYBE I'M PASSED.
YOU STANDING THERE...
MAYBE TO WALK THROUGH ME, UNSEEN LIKE A FOG.
UNHEARD.
I CAN HEAR YOU.
OR MAYBE YOU'RE THE APPARITION.
YOU WANT TO KEEP BACK IN YOUR OWN SPACE.
MY SPACE IS SPLIT APART, I DON'T KNOW ANYMORE THE END OF IT.

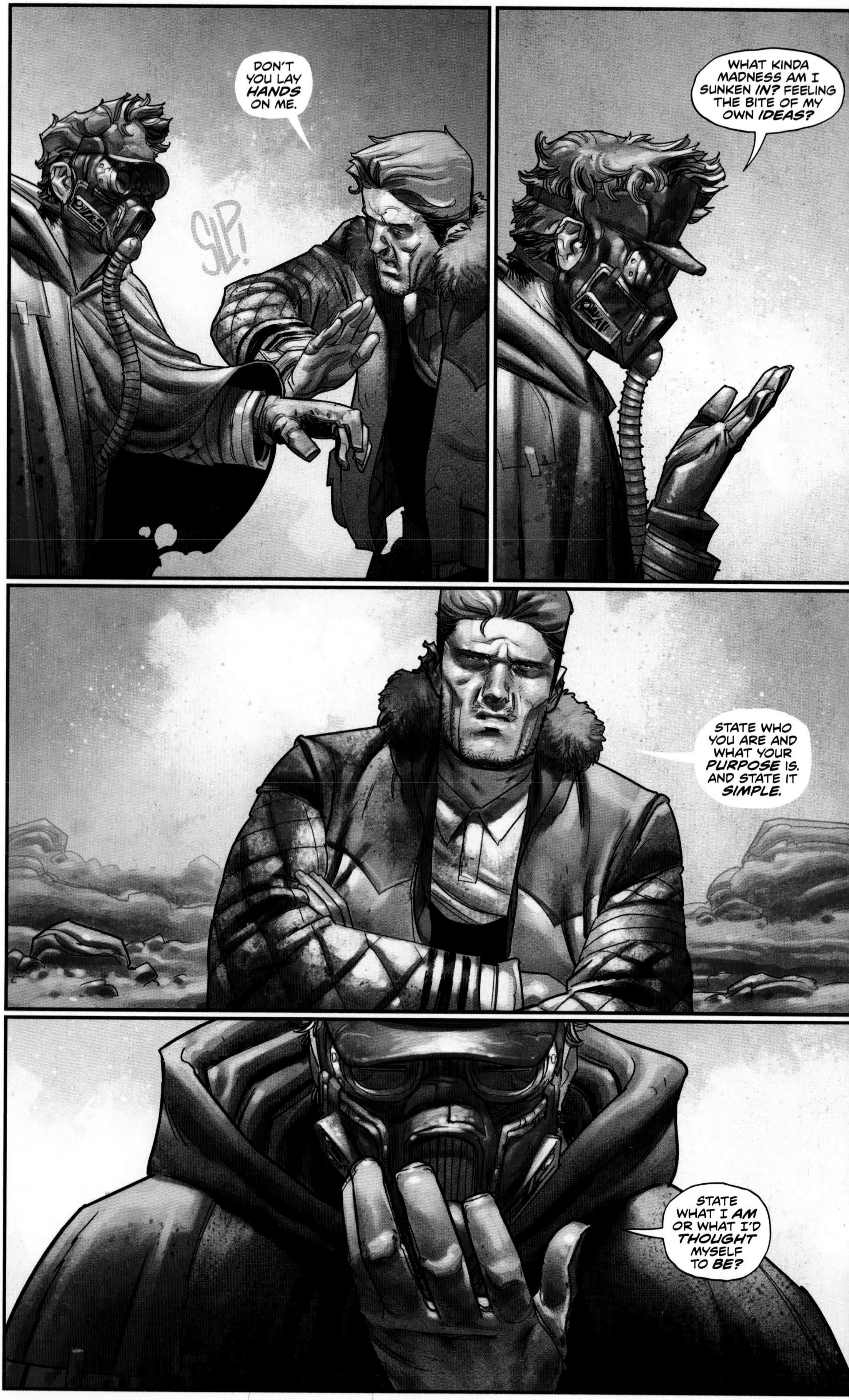
DON'T YOU LAY *HANDS* ON ME.
SLIP!
WHAT KINDA MADNESS AM I SUNKEN *IN?* FEELING THE BITE OF MY OWN *IDEAS?*
STATE WHO YOU ARE AND WHAT YOUR *PURPOSE* IS. AND STATE IT *SIMPLE.*
STATE WHAT I *AM* OR WHAT I'D *THOUGHT* MYSELF TO *BE?*

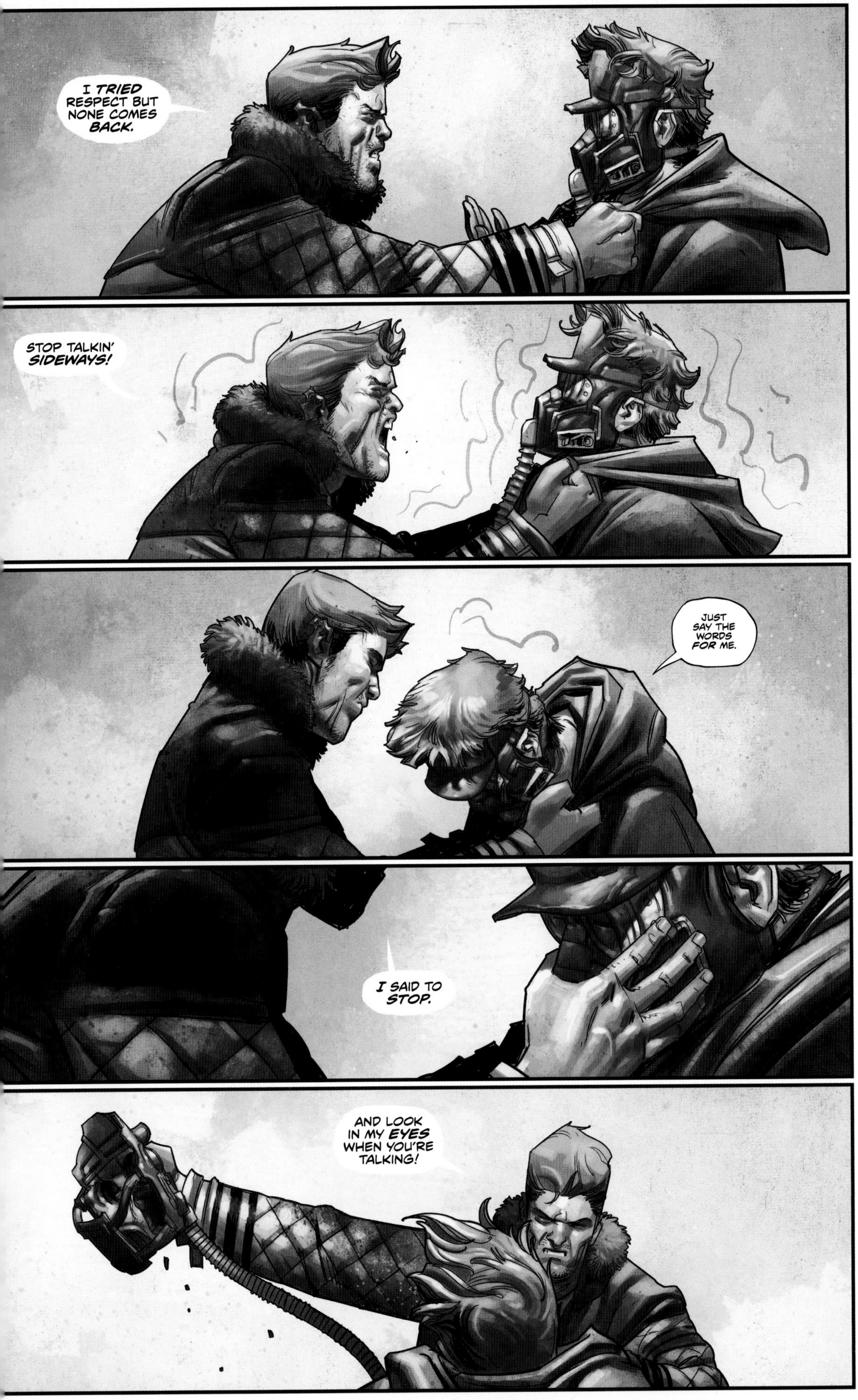
I TRIED RESPECT BUT NONE COMES BACK.
STOP TALKIN' SIDEWAYS!
JUST SAY THE WORDS FOR ME.
I SAID TO STOP.
AND LOOK IN MY EYES WHEN YOU'RE TALKING!

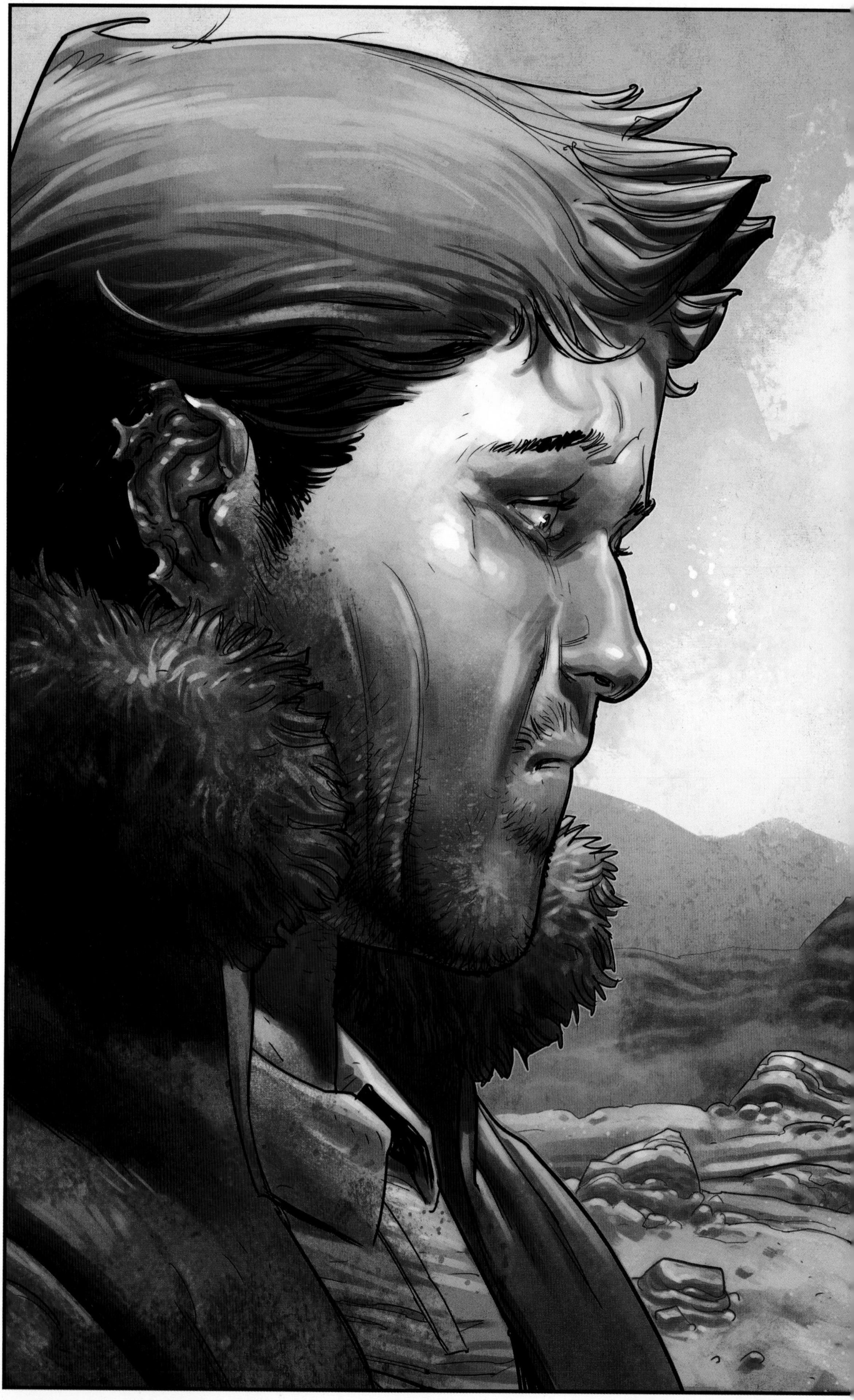

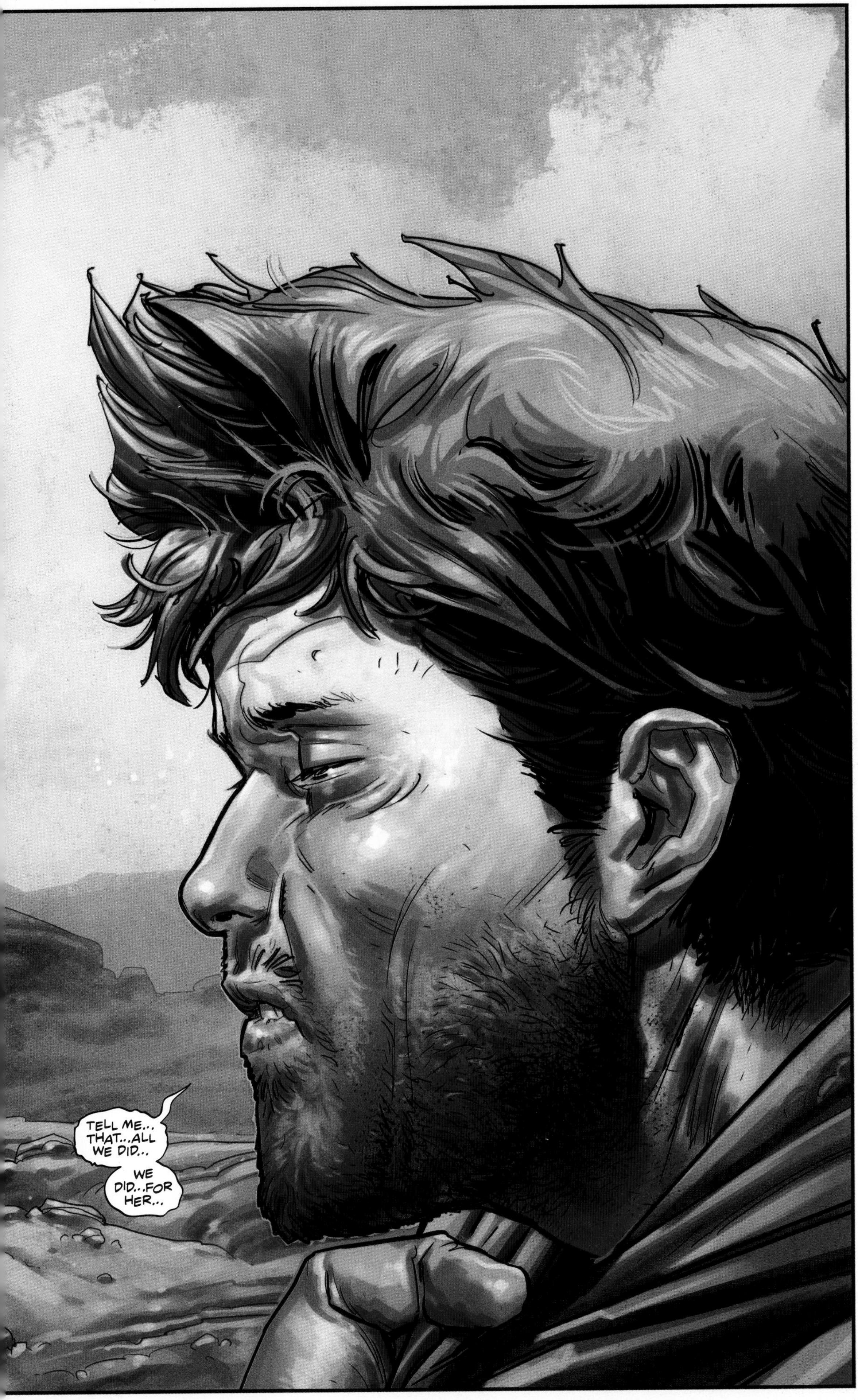
TELL ME... THAT...ALL WE DID... WE DID...FOR HER...

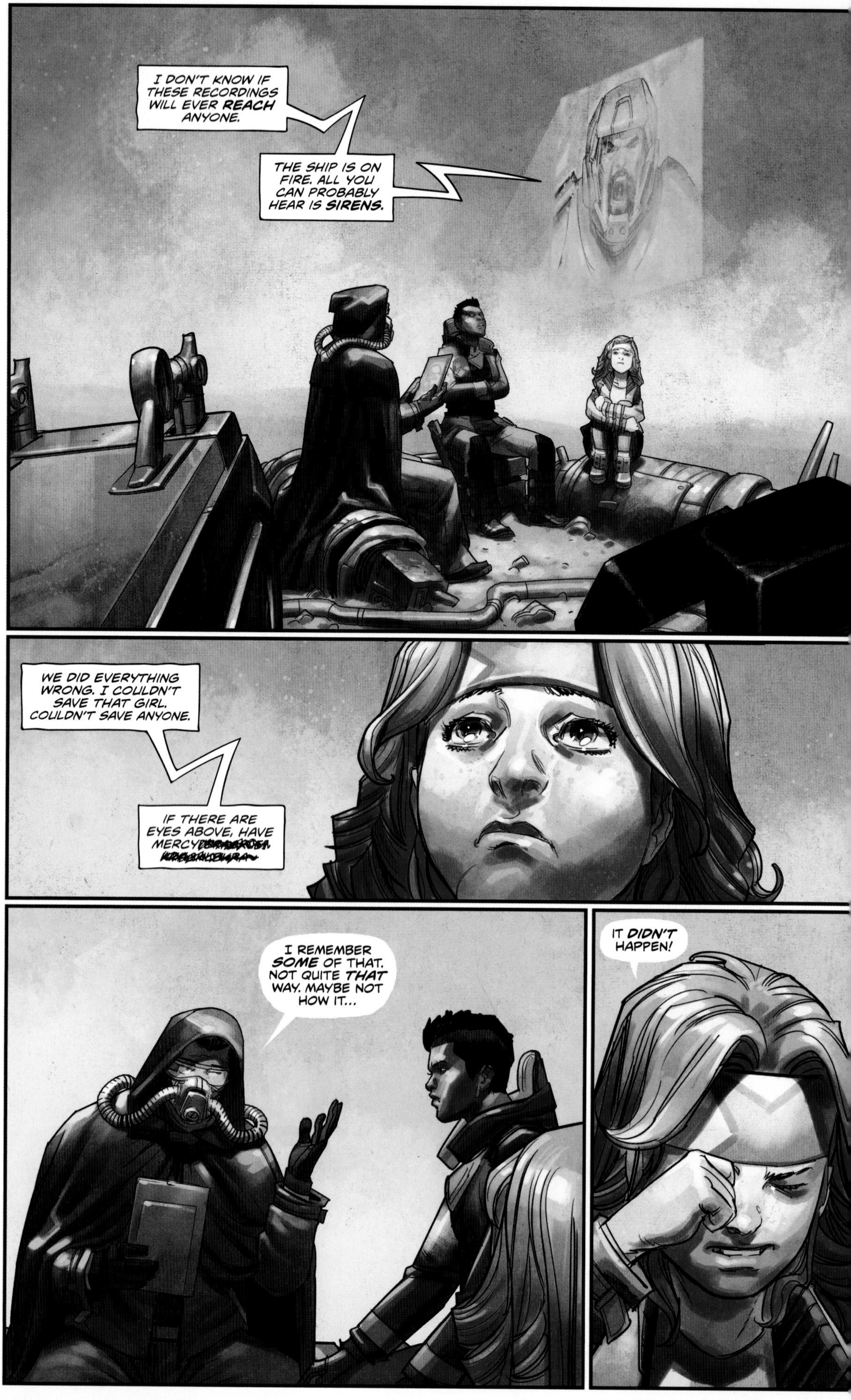
I DON'T KNOW IF THESE RECORDINGS WILL EVER **REACH** ANYONE.
THE SHIP IS ON FIRE. ALL YOU CAN PROBABLY HEAR IS **SIRENS.**
WE DID EVERYTHING WRONG. I COULDN'T SAVE THAT GIRL. COULDN'T SAVE ANYONE.
IF THERE ARE EYES ABOVE, HAVE MERCY
I REMEMBER ***SOME*** OF THAT. NOT QUITE ***THAT*** WAY. MAYBE NOT HOW IT...
IT ***DIDN'T*** HAPPEN!

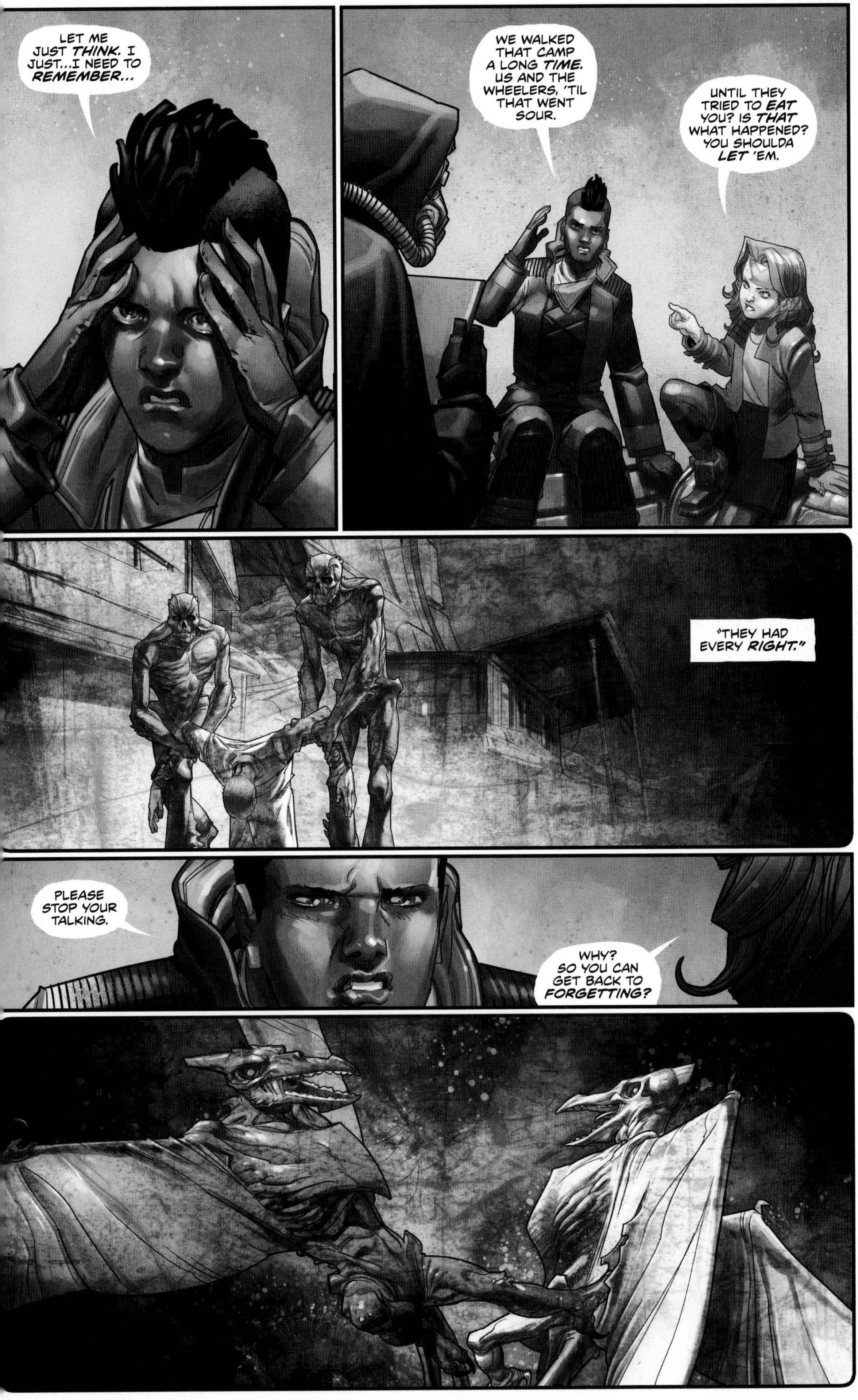
LET ME JUST *THINK*. I JUST...I NEED TO *REMEMBER*...
WE WALKED THAT CAMP A LONG *TIME*. US AND THE WHEELERS, 'TIL THAT WENT SOUR.
UNTIL THEY TRIED TO *EAT* YOU? IS *THAT* WHAT HAPPENED? YOU SHOULDA *LET* 'EM.
"THEY HAD EVERY *RIGHT*."
PLEASE STOP YOUR TALKING.
WHY? SO YOU CAN GET BACK TO *FORGETTING*?

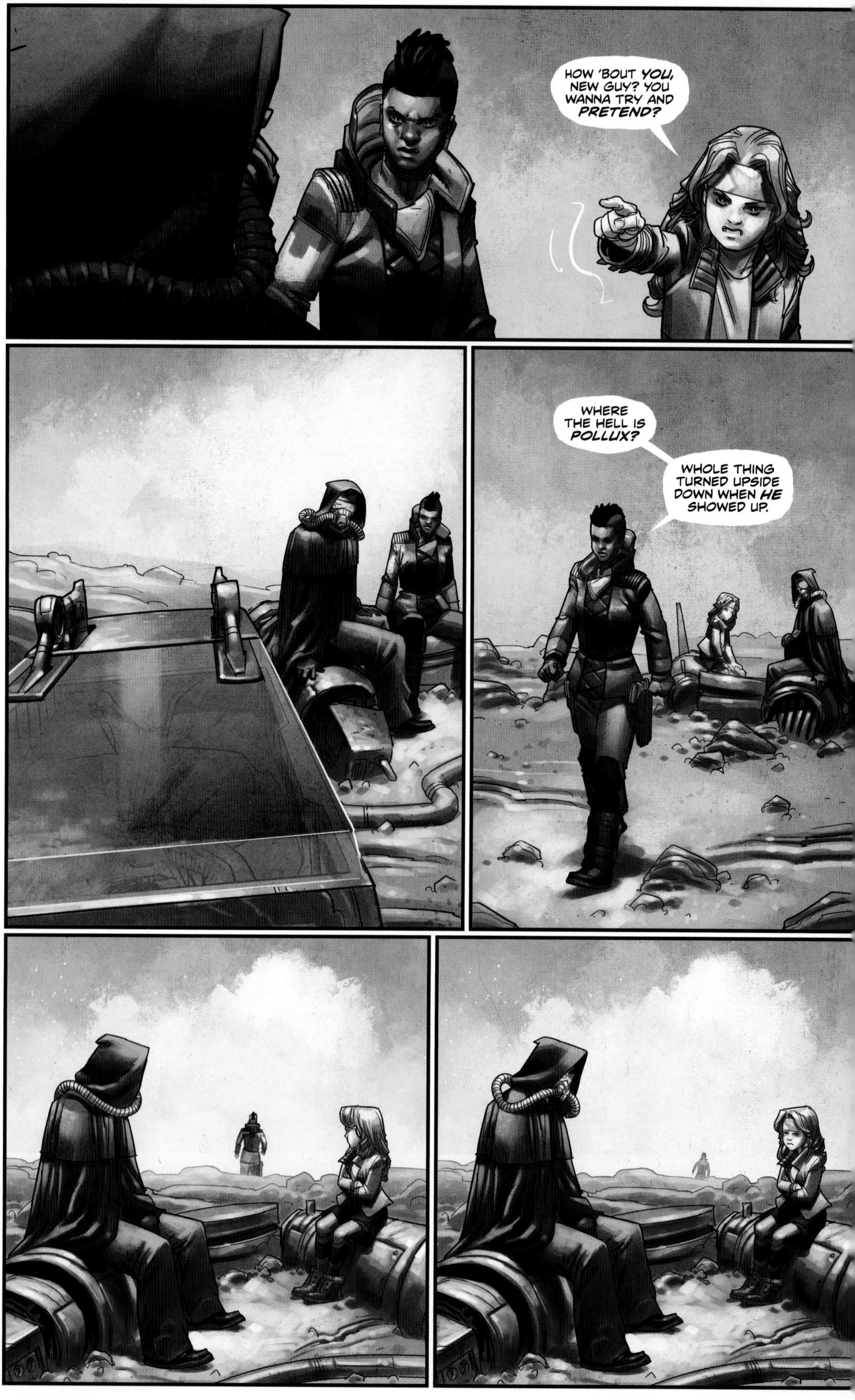
HOW 'BOUT YOU, NEW GUY? YOU WANNA TRY AND PRETEND?
WHERE THE HELL IS POLLUX?
WHOLE THING TURNED UPSIDE DOWN WHEN HE SHOWED UP.

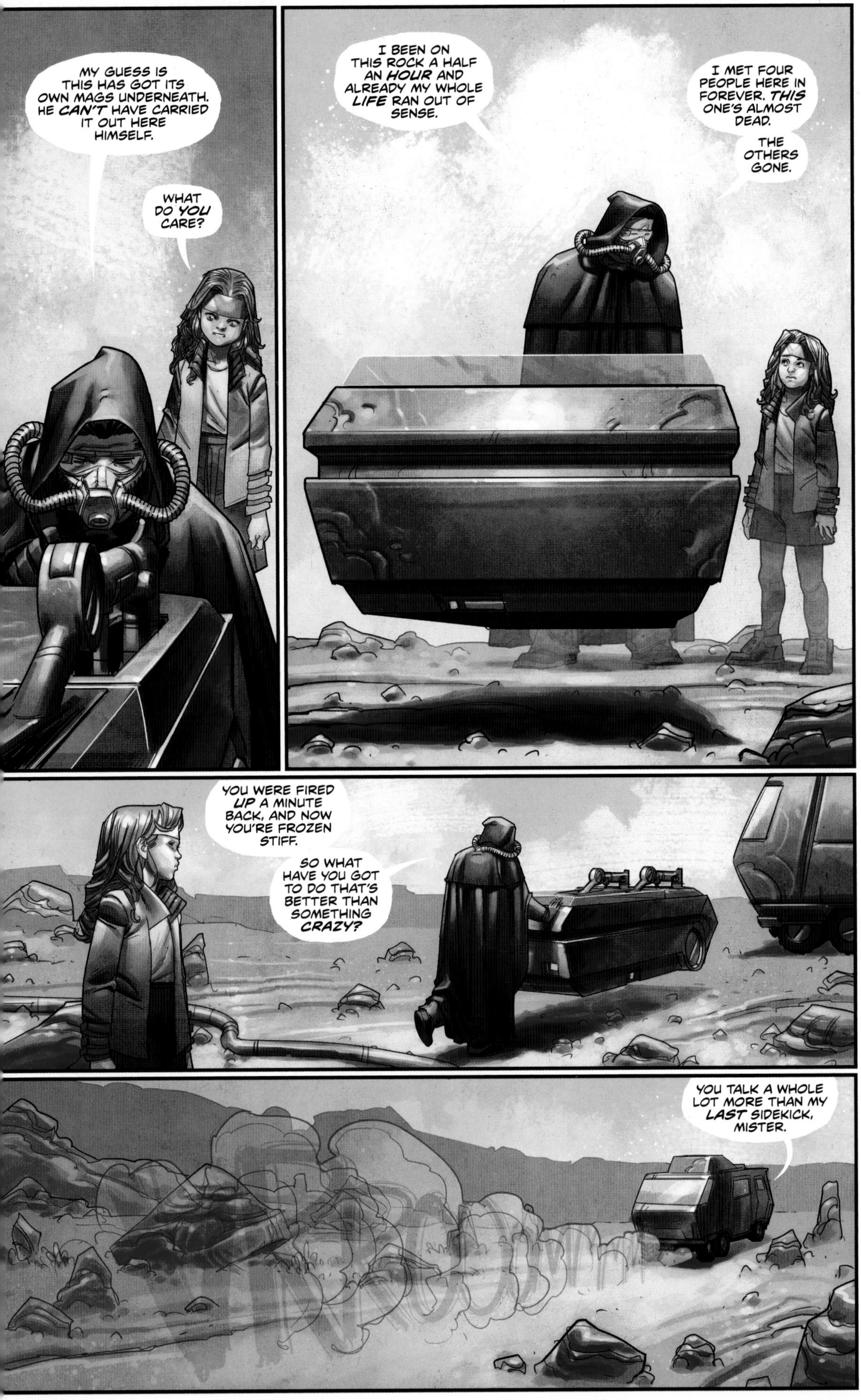
MY GUESS IS THIS HAS GOT ITS OWN MAGS UNDERNEATH. HE CAN'T HAVE CARRIED IT OUT HERE HIMSELF.
WHAT DO YOU CARE?
I BEEN ON THIS ROCK A HALF AN HOUR AND ALREADY MY WHOLE LIFE RAN OUT OF SENSE.
I MET FOUR PEOPLE HERE IN FOREVER. THIS ONE'S ALMOST DEAD.
THE OTHERS GONE.
YOU WERE FIRED UP A MINUTE BACK, AND NOW YOU'RE FROZEN STIFF.
SO WHAT HAVE YOU GOT TO DO THAT'S BETTER THAN SOMETHING CRAZY?
YOU TALK A WHOLE LOT MORE THAN MY LAST SIDEKICK, MISTER.

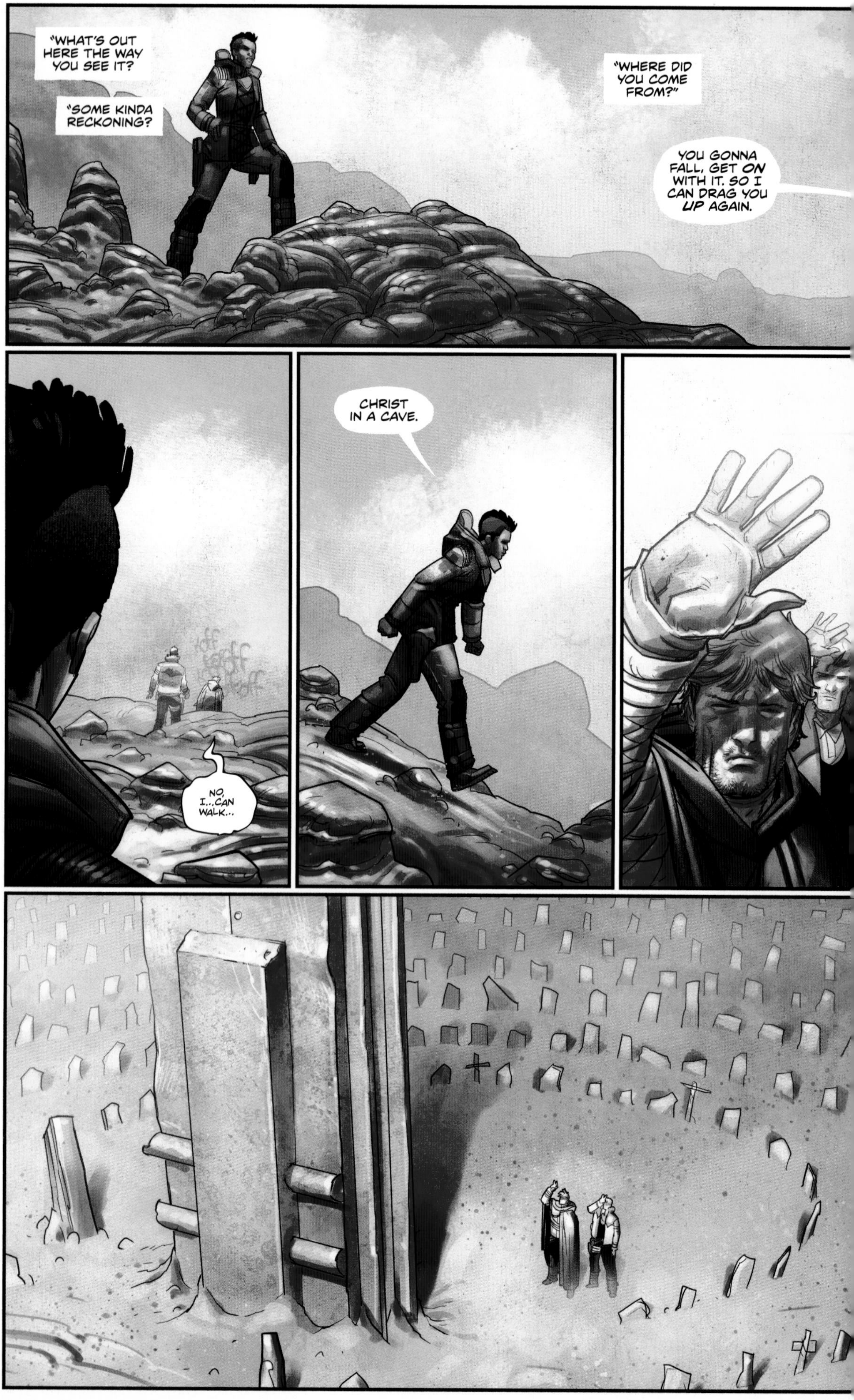
"WHAT'S OUT HERE THE WAY YOU SEE IT?
"SOME KINDA RECKONING?
"WHERE DID YOU COME FROM?"
YOU GONNA FALL, GET ON WITH IT. SO I CAN DRAG YOU UP AGAIN.
NO, I...CAN WALK...
CHRIST IN A CAVE.

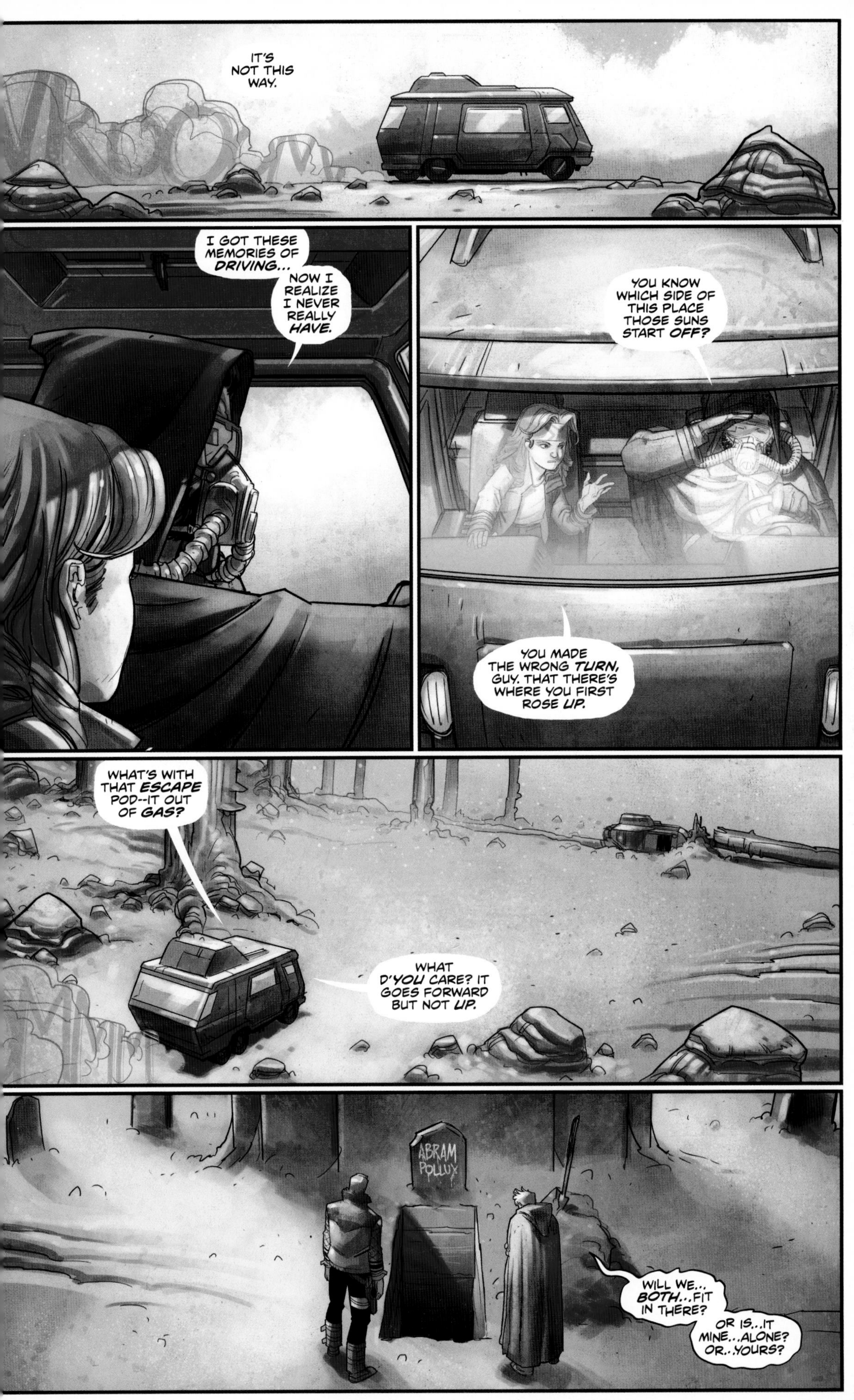

IT'S NOT THIS WAY.
I GOT THESE MEMORIES OF DRIVING...
NOW I REALIZE I NEVER REALLY HAVE.
YOU KNOW WHICH SIDE OF THIS PLACE THOSE SUNS START OFF?
YOU MADE THE WRONG TURN, GUY. THAT THERE'S WHERE YOU FIRST ROSE UP.
WHAT'S WITH THAT ESCAPE POD--IT OUT OF GAS?
WHAT D'YOU CARE? IT GOES FORWARD BUT NOT UP.
ABRAM POLLUX
WILL WE... BOTH... FIT IN THERE?
OR IS... IT MINE... ALONE? OR... YOURS?

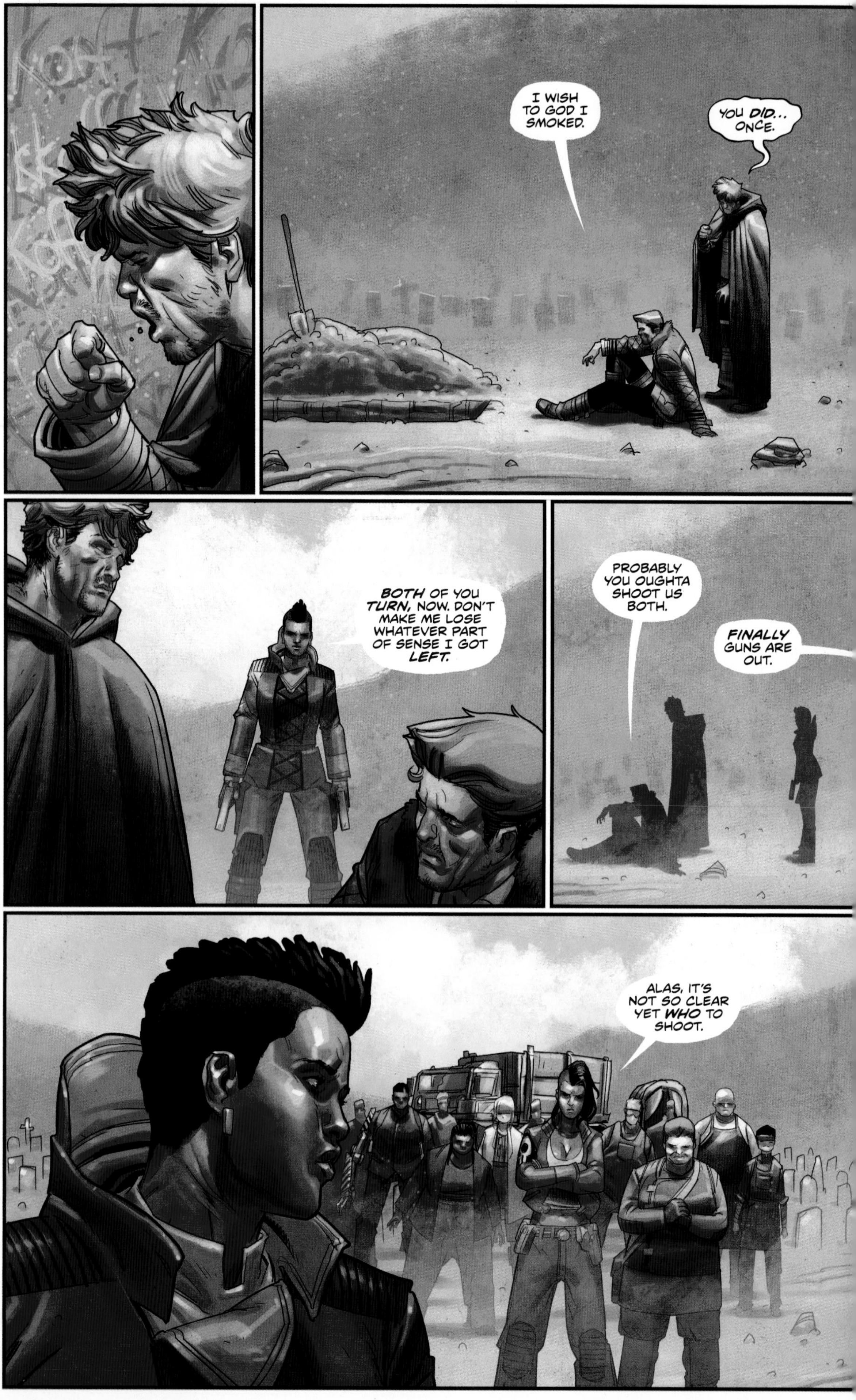
I WISH TO GOD I SMOKED.
YOU DID... ONCE.
BOTH OF YOU TURN, NOW. DON'T MAKE ME LOSE WHATEVER PART OF SENSE I GOT LEFT.
PROBABLY YOU OUGHTA SHOOT US BOTH.
FINALLY GUNS ARE OUT.
ALAS, IT'S NOT SO CLEAR YET WHO TO SHOOT.

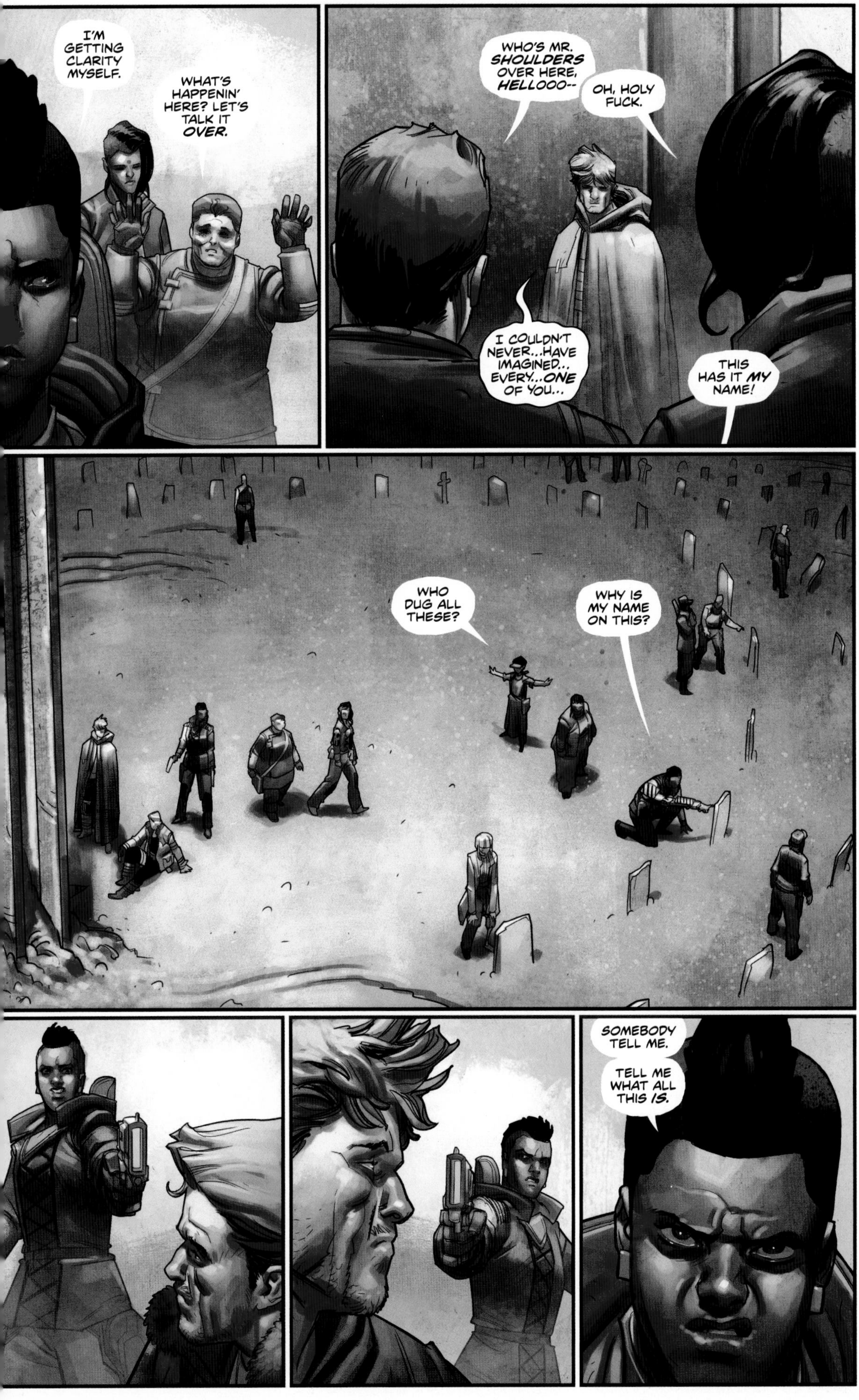
I'M GETTING CLARITY MYSELF.
WHAT'S HAPPENIN' HERE? LET'S TALK IT *OVER.*
WHO'S MR. *SHOULDERS* OVER HERE, *HELLOOO--*
OH, HOLY FUCK.
I COULDN'T NEVER...HAVE IMAGINED... EVERY...*ONE* OF YOU...
THIS HAS IT *MY* NAME!
WHO DUG ALL THESE?
WHY IS MY NAME ON THIS?
SOMEBODY TELL ME.
TELL ME WHAT ALL THIS *IS.*

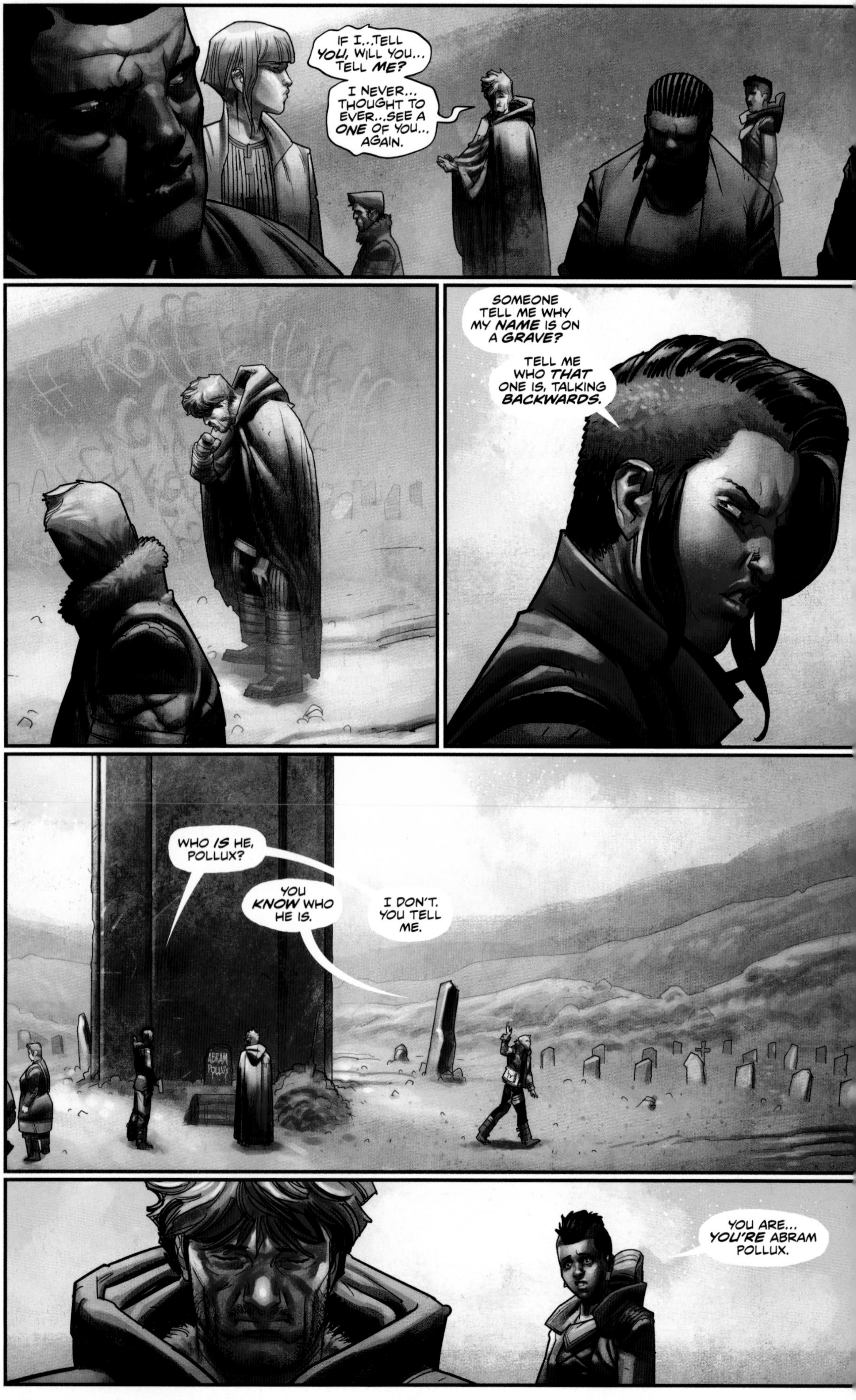
IF I...TELL YOU, WILL YOU... TELL ME?
I NEVER... THOUGHT TO EVER...SEE A ONE OF YOU... AGAIN.
SOMEONE TELL ME WHY MY NAME IS ON A GRAVE?
TELL ME WHO THAT ONE IS, TALKING BACKWARDS.
WHO IS HE, POLLUX?
YOU KNOW WHO HE IS.
I DON'T. YOU TELL ME.
ABRAM POLLUX
YOU ARE... YOU'RE ABRAM POLLUX.

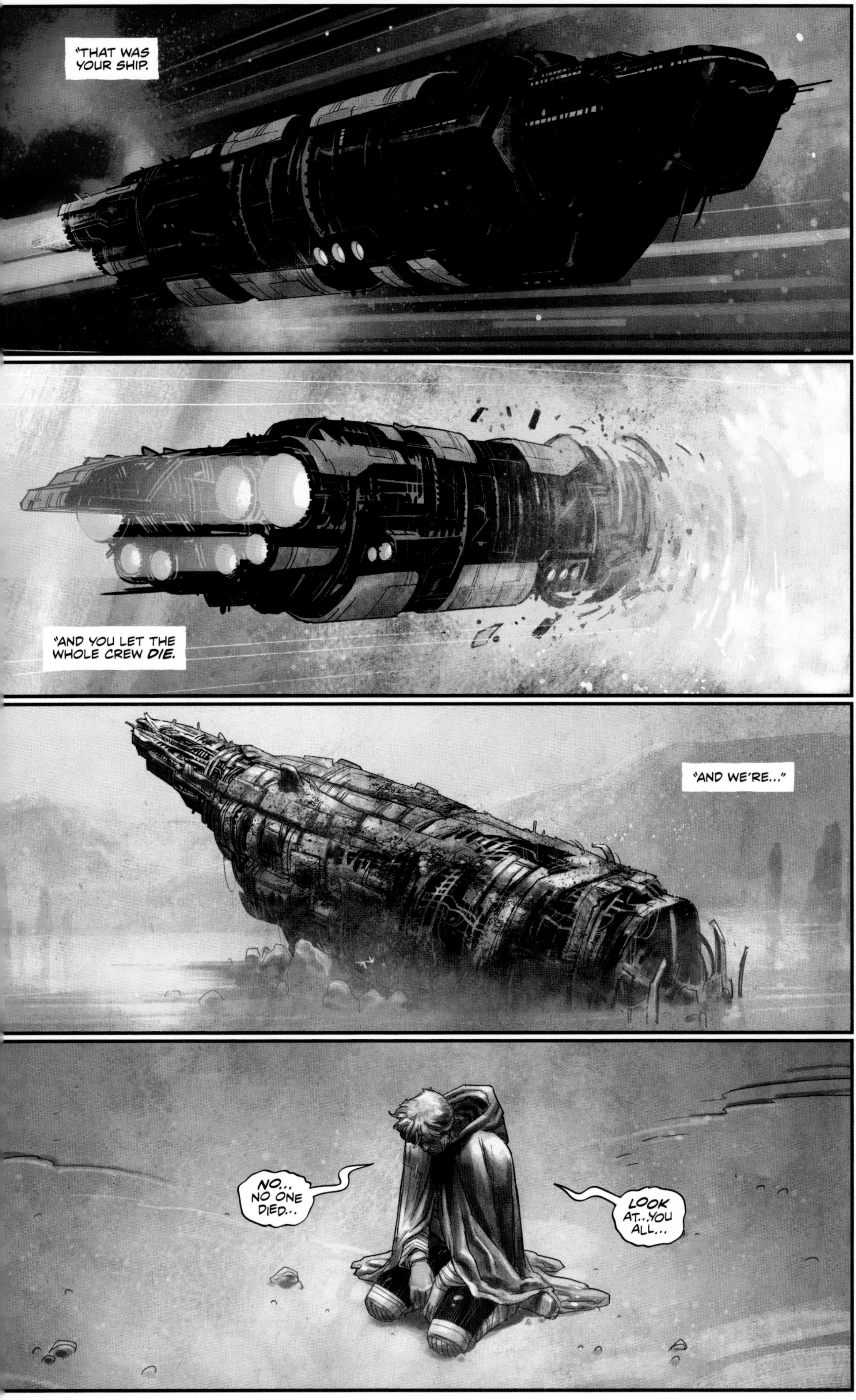
"THAT WAS YOUR SHIP.
"AND YOU LET THE WHOLE CREW DIE.
"AND WE'RE..."
NO... NO ONE DIED...
LOOK AT...YOU ALL...

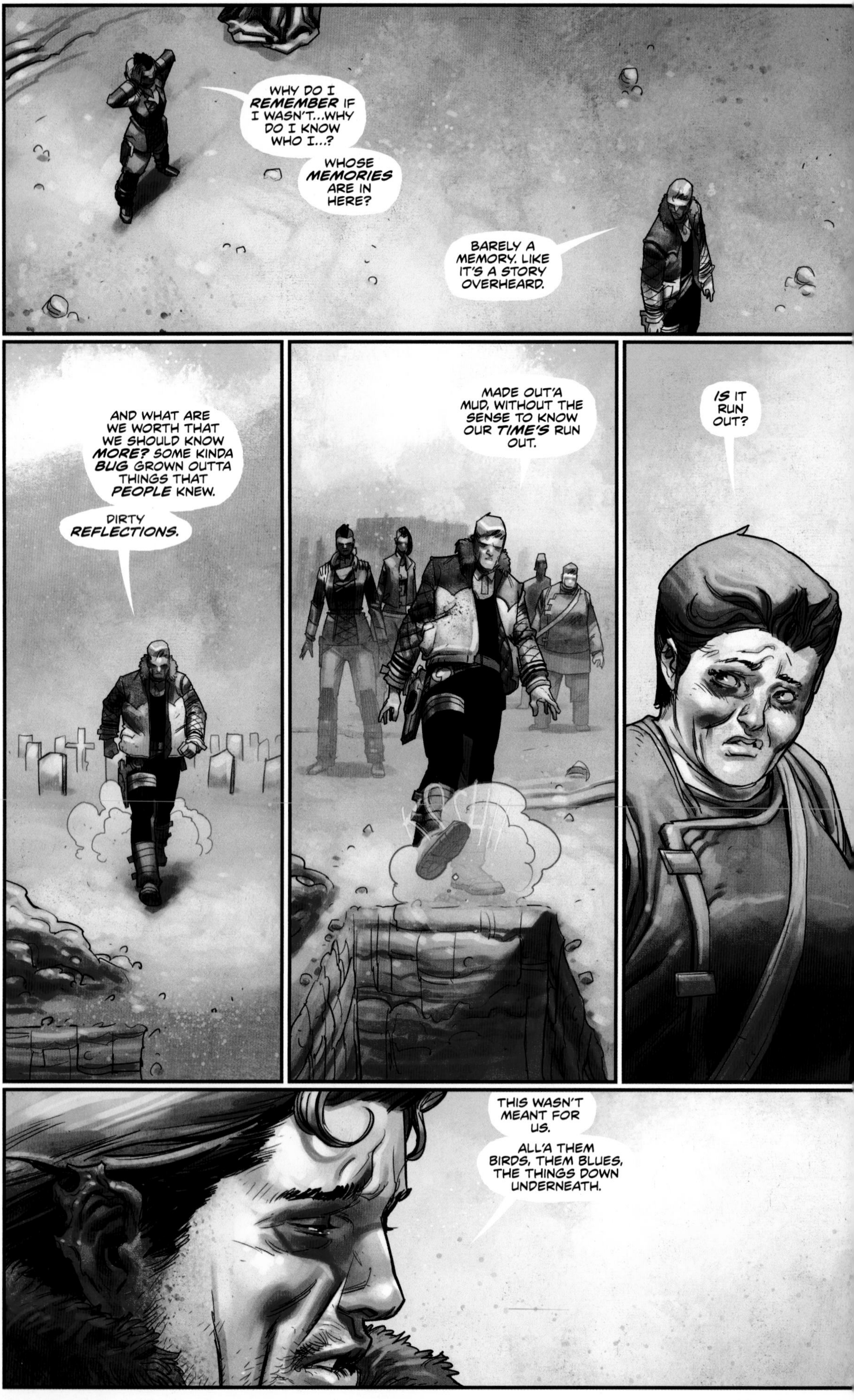
WHY DO I REMEMBER IF I WASN'T...WHY DO I KNOW WHO I...?
WHOSE MEMORIES ARE IN HERE?
BARELY A MEMORY. LIKE IT'S A STORY OVERHEARD.
AND WHAT ARE WE WORTH THAT WE SHOULD KNOW MORE? SOME KINDA BUG GROWN OUTTA THINGS THAT PEOPLE KNEW.
DIRTY REFLECTIONS.
MADE OUT'A MUD, WITHOUT THE SENSE TO KNOW OUR TIME'S RUN OUT.
IS IT RUN OUT?
THIS WASN'T MEANT FOR US.
ALL'A THEM BIRDS, THEM BLUES, THE THINGS DOWN UNDERNEATH.

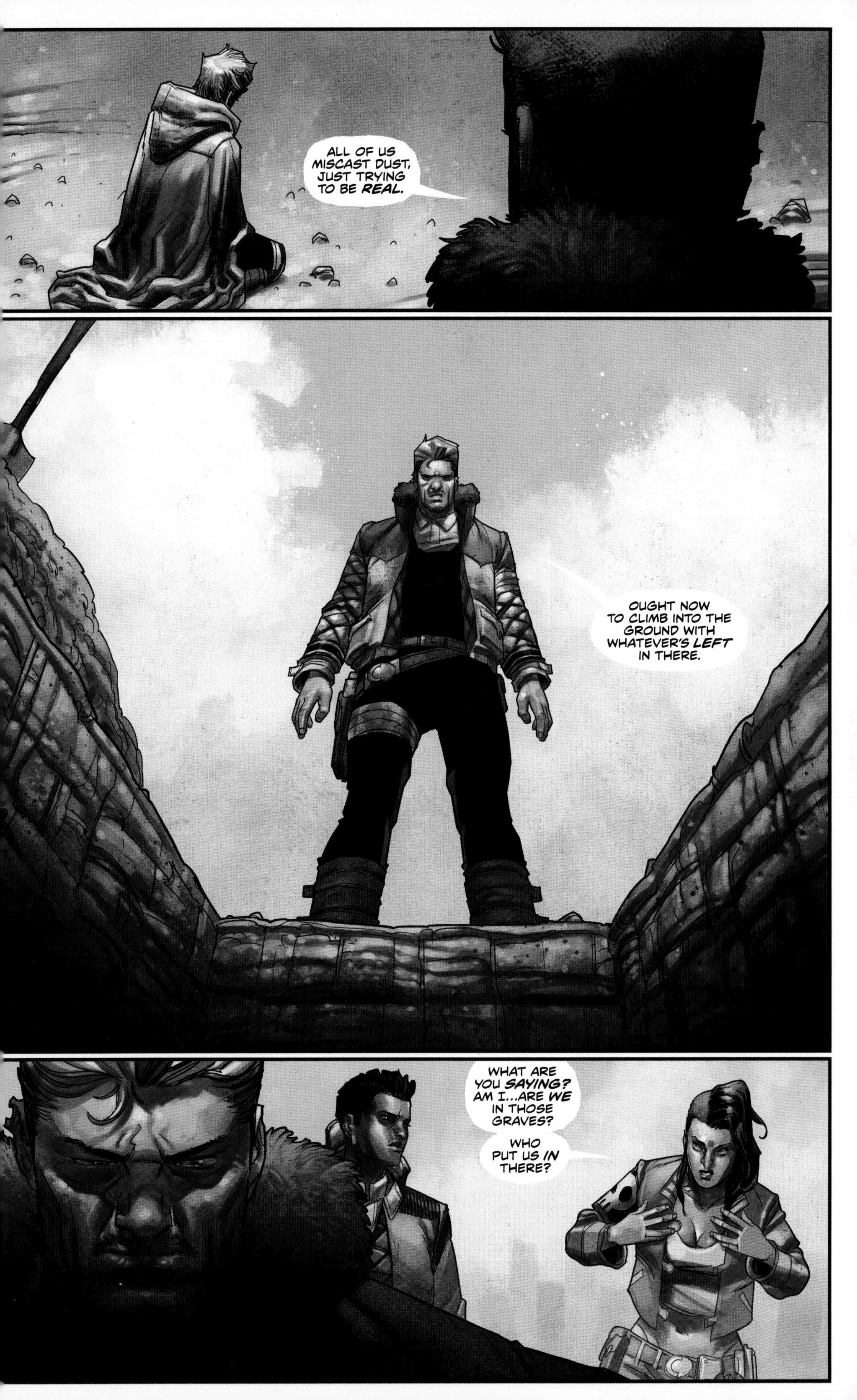
ALL OF US MISCAST DUST, JUST TRYING TO BE REAL.
OUGHT NOW TO CLIMB INTO THE GROUND WITH WHATEVER'S LEFT IN THERE.
WHAT ARE YOU SAYING? AM I...ARE WE IN THOSE GRAVES?
WHO PUT US IN THERE?

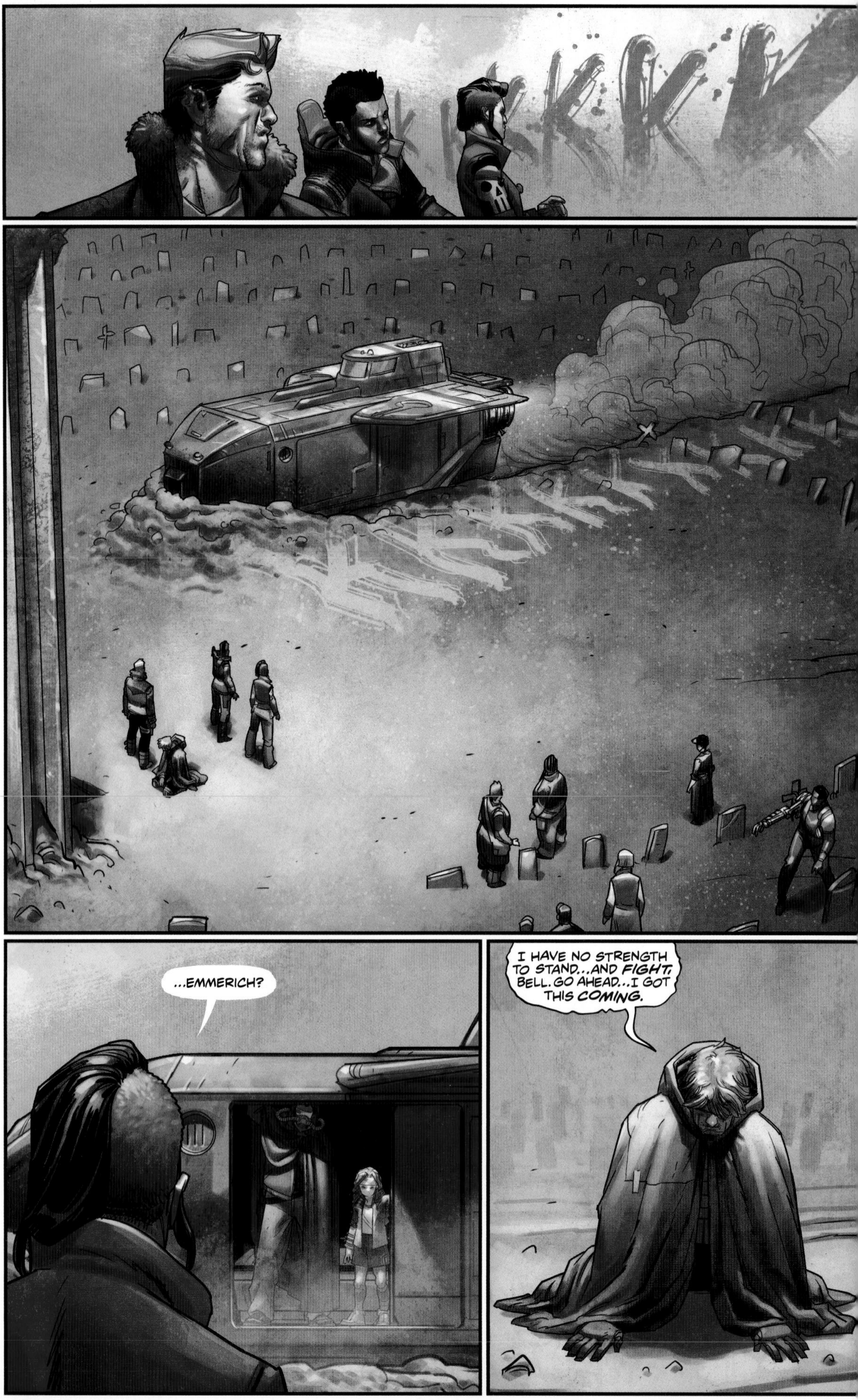
...EMMERICH?
I HAVE NO STRENGTH TO STAND...AND FIGHT, BELL. GO AHEAD...I GOT THIS COMING.

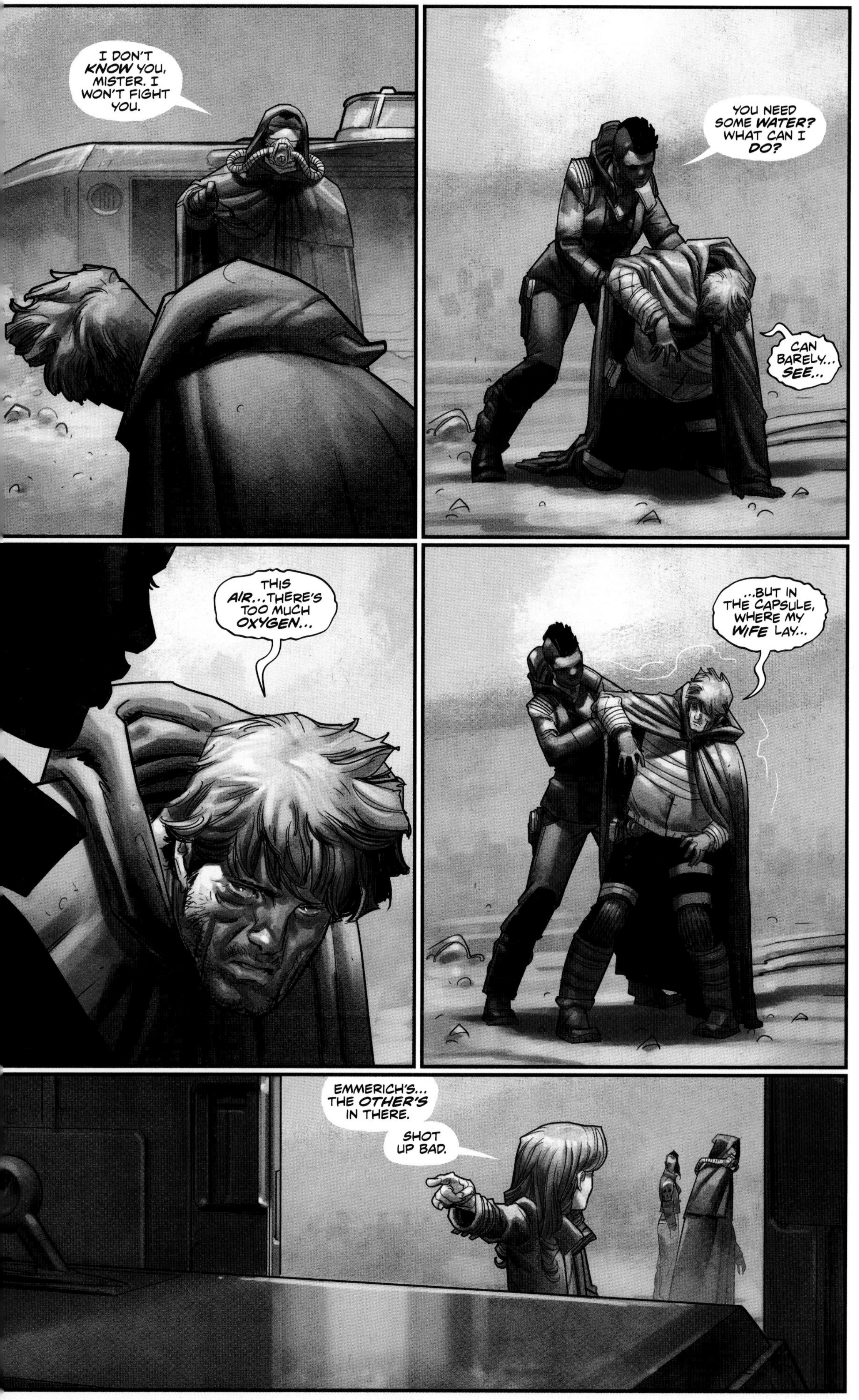
I DON'T KNOW YOU, MISTER. I WON'T FIGHT YOU.
YOU NEED SOME WATER? WHAT CAN I DO?
CAN BARELY... SEE...
THIS AIR...THERE'S TOO MUCH OXYGEN...
...BUT IN THE CAPSULE, WHERE MY WIFE LAY...
EMMERICH'S... THE OTHER'S IN THERE.
SHOT UP BAD.

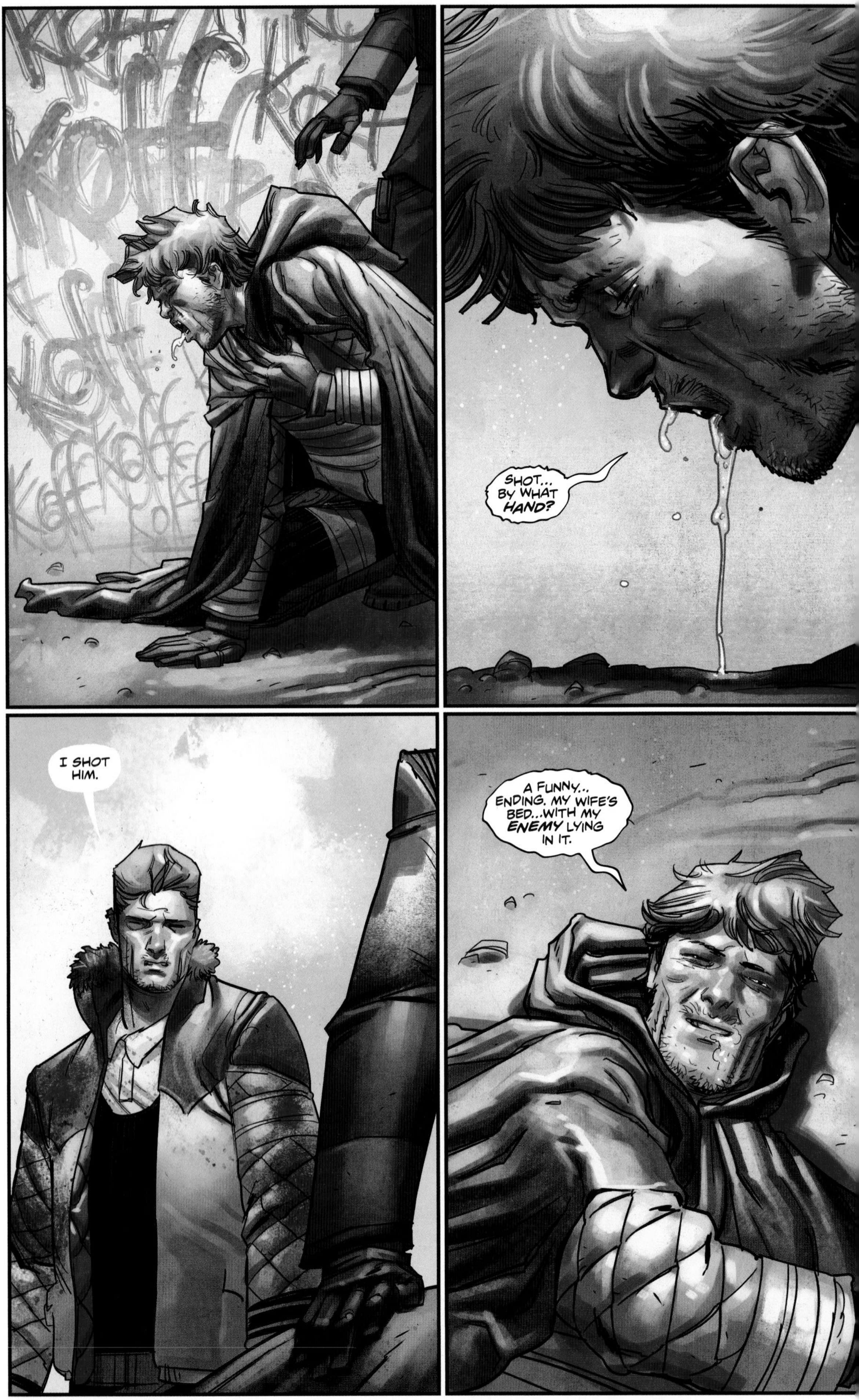
KOFF KOFF KOFF KOFF KOFF
SHOT... BY WHAT HAND?
I SHOT HIM.
A FUNNY... ENDING. MY WIFE'S BED...WITH MY ENEMY LYING IN IT.

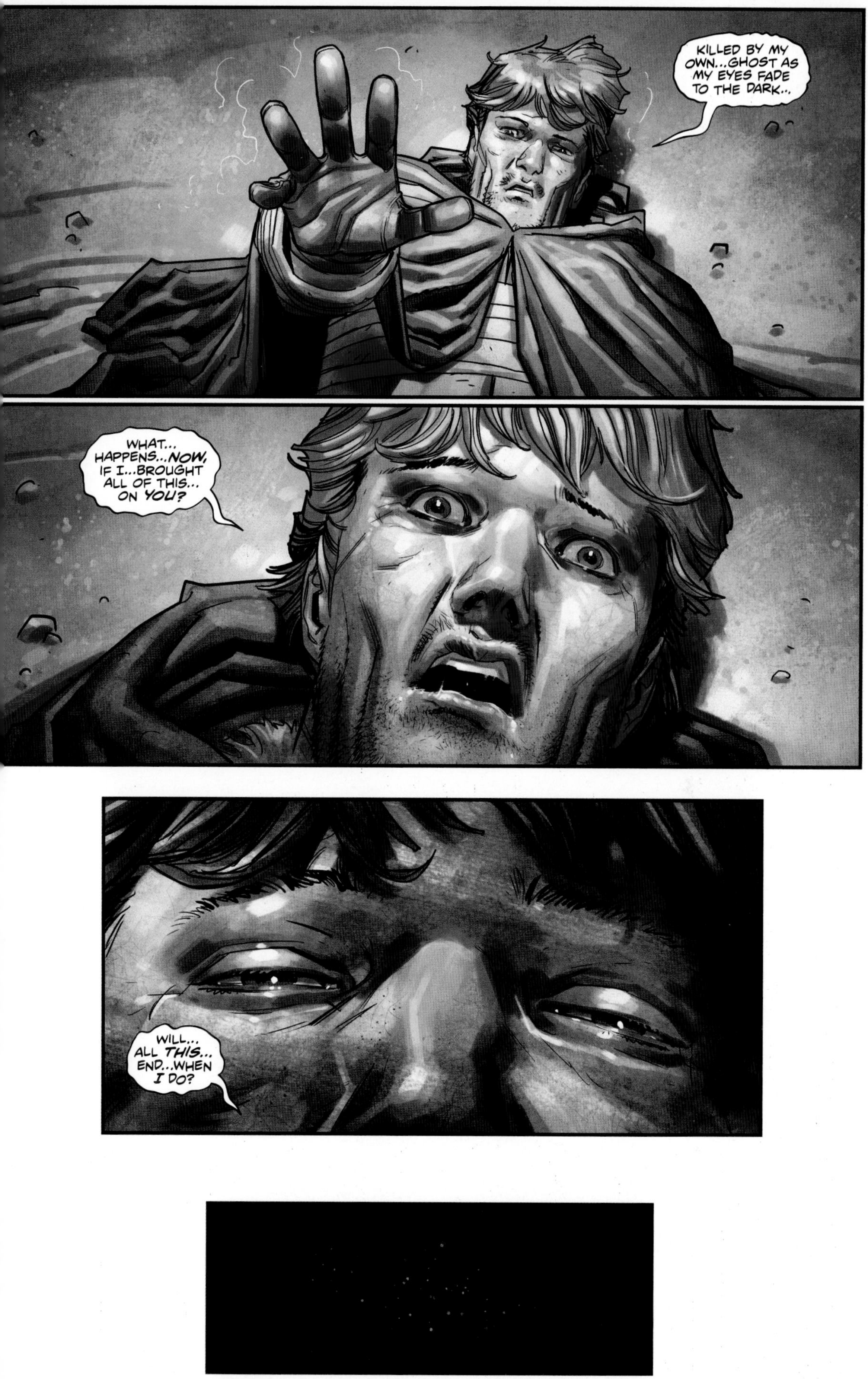
KILLED BY MY OWN...GHOST AS MY EYES FADE TO THE DARK...
WHAT... HAPPENS...NOW, IF I...BROUGHT ALL OF THIS... ON YOU?
WILL... ALL THIS... END...WHEN I DO?

CHAPTER 19
GOODBYE

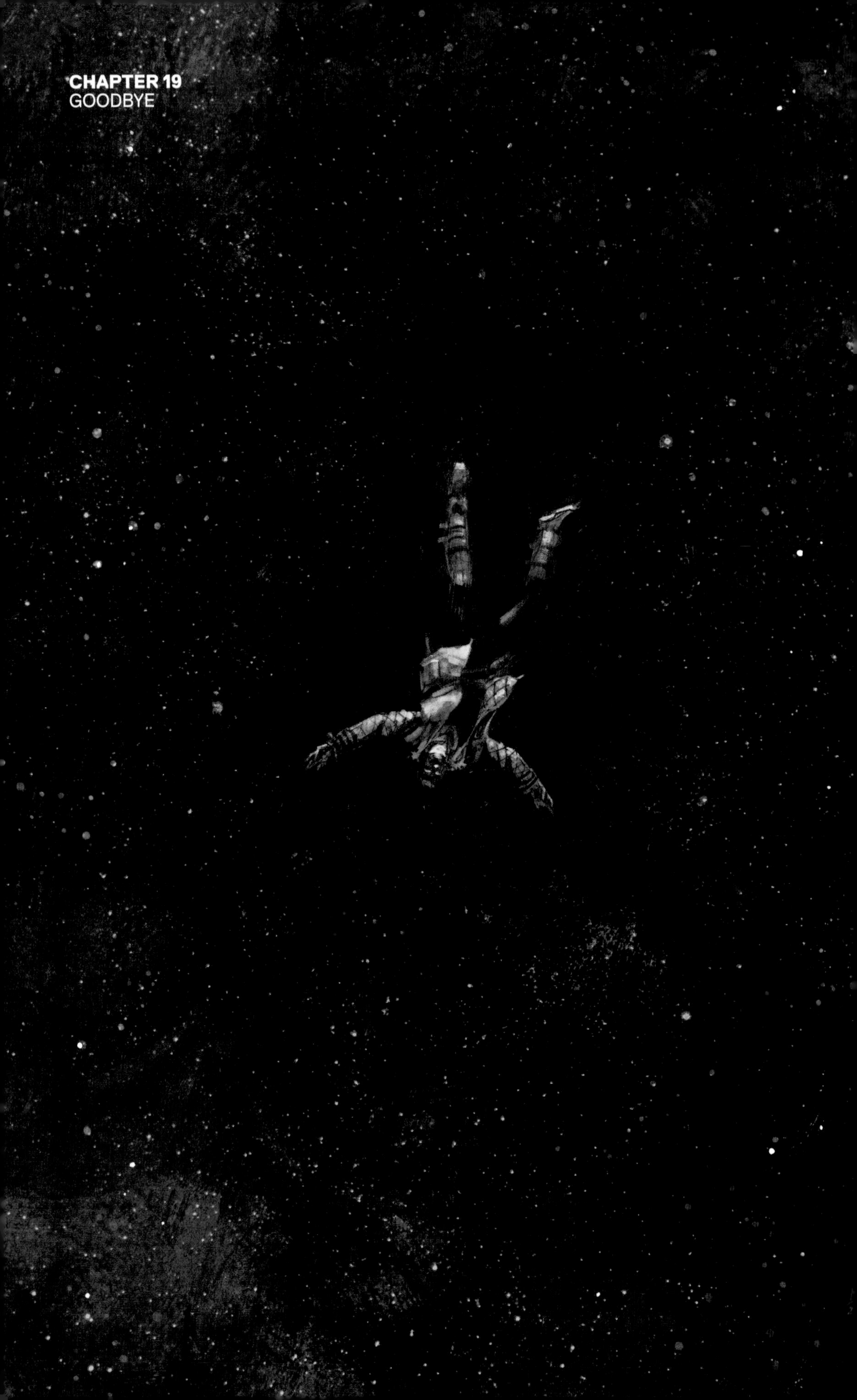

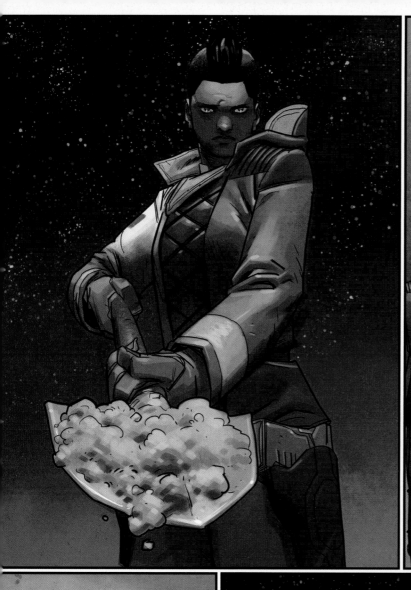

HOW DO YOU FIGURE THAT'D *FEEL*, SEEING THE BACK OF YOUR OWN *HEAD?*

ALL OF THE *WORST* OF YOU, UP ON ITS *HIND* LEGS, FOLLOWING YOU *AROUND?*

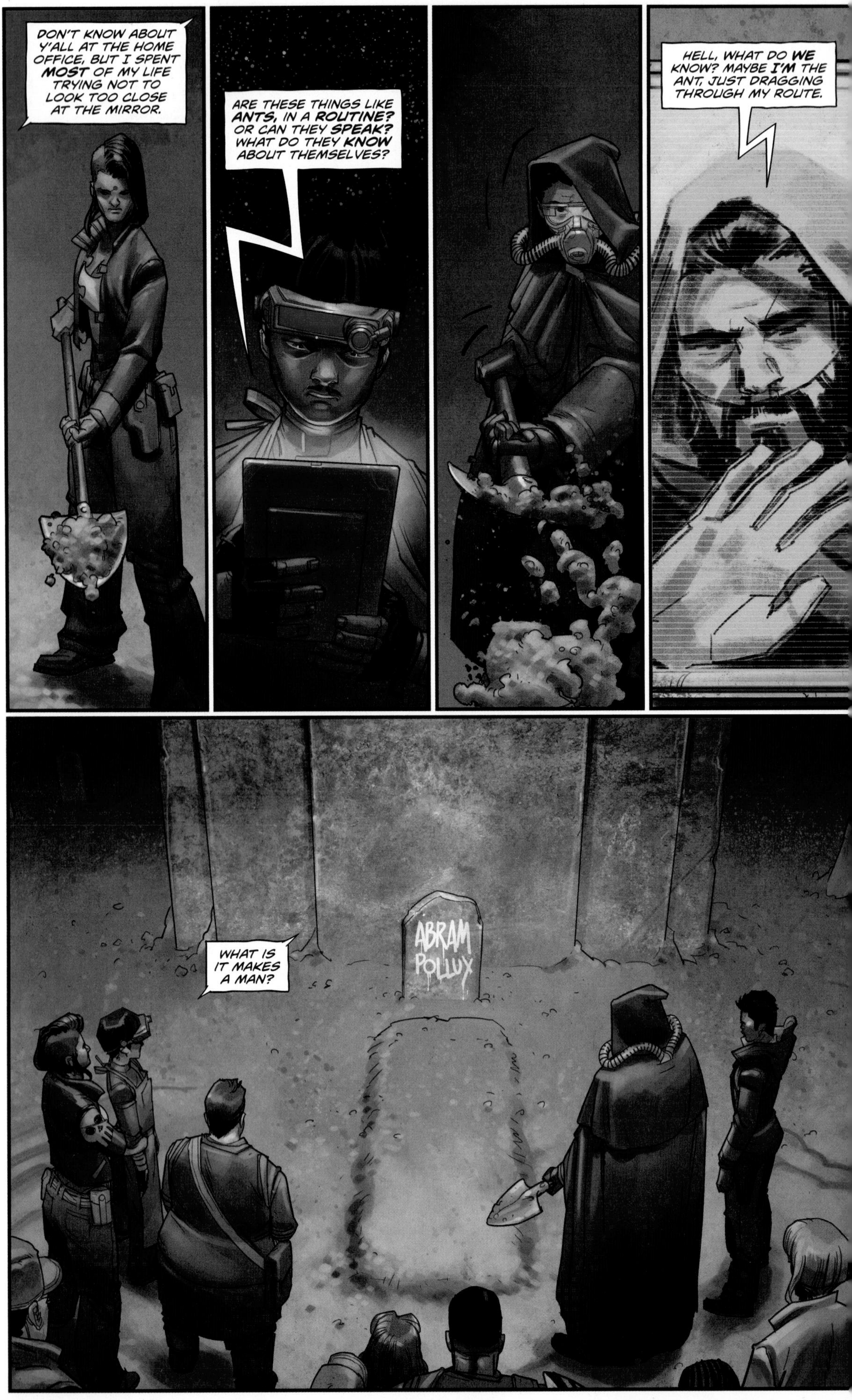
DON'T KNOW ABOUT Y'ALL AT THE HOME OFFICE, BUT I SPENT MOST OF MY LIFE TRYING NOT TO LOOK TOO CLOSE AT THE MIRROR.
ARE THESE THINGS LIKE ANTS, IN A ROUTINE? OR CAN THEY SPEAK? WHAT DO THEY KNOW ABOUT THEMSELVES?
HELL, WHAT DO WE KNOW? MAYBE I'M THE ANT, JUST DRAGGING THROUGH MY ROUTE.
ABRAM POLLUX
WHAT IS IT MAKES A MAN?

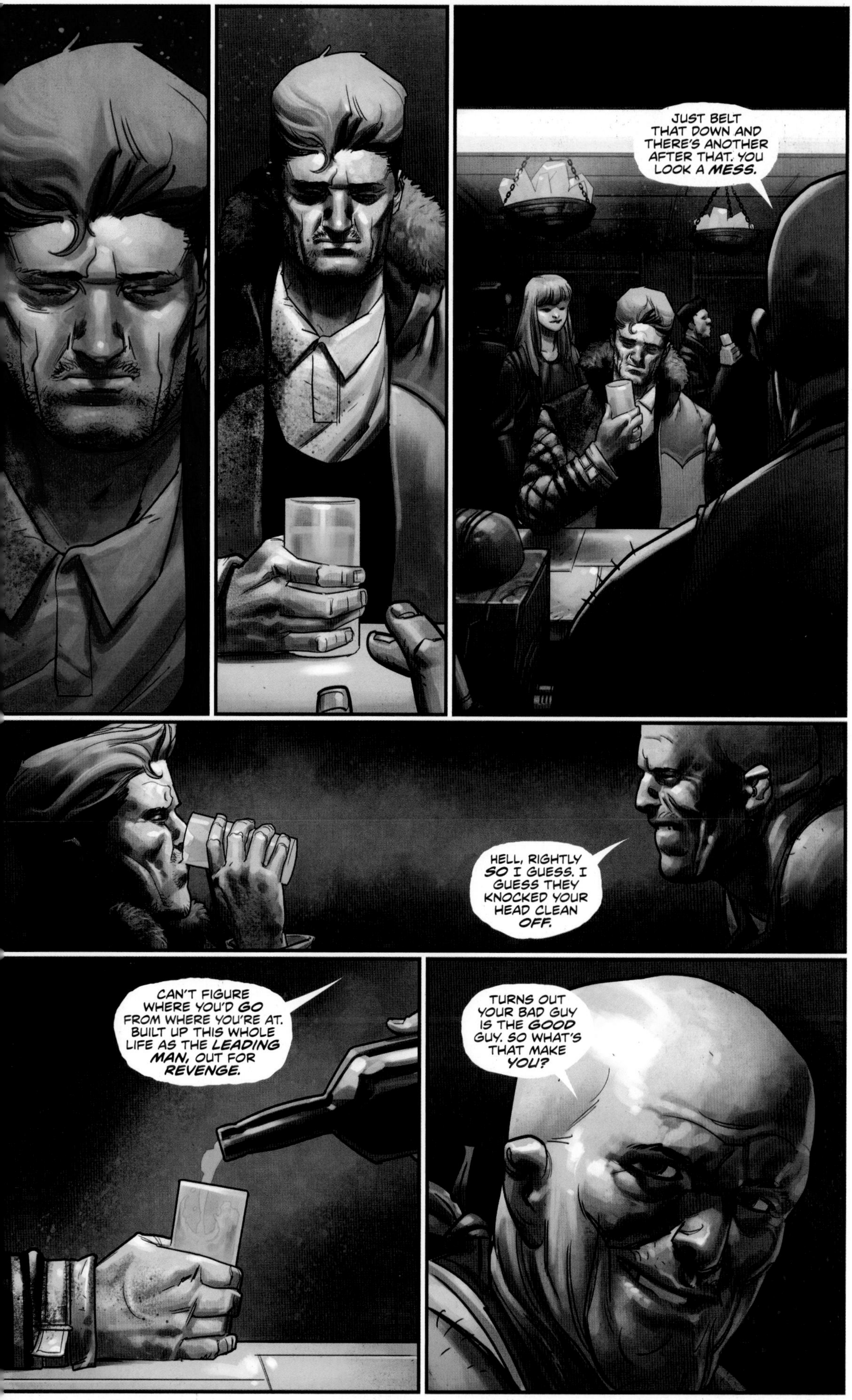

JUST BELT THAT DOWN AND THERE'S ANOTHER AFTER THAT. YOU LOOK A MESS.
HELL, RIGHTLY SO I GUESS. I GUESS THEY KNOCKED YOUR HEAD CLEAN OFF.
CAN'T FIGURE WHERE YOU'D GO FROM WHERE YOU'RE AT. BUILT UP THIS WHOLE LIFE AS THE LEADING MAN, OUT FOR REVENGE.
TURNS OUT YOUR BAD GUY IS THE GOOD GUY. SO WHAT'S THAT MAKE YOU?

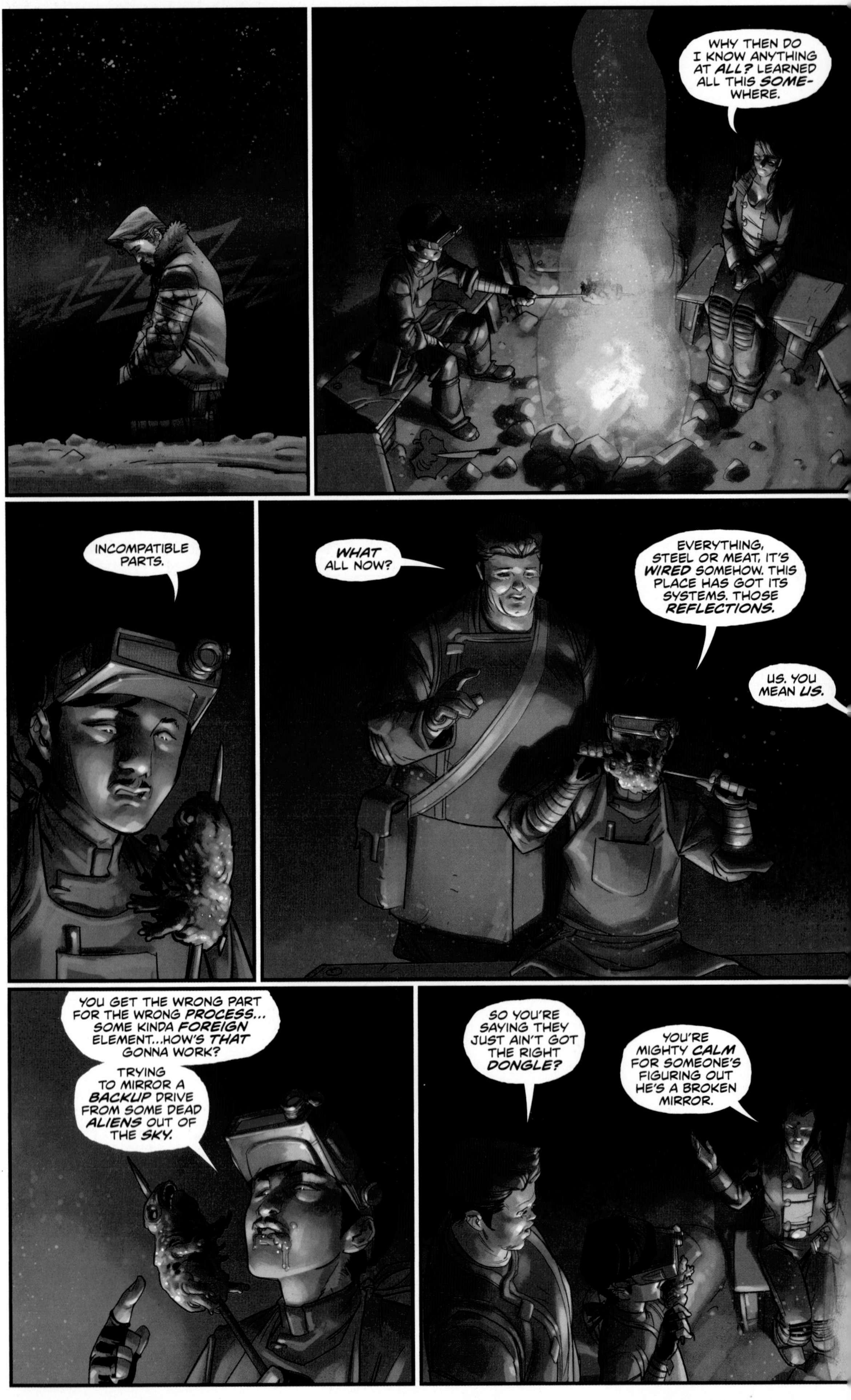
WHY THEN DO I KNOW ANYTHING AT ALL? LEARNED ALL THIS SOME-WHERE.
INCOMPATIBLE PARTS.
WHAT ALL NOW?
EVERYTHING, STEEL OR MEAT, IT'S WIRED SOMEHOW. THIS PLACE HAS GOT ITS SYSTEMS. THOSE REFLECTIONS.
US. YOU MEAN US.
YOU GET THE WRONG PART FOR THE WRONG PROCESS... SOME KINDA FOREIGN ELEMENT...HOW'S THAT GONNA WORK?
TRYING TO MIRROR A BACKUP DRIVE FROM SOME DEAD ALIENS OUT OF THE SKY.
SO YOU'RE SAYING THEY JUST AIN'T GOT THE RIGHT DONGLE?
YOU'RE MIGHTY CALM FOR SOMEONE'S FIGURING OUT HE'S A BROKEN MIRROR.

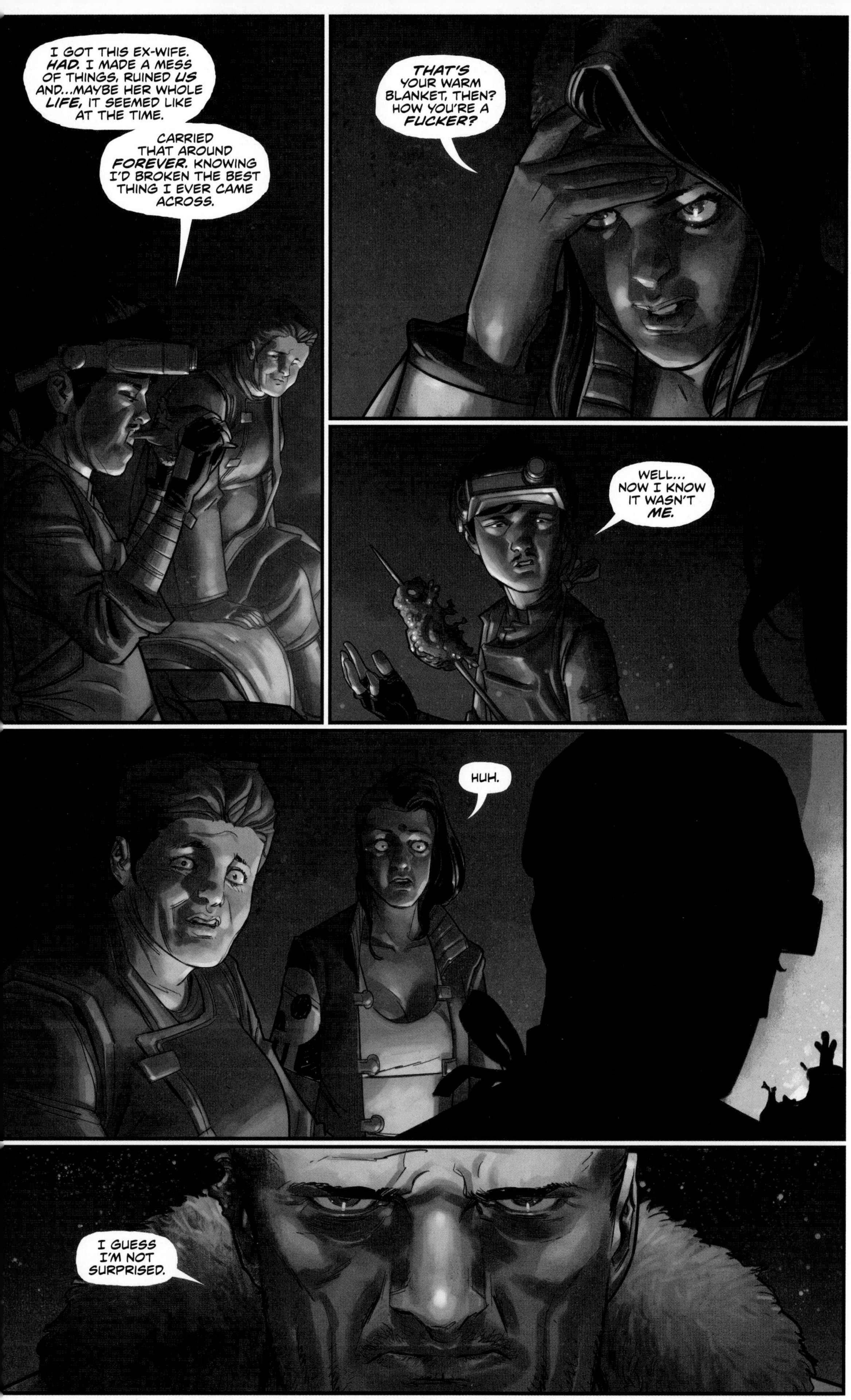
I GOT THIS EX-WIFE. HAD. I MADE A MESS OF THINGS, RUINED US AND...MAYBE HER WHOLE LIFE, IT SEEMED LIKE AT THE TIME.
CARRIED THAT AROUND FOREVER. KNOWING I'D BROKEN THE BEST THING I EVER CAME ACROSS.
THAT'S YOUR WARM BLANKET, THEN? HOW YOU'RE A FUCKER?
WELL... NOW I KNOW IT WASN'T ME.
HUH.
I GUESS I'M NOT SURPRISED.

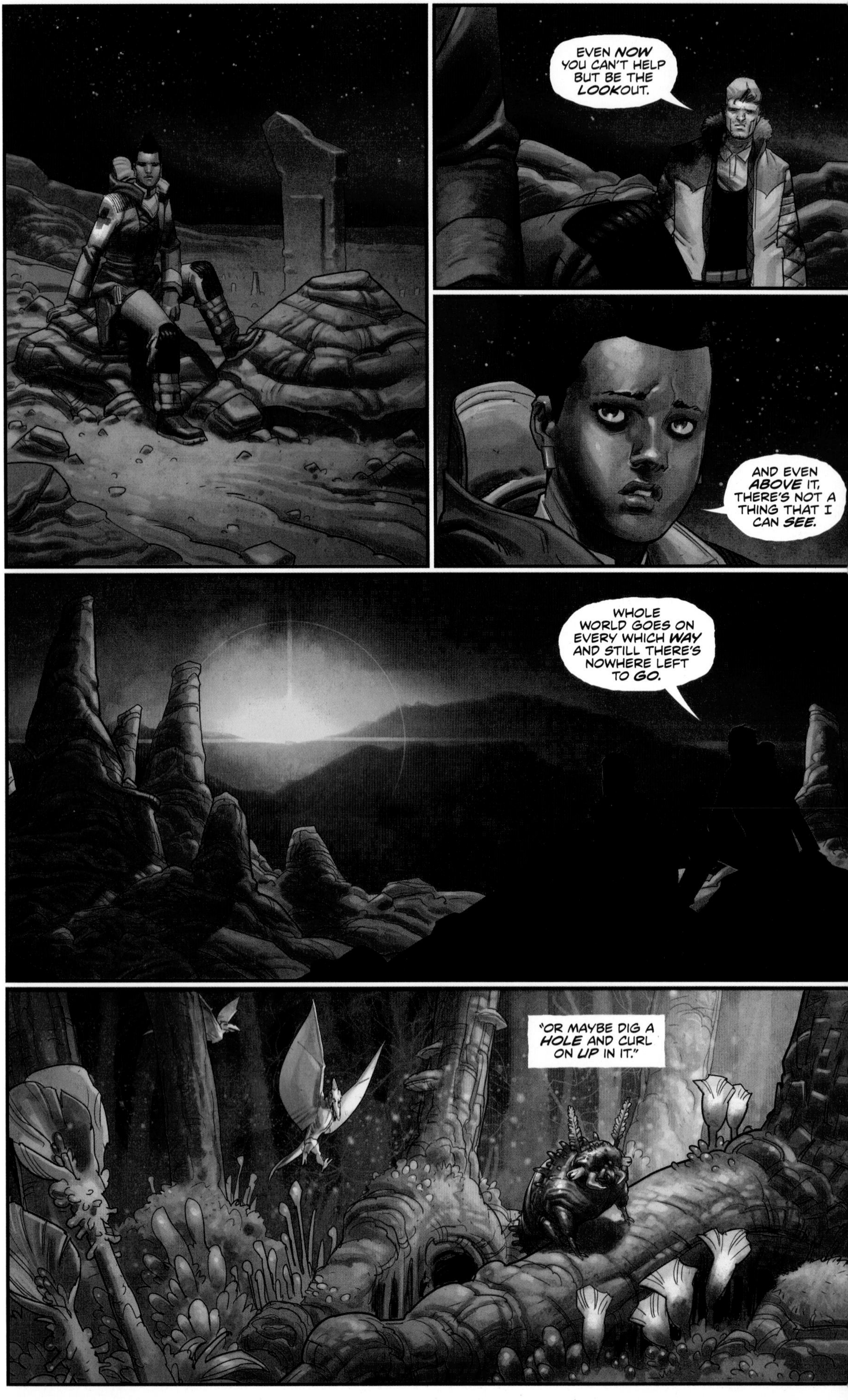
EVEN NOW YOU CAN'T HELP BUT BE THE LOOKOUT.
AND EVEN ABOVE IT, THERE'S NOT A THING THAT I CAN SEE.
WHOLE WORLD GOES ON EVERY WHICH WAY AND STILL THERE'S NOWHERE LEFT TO GO.
"OR MAYBE DIG A HOLE AND CURL ON UP IN IT."

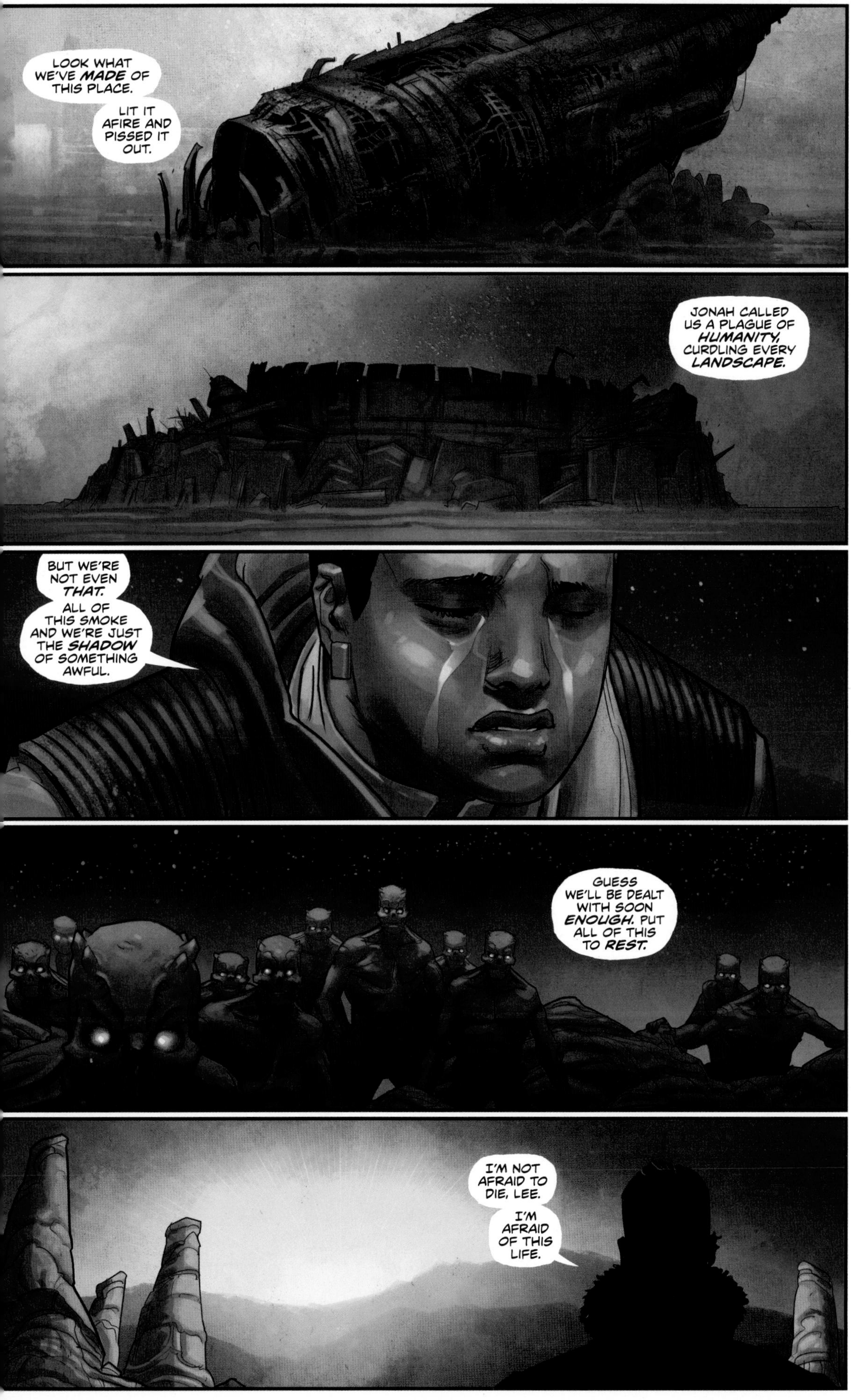
LOOK WHAT WE'VE MADE OF THIS PLACE.
LIT IT AFIRE AND PISSED IT OUT.
JONAH CALLED US A PLAGUE OF HUMANITY, CURDLING EVERY LANDSCAPE.
BUT WE'RE NOT EVEN THAT.
ALL OF THIS SMOKE AND WE'RE JUST THE SHADOW OF SOMETHING AWFUL.
GUESS WE'LL BE DEALT WITH SOON ENOUGH. PUT ALL OF THIS TO REST.
I'M NOT AFRAID TO DIE, LEE.
I'M AFRAID OF THIS LIFE.

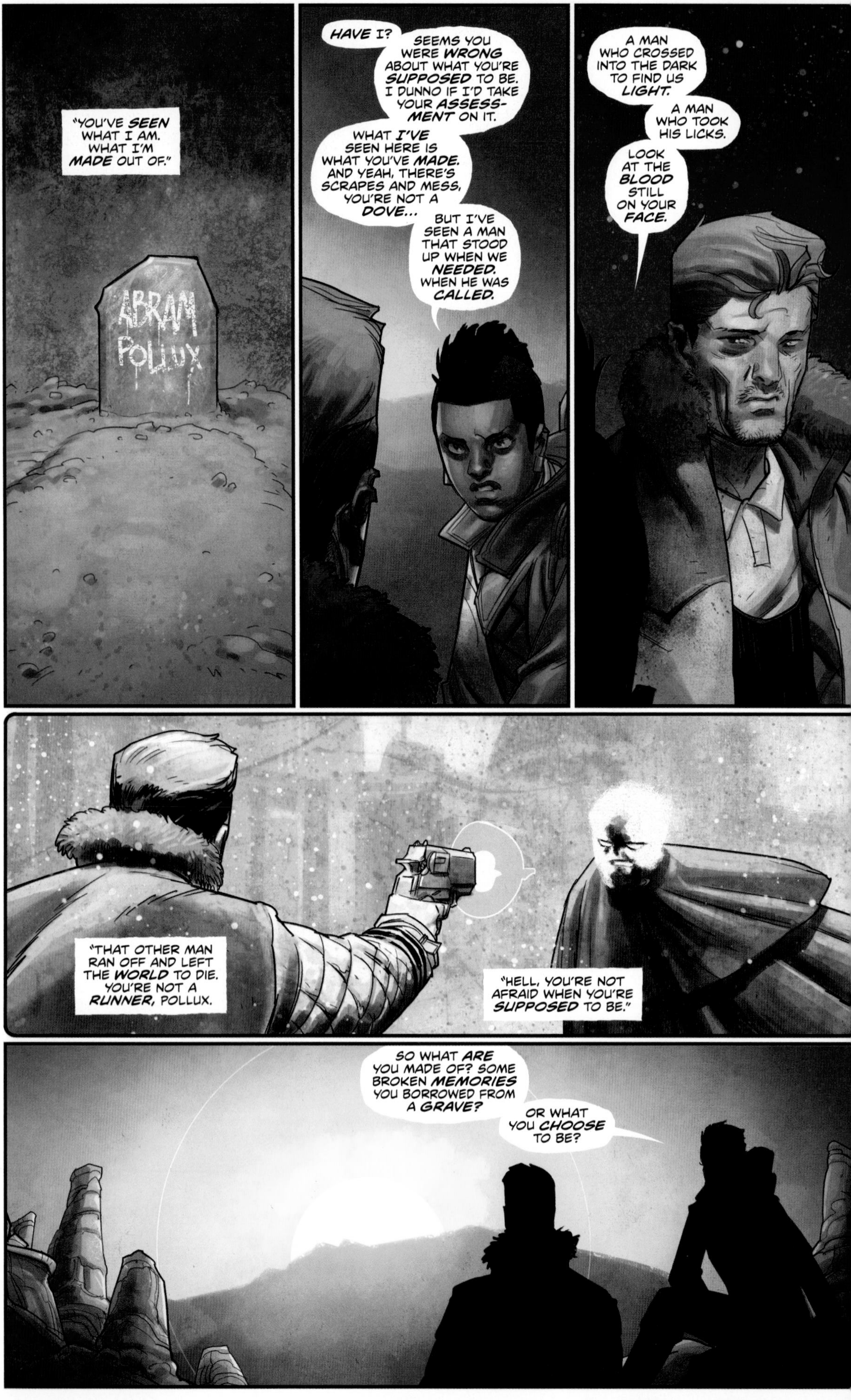
"YOU'VE SEEN WHAT I AM. WHAT I'M MADE OUT OF."
ABRAM POLLUX
HAVE I?
SEEMS YOU WERE WRONG ABOUT WHAT YOU'RE SUPPOSED TO BE. I DUNNO IF I'D TAKE YOUR ASSESS-MENT ON IT.
WHAT I'VE SEEN HERE IS WHAT YOU'VE MADE. AND YEAH, THERE'S SCRAPES AND MESS, YOU'RE NOT A DOVE...
BUT I'VE SEEN A MAN THAT STOOD UP WHEN WE NEEDED. WHEN HE WAS CALLED.
A MAN WHO CROSSED INTO THE DARK TO FIND US LIGHT.
A MAN WHO TOOK HIS LICKS.
LOOK AT THE BLOOD STILL ON YOUR FACE.
"THAT OTHER MAN RAN OFF AND LEFT THE WORLD TO DIE. YOU'RE NOT A RUNNER, POLLUX.
"HELL, YOU'RE NOT AFRAID WHEN YOU'RE SUPPOSED TO BE."
SO WHAT ARE YOU MADE OF? SOME BROKEN MEMORIES YOU BORROWED FROM A GRAVE?
OR WHAT YOU CHOOSE TO BE?

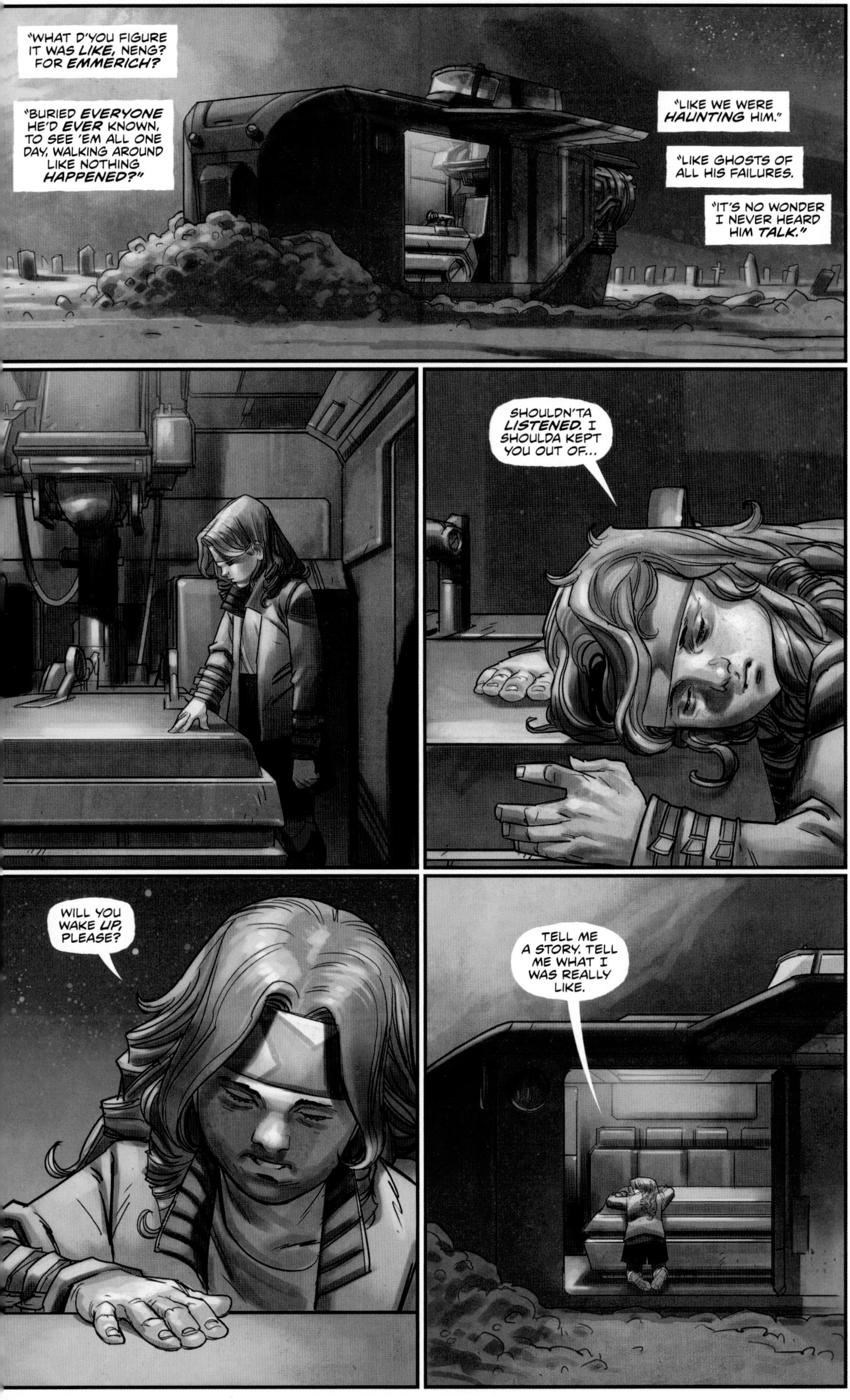
"WHAT D'YOU FIGURE IT WAS *LIKE,* NENG? FOR *EMMERICH?*
"BURIED *EVERYONE* HE'D *EVER* KNOWN, TO SEE 'EM ALL ONE DAY, WALKING AROUND LIKE NOTHING *HAPPENED?"*
"LIKE WE WERE *HAUNTING* HIM."
"LIKE GHOSTS OF ALL HIS FAILURES.
"IT'S NO WONDER I NEVER HEARD HIM *TALK."*
SHOULDN'TA *LISTENED.* I SHOULDA KEPT YOU OUT OF...
WILL YOU WAKE *UP,* PLEASE?
TELL ME A STORY. TELL ME WHAT I WAS REALLY LIKE.

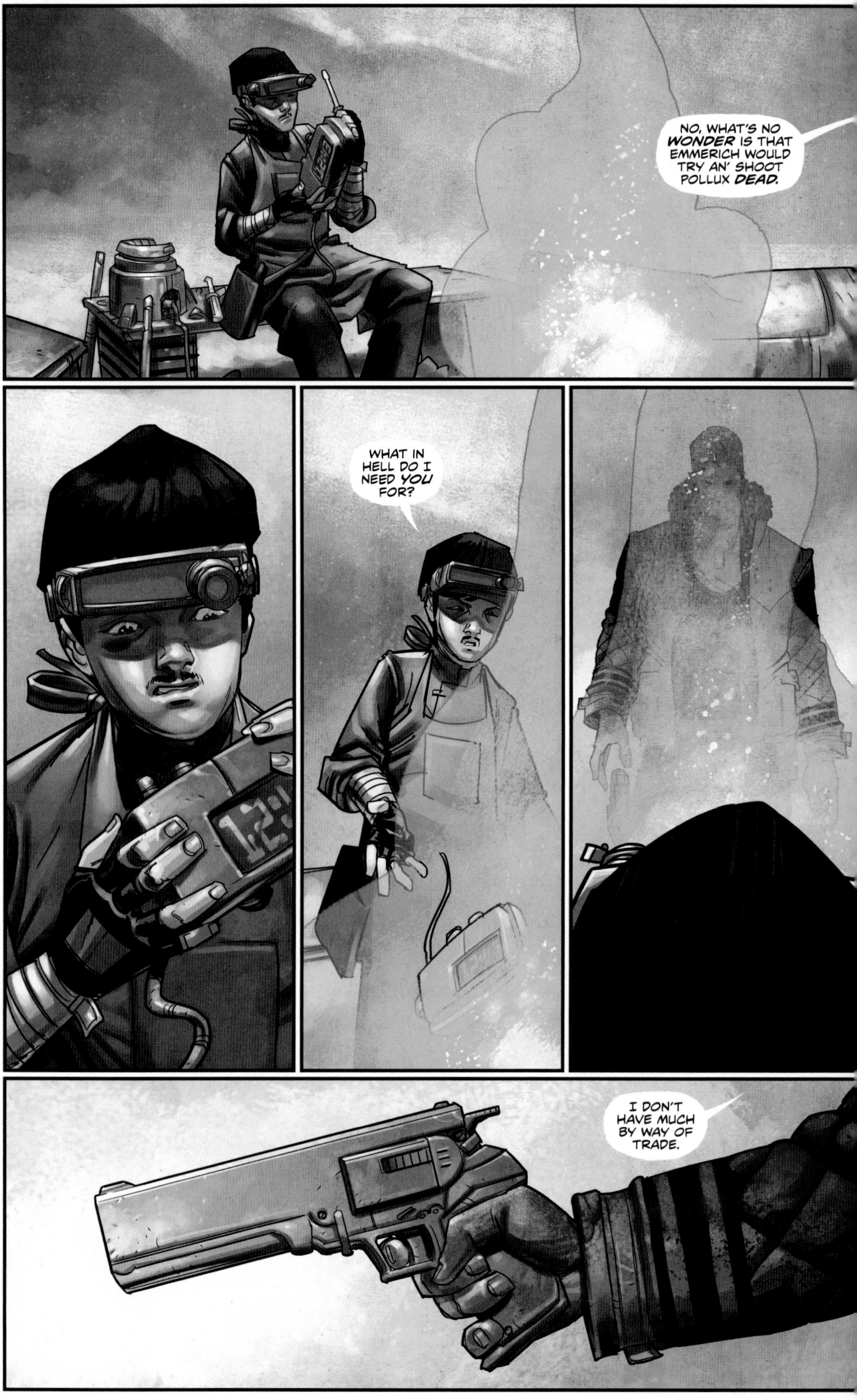
NO, WHAT'S NO *WONDER* IS THAT EMMERICH WOULD TRY AN' SHOOT POLLUX *DEAD.*
WHAT IN HELL DO I NEED *YOU* FOR?
I DON'T HAVE MUCH BY WAY OF TRADE.

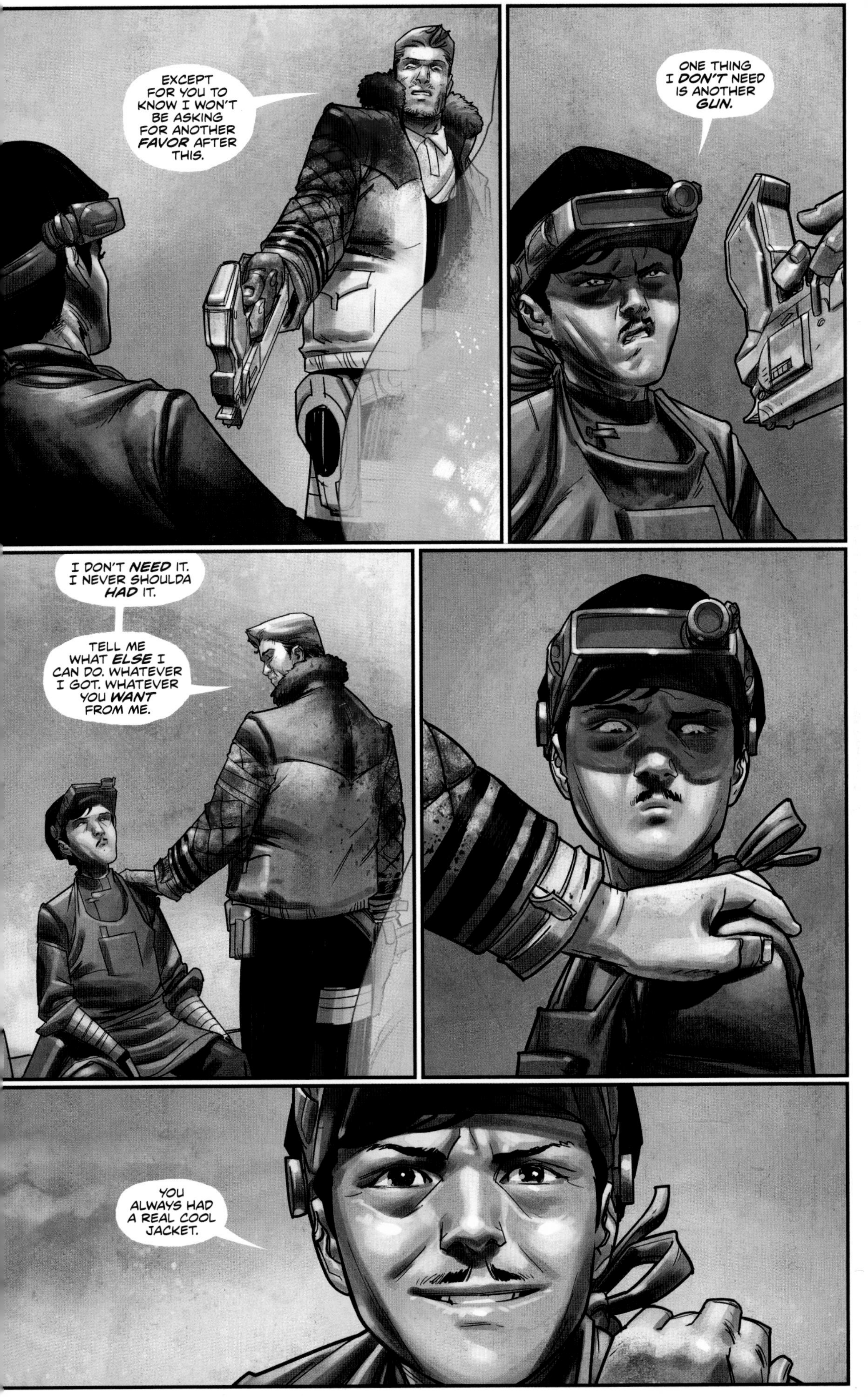
EXCEPT FOR YOU TO KNOW I WON'T BE ASKING FOR ANOTHER *FAVOR* AFTER THIS.
ONE THING I *DON'T* NEED IS ANOTHER *GUN.*
I DON'T *NEED* IT. I NEVER SHOULDA *HAD* IT.
TELL ME WHAT *ELSE* I CAN DO. WHATEVER I GOT. WHATEVER YOU *WANT* FROM ME.
YOU ALWAYS HAD A REAL COOL JACKET.

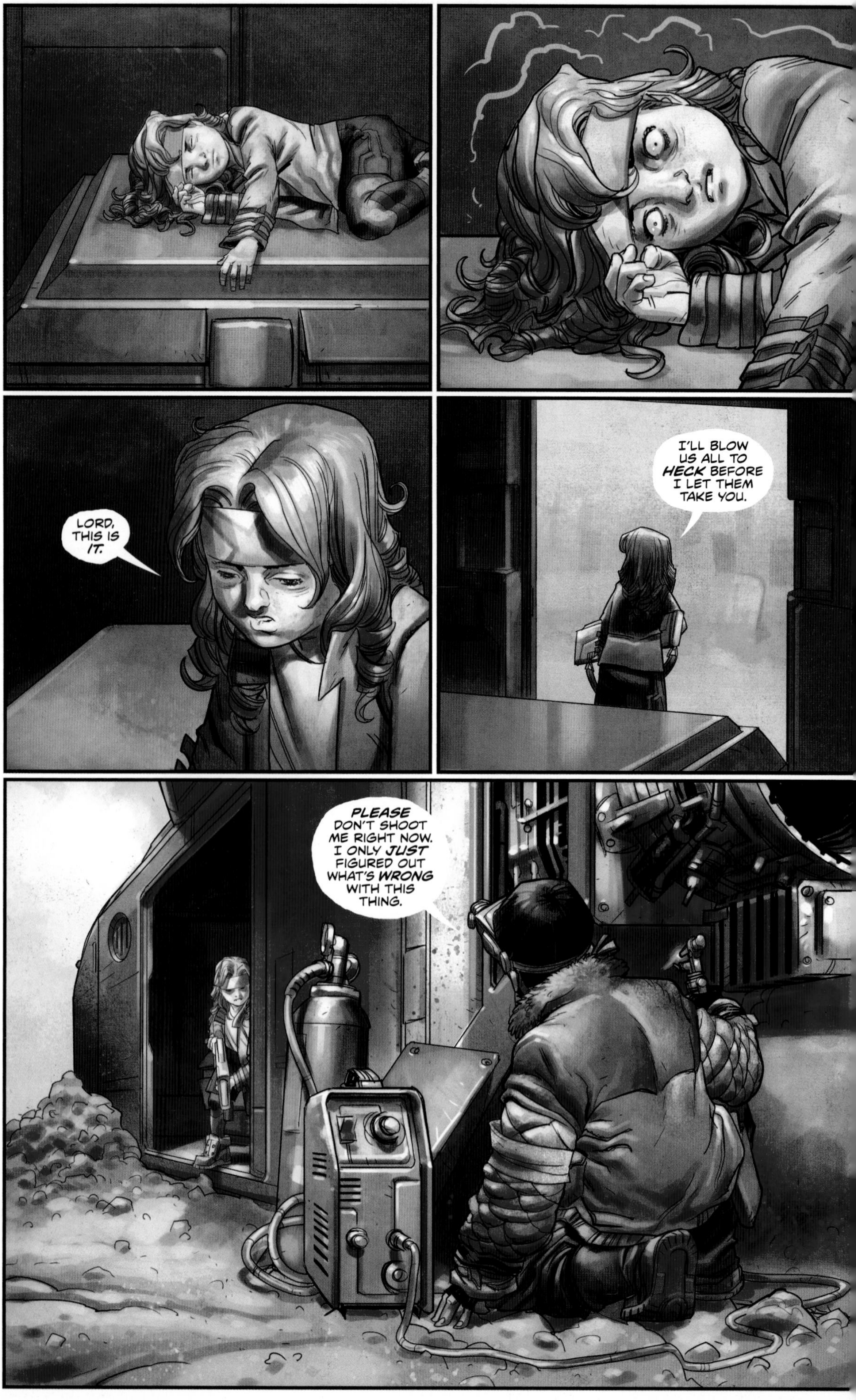
LORD, THIS IS *IT.*
I'LL BLOW US ALL TO *HECK* BEFORE I LET THEM TAKE YOU.
PLEASE DON'T SHOOT ME RIGHT NOW. I ONLY *JUST* FIGURED OUT WHAT'S *WRONG* WITH THIS THING.

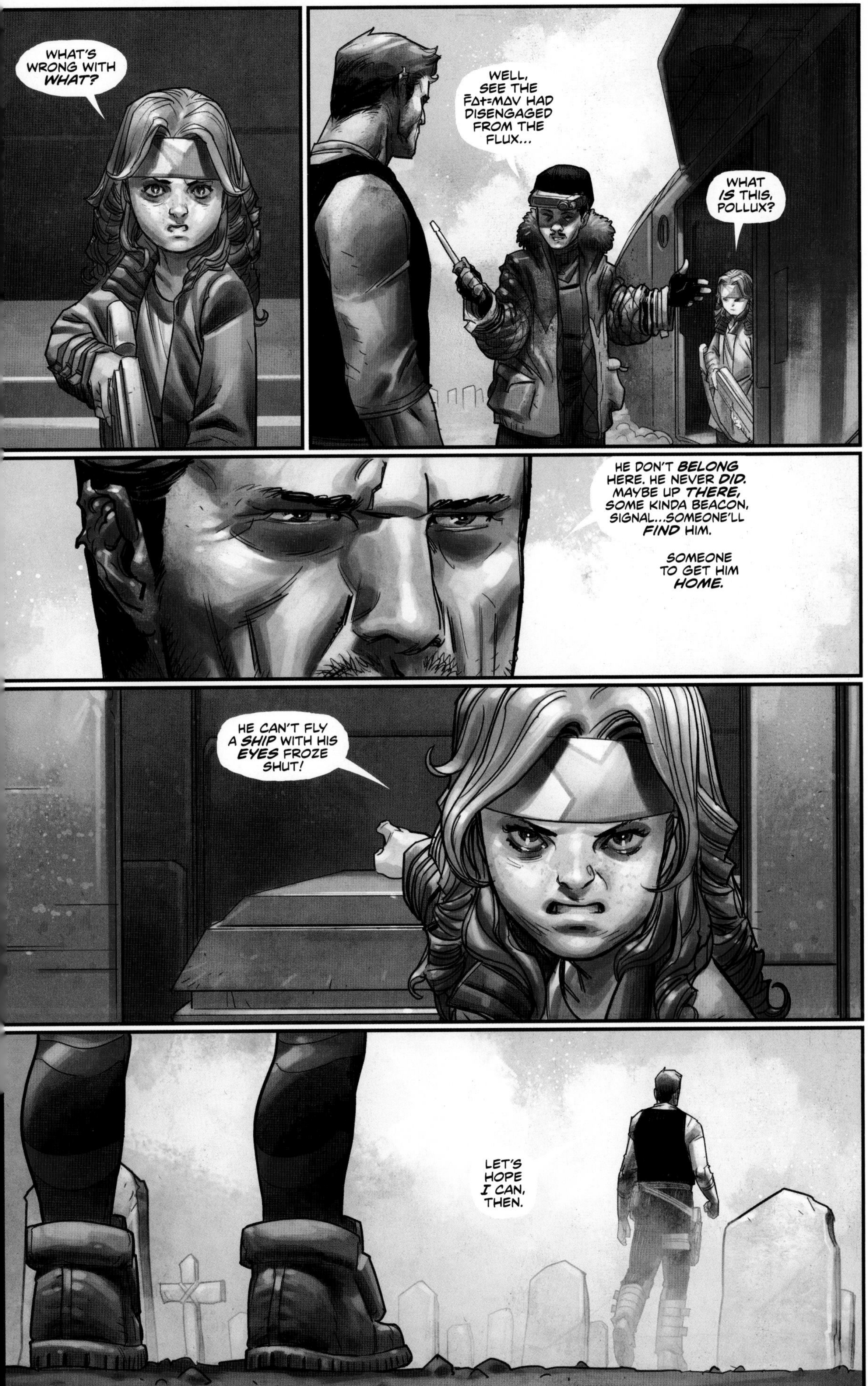
WHAT'S WRONG WITH *WHAT?*
WELL, SEE THE FΔt=MΔV HAD DISENGAGED FROM THE FLUX...
WHAT *IS* THIS, POLLUX?
HE DON'T *BELONG* HERE. HE NEVER *DID*. MAYBE UP *THERE*, SOME KINDA BEACON, SIGNAL...SOMEONE'LL *FIND* HIM.
SOMEONE TO GET HIM *HOME*.
HE CAN'T FLY A *SHIP* WITH HIS *EYES* FROZE SHUT!
LET'S HOPE *I* CAN, THEN.

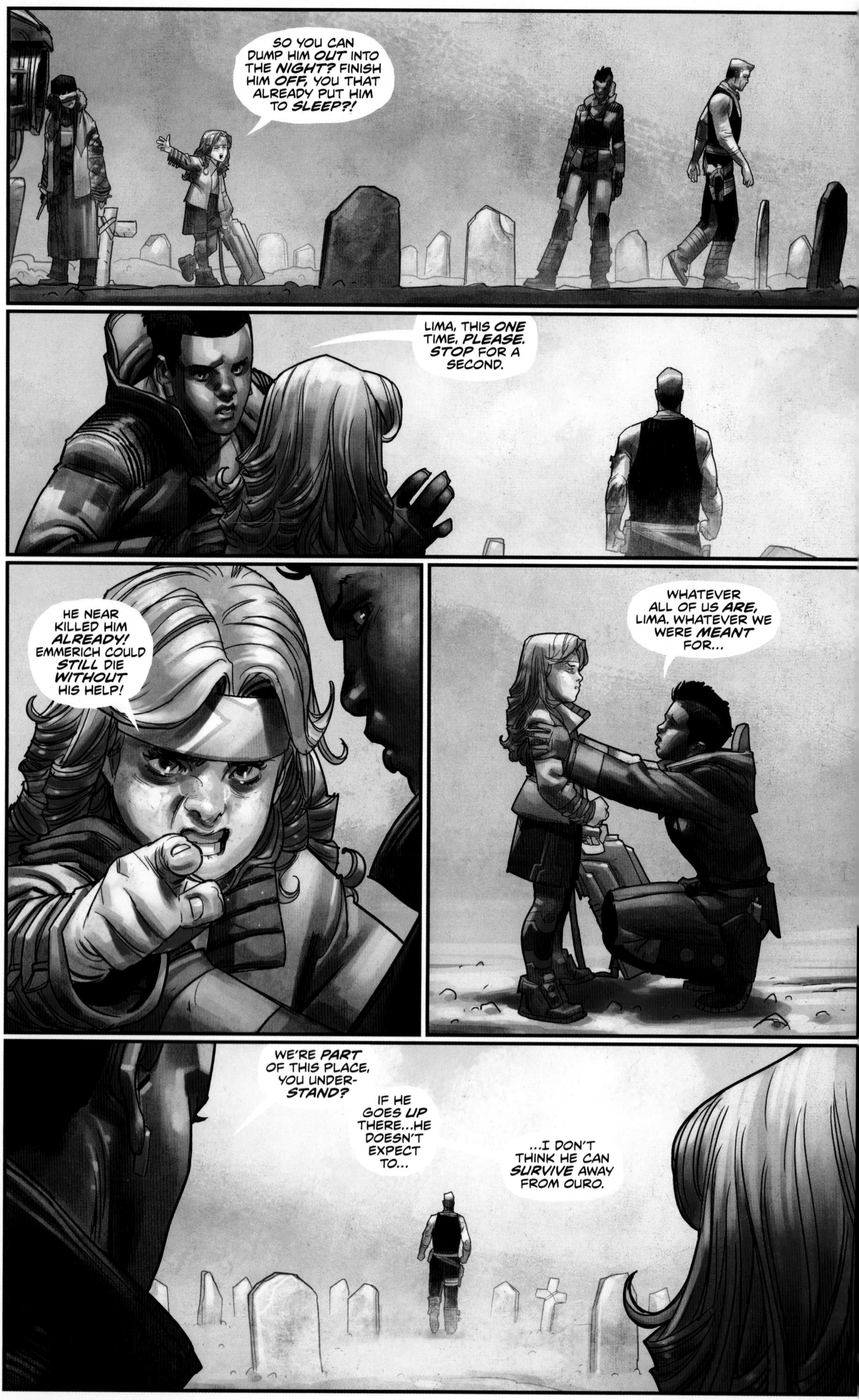
SO YOU CAN DUMP HIM OUT INTO THE NIGHT? FINISH HIM OFF, YOU THAT ALREADY PUT HIM TO SLEEP?!
LIMA, THIS ONE TIME, PLEASE. STOP FOR A SECOND.
HE NEAR KILLED HIM ALREADY! EMMERICH COULD STILL DIE WITHOUT HIS HELP!
WHATEVER ALL OF US ARE, LIMA. WHATEVER WE WERE MEANT FOR...
WE'RE PART OF THIS PLACE, YOU UNDER-STAND?
IF HE GOES UP THERE...HE DOESN'T EXPECT TO...
...I DON'T THINK HE CAN SURVIVE AWAY FROM OURO.

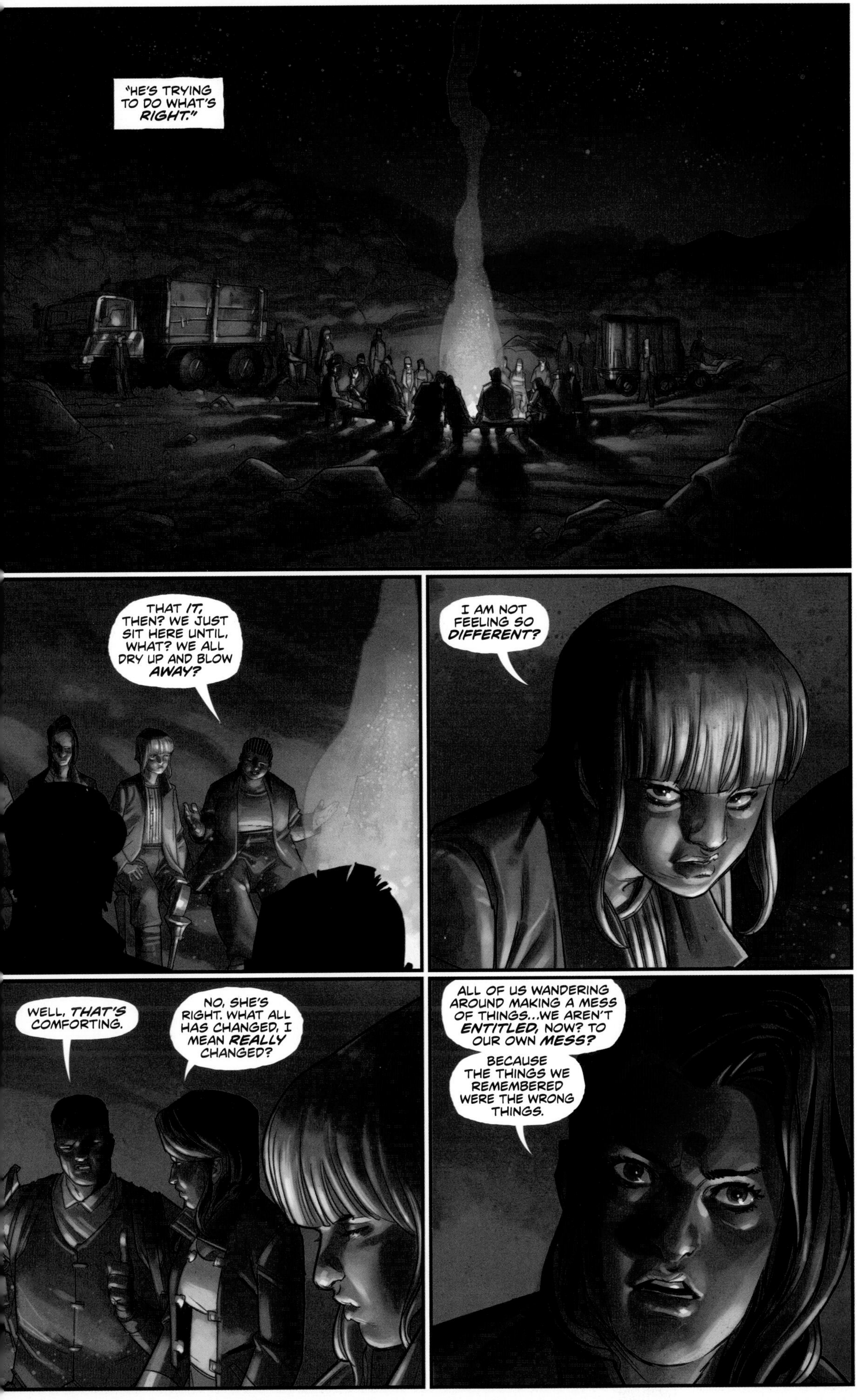
"HE'S TRYING TO DO WHAT'S *RIGHT.*"
THAT *IT,* THEN? WE JUST SIT HERE UNTIL, WHAT? WE ALL DRY UP AND BLOW *AWAY?*
I AM NOT FEELING SO *DIFFERENT?*
WELL, *THAT'S* COMFORTING.
NO, SHE'S RIGHT. WHAT ALL HAS CHANGED, I MEAN *REALLY* CHANGED?
ALL OF US WANDERING AROUND MAKING A MESS OF THINGS...WE AREN'T *ENTITLED,* NOW? TO OUR OWN *MESS?*
BECAUSE THE THINGS WE REMEMBERED WERE THE WRONG THINGS.

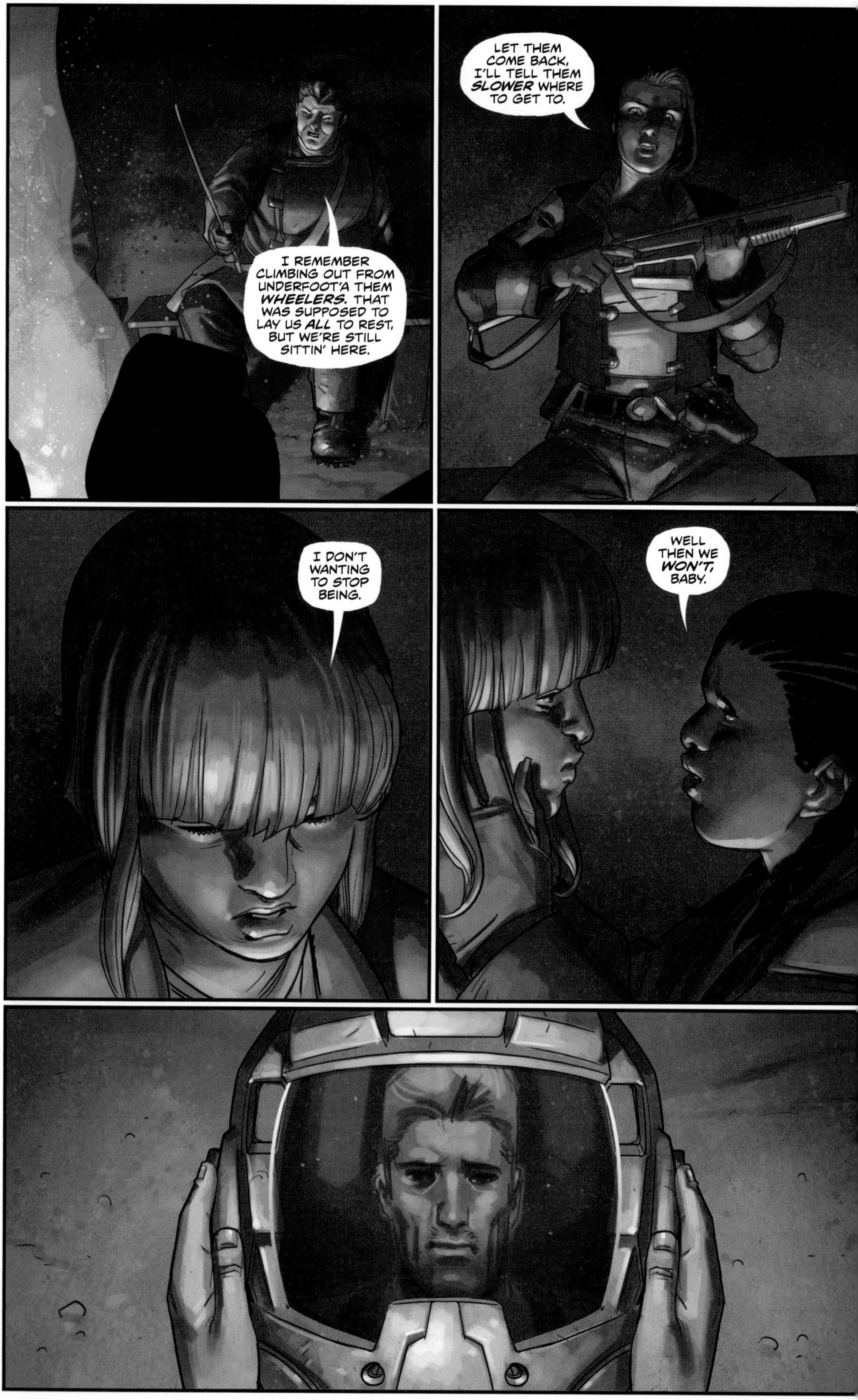
I REMEMBER CLIMBING OUT FROM UNDERFOOT'A THEM WHEELERS. THAT WAS SUPPOSED TO LAY US ALL TO REST, BUT WE'RE STILL SITTIN' HERE.
LET THEM COME BACK, I'LL TELL THEM SLOWER WHERE TO GET TO.
I DON'T WANTING TO STOP BEING.
WELL THEN WE WON'T, BABY.

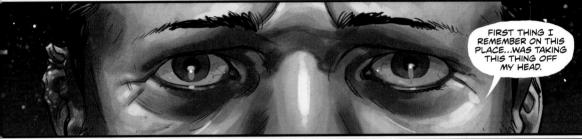

FIRST THING I REMEMBER ON THIS PLACE...WAS TAKING THIS THING OFF MY HEAD.

BUT THAT WASN'T ME. I NEVER *WORE* THIS THING. WHAT IF IT DOESN'T *FIT?*

JUST TRY IT ON.

DON'T NEED THIS ANYMORE.

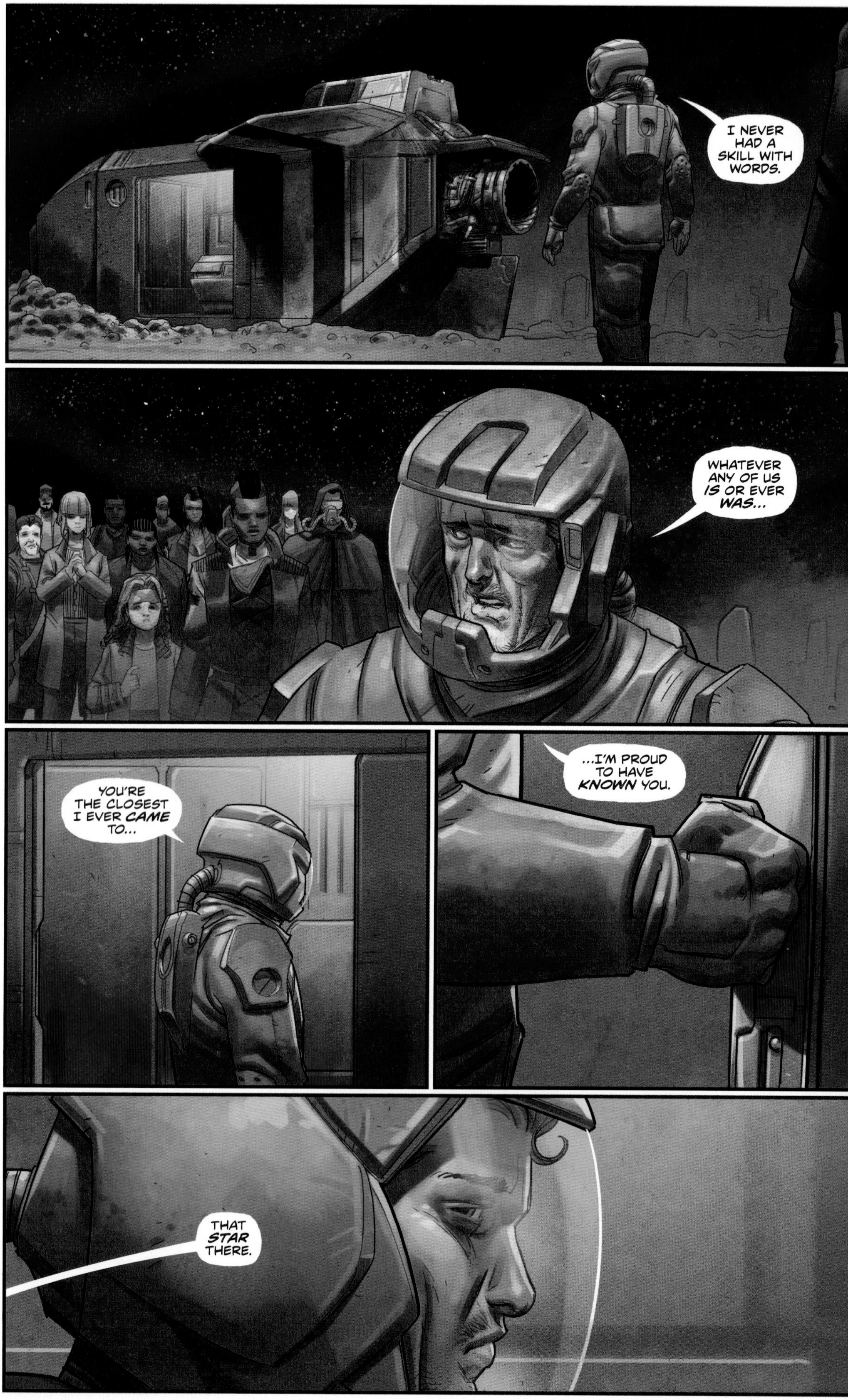
I NEVER HAD A SKILL WITH WORDS.
WHATEVER ANY OF US IS OR EVER WAS...
YOU'RE THE CLOSEST I EVER CAME TO...
...I'M PROUD TO HAVE KNOWN YOU.
THAT STAR THERE.

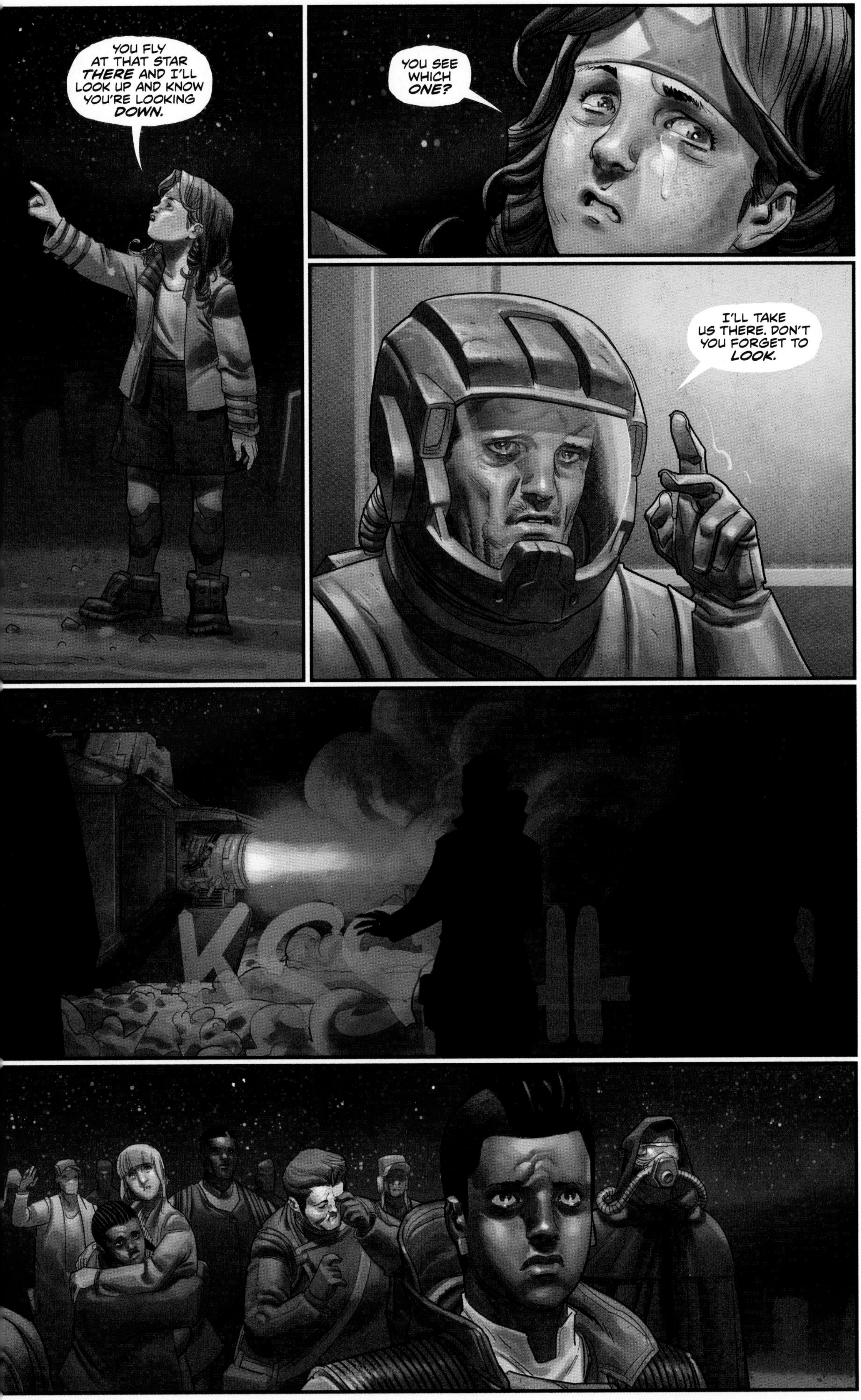
YOU FLY AT THAT STAR THERE AND I'LL LOOK UP AND KNOW YOU'RE LOOKING DOWN.
YOU SEE WHICH ONE?
I'LL TAKE US THERE. DON'T YOU FORGET TO LOOK.

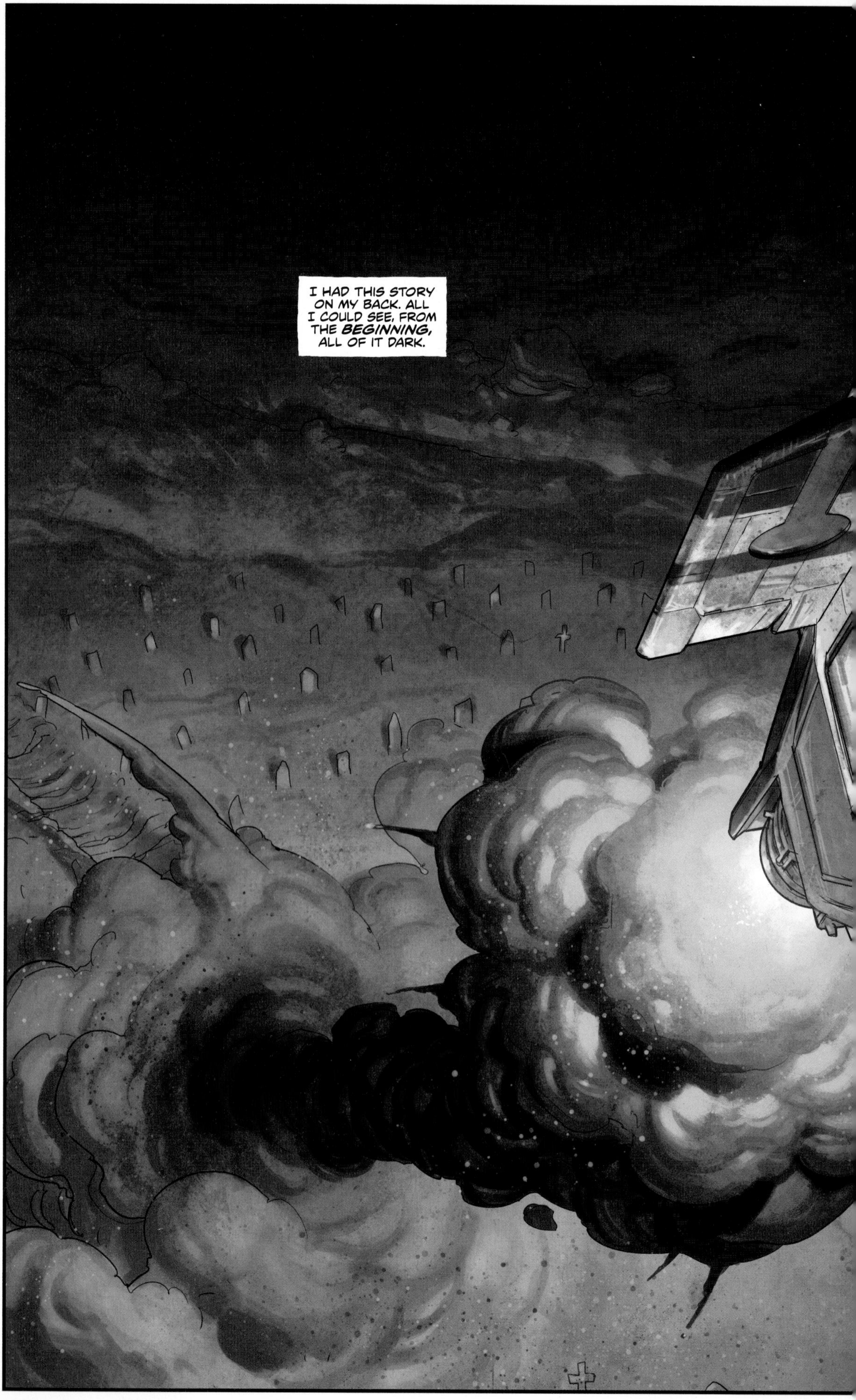
I HAD THIS STORY ON MY BACK. ALL I COULD SEE, FROM THE *BEGINNING,* ALL OF IT DARK.

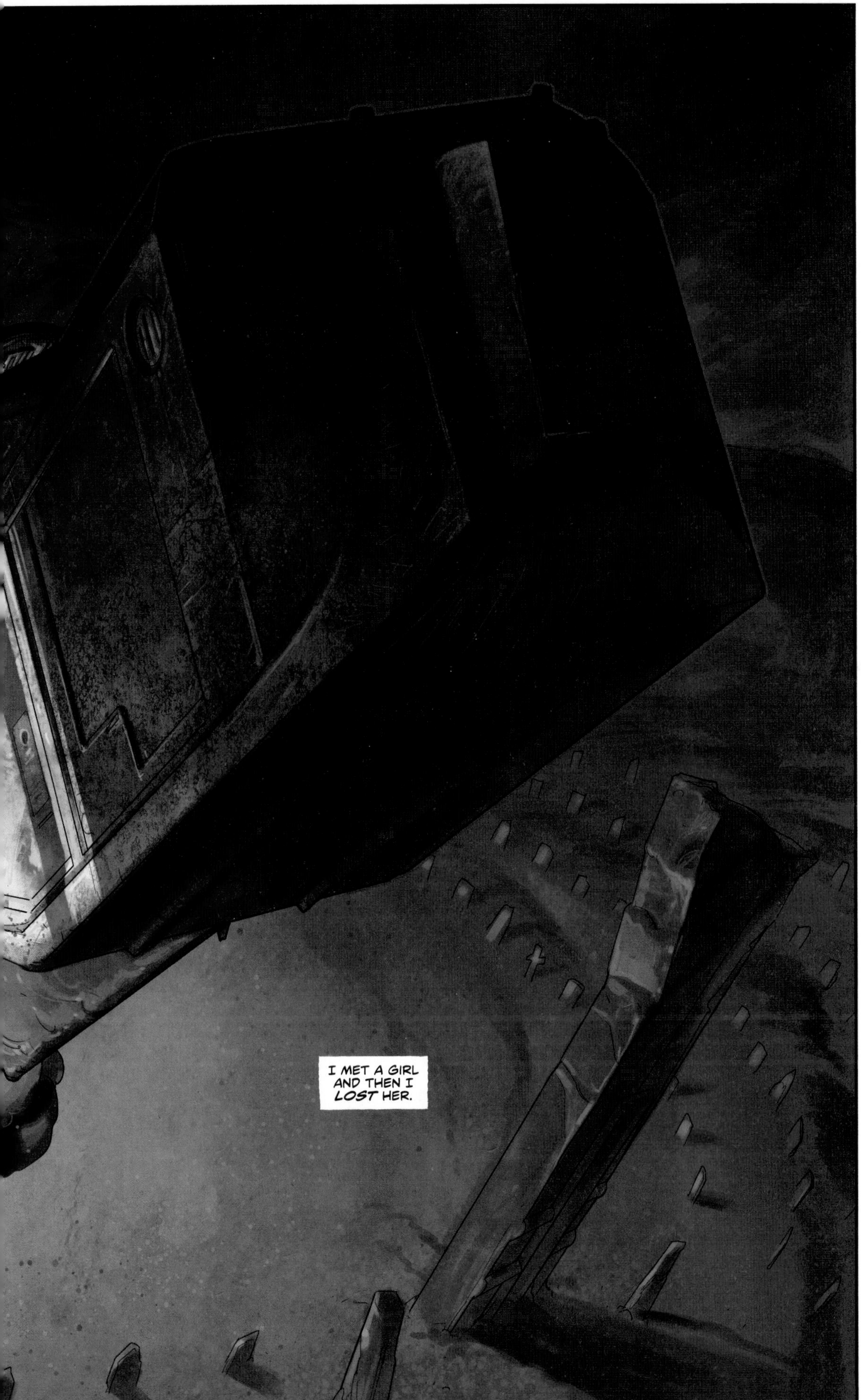
I MET A GIRL AND THEN I LOST HER.

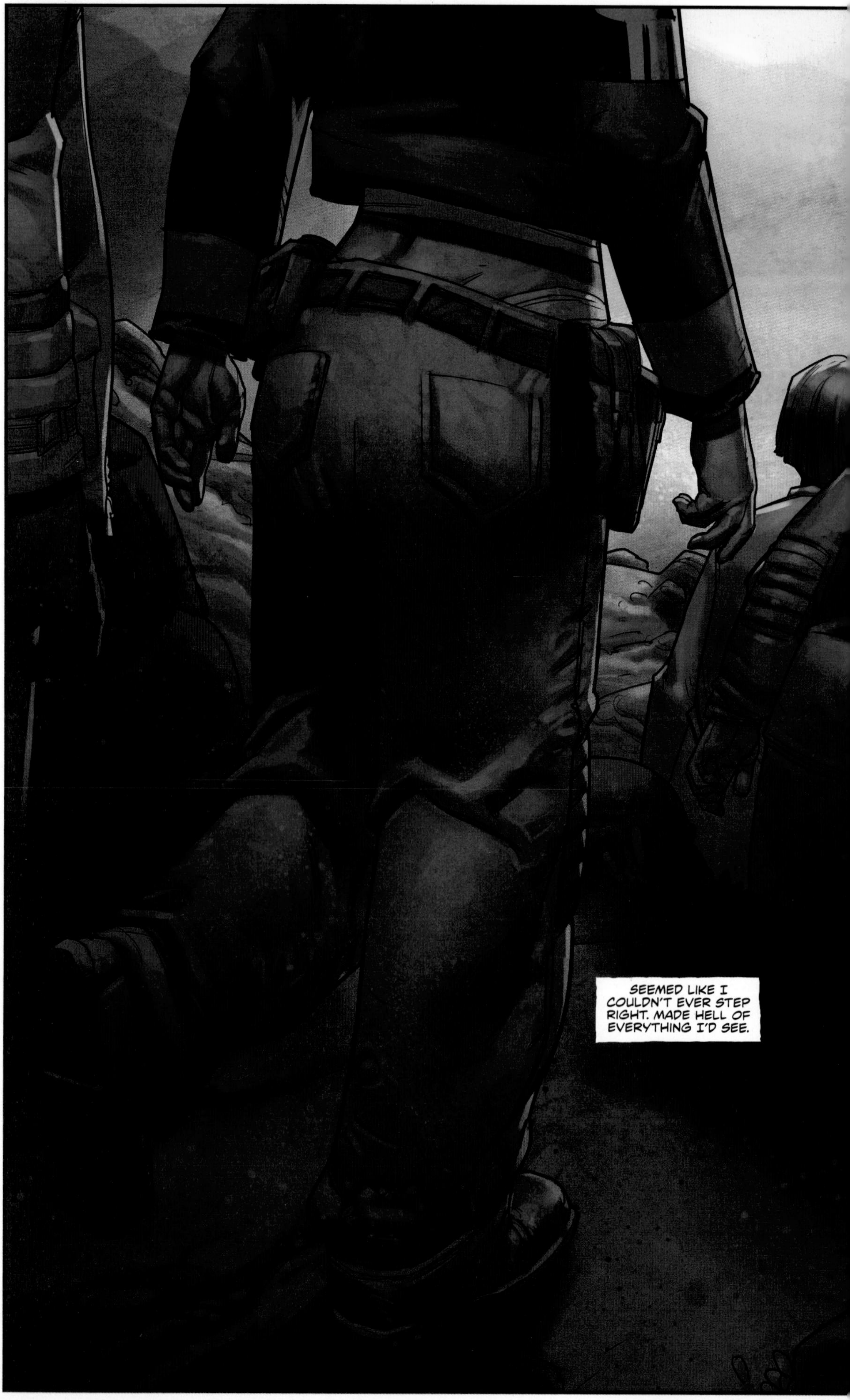
SEEMED LIKE I COULDN'T EVER STEP RIGHT. MADE HELL OF EVERYTHING I'D SEE.

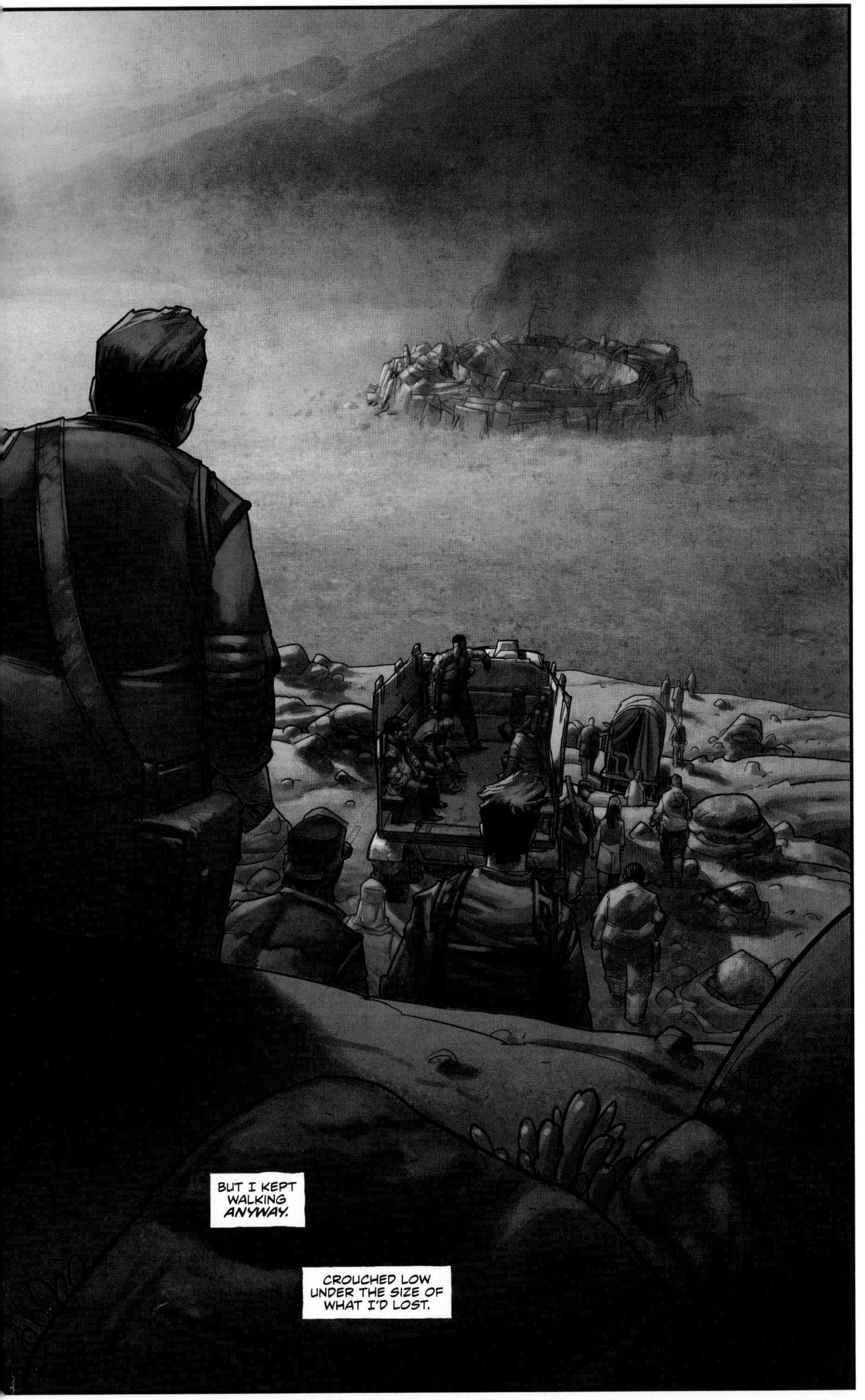
BUT I KEPT WALKING *ANYWAY.*
CROUCHED LOW UNDER THE SIZE OF WHAT I'D LOST.

MAYBE IT WASN'T *ME* THAT DRAGGED EVERYTHING UNDER.

MAYBE I NEVER MOVED THE WORLD AN INCH.

MAYBE I NEVER GOT TO MEET THAT GIRL.

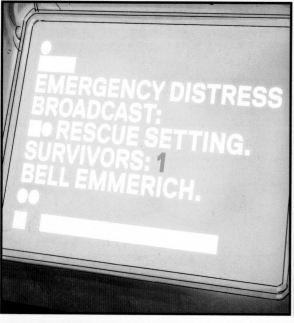

EMERGENCY DISTRESS BROADCAST:
■● RESCUE SETTING.
SURVIVORS: *1*
BELL EMMERICH.
●●
■

I'D NEVER SEEN THE NIGHT BEFORE.

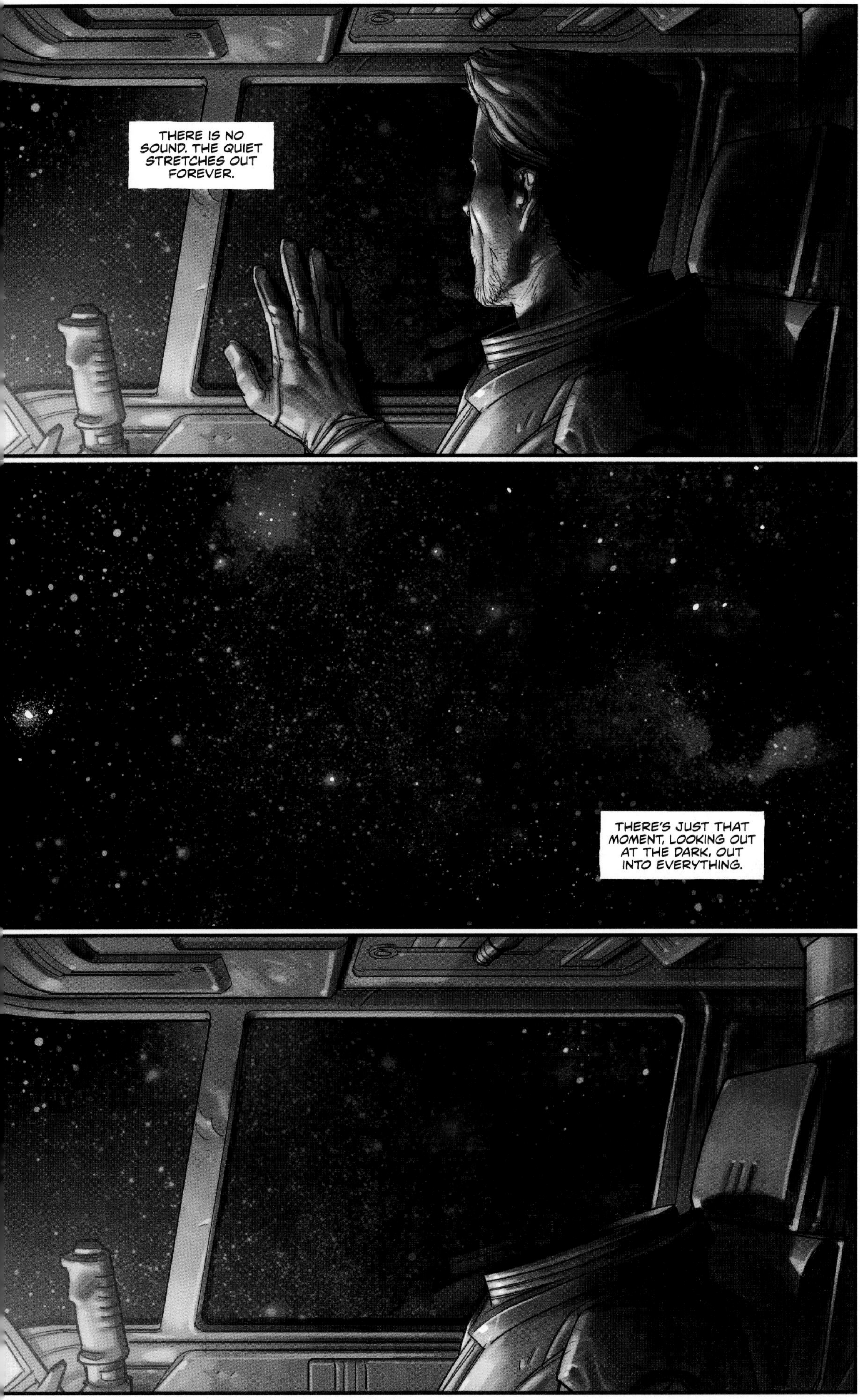
THERE IS NO SOUND. THE QUIET STRETCHES OUT FOREVER.
THERE'S JUST THAT MOMENT, LOOKING OUT AT THE DARK, OUT INTO EVERYTHING.

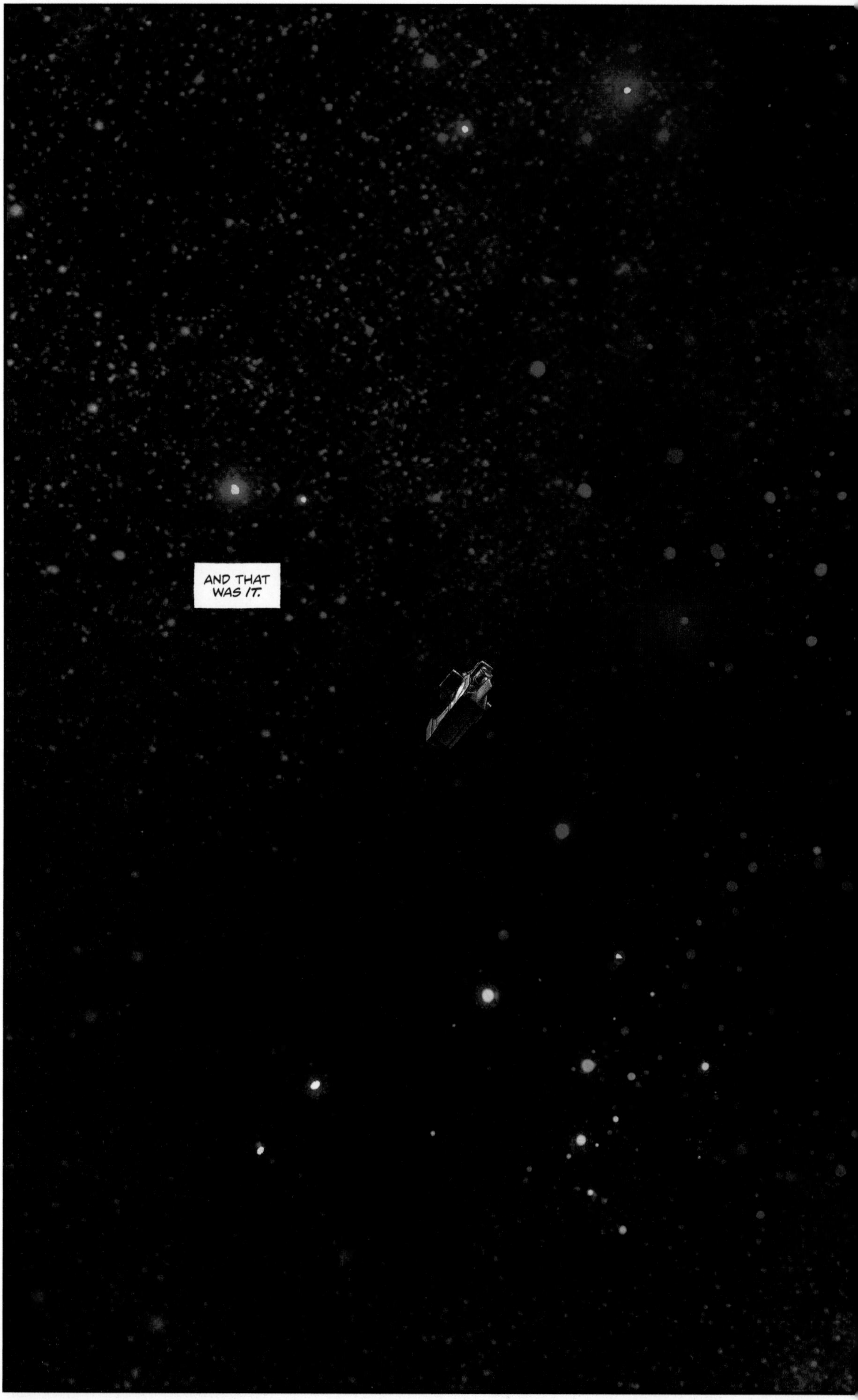
AND THAT WAS IT.

THE END

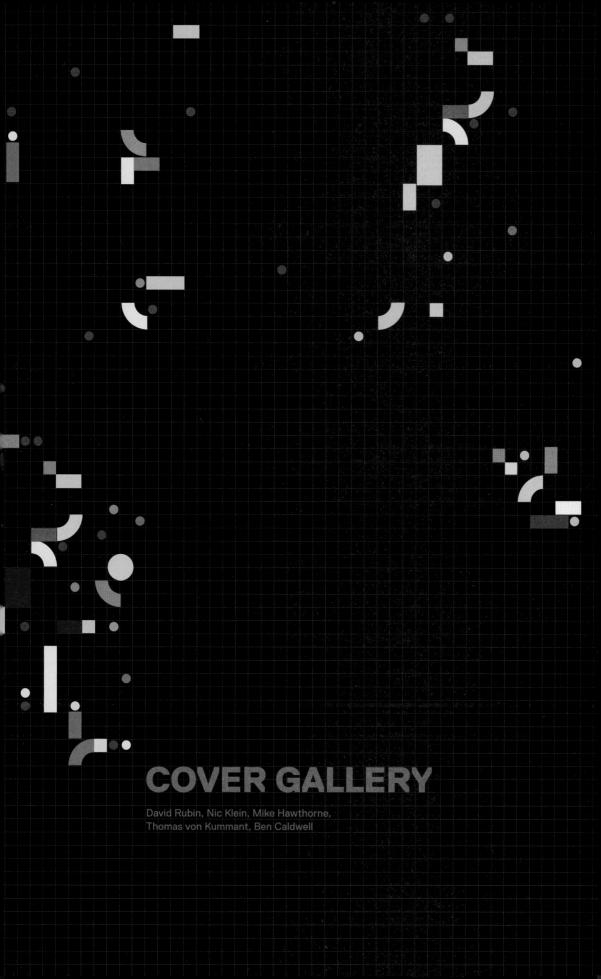

COVER GALLERY

David Rubin, Nic Klein, Mike Hawthorne,
Thomas von Kummant, Ben Caldwell

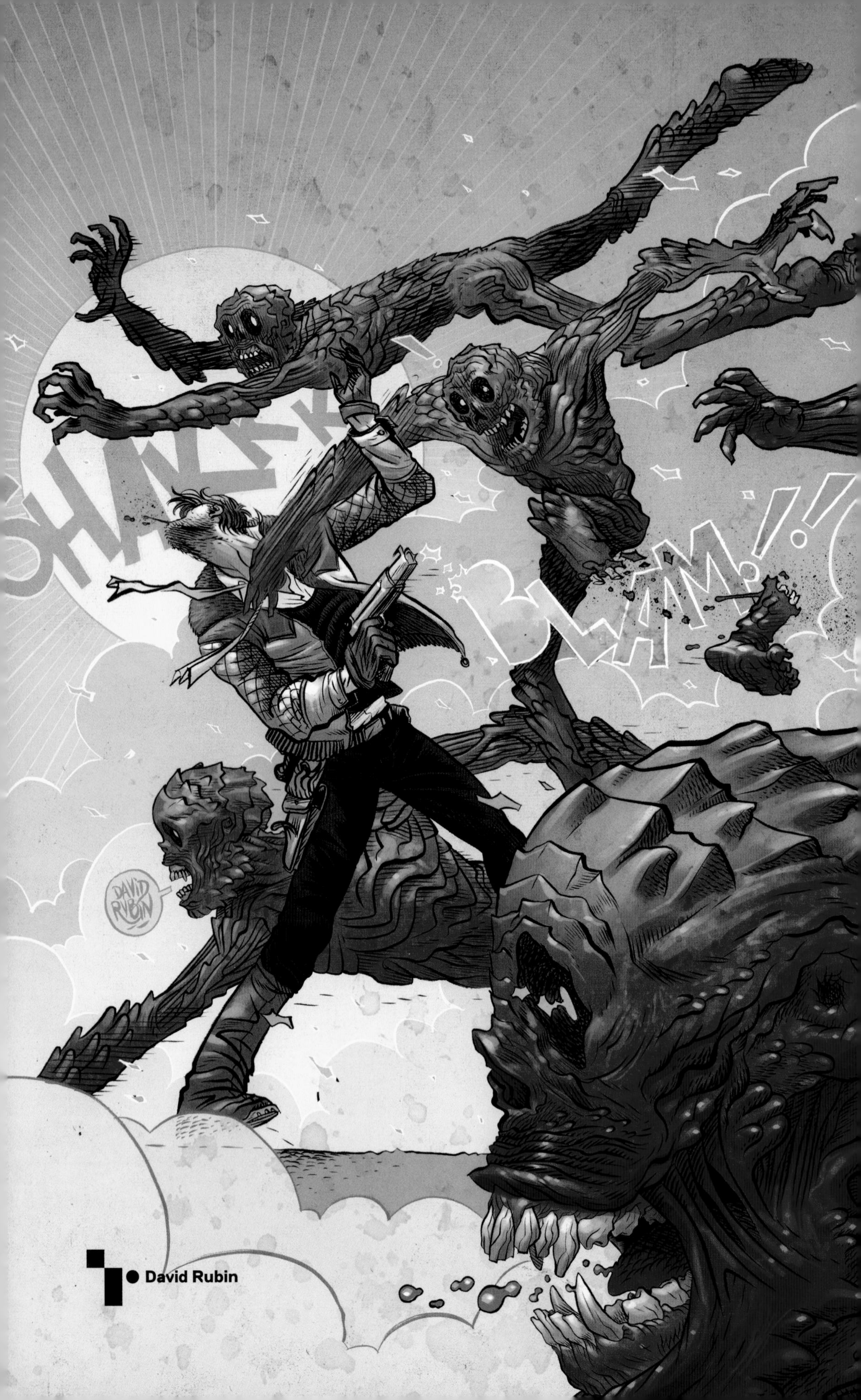
BLAM!!
DAVID RUBIN

David Rubin

Nic Klein

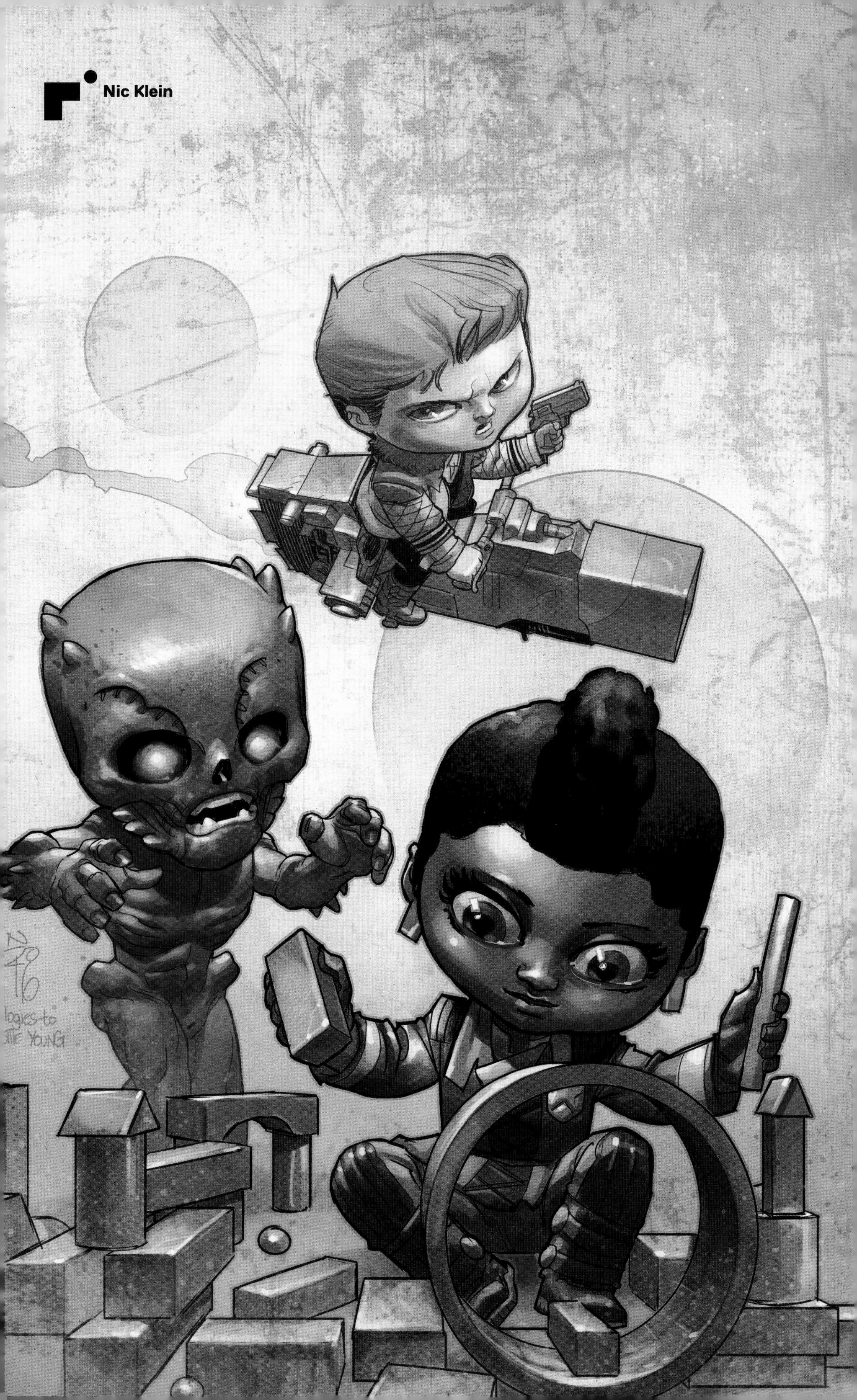

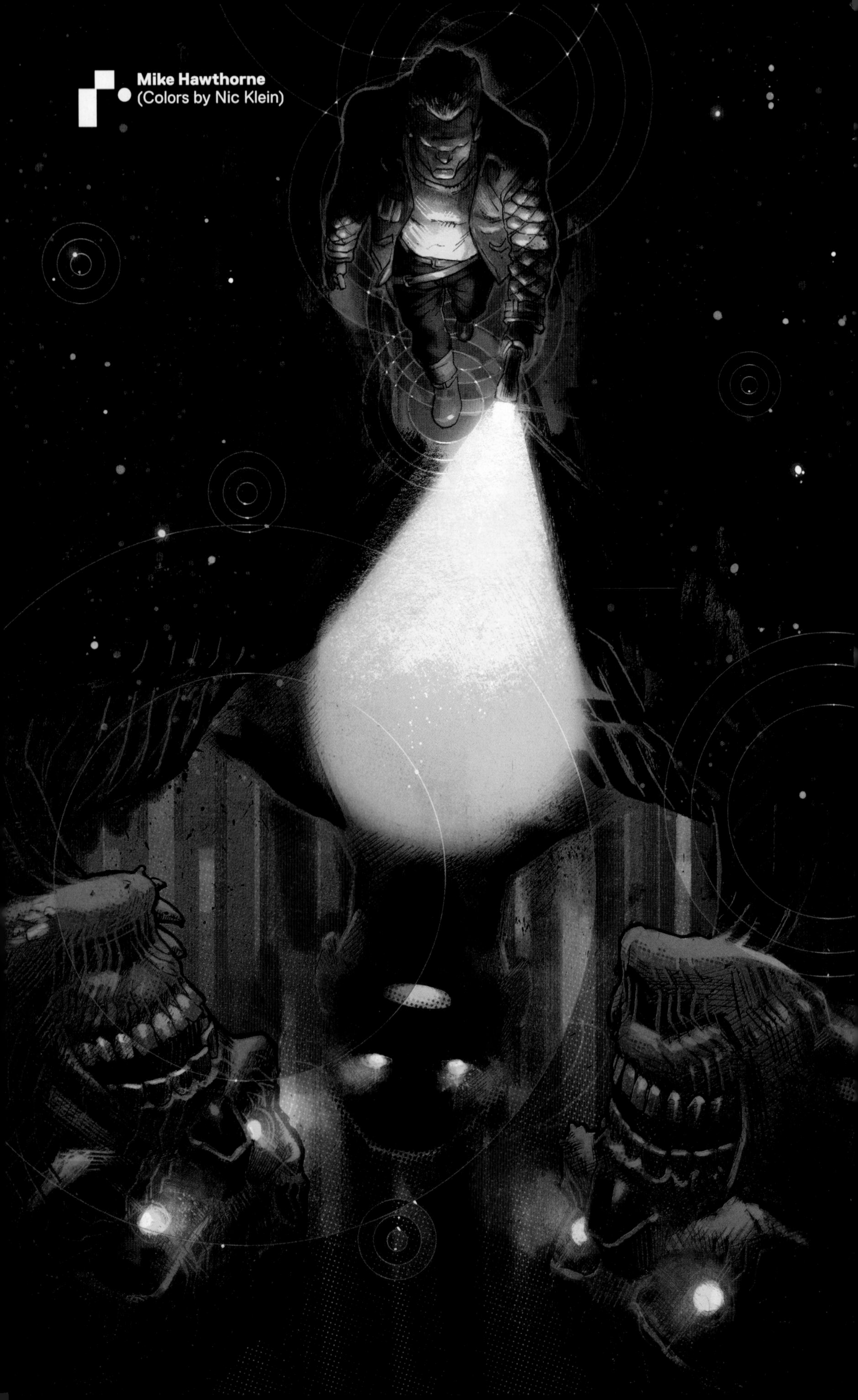

Mike Hawthorne
(Colors by Nic Klein)

Thomas von Kummant

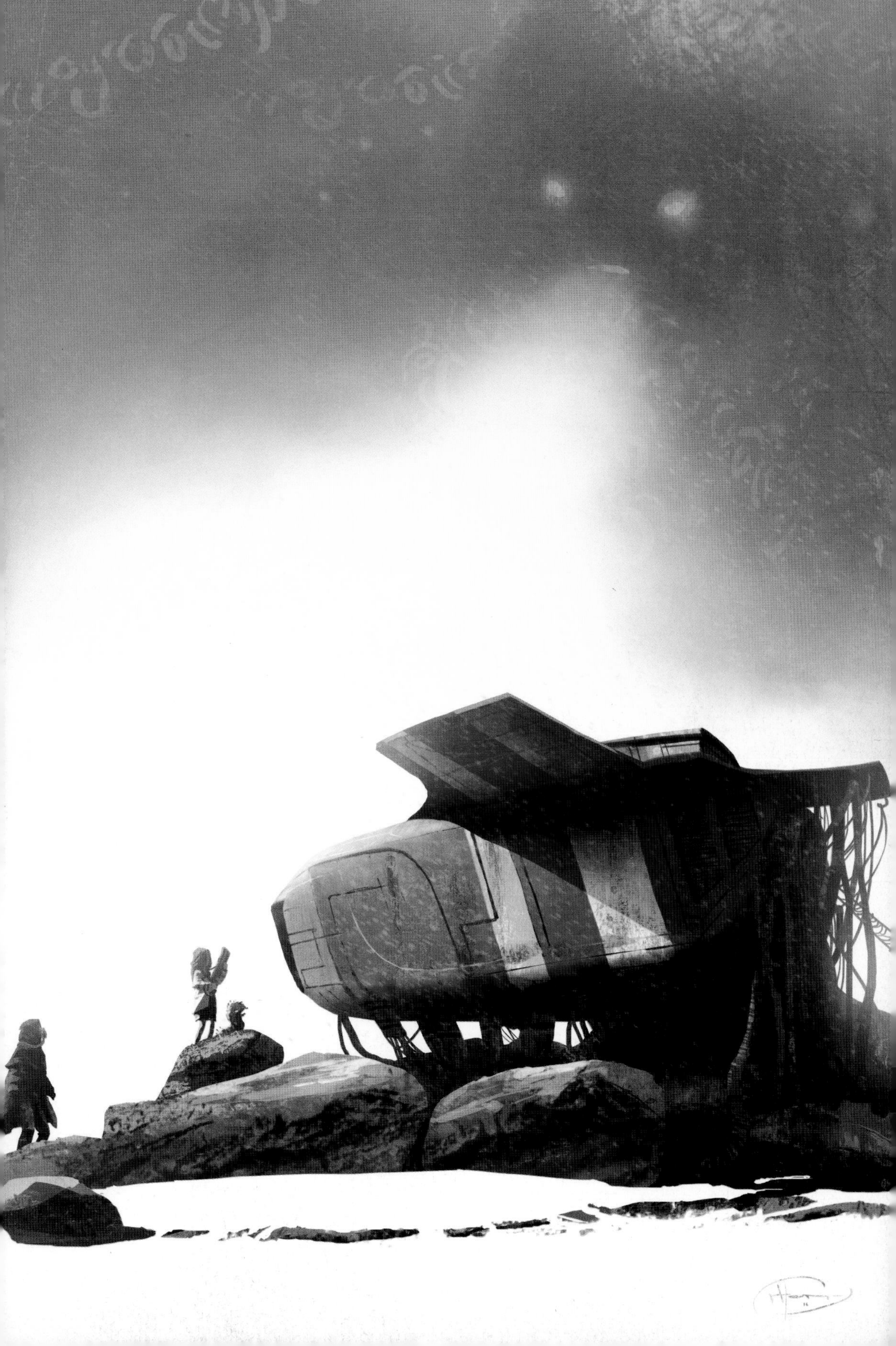

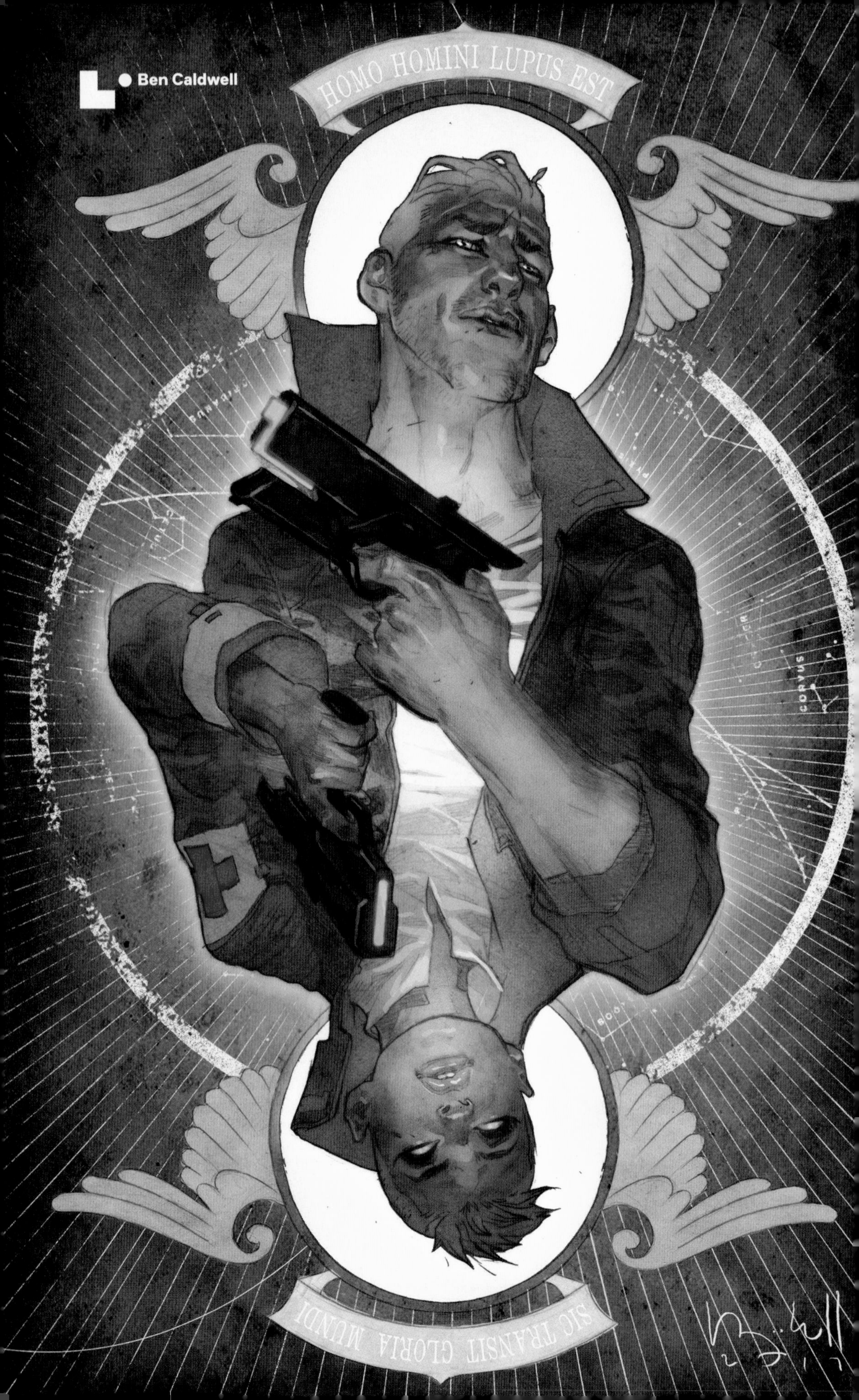
Ben Caldwell
HOMO HOMINI LUPUS EST
CORVUS
SIC TRANSIT GLORIA MUNDI

Nic Klein

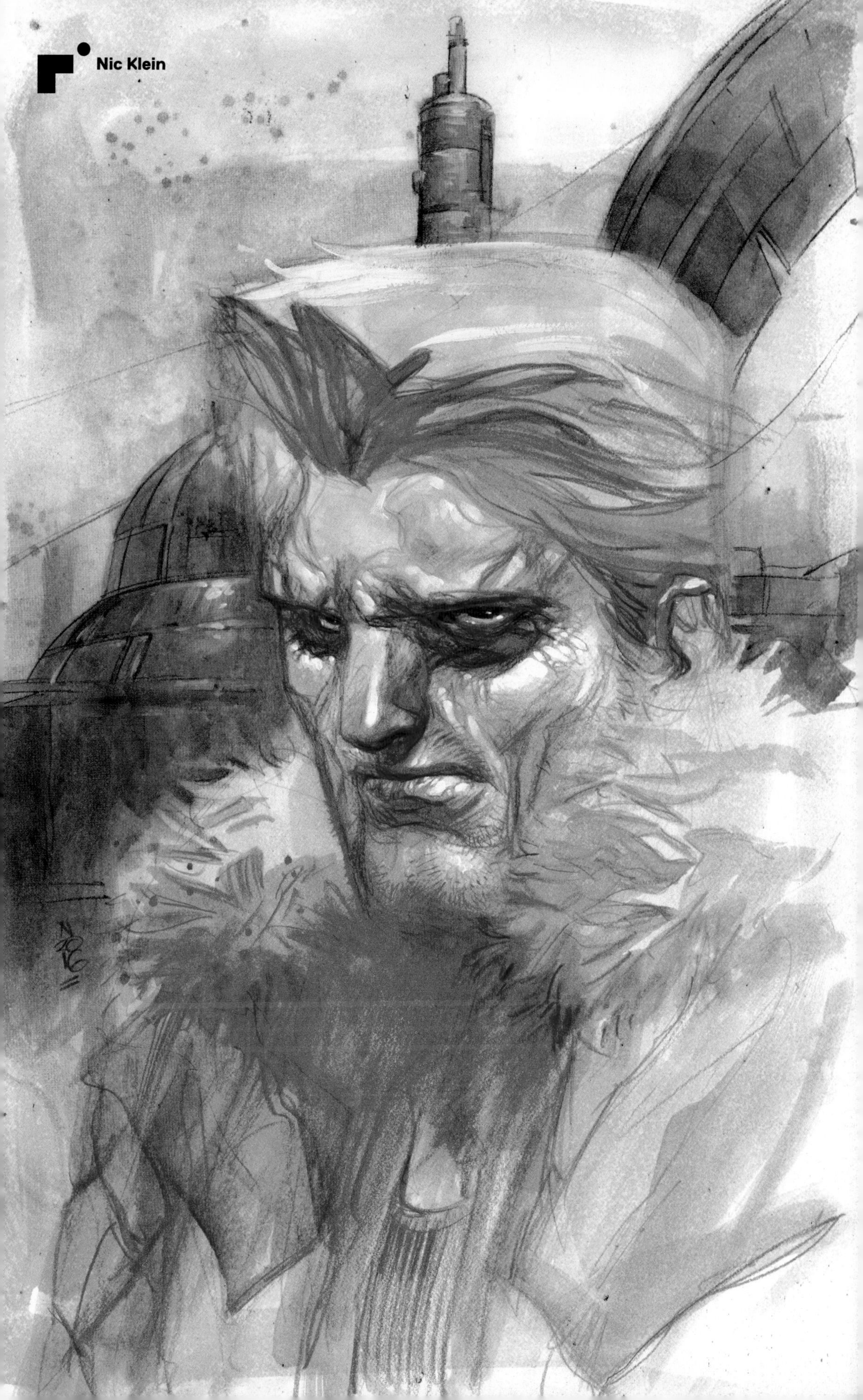

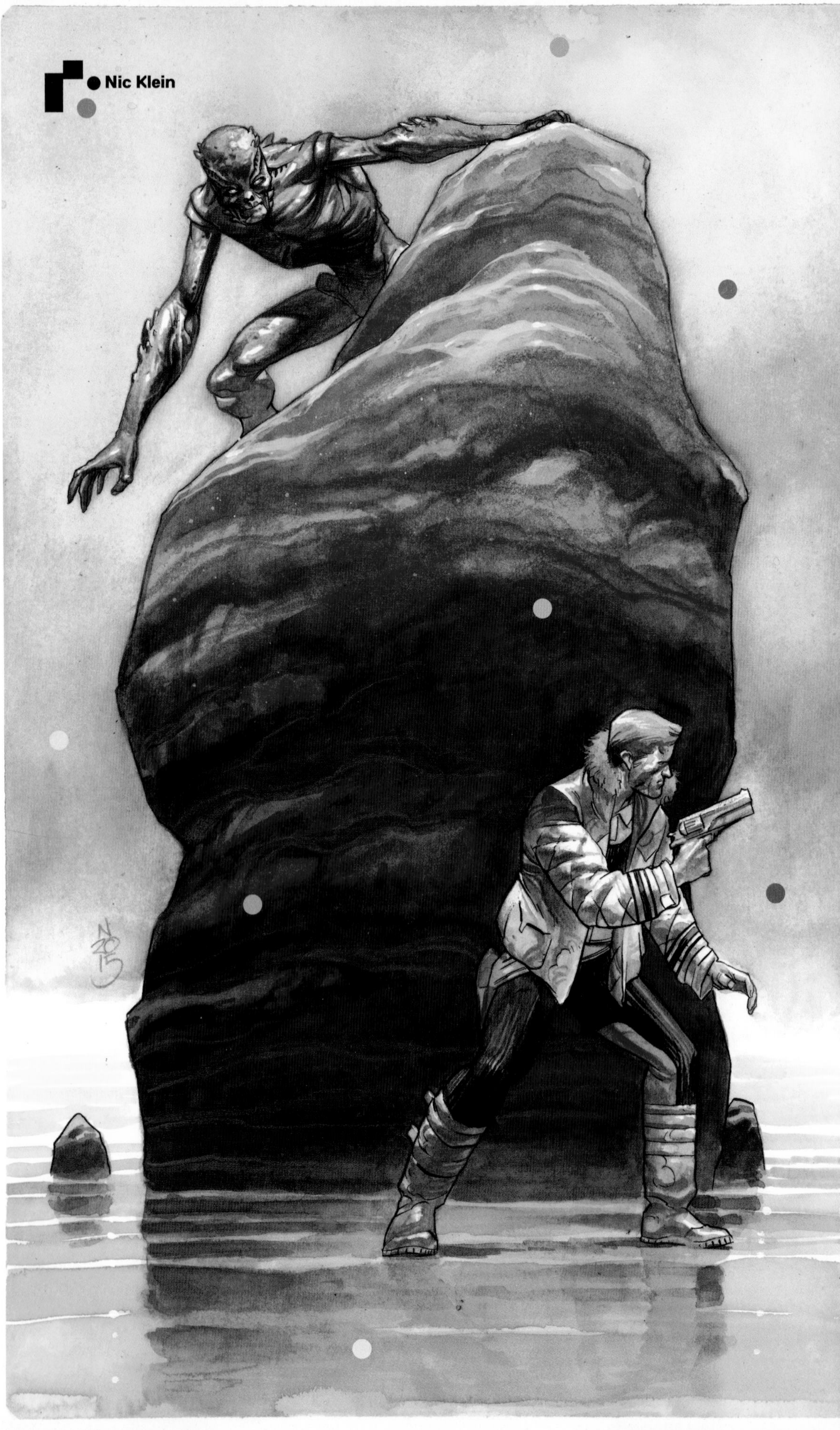
Nic Klein